The Minister's Daughter

The Minister's Daughter

A NOVEL BY

Jennifer Wixson

BOOK 4 IN

The Sovereign Series

PO Box 4
Troy, ME 04987
whitewavepublishing@gmail.com

For more information on *The Sovereign Series* visit:
www.TheSovereignSeries.com

10 9 8 7 6 5 4 3 2 1

ISBN 978-0-9962237-0-6
eBook ISBN 978-0-9962237-1-3

For Mom ~
Inspiration, Role Model, Philanthropist, Grammie Ro
and ..."Rowena the Boss."

Let me live in a house
by the side of the road,
Where the race of men go by-
The men who are good and the men who are bad,
As good and as bad as I.
I would not sit in the scorner's seat,
Or hurl the cynic's ban;-
Let me live in a house by the side of the road
And be a friend to man.

Sam Walter Foss (1858-1911)

Acknowledgements

My thanks go first to the loyal group of fans (and you know who you are) whose kind words and enthusiastic encouragement keep me writing long into many a winter night when I would much rather snuggle up in bed next to my husband, the Cranberry Man. As devoted readers of the Sovereign Series know, I was planning to bring the series to a close—wrapping up all the story lines—with *The Minister's Daughter*; however, you have convinced me via your messages, emails, and book reviews to continue this wonderful journey we began in 2012 with the publication of *Hens & Chickens*. And so, thanks to *you* my loyal fans, there will be at least two more Sovereign Series novels coming down the pike at some point in the future.

I'd like to take this opportunity to thank my editorial team, many of whom have been with me since the beginning: my stepmother Marilyn Wixson; my lovely niece Laurel Wixson McFarland; "Aunt" Wini Mott over on Paris Hill; and my husband, Stan the Cranberry Man. New to the editorial team this year is my old friend Nancy McCallum, who brought with her four decades of professional writing and editing experience. (I'm not sure how that can be possible since we're only thirty-seven.) Nancy's straightforward and often thought-provoking comments were always helpful and illuminating. My father, Eldwin Wixson, not only added his two-bits to the first draft of this book, he also gave me a great idea for the main plot of Book 5, *Maggie's Dilemma*. I think I'd better put Dad to work on all my books henceforth!

This year rather than ask individuals around the country to be our Advance Readers, I approached the neighborhood book group of my childhood chum Sue Simoneau of Wells, Maine. The Spruce Neighborhood Book Group agreed to read *The Minister's Daughter* and provide honest reviews. I'd like to take the opportunity to thank them individually for their kind and thoughtful words: Sue Simoneau, Betsy Shelley, Brenda Vitali, Kim Lord, Nicole Ianniello, Nicole McAlister, Joan Haskins, R. Hinkley, Brenda Bacon, Megan Kreie and Erin Simoneau. Thanks also to my other two advance readers: Becky Soble and Julie Theroux. Last, but certainly not least, I'd like to thank my cousin Adeline Wixson, who read *The Minister's Daughter* with me as I wrote it, chapter by chapter, providing me with valuable instant feedback (which was sort of like instant gratification, except when it was an instant reality check.)

Kudos to my creative design team Peter Harris Associates—consisting of Peter Harris and Greg Elizondo—who provided us with the lovely cover of *The Minister's Daughter.* This is the fifth cover Peter has done for my books (the fourth cover in the Sovereign Series) and my plan is to keep him from retiring until he's done the covers for Book 5, *Maggie's Dilemma*, and Book 6, *To the Waters & the Wild.*

Without further ado, let me introduce you to Nellie Walker—*The Minister's Daughter.* Enjoy!

Jen Wixson
Troy, Maine
August 5, 2015

Table of Contents

Prologue

A middle-aged woman, her face puffy and streaked from weeping, huddled over the kitchen table, clutching a ballpoint pen in her right hand. Her left hand absently fingered the white hairs on her head, downy as a duck's underbelly and new since the chemotherapy. A yellow legal pad rested in front of her on the checkered Bates Mills tablecloth; however, rather than concentrating on her writing she gazed listlessly off into space.

The country kitchen, normally cheerful and welcoming, appeared this August morning to mirror the woman's apathy. Dirty dishes cluttered the sideboard; unopened mail littered the stenciled pine chiffonier; and a pile of half-folded laundry—men's briefs, cotton socks, and navy-colored T-shirts—jumbled together on the opposite end of the table. Four or five funeral arrangements of flowers emitting a sickly sweet perfume grouped awkwardly atop the cold black woodstove like mourners at the graveside.

The woman's eyes happened to focus on the funeral arrangements. She dropped the pen and heaved forward as though struck from behind. A violent, heart-rending wail escaped her. She began to sob uncontrollably. After several minutes, the waterworks ended and she was able to pull herself together. Lethargically, she removed a crumpled lace handkerchief from her purse and dried her eyes. She spread the damp hanky in the flat of her palm and traced the purple embroidered initials—ALR—with her index finger, taking satisfaction in the feel of the raised silken thread against her skin. "It never gets any easier, does it, Addie?" she said, sadly.

She thought of all the thousands—maybe hundreds of thousands—of whispered words of condolence, commiseration, and reassurance she had uttered over the years to the bereaved and realized beyond a shadow of a doubt that none had been efficacious. What a fool she had been! To think that she, Maggie Walker, could make a difference where death was concerned!

She nearly gave way to weeping again, but suddenly recalled a late friend's exhortation to her: "This too shall pass!" She was struck by the powerful simplicity of Miss Hastings' four simple words. "This too shall pass," she repeated, aloud. "This too shall pass!"

Hastily, she retrieved the pen. She scribbled a short burst of writing and set the pen down to reread what she had written:

Words can't begin to describe the pain I feel. I can hardly stand up straight. 'The sorrow of life itself has entered into my soul.'

I feel as though I need to perform some act of contrition so I'm going to try and walk the Way of St. James. I'll write again as soon as I am able. In the meantime, I thank my darling Nellie for coming home to take care of things for me.

Love, Mom

The note wasn't much, but it was the best she could do. She heard the toot of a horn out front and knew her ride had arrived. She pulled herself up from the table and stepped into the adjoining room where she placed the legal pad on the writing surface of her ancient roll-top desk. She retrieved two checkbooks and her keys from her purse and placed them on the yellow pad. She hesitated a moment before removing her smartphone. She shut the phone off, added it to the pile, and rolled down the cover of the desk.

The taxi tooted a second time. She hooked her purse strap over her shoulder and grasped the handle of her suitcase. With an obvious effort she straightened herself up. She inhaled, squared her shoulders, and stoically exited the kitchen and attached shed without a backward glance at the unopened mail, the dirty dishes, the half-folded laundry—or the funeral arrangements of flowers.

CHAPTER 1
Nellie's Return

For Nellie Walker coming back to Sovereign was like being thrown unwittingly into the pages of a nineteenth century novel, complete with eccentric local characters, crazy Maine weather, and singular circumstances that happened nowhere else on earth yet were accepted as perfectly normal events. Except for the lack of an ocean (Sovereign was, unfortunately, thirty-five miles from the coast), her mother's primitive, cobbled together cottage—formerly the town's first one-room schoolhouse—might have issued straight from Sarah Orne Jewett's fictional outpost of Dunnett's Landing. Nellie's heart sank as from the top of the hill she spied the rusty tin roof of the old schoolhouse. She had once sworn she would never return to Sovereign, and now—here she was.

They bumped down the dry, washboardy dirt road, a plume of dust barreling behind their pickup like a sandy shadow. Metcalf swung into her mother's driveway and shut off the engine. "Roll up your window, quick," he advised, and Nellie complied, cranking on the old window handle. The soft dust washed over the vehicle and disappeared in search of its final resting place. She peered through the dirty windshield to inspect her mother's house, attempting to gauge what had changed since her last visit. The white wooden clapboards on the original fourteen-by-twenty schoolhouse and ell extension had been recently painted, she noted, and the leggy lilacs framing the living room windows had been lopped down to an appropriate size. Uncle Peter's handiwork, most likely. In addition, the traditional old-fashioned daylilies in front of the attached shed had been thinned and weeded. The lilies' vivid orange blooms popped against the gray weathered shed.

"Don't look now, Nellie, but here comes your welcoming committee," Doctor Bart said evenly. "Wendell must have seen us go by. I noticed Mom's car at their place, too."

Nellie glanced over her shoulder and spied a second wave of dust somersaulting down the hill, foretelling the approach of another vehicle on the rarely-used back road. Without a moment's hesitation, she opened her door, grabbed her backpack, and darted into the large attached shed, which she knew would be unlocked.

The inner door creaked as she let herself into her mother's quaint country kitchen. The familiar floral papered walls were hung as always with Maggie's cast-iron cookware, cabbage choppers, and a host of other antique kitchen utensils. Three multicolored braided rugs adorned the battle-scarred pine floor and hanging bunches of herbs added a musty sweetness to the stuffy, closed-up room. Most prominent in the kitchen, however, was the old oak table, upon which Nellie used to do her homework and where her mother often worked on her Sunday sermons.

She examined the rest of the kitchen, taking in the dirty dishes on the sideboard, a stack of unopened mail on the stenciled pine chiffonier, and a pile of half-folded laundry on the table that had somehow never found its way to the dresser. She spotted four or five mostly dead funeral arrangements on the cast-iron woodstove and her eyes immediately filled with tears. She would not cry! She must not cry. Uncle Peter was dead; he wasn't coming back.

She heard the murmur of voices in the front yard and knew it was only a matter of moments before she was joined by her mother's well-meaning friends. She heaved a sigh of self-pity, and pulled up a chair at the oval oak table, setting her backpack in the chair beside her. She pushed aside a cut-glass sugar bowl that served as a spoon holder and two bronze trivets, securing a spot for her elbows on the table.

She glanced up and spied stern-looking stoneware platters and pitchers glowering at her from atop the Shaker-style cabinets, as though rebuking her for having her elbows on the table—and for staying away so long. She quickly hid her wan face in her hands. Her long blonde hair cascaded down, effectively screening her from the glares of the stoneware and from the anxious gazes of her mother's friends, now trooping into the kitchen: Wendell and Rebecca Russell (Maggie's neighbors), 'Aunt' Jane Lawson (her mother's best friend from Albion), and Aunt Jane's son, Metcalf Bartholomew Lawson, (the local country doctor and her chauffeur).

"We're so sorry, Nellie dear," said Mrs. Russell, entering the kitchen first.

Nellie, her face still hidden, simply nodded in response. She bit her lip as they appropriated consolatory positions around the kitchen. Rebecca Russell selected Maggie's rocker while her husband, Wendell, a Sovereign stalwart, stood awkwardly on the edge of the small braided rug in front of the sink, holding his cap in his hands like a supplicant. Aunt Jane sat down in one of the mismatched straight-back chairs across from her and Doctor Bart leaned against the living room doorframe. For several moments, no one spoke.

"My, that road is dusty," remarked Aunt Jane, breaking the awkward silence.

Wendell Russell leaned back against the cast-iron sink unit and crossed his arms over his chest. "Wal, you know, she needs some calcium chloride to nail down them fines."

"Fines?" queried Aunt Jane.

"Thet's the good top dirt, you know, the fine stuff. I'm surprised Asa ain't been 'round with the salt yet."

"Today would have been the perfect day to spread, too," Doctor Bart said. Seeing the perplexed faces of the two older women he added: "At 77°F and 75% humidity—which is about what it is today—calcium chloride absorbs more than twice its weight in water. If Asa had spread this morning the salt would have pulled enough moisture from the air to keep the fines from becoming dust."

"I see," said Rebecca, who had not even attempted to follow Metcalf's explanation. "Well, I'm just glad we live on a paved road."

Nellie stole a glance at the regulator wall clock, which was tossing desultory ticks of time into the stuffy room much like she used to toss bread to the wild birds out back. Oh, God—was it only three o'clock? How long did they intend to stay? What did they want from her? Surely they weren't there to talk about the road dust, which occurred every year like a sixth season after mud season and summer?

Nellie straightened up in her seat. Her eyes happened to land on the oak mirror propitiously situated next to the inner shed door, sited there so her middle-aged mother—her only parent and minister of the local church—could check her hair and teeth before sallying forth to do battle with the world. In a flash, Nellie recollected the year (she must have been about thirteen) when Maggie had banished all mirrors from the house. "Apostles of vanity," her mother had declared, hefting, with a little grunt, the offending oak mirror down from its square-headed nail. "Vanity of vanities … all is vanity!"

"I thought you hated Ecclesiastes," Nellie had remarked, looking up from her laptop. She was huddled under a crocheted throw, sitting cross-legged in the chair next to the toasty woodstove, laptop on the table. Her classic face with its high cheek bones and aquiline nose was pale from lack of heat and winter daylight. She had always been cold in this primitive place, especially in winter. "That's what you've said, isn't it, Mother?"

With a little thud, Maggie set the mirror down. She turned its liquid silver face to the wall, punishing the mirror as though it was one of the errant schoolchildren responsible for all the scars on the wide pine floor. "Never mind that—we pay way too much attention to our appearance around here."

Nellie shrugged. "No problem," she said. She tapped a key on the laptop and the screen flashed back up. She returned her chin to her hand and went back to her homework.

"Have you ever noticed how many times during the day we seek the reassurance of a mirror?" Maggie pressed onward. "How they've crept into our lives as slyly as television and telephones, almost?"

"Not really."

"Mirrors have tricked us into believing our self-esteem lies outside us, rather than inside ourselves. The more mirrors we depend upon in our daily life—bathroom, kitchen, car; why they're everywhere!—the lower our self-esteem. 'What is crooked cannot be made straight', especially by looking in a mirror." Maggie scribbled a few lines onto a yellow legal pad. "Are you listening to me? I mean it, Nellie, not even a mirror in your purse."

"I don't have a purse," Nellie said. She closed the laptop and stood up, slipping it under her arm. "I'll just go to the living room while you work on your sermon, Mom." As Nellie exited the kitchen she heard her mother mutter under her breath: "Damn Theological Offspring!"

That was probably the moment, Nellie realized now, when she had decided to look for a preparatory boarding school so she could live away from home during high school. Home? That was a laugh! When had she ever thought of Sovereign, Maine as home?

Sixteen years ago when her mother had announced they were moving to Sovereign, Nellie had been horrified. Over the years she had tried to figure out why her college-educated, Seminary-trained mother had wanted to relocate from the hip Portland area to this unprogressive rural farming community—but failed. Now, however … now that Uncle Peter (Maggie's husband and Nellie's stepfather) was dead and her mother had decamped for parts unknown, Nellie suddenly realized her mother had always been just as weird as the rest of the bunch. She allowed a little groan to escape her parted lips.

"We're so sorry, dear," Rebecca repeated, misinterpreting Nellie's articulation for an expression of grief over the unexpected loss of her stepfather, Peter Hodges, who had died in his sleep of heart failure ten days ago. Nellie had not made it home in time for Uncle Peter's funeral and her mother had apparently bolted after the special memorial service held at church the following day. Rebecca lurched up out of the rocker and gave Nellie a motherly hug. Nellie felt the older woman's hot tears fall on her neck and cool as they slid down past her shoulder blades. A lump formed in Nellie's throat and she almost gave way to tears herself.

Rebecca turned from Nellie to the consoling arms of her husband. "They-ah, they-ah, de-ah," Wendell said, patting his wife as though she were a child.

Doctor Bart broke the maudlin spell. "Nellie knows how sorry we all are about Peter," he said, to the group at large. "I told her that on the drive home from the bus station. The more important thing is—what should be done now? Maggie's left a lot of things in the lurch, stuff Nellie shouldn't have to deal with by herself."

Doctor Bart—Metcalf—had always been Nellie's champion, an older brother of sorts. Since she could remember he had been her self-appointed guardian, looking out for her best interests, especially when Maggie was too busy saving souls to parent her daughter. The Lawsons, who were from Albion, and the Walkers, who were from, well, nowhere, had remained close no matter the distance between the two families. But on Nellie's last few visits home she had begun to detect more than brotherly affection in Doctor Bart's manner, an unfortunate turn of events most likely stemming from her mother's legendary match-making. While Nellie was grateful for Metcalf's affection, she certainly wasn't looking for a romantic relationship in that direction. He was far too stodgy and serious for her. She was glad she hadn't offended him during those few feeble romantic overtures, however; since with Uncle Peter gone there was no one else in the world she could count on for support.

Uncle Peter had always been kind, good-natured, and encouraging. As she thought of her stepfather, Nellie once again fought back tears. The news of Uncle Peter's death was still so raw she could barely believe he wouldn't come walking into the kitchen any moment with his cheery voice, salt and pepper hair, and smiling blue eyes. The only father figure she had ever known was—dead.

"How stuffy it is in here," Aunt Jane cried, hopping up from the table. She threw open the double-hung window over the sink and propped it up with the stick. A welcome burst of fresh air entered the room.

"That's OK until the next car goes by, Mother," Metcalf pointed out, somewhat drily.

"I'll close the window if anyone comes. That road is so bad we'll be able to hear a car half a mile away. Tea, anyone? Nellie?"

"Sure. Why not."

Aunt Jane moved to the two-burner propane stove and switched on the gas under the copper tea kettle. "Iced or hot?"

"Hot, thanks."

"Me too, please," said Rebecca. She straightened the folds of her pretty white maternity blouse. "Wendell and I will be glad to help Nellie," she offered. "At least until the baby comes. But surely Maggie won't be gone as long as that?"

"When are you due?" Nellie asked, politely. She was grateful for the opportunity to shift the focus of attention away from herself.

"Not until November. But let's hope I go early—I'm so fat, already!"

"Wal, you know, you look jest right to me, Mrs. Russell," replied her gallant husband.

Nellie mentally rolled her eyes. Mrs. Russell? How pathetically quaint!

"Black tea or herbal?" Aunt Jane interrupted.

"Herbal for me please," said Rebecca.

"Ditto," added Nellie. "I'm cutting back on caffeine."

"You must be the only young person to do so! Metcalf can't live without his six cups of coffee a day," said his mother.

Nellie smiled to herself. It was so like Aunt Jane to consider her and Metcalf peers. How silly was that? He must be thirty by now, at least.

She glanced over at him—he was frowning at his mother. Nellie remembered that since he had started working at the medical clinic in Unity, he preferred to be called 'Doctor Bart,' dropping his conspicuous first name altogether. Her mother had told her that interesting tidbit in an email, but obviously no one had told Doctor Bart's mother.

Metcalf straightened up. "Unfortunately, we don't know how long Maggie will be gone," he replied gravely, speaking to Rebecca. He absent-mindedly ran his long fingers through his rust-colored curls. "Her message to Nellie asked her to return home as soon as possible but implied nothing about Maggie leaving town. I tracked down the taxi driver who took Maggie to the airport, too, but she didn't mention to him her final destination or how long she might be away."

"That's so like Maggie," said Aunt Jane, who was not Nellie's real aunt but rather a second cousin to Maggie. The three—Maggie, Aunt Jane and Uncle Peter—had played together as children on Peter's family farm in Winslow. "I always called her a 'hotel griever' because she'd take off by herself to some hotel room or other whenever she lost anything she loved. When we were in college I didn't see her for nearly a month after her dog died."

"Goodness!" exclaimed Rebecca.

"Oh, God," said Nellie.

Wendell Russell flashed his signature gold-toothed grin. "Thet must'a ben a big hotel bill!"

"Not really. She waited tables at Pride's Restaurant in Greenville in exchange for her room and meals. Maggie always knew how to make her dollar go about as far as five of Peter's and mine. I think she came back to the dorm with more money than she left us with."

"You don't say," said Wendell, further impressed.

"I just thought of something," Rebecca broke in. "What about Maggie's chemotherapy?" She glanced anxiously at Doctor Bart.

"She finished her chemo in July. Her last CT scan was Tuesday and it was clean."

"Thank goodness!"

"That doesn't mean she's entirely off the hook—breast cancer has a bad habit of popping up someplace else in the body. Hence the radiation and chemo. She'll need a follow-up CT scan in three months, but nothing else at the moment."

"When did you last see your mother?" Aunt Jane asked, as she set a fragrant, steaming mug of Maggie's homegrown spearmint tea on the table in front of Nellie.

Nellie felt the hot flush creeping up her neck. Even though she cared little for the opinions of her mother's friends, she was embarrassed to admit she hadn't seen her mother in nearly a year. After spending her Christmas holiday with one set of friends and welcoming in the New Year 2014 with another, Nellie had travelled to Argentina and Nicaragua to intern with Clean World Water, a non-profit organization providing clean drinking water to developing nations. When the internship ended in May, she had been offered a job with them and had stayed on in Nicaragua, even though it had meant missing her own college graduation. Maggie had been upset over that.

Nellie hadn't realized how much her mother had been looking forward to her graduation from Columbia. She wondered now whether her mother had taken flight to a hotel room after hearing that news; but, no, she'd been married to Uncle Peter by then, so she would have sought consolation at home.

Wendell bent his bear-like frame down close to Nellie's ear. "Thet honey's awful good in yore Ma's tea." He pointed to the glass jar sitting in the middle of the table. "I jest extracted 'er t'other day." The jar captured a slanting golden ray of the mid-afternoon sun and the honey was now aglow, as though illuminated from within.

"Tea with Wendell's honey is the most common remedy at our house," Rebecca said proudly. She hooked elbows with her husband, and gave him a fond glance.

Nellie, glad to have something to do, reached for the cut-glass spoon holder and selected a teaspoon. The spoon holder refracted the mysterious August sunlight, splashing multicolored sundogs against the patterned wallpaper. She idly watched the brilliant lights for a moment before exchanging the spoon holder for the jar of honey. Nellie added a modest dollop of the thick elixir to her tea and returned the jar to the table.

"'Tain't 'nuff," Wendell remarked.

She duly spooned out more honey, fighting back what would have been an ironic chuckle. She had always been a bit in awe of Wendell Russell, the town's old-time chicken farmer, with his bulky frame and odd phrases. But the image of a mother hen fussing over her chicks had suddenly popped into her head, and as a result Mr. Russell seemed more approachable than he'd ever been in all the years she'd known him. She flashed him a radiant smile—the smile that opened doors for her around the globe—and the bashful farmer stepped back and nearly tripped over the braided rug.

"Careful," Rebecca cautioned, tightening her grip on her husband.

Doctor Bart cleared his throat. "When *did* you last see your mother, Nellie?" he asked, resuming his role of lead arbitrator.

Nellie rattled the spoon around the ceramic tea mug, dispersing the honey. "Not since before Christmas," she admitted. "You know I've been in Nicaragua. We work in remote villages—without phones and internet—setting up clean drinking water stations. I didn't get Mother's message about Uncle Peter until Sunday, the day she left, apparently." She shook off the silver-plated spoon and set the wet utensil onto the nearest napkin.

"That's odd. Your mother told me you were in Argentina," Rebecca puzzled.

"I was in Argentina for a short while but was reassigned to Nicaragua. I'm sorry I wasn't here for the funeral, but …"

"We missed you, dear," Aunt Jane cried.

"… but I headed home as quickly as I could. I called Maggie as soon as I got her message, but when I couldn't reach Mother on the phone—even though I kept trying and trying—I finally called you to pick me up at the bus station."

"And your mother had already left—tragic!"

"Wal, you know, Nellie done the best she could to git home," Wendell interjected. His defense of her further enhanced Nellie's opinion of the old chicken farmer.

"Nobody's censuring, Nellie," Doctor Bart reassured Wendell. "We're all here to support her. Right, Mother?"

Jane looked contrite. "Oh, certainly, Metcalf."

"But there are things to attend to: bills to pay; Maggie's duties at the church to cover; the house and garden to take care of …." Doctor Bart broke off and gestured meaningfully at the dirty dishes piled up in the sink. "Most likely there are some of Peter's affairs to wrap up, too."

"Do we know who Peter named as his administrator?" Aunt Jane asked.

"Maggie."

There was a mutual drooping of faces around the room. "But the situation could have been worse," Doctor Bart continued. "It turns out Peter had already deeded over Oaknole Farm—land, cows, machinery, everything—to Bruce and Amber not long after he and Maggie were married. I had a chance to talk with Bruce after the funeral—poor guy, he was heartbroken! He and his uncle were like father and son. Anyway, Bruce said they have Peter's affairs at the farm under control and he offered to help with whatever was needed here."

"Without Maggie, I don't think there's much any of us can legally do," said Jane. She worked at the state law library in Augusta and considered herself somewhat of an expert in all things legal. "Would you like me to check the statutes tomorrow?"

"Perhaps first on the agenda should be a consultation with Ryan," Doctor Bart replied.

"Oh. Of course."

Ryan MacDonald was the town's sole attorney, a former big-city lawyer who had flown the coop and married a local farm girl, settling down in Sovereign to sell butter, milk and cheese and, in his spare time, draw up wills and deeds for the locals. "I know he's Maggie's attorney," Metcalf continued, "because she asked Ryan to put her affairs in order when we first discovered the cancer."

"Poor Maggie," lamented Rebecca. "I'm sure she thought she'd be the first to go, after that awful cancer diagnosis. It just reminds us how powerless we are in this world."

"It's a blessing none of us knows who's going to be next," exhorted Jane, with some eloquence.

"All the more reason for us to be kind to one another," declared Rebecca. She gave her husband's arm a squeeze, and then dropped it summarily. "Now … I'll take care of these dirty dishes. Wendell, could you fill the woodbox? We've had some cold nights already and Nellie might need a fire."

"Ayuh," he replied, good-naturedly.

"I'll go get the rest of your things from the truck, Nellie," Jane offered.

"Thanks, Aunt Jane. But I don't have anything except my backpack here." Nellie patted the blue backpack that occupied the chair next to her.

"Oh, my! You young people are certainly different than we were at your age. Maggie and I took four suitcases with us on our trip to Paris when we graduated college."

"Our generation believes in leaving a light footprint," replied Nellie, unable to keep a note of smugness from her voice.

"Well, then—you wash and I'll dry, Rebecca. Hand me that dish towel."

Doctor Bart glanced out the window at Maggie's straggling, dust-covered mailbox. "I'll go get the mail," he said.

"There's more?" Nellie asked, with a quick glance at the pile on the chiffonier.

Metcalf shrugged. "Most likely." He smiled and disappeared through the shed door.

While the others were thus occupied, Wendell turned to the counter and carefully removed a bag of cookies from Maggie's porcelain cookie jar. He held the bag out for Nellie's inspection. "'Tain't right fer these to go to waste," he said, with a boyish grin.

Nellie eyed the cookies closely. "Hey—are those molasses?"

"Ayuh."

"They're my favorite!"

Jane turned around, dripping dinner plate in hand. "Your mother must have baked them specially for you. That's so like Maggie! To take off and leave you by yourself, but bake your favorite cookies as a consolation prize."

"And so like Wendell," laughed his wife, elbows deep in soap suds. "He knows what's hidden in every cookie jar in Sovereign."

Nellie accepted the bag of cookies from Wendell. She smiled—sincerely this time—at the old chicken farmer. "Thanks, Mr. Russell."

"Wal, you know, you kin call me 'Wendell'," he suggested, somewhat bashfully. He hitched up his jeans.

Nellie availed herself of two thick cookies and placed the bag across the table. "Cookie … Wendell?"

"Don't mind if I do," he replied. He winked.

CHAPTER 2
Memories

The sun was setting by the time her mother's friends departed and Nellie had to admit she was grateful for their efforts. The dishes were done up, stove and counter wiped down, floor swept—leaving the kitchen neater and cleaner than Nellie had seen it in many years. The funeral arrangements and Peter's laundry had been discreetly removed. Aunt Jane and Rebecca had then proceeded to straighten up the rest of the house—tackling first the all-important upstairs, Maggie and Peter's bedroom—before moving down to the first floor. Doctor Bart carefully sorted the mail for inspection by Nellie and Ryan at a later date and Wendell did whatever his wife asked him to do. Before they departed, Aunt Jane offered to stay overnight, but Nellie assured her—assured them all—she would be fine by herself.

"I like to be alone," she said, not untruthfully. "It'll give me a chance to get myself together before Ryan comes." Metcalf had been able to reach Maggie's lawyer in the barn during his evening milking and the farmer-cum-attorney offered to stop by the old schoolhouse the following day.

"Is one o'clock OK, Nellie?" Metcalf had asked, covering the black rotary receiver with his hand.

"Sure. Why not," Nellie replied, shrugging. The cat—a gray feline with white boots who had been added to the household since Nellie's last visit—came up and rubbed against the side of her leg. She leaned down and ruffled the animal's fur and the cat began to purr loudly. "What else to I have to do, except play with the cat," she added under her breath.

It seemed strangely comforting to be by herself in the old place. When she was younger, seven or eight, she had been afraid of being left alone during the times her mother was out making visitations or saving souls or consoling the bereaved. But when Nellie was older she had looked forward to those hours of restful solitude, especially the Sundays she had been allowed to stay home from church. She used the opportunities to dream about her future, fantasizing about all the globe-trotting she would do when she was old enough to get away from Sovereign. Now that she had done much of that globetrotting she was surprised how small—and yet how rich in memories—the old schoolhouse felt.

She poked her way through the cottage examining new photographs of her mother and Uncle Peter, discovering masculine additions to the household, petting familiar furniture friends. As she moved along she felt as though the house was watching her, perhaps inspecting her just as much as she was inspecting it. She wondered if the old place would give her a passing grade. Probably not.

She found a new framed photograph on her mother's roll-top desk in the living room, a four-by-six picture of Maggie and Uncle Peter, with Peter's nephew Bruce and Bruce's wife Amber. The picture was obviously taken at the ribbon-cutting ceremony for the opening of the Sovereign Corn Shop Museum, which was held not long before Uncle Peter had died. The corn shop, an old sweet corn processing facility, had once employed nearly all of the town's residents but had been shuttered for more than forty years until Bruce and Amber discovered some new Emily Dickinson material in an old carriage house. The sale at auction of those rare literary collectibles penned by the eccentric poet had subsidized the corn shop's renovation into a museum. Her mother, Uncle Peter, Bruce and Amber had been the driving force behind the museum and Maggie had been disappointed when Nellie hadn't returned for the museum's grand opening. Nellie did feel badly now she had missed the event, mostly because it would have given her one last opportunity to see Uncle Peter. She would have liked to have told him how much he had meant to her. Unfortunately, she had waited too long.

Because of her decision to stay in Nicaragua, she had also missed Miss Hastings' funeral in May. Miss Hastings, a retired music teacher whose father had been superintendent of the corn shop, had been an institution in Sovereign, the heart of the little community. At the time, Nellie had regretted not being there to say 'goodbye' to her piano teacher. She had heard from her mother that Miss Hastings had willed the sweet family cottage on the Russell Hill Road next to Wendell's house to Metcalf, and she was able to mention the propitious inheritance to Doctor Bart as he was departing, the last of the little group to leave.

"In my wildest dreams, I never thought she'd leave the place to me," Metcalf admitted, pausing on the granite stoop outside the shed. A late-day summer shower had nailed down the road dust, leaving the evening air fresh and sweet smelling. "Miss Hastings told me I could have her Seven Sisters rose—I've been tending her mother's old-fashioned rose garden, you know. No, you probably don't know. But anyway … the house and land? No way." He shook his head, still bemused by his unexpected inheritance.

"Are you going to live there?"

"I'm living there now. Everything's gone through probate. Ryan gave me the keys about six weeks ago."

"Very cool."

Doctor Bart hesitated. His thoughtful visage was only partially visible in the dusky folds of the late-summer twilight yet it was obvious to Nellie, who knew him well, he had something else on his mind. She hoped he wasn't going to ruin everything by proposing she share his life at Miss Hastings' house.

He unconsciously twirled his tweed driving cap round and round in his hands. "You might be interested in my idea for the place, Nellie," he said, finally. "I've thought about it for quite a while. I haven't mentioned it to Mom or anyone, but …." Suddenly, he broke off, and stopped twirling. "But … maybe another time. I'd better get going."

Nellie's curiosity was piqued. What was he thinking of for Miss Hastings' house? Obviously, he wasn't going to give piano lessons there, like the late music teacher had done in her studio. But what else was an odd place situated in the middle of nowhere useful for?

Had she still been ten and he eighteen, she would have pressed him for more information. But since she had detected those nascent symptoms of romantic love she was careful not to encourage him. She was honest enough not to want to give him false hopes and, more importantly, she didn't want to risk losing the one true friend she had left in the world. "OK. Thanks for picking me up at the bus station and, you know, helping out."

"No problem. I'm just sorry Aunt Maggie has left you in such a mess."

Nellie shrugged. "That's Maggie."

A frown flitted across his freckled face. "In her defense, Nellie, she was inconsolable when Peter died," he rebuked her, gently. Doctor Bart gazed across the scrubby field next to the house, where the sunset's last gasp illuminated a stretch of fading goldenrod blooms in a mysterious, rose-colored light. "They really loved each other, Aunt Maggie and Peter. For her, when he died, it was as though the sun went down and never came back up." He turned back to Nellie. "I shouldn't tell you this—medical ethics and all—but I had to sedate her for the first day or two."

Nellie felt a pinprick of empathy for her mother. But that rare emotion was soon supplanted by her ever-present anger toward her only parent. She remained stoically silent.

"Anyway, I'm just glad you're home now," Doctor Bart concluded. He popped the driving cap over his unruly curls and smashed it down. "I'll call you tomorrow."

"OK, I'll probably be here."

The cat slipped out the open door, hopped down onto the stone step, and rubbed against his leg. "Get back in there," Doctor Bart said, reaching down and snatching up the cat. He tossed the wiry feline back into the shed. She meowed loudly in protest. "You know you're a house cat."

"Is she?"

"According to Peter—he brought her here from the farm a couple of weeks ago. He told your mother to keep her in because he found coyote scat in back of the shed. Sorry, I can't remember her name."

"She looks like a 'Boots' to me."

"She'll probably answer to anything, as long as you feed her. Look, be sure and let me know if you need anything Nellie." Before she knew what he was doing, he leaned over and gave her a brotherly peck on the cheek. "I'm just up the road now." He smiled, reassuringly.

"Sure, thanks."

Nellie closed the outer door behind him. She leaned her back against the paint-chipped wood, and listened to his footsteps crunching down the gravel path.

What a disappointment! While she certainly hadn't wanted Metcalf to take her in his arms and kiss her, he had wasted a perfectly good opportunity to show off his manly side. But that was so like Metcalf: slow, fussy, and pedantic. No wonder he was still unmarried!

But why did she care how manly he was? Hadn't she always thought of him as too old and too boring a life partner for her? And—most damning of all—wasn't Metcalf her mother's choice of husband for her?

It was at this point Nellie had begun her inspection of the silent, watchful house. Her gaze came back to the corn shop museum photo she still held in her hands, and she hastily set the picture back onto her mother's desk. She moved next to the bathroom, where she discovered poignant evidence of Uncle Peter that Aunt Jane and Rebecca had somehow overlooked: his hand razor, a can of shaving cream, and a tiny mirror on a shelf above the sink. A worn T-shirt hung from a hook on the back of the door and Nellie held the navy cotton shirt to her face, inhaling her stepfather's reassuring scent. Her heart constricted. She had been stoic about her loss until that moment—not having cried a single tear—but she was unable to forbear against the sight and smell of her stepfather's personal items, which suddenly had empowered Uncle Peter to rise up and touch her beyond the grave. Nellie sat down on the closed toilet lid and put her face in her hands. She wept.

Later she unpacked her few belongings from the backpack into the painted dresser in her purple bedroom, which was still the same as she'd left it when she departed for Hathorne, the distinguished New Hampshire boarding school, eight years earlier. Her mother had changed nothing. Her favorite books were just as she had left them on the shelf, silly schoolgirl pictures from magazines were taped to the walls, and her equestrian trophies held down their customary spot on the small maple desk. For the first time in her life Nellie wondered where her mother had gotten the money to pay for her riding lessons. Nellie opened the closet door to hang up two shirts, and laughed out loud when she came face to face with the life-sized poster of Brad Pitt. How she had changed since those days! But then, how Brad Pitt had changed, too!

The timer went off and Nellie returned to the kitchen to withdraw a pasta casserole from the gas oven. Rebecca had defrosted and begun reheating the casserole for her supper ("Aunt Hannah's Company Casserole," she had informed Nellie). Rebecca had also found some yeast rolls in the freezer and Nellie had removed them from the oven earlier. The pasta, tomato sauce and ground beef, and cream cheese casserole, one of many brought to Maggie after Peter's death, was delicious—Nellie knew if nothing else the women of Sovereign were outstanding cooks—and she consumed the moist meal hungrily, figuring that, as a primary griever for Uncle Peter herself, she might as well make use of these savory offerings.

After cleaning up from supper, Nellie texted some college friends about her odd welcoming committee and checked her work email. At nine o'clock she prepared for bed. With the fond excitement of seeing an old friend for the first time in years, she perused her favorite books and finally made her selection. She curled up in her twin bed caressing the novel, enjoying the tactile feel of the hardbound book. She pressed her warm cheek against the cool binding and inhaled the book's leathery fragrance. In a flash, she was young again, sprawled on a blanket beneath the pine tree on a hot summer day, meeting for the first time the girl Anne of Green Gables and her grave new custodians, Marilla and Matthew.

How wonderful life had been in those days! Her mother had always known where to find her that summer because she had spent every waking moment in Avonlea. Her first love had been Gilbert. Her first kiss, a birch tree. Funny, she had never noticed back then how much Avonlea resembled Sovereign, and Matthew, Wendell. Perhaps that was because she hadn't yet gained enough perspective to see the similarities between their differences, like the shadows in a summer woods.

She read for about an hour, until the cat hopped up and managed to worm its way between her face and the book, forcing Nellie to pay the feline its due respects. She marked her place with a bookmark and set the novel down onto the dresser. "OK, you got my attention," she said. "Enough memories for one day." She began to rub the cat's fur backward and forward in a rough fashion. The dry gray hair crackled with static electricity. She snapped off the table lamp and slipped deeper into the warm bed. The house was so quiet she could hear a cricket chirp from the living room. The cat curled up in a contented ball next to her and purred loudly, accompanying the cricket. Nellie felt herself relax, and before she knew it, she slept.

CHAPTER 3
Visitations

The next morning Nellie was barely out of bed when she heard a knock on the outer shed door. She was surprised—and somewhat nettled—to discover Rebecca Russell standing on the granite step. "Mrs. Russell?"

"Oh, please call me 'Rebecca'. Mrs. Russell makes me feel so old. May I come in?"

"Sure, if you don't mind I'm still in my PJs …?"

"Oh, dear! Did I get you out of bed?"

"Not quite." Nellie opened the door wider and Rebecca stepped carefully inside, making her way familiarly into the kitchen. She was a short, attractive woman, with soft brown curls that bounced below her shoulders. She was wearing an oversized long-sleeved print blouse and maternity jeans, and looked fresh, happy, and pretty. Nellie had always wondered about Rebecca's relationship with Wendell Russell, which had been spawned after Nellie had left home. Rebecca had relocated to Sovereign from Boston in 2012 with a friend, Lila Woodsum, at the encouragement of Miss Hastings. Lila had shortly married and moved to northern Maine but Rebecca had stayed to become the wife of Wendell, the long-time bachelor and chicken farmer, who was about twenty years her senior. Rebecca had brought her college-age daughter, Amber, to Sovereign with her and she and Maggie had attempted to promote an intimacy between their two daughters; however, the forced friendship attempt had failed. Amber had recently married Uncle Peter's nephew Bruce and was now living in Winslow at Oaknole Farm.

"May I sit down?" Rebecca asked, poised at the table.

Nellie nodded. "Sure. Why not?"

"Don't worry, I won't stay long." She settled herself into one of the straight-back chairs.

Nellie, not wanting to encourage greater intimacy with her mother's neighbor, forbore taking a seat. Instead, she leaned back against the counter. The cat rubbed up against her legs and she reached down to ruffle the pet's fur. "Are you on your way to Ma Jean's?" she asked. The last thing Nellie knew about Rebecca was that she and Gray Gilpin's grandmother were running the local eatery.

Rebecca shook her head. "No, once Wendell found out I was pregnant he put the axe to that. To tell you the truth, the restaurant was more work than I expected and I think even Maude was ready to bow out. Jessica Gould is running Ma Jean's now, and Shirley Palmer's niece, Sarah Louise, is helping her wait tables."

Nellie, not knowing what to say, recalled one of her mother's pet adages: "When you don't know what to say—say nothing at all."

"I hope you're not offended, Nellie, but I'd like to give you a little advice," Rebecca continued, anxiously. She folded her hands atop the table.

Nellie barely caught herself from rolling her eyes. She pulled out the chair across from Rebecca and plopped down, crossing one leg over a slim thigh. "OK, what's up? Did something else happen I should know about?"

"No, no—not that. But I wanted to be the first one here today because I know you will be visited."

"Visited? You mean as in: 'You will be visited by three ghosts'?"

Rebecca laughed at the allusion to Dickens' 'A Christmas Carol.' It was a cheerful, open-hearted laugh. "I can assure you these ghosts are very much in the flesh," she replied. "And while they might seem a bit overwhelming at first, like Dickens' ghosts their attentions are well-meant."

"I suppose you're alluding to the fact that all the little old ladies in Sovereign will shortly turn out and smother me with cakes and cookies?"

"Yes, exactly. I see you're familiar with the tradition of trying to suffocate sadness with food. I suppose I should apologize in advance for not getting up at five o'clock and baking you a nice custard pie …?"

"Not necessary," Nellie said, allowing the briefest of smiles. "Thanks for the heads-up, but the little old ladies probably won't bother with me. They don't even know me, why would they care about me?"

"But don't you see—that's what makes Sovereign so special, Nellie," Rebecca cried. "They don't need to know you to love and accept you. Your mother once called Sovereign a 'frost pocket of goodness' just for this very reason."

Nellie shrugged. "Suum cuique. To each his own," she said, fingering the handle of her coffee mug. Seeing the puzzled expression on Rebecca's face she added, "I studied Latin at Hathorne Prep."

At the mention of the exclusive New Hampshire prep school, Rebecca hesitated. "I know you've never felt as though Sovereign was your home, Nellie, but maybe this time it will be different for you?"

Nellie frowned. No amount of time would be long enough for that!

"Oh, actually, there is some news. You have a new neighbor. The Lovejoy place changed hands. I don't think you'll have to worry about Mr. Trow visiting you, though, because Wendell says he's a bit of a grump."

"So … the heirs finally settled?"

"I believe there was a court order to sell but I don't keep up with the particulars of all the real estate transactions in town like Wendell does. Would you like me to ask him?"

"Thanks anyway, but I probably won't be here long enough to meet the new owners. It's too bad the place went out of the Lovejoy family, though, after two hundred years. I used to visit old Mrs. Lovejoy but I never met any of her grandchildren. They all live out of state."

Rebecca patted her protruding belly. "That's why I'm so thrilled about my little menopausal baby—sorry! I didn't mean to embarrass you. I forgot for a moment you're not Maggie. Anyway, it's a wonderful gift knowing there's another Russell coming along to care for the old homestead. Otherwise, frankly, I'd be tearing my hair out, pregnant at this age."

No sooner had Rebecca departed than Shirley Palmer, the town's retired postmistress responsible for keeping most Sovereign secrets for fifty years, rapped loudly on the outer door. Nellie rose from the kitchen table to answer the knock, but was startled when the spry elderly woman walked right in without waiting for an invitation. She was dressed in what appeared to be full Sunday regalia.

"I ain't agoing to stay, dearie," Shirley declared, setting a rectangular plastic tub onto the kitchen table. She straightened her hat over tight gray curls. "I jest brought you a little something." She peeled back an edge of the plastic cover to reveal a scrumptious-looking chocolate cake.

Nellie smiled to herself. She snuck a peek at the cake and instantly forgave the former postmistress her intrusion. "Thanks, Mrs.

Palmer. But you shouldn't have done that—Mother's freezer is full of food."

Shirley waived aside her objection. "'Tain't nuthin', dearie. I told Asa when I heared you come home to find yer Ma vamoosed I was agoing to bake you something sweet." Shirley's husband, Asa Palmer, was the town's road commissioner, noted for driving the town's grader down to Gilpin's General Store for donuts and coffee whenever his truck wouldn't start. "Ain't nuthin' like a chocolate cake to pick up one's spirits," she proclaimed, heartily.

"That's for sure!"

"But I told Asa I warn't agoing to stop. You've got plenty to do without me taking up yer valuable time—My! I ain't never seen Maggie's kitchen so clean before!—'cause no doubt, as I said to Asa, I'd have time for a good long chat with you at the meetin' Monday afternoon." She paused, cordially awaiting Nellie's reply, taking the opportunity to pull up her gloves in preparation for her departure.

"What meeting?"

"Why, the Ladies Corn Shop Museum Auxiliary meetin', course! I was shore you'd notice it on yer Ma's calendar." Shirley stepped to the hanging wall calendar and pointed out the encircled date. "Probably you ain't hed time to look, though, poor dearie."

Nellie politely inquired about the time of the meeting, realizing the moment her question was broached she had made a serious mistake. The inquiry loosened Shirley's loquacious tongue.

"Wal, now," Shirley began, her furrowed brown face lighting up, "course you know the Ladies Auxiliary always used to meet the second Wednesday of the month at seven o'clock but for one reason or 'nother we begun meetin' the second Monday of the month at one o'clock in the afternoon. I think them men of ours hed something to do with that change. They don't like drivin' at night. Not that they'd be drivin' any of us to whar we needed to go—Oh, no! We change meetin' places every time, you remember, dearie. No, them men'd be agoing 'bout thar own business, getting themselves pie 'n donuts and acting like a silly bunch of schoolgirls while we ladies all gets together and does the actual work. They got their club and we got ours, I guess you could say." She paused and straightened her hat.

Nellie glanced at the hanging calendar. "But the second Monday of the month was this past Monday."

"Oh, yes! I was gettin' to thet. Wal, we changed the date on account of Peter's funeral and memorial service 'n all—we're all jest as sorry as we could be 'bout Peter! So out of respect 'n all we moved the meetin' to next Monday. You will come, now, won't you, Nellie? My great-niece—Sarah Louise, Myron's girl, you know; she's livin' with us now—is dyin' to meet you. You two gals is about the same age."

Nellie suspected she'd much rather attend the men's club and eat donuts than attend the women's group and listen to the ladies' charitable endeavors; however, she glanced again at the plastic tub. She groaned to herself. Was every act of kindness going to be accompanied by a reciprocal request?

"Sure. Why not," Nellie replied, vowing to herself she would say 'No' next time—no matter what the request.

During the forenoon two other matrons stopped by with a cake and casserole. Nellie politely accepted the offerings. Recognizing each of the women from her church-going days, she had invited them in. Fortunately, both ladies declined, and neither pressed invitations upon her. Perhaps there was going to be some consolation after all!

Ryan MacDonald, her mother's attorney, arrived as scheduled at one o'clock. He was dressed in blue jeans, LL Bean boots and a flannel shirt, and carried a leather briefcase. Ryan was a tall, handsome man, self-confident, as anyone would expect of a former high-powered Boston attorney. Nellie had always had a secret crush on him. Now, if her mother had picked *him* as a potential partner for her daughter, Nellie might have come home more often!

Strange that someone with Ryan's looks and talents would choose Sovereign, Maine as his home, however, when he could live anywhere in the world. And to take up with Trudy Gorse—when he could have any woman in the world! A commonplace farm girl whose biggest claim to fame was she made the best butter in Maine! But somehow the two had gotten together. Maggie had told her the couple had had their first child in February—a cute photograph of little Alice Rose was posted on the superannuated white fridge, along with many other of Maggie's 'kids'—and apparently they were happy, even though they were living at Scotch Broom Acres with Trudy's father, Leland Gorse, who certainly wouldn't be Nellie's first choice of a father-in-law.

Nellie didn't begrudge Ryan and Trudy their happiness, however. She just couldn't comprehend the attractions for a worldly man like Ryan MacDonald.

Ryan set the briefcase on the table, and made himself at home. "Here's the deal, Nellie," he began, somewhat abruptly. "Your mother put all of her affairs in order this summer." He pulled a sheaf of stiff ivory-colored papers from the leather briefcase and spread them on the tablecloth in front of her. "This is her Advance Health Care

Directive and this—important for our discussion here today—is her Durable Financial Power-of-Attorney. Maggie named Peter as attorney-in-fact in both documents; however, in the event Peter predeceased her, your mother designated you as her alternate attorney-in-fact."

Nellie lifted the stapled Durable Financial Power of Attorney and pretended to peruse the legal mumbo-jumbo on the top page. She returned the stiff document to the table. "Great," she said. "What does it mean?"

"It means that Maggie has given you the authority and power to undertake and carry out any and all acts which may be necessary in the management of her affairs, in every respect as full and complete a manner as she herself might do. You can pay her bills. You can enter into contracts on her behalf. You can do whatever you think right and proper, until she returns to take up her own affairs. Most Powers of Attorney such as this are never activated until a person dies or becomes incompetent, but in this case …"

"In this case I think we could say Mother is basically incompetent," Nellie interrupted, unable to restrain her growing anger at her only parent.

Ryan's brown eyes opened wide and a surprised expression overcame his tanned visage. Nellie blushed. "I didn't mean that like it sounded," she added, lamely.

"Don't apologize, Nellie," he said, in a penitential tone of voice. "I'm an unfeeling idiot—to rush right into business! Trudy is always reminding me I'm not in Boston anymore. This must be an extremely difficult time for you. Everyone who knew him loved Peter, but he wasn't *our* father."

He wasn't mine, either, thought Nellie, sadly. This time, however, she managed to hold her tongue.

Hot tears filled her eyes. Suddenly, she felt like she was five years old again, much like the time when her mother had taken her into Portland and, in the middle of downtown, handed her two letters to mail. Nellie had skipped happily across the street, but when she had returned from posting the letter in the ubiquitous blue metal mailbox, she'd been shocked and dismayed to discover her mother had disappeared, leaving her by herself. Years later, Maggie had told her that her disappearing act was a 'growth opportunity,' and she had been watching her daughter the whole time from a discreet distance. "You were never alone," she'd emphasized.

Wasn't I? Nellie thought bitterly to herself. Wasn't I always alone?

She leaned forward, covering her face with her hands, commanding herself not to bawl, as she had done that day in downtown Portland.

"Go ahead and cry, Nellie," Ryan urged, kindly. "You'll feel better afterward."

Oh-my-God—she had forgotten all about Ryan MacDonald! Nellie choked back the tears. "I'm fine," she said, straightening up and flipping her long blonde hair back over her shoulder defiantly. "What's next?"

When Ryan left Nellie wandered into the living room and once again took up the photo of her mother and Uncle Peter at the Corn Shop Museum opening. The tears came freely now. She heartily repented her stubborn pigheadedness in not returning home for that event. She only hoped that in Heaven Uncle Peter knew how much she loved him.

Nellie continued to receive visitors throughout the week. Empathetic fussing matrons and two or three hoary farmers holding stained, dusty caps appeared on her doorstep with offerings of food, condolences, and kind words about her mother and Uncle Peter. She was therefore relieved and gratified when she opened the shed door Thursday night and discovered her young friend Gray Gilpin catching rain from the eaves in the bright white of the outdoor light.

"Gray! God, it's good to see you. Get in here before you drown."

Gray stepped inside and shook himself off. He removed his baseball cap and knocked it against the door frame. Water sprayed everywhere. "Sorry I'm here so late but I couldn't get away until the store closed."

"Don't even think about it. I'm just glad to see someone under seventy. Come in and get warm by the stove."

The two young people were soon settled at the kitchen table. Some small talk ensued. Gray unsnapped his coat and suddenly launched headlong into a prior conversation from Nellie's last visit home. "Remember when ya told me ya thought yer Dad was a beach bum? Well, I been thinkin' bout thet lately."

"Oh? Why's that?"

"Ya know—Uncle Peter 'n all." He slipped out of his jacket and draped the raincoat around the back of the oak kitchen chair. In point of fact, Peter Hodges had been Gray's great-uncle, brother to the youth's grandmother Maude Gilpin.

Nellie attempted to recall the specifics of the conversation he alluded to, which confab had occurred the prior winter when he'd come over to shovel snow off the roof. "I think, Gray, what I said was my mother probably used a sperm donor, and I jokingly alluded to the fact my father might have been a surfer from California or a theoretical physicist."

"Yeah, like Stephen Hawking."

"Like Stephen Hawking."

"But what if he ain't like Stephen Hawking?" Gray continued, leaning forward and resting his skinny forearm on the table. "What if yer Dad's, like, the Organic Kidd?"

Tom Kidd was a thirty-something certification guru with the Maine Organic Growers Group (MOGG) headquartered in Unity. His shady reputation was well-known to everyone in Sovereign, including Nellie. "Don't be stupid, Gray. Tom Kidd is even younger than your father. He can't possibly be my father."

"Just sayin'," Gray replied, unfazed. "Got any cake left?"

Nellie had already informed her visitor of the townspeople's generosity. "No. Want a cookie?"

"Sure."

She retrieved some cookies from the pantry and set the plastic tub on the table in front of Gray. "These are your mother's. What's up with her and Mr. Nutter, anyway?"

Gray helped himself to a stack of four cookies and pushed the tub across the table toward Nellie. "What do you mean—what's up? She lives on the farm with him, that's all. Got any milk?"

Wordlessly, Nellie got up and poured her visitor some cold milk from a glass jar affixed with a Scotch Broom Acres label that Ryan had brought her along with milk, eggs and butter. She had not yet needed to visit a grocery store, thanks to the outpouring of food Rebecca had warned her about and the contents of her mother's larder. Nellie set the glass on the table in front of Gray and resumed her seat. "And you have a new half-sister?"

"Yeah, Olivia. She's OK. Kinda cute."

"How's school going?" Nellie knew that Gray had started Thomas College in July.

"Pretty good, 'til Uncle Peter died. Now I'm missin' classes left 'n right 'cause Grandpa and Grandma are ovah at the farm with Dad and Amber. I'm runnin' the store by myself, now, so I ain't got much time for school."

"That's too bad. An education is an important stepping stone to breaking the cycle of poverty."

"Aw, I ain't missin' much—and we ain't poor, neither. Besides, I like runnin' the store by myself, makin' all the decisions 'n stuff."

"I guess you'll probably take over the store from your grandfather someday?"

"Yep. But Grandpa ain't dead yet. He's got a lotta life left in him."

"That's what we all thought about Uncle Peter."

"Right." Gray's face fell.

Nellie saw the youth was fighting back tears. She hesitated, and then got up and poured him some more milk. "I miss him too. He was the only father I ever knew."

Gray dashed the tears away with the back of his hand. "Yeah. So … ya gonna find yer real Dad, now?"

Nellie, who was in the process of returning the milk to the fridge, stopped in her tracks. She felt a sick feeling in the pit of her stomach. "Why do you say that?"

"No reason. Jest thought 'twould be what I'd do."

She finished her task and resumed her seat. "I've thought about trying to track down my father," she said slowly. "But then I think that might be opening up a can of worms. I've got a college friend who found her father and now wishes she hadn't. Who needs another problem?"

Gray chuckled. "Aw, ya don't gotta worry none, Nellie. Jest look in the mirror! Yer Dad ain't gonna be a problem. Most likely he was some college kid from Away who needed a few extra bucks 'n donated his sperm and now he's my algebra teacher."

Nellie found herself smiling. "Maybe I'll sign up for one of his classes, then, just to see what he's like. Seriously, I wish there was a way of being a fly on my father's wall before introducing myself—just in case."

"Seems creepy to me—spyin' on yer Old Man."

"What! Did you take an ethics class at Thomas?"

Gray shrugged off her jab. "Maybe I been doin' some thinkin' on my own since Uncle Peter died. Didja evah think how different yer life might-a been if yer parents was like, regular folks?"

"Sure. When I was eight or nine. I thought having a married mom and dad would be the greatest thing in the world. When I was a teenager, though, and saw all my friends' parents getting divorced—nothing personal meant, Gray…"

"Nothin personal taken."

"... and saw how screwed up they all got, I thought maybe a 'normal' family wasn't so hot."

"Do ya think ya'd be different?"

"If I'd grown up with a father? Sure. Do you?" Gray's father had rarely been home during his childhood, having been off fighting the wars in Iraq and Afghanistan for ten years.

"Yeah. I think so. I know so."

"But you're so much like you're grandfather, Gray!"

"Yeah, well maybe I would'a been more like my Dad if he'd been around more, doncha know? Sometimes I did stuff, too—stupid stuff—jest 'cause I was angry at him."

"Like acting out?"

"Yeah. Ya must'a done some of thet stuff, too, Nellie ...?"

If Gray's question had been a comment rather than a question, she would have taken it as an accusation, and probably refused to answer him. Instead, Nellie heard the remark as nothing more than the commiseration of a comrade. "I probably did some acting out of my own," she answered, honestly, "although I can't think of anything specific at the moment."

"What 'bout not comin' home for Miss Hastings' funeral? What 'bout not comin' back for the corn shop museum openin'? What 'bout ..."

She gestured for him to stop. "OK, I get it. You don't need to list all my transgressions, Gray. God, you must have taken that ethics class!"

He shrugged again. "If the shoe fits ..."

CHAPTER 4
Of Grandmothers and Roses

On Friday morning Nellie sat down to pay her mother's bills, many of which were overdue. Ryan had informed her that Maggie had added her name to her mother and Peter's checking and savings accounts so she needn't provide the bank with a copy of the Durable Financial Power of Attorney. "Just stop into the bank sometime and give them your signature so they have it on file," the lawyer advised. "I've already given them a copy of Peter's death certificate." He explained that the accounts were joint tenants with rights of survivorship, so what was once Maggie and Peter's jointly was now Maggie's—and Nellie's—without having to pass through probate.

She had discovered two checkbooks inside her mother's roll-top desk, obviously left for her to find. She had rolled back the cover of the antique oak desk, which had once belonged to Maggie's grandmother, and had found the checkbooks, her mother's keys—and her cell phone. The cell phone was shut off. "No wonder she never answered any of my calls!" Nellie fumed.

Underneath everything was a yellow legal pad with what appeared to be the scribbled beginnings of one of her mother's sermons. Nellie set the pad aside without reading it and poked through the papers in the desk, uncovering a raft of unpaid medical bills. She made a quick search of the small upper drawers and slots and located Maggie's savings book. She flipped through the pages of the green passbook and noted her mother had made several big withdrawals over the past few months, no doubt to cover the copays of her breast cancer treatment. Nellie reached for the calculator and added everything up. In total, her mother had less than five thousand dollars to her name—and her medical copays would take a third of that!

How was Maggie going to pay for her grief junket? What if she didn't come home for a month or more? Would the church continue to pay her salary? Her medical insurance?

Nellie recalled Aunt Jane's tale of Maggie waiting tables at Pride's Restaurant in Greenville and she nearly laughed out loud. Her mother had gained thirty pounds since college and certainly wasn't spry enough to wait tables. "She might wash dishes," Nellie mused to herself. "But that's about it."

The cat jumped up into her lap and pushed between her and the desk. Nellie slid the wheeled desk chair back a few inches so she could pull the cat's tail. "What do you think, Boots?" she asked. "Maybe we'll both have to eat cat food." The cat meowed what sounded like a mournful cry of commiseration.

Nellie realized she would probably need to get a job as soon as possible, that is, if she was going to remain in Sovereign. But what other choice did she have? Someone in the family had to be responsible.

She sighed. Why did *she* always have to be the mature one?

After a lunch of leftovers, Nellie decided she would walk up and visit Doctor Bart. She lifted a light-weight fleece jacket she'd left hanging on the Shaker-style wooden peg rack in the shed and slipped into it. The fleece wasn't something she'd be caught dead wearing in public, but for the backwater of Maine the green jacket was perfectly acceptable.

Nellie hadn't seen Metcalf since her first evening home, but he had called her several times and had invited her to stop over Friday afternoon, his day off from the clinic. Barring any unforeseen medical emergencies—he was on-call—he would be at home, he said. Nellie was beginning to get lonely, despite the never-ending stream of visitors, and was longing for intelligent conversation. She had accepted Doctor Bart's invite even though it went against her better judgment.

But why shouldn't she spend time with him? What would be the worst thing that could happen? Metcalf would ask her to marry him and she would graciously—but respectfully—decline. She might as well get it over with, sooner rather than later.

Besides, she told herself, she wanted to consult with him about Maggie's financial situation. In addition, she was curious to see the place she was so familiar with—Miss Hastings' house and studio—which was now entrusted to Doctor Bart's care.

The old schoolhouse where Maggie lived was situated about half way down the Cross Road, the isolated dirt road whose sole purpose now was to connect the Russell Hill Road to the Ridge Road where, among others, Ryan MacDonald and his family lived. The Cross Road had once been part of the old stagecoach line leading from

Augusta to Bangor, however, so the road bed was laid out straight and narrow. The road was lined with a mix of mature maples, birch and balsams, which crowded up to the gravel ditch and stretched their branches across the road as though trying to hold hands. The recent hard rain had left the road damp and musty smelling. Just prior to the rain Asa had motored past in the town's truck scattering calcium chloride pellets. The dirt road was now streaked with salt, turning the hard-packed track prematurely aged white.

A pair of distrustful crows preceded Nellie's progress up the road, flapping their black wings and loudly cawing out a warning to any interested party. The land on either side of the road had belonged to the Lovejoy family until recently but now was owned by the newcomer Henry Trow. Nellie had always felt connected to the Lovejoys, not only because they were neighbors but also because the land for the old schoolhouse had been carved from the Lovejoy family's original purchase. Asa Lovejoy, the first minister, had married a member of the prominent and wealthy Wentworth family, and their monies had built the town's first church and the school. Although the church had been built on the main road, land for the schoolhouse had been cut out of the Lovejoy property. When, in the twentieth century, Sovereign's many one-room schools had been consolidated into one larger building, the Lovejoy heir had added nine more acres to the property, which was then auctioned off to raise money for the town. By the time Maggie purchased the place in 1998, it had changed hands nearly a dozen times and the odd assortment of sheds and outbuildings had been cobbled onto the one-room schoolhouse.

As Nellie hiked along she suddenly noted that the trees lining the road were tacked with a slew of ugly yellow "No Trespassing" signs. She made a little face. Why was it everyone from Away immediately had to post their land? By contrast, the Lovejoy family had always kept their land open for public access, something Maggie and Nellie as neighbors and abutters had always appreciated and respected.

As Nellie hoofed up Lovejoy Hill, enjoying the dappled sun on her face and the fragrance of the musky woods in her lungs, she suddenly spied a tall, bearded man making his way through the thick forest about a hundred yards to her right. She paused and watched for a moment, long enough to distinguish that the man was not hunting but rather was preoccupied with the ground. He scooched down and gathered something into a wicker basket and Nellie realized he was mushroom hunting, a common pastime in Maine from late summer through the early fall. She surmised the bearded stranger to be her new neighbor, Henry Trow, and would have stopped to introduce herself had he not been so far away and so engrossed by the mushrooms.

At the intersection of the Russell Hill Road, the Cross Road abruptly ended, having done its duty by connecting the two paved secondary roads. Nellie paused at the top of the hill to catch her breath, taking the opportunity to enjoy the variety of views. To the south, the distinguished-looking two-story brick Lovejoy house perched atop the ridge like a watchful sentinel. The venerable brick house, built circa 1840 by the second son of the second generation, rested on huge blocks of granite and featured impressive granite eyebrows over the windows and doors. To the west, gently sloping hayfields stretched down to meet an indistinguishable line of balsam firs, spruce, pine, and other softwoods. On the eastern side of the road and at the very summit of Russell Hill, sprawled the Russell Hill Cemetery, where Miss Hastings and most residents of Sovereign were buried. The graves closest to the road were the oldest, of course. The headstones, weathered gray sentinels, faced west, some leaning forward as though genuflecting, a few others prostrate on the ground. Nellie paused momentarily at the entrance to the cemetery, silently promising Miss Hastings she would return soon to pay her last respects.

From the cemetery, it was a short walk down the hill to Miss Hastings' house. When Nellie reached the little yellow cottage that had formerly belonged to the retired music teacher, she spied Metcalf at work in the old rose garden. The garden had been planted on a slight rise of land behind the house by Miss Hastings' mother, a rose enthusiast, who with her husband had emigrated from Russia, bringing to the new country some antique roses from the old.

Metcalf straightened up when he saw Nellie approach, raising a leather-gloved hand in greeting. "C'mon up—but watch the thorns," he called.

Nellie hiked across the grassy sward, slowing when she reached the white painted gate leading into the overgrown garden. She gently pushed her way through creaking gate, ducking away from several thorny vines that reached down through the wooden arbor as though trying to snatch her silky blonde hair. Once inside the garden she gazed around in amazement at the mess of entangled vines, fragrant rose blooms, and overgrown bushes. "Wow! I haven't been up here since I was a kid. I can't believe how wild it's gotten since then."

"Miss Hastings hadn't been able to take care of the roses for a long time," Doctor Bart said. "She wasn't much of a rosarian anyway. And Gray, who always mowed her lawn and weeded the flowers around the house, avoided this place like the plague. He was smart—smarter than me."

"I doubt that." A friendly chickadee flitted to the top of a stalwart, wine-colored sucker and cocked its black-capped head, examining her closely. Nellie felt an unusual thrill of happiness pervade her being. She stretched out a bare hand toward the chickadee, but it flew away.

The breeze ruffled Metcalf's loose, reddish-blond curls and he unconsciously removed his glove and straightened his hair. He shifted his stance, and when he turned, Nellie noted an ugly-looking scratch across his right cheek, which was just beginning to ooze blood. "You cut yourself," she pointed out.

"I did?" He lightly touched his cheek, and examined the blood on his fingers. "I didn't feel it."

"Too bad you don't know a good doctor," Nellie joked. They both laughed. The feeling of happiness radiated throughout her body, endowing her with an unfamiliar sensation of contentment.

Doctor Bart daubed the blood from his cheek with the tail of his flannel shirt. "You'd never know I've been working in here off and on for the past few months, trying to bring some order to this chaos."

She stared at him, as though seeing him for the first time. He seemed so natural, so at ease, so confident in himself. Had he changed? Or—God forbid!—had she?

"I didn't know you were into roses," she remarked. "Do you have any yellow ones? I love them best, probably because yellow roses are so different."

"Not yet, but there's an old-fashioned yellow bush at the farm I'm going to clone next year. I couldn't find a good piece to transplant or I would have brought it up this summer. Take a look at that…"

He jerked his thumb to the right and Nellie's gaze obediently followed his direction. She spied a delicate rose bush and could tell by the rich black soil around the base that the plant was a new addition to the garden.

"That's the Metcalf Rose," he explained. "It's a hot pink rose—about the color of Canada mints—with a wonderful old-fashioned scent. It was propagated by my great-great-great grandfather Metcalf in Albion. I moved a piece of it up from my grandmother's farm a few weeks ago. The woman who bought the place gave me permission to dig it up."

Nellie was duly impressed. "Must be nice! Most people don't have a rose named after them."

"Most people don't have a baby cow in their first name, either."

Nellie laughed. "Touché."

"And it's actually the other way 'round—I'm named after the rose; the rose isn't named after me. But that's not why I love roses. They have so many uses: medicinal, culinary, household, to say nothing of the beauty and fragrance of a bouquet of fresh cut roses. See these rose hips?" Doctor Bart latched carefully onto one spindly arm of a multi-headed scrubby bush full of bright orange rose hips. "They're loaded with vitamin C. I've dried a bunch already. We can have some rose hip tea when we go in. Maggie usually harvests Miss Hastings' rose hips for her herbal teas but she's gonna have to fight me for 'em this year."

"I must say, I'm not usually interested in all things botanical, but, really, you make it sound so intriguing."

Doctor Bart released the vine. "Your mother probably tried to push her herbs onto you when you were a kid, and you rebelled."

"Most likely."

"You always were a rebel, Nellie. Always had to do everything your own way. Now, if you'd had a grandmother who wanted to teach you about herbs … that would have been a different story altogether. When I was a kid, I wouldn't weed our vegetable garden but I'd help my Grandmother Metcalf with things you wouldn't think a boy would be caught dead doing. We used to make rose beads with some of her *Rosa gallica officinalis*—that's the Apothecary's Rose—beautiful dark beads we'd string together into a necklace. She put them in her handkerchief drawer to keep her hankies smelling fresh. We made rose water, too. We'd pick a basketful of fresh blooms each morning—when the dew was just off the roses—and simmer the petals in distilled water in one of those big white enamel pots she had. Gram concocted one of her more popular remedies by adding Valerian Root to the rose water, which she then handed out to all her female friends as a restorative."

"Did it work?"

He chuckled. "Let's just say there was no danger she would put old Doc Thompson out of business. Although Valerian Root does have a calming effect," he added, as an afterthought. "Most women of Gram's day cooked with their rose water, too. Grandma Metcalf baked the best rose custards and creams you've ever eaten in your life."

Metcalf had warmed to his subject and a flush of enthusiasm spread across his freckled face. His hazel eyes sparkled. He was dressed in a pair of faded blue jeans that hugged his thighs and a plaid flannel shirt over a Henley that helped give substance to his bony shoulders. Nellie thought she had never seen him look so attractive before.

"One July when I was about thirteen we tried to make attar of roses," he continued. "I was into chemistry at the time and Grandma found some old distilling equipment—somebody's old bootleg hooch operation—at a yard sale. We set it up in her old kitchen and went to work." He smiled at the recollection. "Do you know how many rose petals it takes to make one ounce of rose oil? You'll never guess, so I'll tell you. Sixty thousand blooms! We worked our butts off all day—nearly burned the place down—and still only managed to squeak out three drops of rose oil."

"Oh-my-God."

"Still, that was the highlight of my summer," he concluded, cheerfully.

His words reminded Nellie of the difference in their family situations, and a sharp pang of reality burst her light-hearted bubble. "I never had a grandmother," she said, enviously.

Doctor Bart's face fell. He was immediately contrite. "I'm so sorry, Nellie—I forgot Maggie's mother died before you were born. And here I am babbling on about my grandmother like an idiot."

She shrugged. "I'm used to being different. It's no big deal."

"It *is* a big deal, Nellie," he said, seriously. He reached out and took her hand. "Grandparents are some of the few people in our lives who will love us unconditionally, no matter what we do, no matter what we say. None of us ever have enough of that." He gave her hand a reassuring squeeze and let her go.

Nellie frowned at the ground, stubbornly refusing to be placated. A fat caterpillar was squirming across the short stretch of grass that constituted the path, yet she failed to see what was just before her eyes. "The worst thing is," she said, her tone hard and accusatory, "I could have a grandmother living at this very moment. She might be walking around Winslow or Albion and even growing roses for all I know! But I'll never get to know her because I don't know who my father is."

Metcalf stared at her intently. "Have you ever asked Aunt Maggie?"

"Who my father is? No. I've never asked her that question point blank. I figured if she wanted me to know, she would have told me by now. And I'm *way* too proud to start asking questions at this point in my life!"

"You know what they say—'Pride goeth before a fall'."

"Yeah, right." A singular idea popped into her head. She glanced up at him, pulse quickening. "You don't know who my father is, do you?"

"What—me?"

"You're her doctor."

"Sorry, Nellie, but Aunt Maggie never confided in me about her private life, especially anything as personal as who your father is." Doctor Bart paused a moment. "Funny, now that you mention it," he added, "my mother has never said anything to me about your father, either."

"So, it's a taboo topic with Aunt Jane, too. That figures. Then I'll never know who my father is," she stated, bitterly.

"That doesn't necessarily follow. There are legal ways to find out one's parentage. Who's listed on your birth certificate? Have you seen it?"

She nodded. "Of course. I needed my birth certificate to get my passport. No one's listed, except my mother."

"Maybe your father wanted to remain anonymous? Maybe he doesn't want to be found?"

"I don't think that's the case. From the things Mother's let slip over the years I'm almost positive he doesn't know I exist."

"Well, you're probably right. If your father knew about you he certainly would have come forward to claim you before now. Who wouldn't want such a smart, sophisticated young woman for a daughter?"

"My point exactly," Nellie said. They both laughed.

"I can make some inquiries for you, if you want?" he offered. "Find out what you need to do to start the ball rolling?"

Nellie felt the inveterate anxiety. This was always the sticking point! On one hand she wanted to know who her father was yet on the other hand she was afraid to know the truth. She had heard way too many horror stories about people who had tracked down their natural parents only to wish they hadn't.

"Come, Nellie, what's the problem?"

"What if I find out he's a dump truck driver who collects trash for a living? Or a drunk? What if I don't like him?"

"What if you find out he's an astrophysicist with a new take on string theory?"

Nellie smiled faintly. "Sure. That's the one."

"Finding out the truth is a risk you'll have to take. But I know how brave you are. You can do this. Besides, I can't see Aunt Maggie picking a drunken dump truck driver for your father, not when she always had a steady guy like Peter waiting in the wings."

"That's true. Poor guy! She led him on for years."

He let the slur against her mother go without rebuking her. "Speaking of Peter … you're sure it's not him?"

"Absolutely. He told me so himself. Precocious me—I asked him when I was about eight."

"Too bad you didn't think to ask him who your father was. He probably knew."

"I so wanted it to be him! When I found out Uncle Peter wasn't my father, I just let the whole thing drop." She sighed. "Oh, well. Can't ask him now."

"Let me be Peter's stand-in," he urged. "What do you say, Nellie? Shall I make some inquiries for you?"

The friendly chickadee returned to its perch. Nellie held out her hand and this time the little bird did not fly away, merely cocked its black-capped head and glanced inquisitively at her. Nellie took that as a positive sign. "Sure. Why not?"

Metcalf reached around her to swing open the wooden gate. The bird fluttered off. "Good girl. Let's go in and get that cup of rosehip tea."

CHAPTER 5
"Whose Woods These Are"

It was a given Nellie would go to church on Sunday. She had received word late in the week from Shirley Palmer that a guest minister would fill in for her mother and also that there would be a meeting of the church's ministry committee after coffee hour. Shirley informed her that the impromptu meeting had been called to discuss how the Sovereign Union Church would proceed in the short term without its settled pastor. Nellie knew given the circumstances of Maggie's disappearance it was necessary she attend both church and the meeting.

How Nellie would get to church was not a given, however. Although Maggie had left her car at the house, Nellie, a self-avowed urbanite, had never learned to drive. In the city—or even while working for Clean World Water—this had not been a problem. But there was no public transportation or handy shuttle bus in Sovereign, Maine. Nellie momentarily kicked herself for her youthful decision not to take Driver's Ed, a decision she knew she had made mostly because it would annoy her mother.

Annoyed Maggie was. "I won't continue to drive you around like you're in middle school," her mother had warned after Nellie had told her in a telephone conversation that she was skipping Driver's Ed at Hathorne yet again. "We live in the country, Nellie, not in New York City. You know there's no public transportation here. How will you get around when you're home?"

"Don't worry, Mother, I'm perfectly capable of finding my own rides."

"Now, that's a relief!" Maggie had replied sarcastically. "Do you think I'm a fool? I know how it is with teenage boys and cars, Nellie. They drive too fast. They drink too much. And they like to get you into the backseat."

"If this is going to turn into a treatise about sex, Mother, you can just skip over that. I know all about it."

"Oh, I can skip over that, can I? Listen young lady, you're still my daughter. And until you're eighteen, you'll listen respectfully to whatever I want to say to you—whether it's about sex or anything else—and whether you want to hear it or not. You might think you've gotten out from under my thumb by getting a full scholarship to that swank prep school but never forget I can yank you home anytime I please."

Nellie had felt panicked then. "OK, OK. I'll be careful who I ride with, I promise. I just really … I don't feel like learning how to drive is all."

Maggie had appeared slightly appeased. "Well, I'm sorry to hear that because independence is an important thing for a young woman. And while I can't make you take Driver's Ed, I can guarantee you'll regret this decision someday."

Although she would never admit it to her mother, Nellie had almost immediately regretted her decision not to learn how to drive. There had been times—especially at Hathorne but even at Columbia—when she had experienced a demeaning feeling of dependence, begging for rides from those whose company she would not otherwise have kept. And how much easier her life would be now if she had learned how to drive!

On Saturday, Doctor Bart, upon learning of her predicament, offered to give her a lift to church. "I need to go to church more often," he allowed. "Your mother's been very good since I moved to town—she never says a word to me about not seeing my smiling face in her pews. But I know she feels it."

Nellie had politely refused Metcalf's offer, not wanting to be seen together at church with him. She had already picked up from some suggestive remarks from a few of the little old ladies who visited that there was a general belief in town she and Doctor Bart were an item. She certainly didn't want to give substance to that rumor!

Later that same day Rebecca phoned to invite Nellie to go to church with her. Suspicious that her neighbor had been prompted by Doctor Bart, Nellie stubbornly declined that ride, too. "If it's a nice day, I'd rather walk."

"But it's nearly three miles!" Rebecca protested.

"Not if you go through the woods—it's only a mile and a half."

"For a city girl, you sure make yourself at home in the country, Nellie!"

"I like to walk in the woods," Nellie remarked, perhaps not recollecting how many years it had been since she'd actually taken a stroll in the Maine woods.

Sunday morning Nellie dressed for church with uncharacteristic carelessness, electing to wear a pair of ugly polyester pants her mother had bought for her years ago and which had been hanging in her closet ever since. What did it matter what she wore? There would be no one she cared about to see her. She found a knit ribbed shirt in her dresser and a pair of leather ankle boots in the back of her closet. It had rained again overnight and she suspected it would be cold and damp in woods so she borrowed one of her mother's wool sweaters. The over-sized, coffee-colored sweater, which fell considerably below her slim hips, was embellished with puce trim around the neck and wrists and decorated with large, matching florets. Nellie made a face when she saw her reflection in the full-length bathroom mirror. "I look like something straight out of 'Little Miss Sunshine'," she told the cat, who was weaving about her ankles during the entire dressing process, a silent, sympathetic partner. The cat replied with her usual mournful meow. Nellie's habiliment complete, shortly after ten o'clock she set off through the woods for church.

The woods nearby was comprised of balsam fir, white pine, and some hardwoods and had been intermittently logged by the Lovejoys since Nellie and her mother had moved to town. Remnants of old logging roads crisscrossed the land and she struck out on one of these now, feeling confident she could find her way. Many times in her younger years she had hiked to the Millett Rock, a giant boulder deposited upon Wendell Russell's property during the last Ice Age and a popular picnic spot. From the Millett Rock Nellie knew she could find the well-trod path that led up to the Russell Hill Road, and from there it was only about half a mile to the church.

She hummed to herself as she set off up the woods road, lightly pushing aside the damp branches of several young balsams screening the entrance. The woods smelled like fresh earth and decaying leaves. Cooler August nights had turned the swamp maples, always the first to display their foliage, a flaming red and they cast their resplendence upon the rest of the forest. As she walked along she heard the sound of trees weeping. She glanced upward at the towering, moist canopy and spotted a lone maple leaf spiraling earthward. She captured the damp supple leaf before it hit the ground and inspected it, enchanted by its diversity of color. The rose-orange leaf looked as though it had swallowed the prior evening's spectacular sunset.

She began to notice little things in the forest, things she had never seen before: an abandoned wooden tree-stand, moss-covered and rotted; the bold zebra striping of a patch of young birches; three rusty spikes entombed in a giant oak, evidence of a former but now forgotten glory; and dozens of strange-looking, colorful mushrooms, suddenly as ubiquitous as salt and pepper shakers on a dining room table. Nellie stooped over to examine a patch of conspicuous-looking, rusty-red mushrooms popping up at the base of a gigantic pine tree. She lightly touched one of the moist, furry caps, wondering if the queer-looking thing was edible. She broke the red cap off from its rubbery stem and sniffed it. The woodsy scent made her taste buds tingle. Perhaps on her way home from church she would pick some mushrooms to fry up for her supper. But … were these mushrooms safe to eat?

"They're safe," said a well-modulated masculine voice behind Nellie, as though its owner had read her thoughts.

Startled, she dropped the mushroom like a guilty child. "I … I didn't hear you coming," she said. Suddenly, she felt very vulnerable. She instantly recognized the figure as the tall, bearded man she had seen in the woods while walking to Doctor Bart's. At the time she had felt a neighborly urge to stop and introduce herself to Henry Trow. Now, however, she wished he would simply disappear back into the woods, allowing her to continue on her way unnoticed. It was one thing for a young woman to make conversation with a new neighbor alongside a road, even a dirt road; it was an altogether different thing when trapped alone with a stranger in the deep woods! There was an intimacy projected by the encroaching trees and fertile-scented soil that made Nellie uncomfortable.

"Sorry I scared you," he said. His right arm clasped a wicker basket, which hung from a leather strap slung over his shoulder. "You looked as though you were wondering if that painted bolete was safe to eat. It is."

"I'm the one who should apologize," Nellie replied, recovering her equanimity. She made a quick assessment of the man. He was dressed like a woodsman, yet he was unlike any Maine woodsman Nellie had ever met. His face was obscured by a bushy brown beard and moustache, but his beard was trimmed and well-kept, and his light brown hair, which just touched the back of his shirt collar, was clean and neatly combed. His hands were slender yet strong-looking, and his fingernails had been recently clipped. Although it was difficult to tell because his beard made him appear older, Nellie suspected he was only a few years older than she was. He was wearing a plaid flannel shirt, newish jeans, and leather boots. Yellow lights flickered in his brown eyes, as though something she had said or done had amused him.

"Why should you apologize?" he asked. He unhooked the lid to the wicker basket, flipped open a jackknife and scooched down to cut several painted boletes. He carefully added them to the basket and stood up. "You've done nothing wrong." He closed the jackknife with a snap and returned it to his shirt pocket.

His voice was even and his pronunciation free from an embarrassing Maine accent, which Nellie had worked hard to scrub from her own speech. He also spoke using correct grammar and she immediately perceived he wasn't from the state. "I was stealing your mushrooms," she pointed out.

"They're not mine. The 'shrooms belong to everyone."

"Thanks. That's very generous of you. The Lovejoys always used to let us use their property. I'm glad to see …" Nellie broke off, confused. A disdainful expression had flickered across his bearded countenance. For some reason, the image of the newly-plastered "No Trespassing" signs she had seen alongside the Cross Road popped into her mind. "I … I've made a mistake, haven't I? You're not …?"

"Henry Trow? The new land baron? No. But that wasn't your mistake. Your mistake was in thinking this land can be owned by anyone—the land owns us, not the other way 'round. Didn't they teach you anything in your Maine history class?"

"I'm sorry—what?"

"Don't you remember that little footnote about the Native Americans?"

Nellie recognized he was having sport with her. She understood perfectly well his allusion to land ownership and the sarcastic footnote. Both related to the unique relationship Native Americans shared with the earth, which they believed owned them and not the other way round. Nellie remembered from her early American History classes that during the sixteenth and seventeenth centuries in New England Indians had signed many deeds to various parcels of land, thinking they were selling the Europeans the same access to the land they held. The Native Americans didn't realize they were deeding the land entirely away, because they didn't understand the European concept of land ownership.

But what nettled Nellie worse than the stranger having sport with her was that he had mistaken her for one of the locals. She squared her shoulders and tossed back her gleaming blonde locks.

"For your information, I didn't go to high school in Maine. I attended Hathorne Prep. I graduated from Columbia in May."

"More shame on you, then. If nothing else, Hathorne should have taught you to think for yourself."

Nellie bridled. "Who says it didn't?"

"You do. Talking as though we needed 'permission' to be here." He indicated the wider woods with a wave of his hand. "Permission! To enjoy God's green earth? Something that was freely given? You must be joking."

"I'm not sure you've got the 'freely given' part correct but I concede your point. Still, there is such a thing as the law."

"This country's capitalist-driven laws about land ownership simply reinforce the wealth and privileges of the one percent," he retorted, with increasing energy. "Maine in particular has a long history of being raped by capitalists. Laws aren't made to protect the innocent. Laws are made to protect the privileges of the rich. 'Whose woods these are I think I know. His house is in the village, though.' Why? Why is his house in the village? Did you ever stop to wonder about that?"

Nellie felt herself mentally grasping at straws. She was familiar with the Robert Frost poem. Who wasn't? But what was the stranger talking about? Where was he going with this line of reasoning?

"Why wasn't the owner's house next to his woods?" he continued, as though reading her mind. "Why does he live in the village? Is this his woodlot? If so, why does he need a woodlot if he lives in the village? Is this an investment property for him, then? See, when you really dig deeper there's a lot to unpack in that poem, stuff that's just taken for granted like we used to take for granted that blacks should ride in the back of the bus."

"Oh-my-God—you're comparing 'Stopping by the Woods on a Snowy Evening' to inherent racism? I'm sorry; I can't let that pass without an argument."

"Then rebut my argument, if you can." The stranger's brown eyes were alive with the enjoyment of a good debate.

Nellie, who had been a star member of the debate team at Hathorne, racked her brains for a sharp retort or smart setback. Unfortunately, she couldn't think of anything appropriate on such short notice.

"You can't, can you?" he cried, a note of exultation in his voice.

"Give me a minute! I haven't had time to think about it, like you obviously have. I never thought about doing an exegesis on Robert Frost before."

"And that circles back to my first point—whether or not Hathorne taught you to think for yourself. Public schools have long since abdicated responsibility in that regard. Can you imagine anyone today with the perspicacity to pen 'The Declaration of Independence' or 'The Gettysburg Address'? Instead, the so-called 'good citizens' of this country learn to take the status quo for granted. Are you a good citizen?"

"No. Yes, that is—I don't know. I'd have to know your basis for what constitutes a 'good citizen'."

He glanced up at the sun, which was just breaking through the canopy of the tallest pine tree to the east. "Look, I'd love to stay and debate more with you but I'll have to take a rain check. Unfortunately, 'Time and tide wait for no man.' I need to get these," he continued, patting his basket "to the post office before it closes. Thanks to our capitalist-driven economy, the window hours at the Sovereign Post Office have been slashed in half. She's only open two hours in the morning and two hours in the afternoon, now."

"Really? I had no idea," Nellie replied, feeling completely ignorant. She had taken the post office for granted, much like she had always taken the simply beauty of Robert Frost's poems for granted. She kicked herself for having been caught flat-footed—and in the Maine woods, at that!

"Like I said, the red boletes are safe to eat but be careful about any other 'shrooms you see around here, particularly anything white," he cautioned. "That could be the Destroying Angel, a pure white Amanita that will make you very, very sick." He turned on his heels to leave her, and then paused. "By the way—nice sweater," he remarked. "Did you pick that up at Hathorne, too?"

Infuriated, Nellie felt like stamping her foot. But she knew it would be a useless gesture since the soggy pine needles beneath her wouldn't give her any satisfaction. She touched a hand to her hot cheeks. Why had she worn these horrible old clothes? What must he think of her?

But then, why did she care? She didn't know who he was and she certainly hoped she'd never find out!

Nellie knew instinctively the stranger was deliberately disregarding the "No Trespassing" signs, in effect stealing the mushrooms. After being on the receiving end of his lecture about land ownership, she knew he would never condescend to ask the real Henry Trow for permission to harvest them.

But then she realized with a little shock that she, too, was trespassing! She had also disregarded the "No Trespassing" signs—albeit unconsciously—assuming that because she had always used this land she could continue to do so. How vexing!

Nellie made a mental note to secure an introduction to Henry Trow as soon as possible. However much she might silently agree with some of the annoying stranger's views, she was not one to break the rules.

For a moment Nellie experienced a feeling of admiration, and perhaps envy, that he could so easily step out-of-bounds. Who was this man who dared to break the law? And why—out of all the places in the world—was he here in Sovereign, Maine?

CHAPTER 6
The Little White Church

Like so many little churches dotting the rural New England landscape, the Sovereign Union Church was perched like a white dove on a prominent knoll in the center of town. The church had been built by the original settlers of Sovereign, who, at the time of construction, were of the Calvinist persuasion. The soft-hearted townspeople never felt quite comfortable with the doctrine of double predestination, however, having an idea that a god who randomly saved some souls while condemning the rest to Hell wasn't a god whom they felt inspired to worship. Thus when the first flush of universal salvation spread across the land (not long after Asa Lovejoy had gone to claim his Great Reward) the congregation eagerly abandoned their Calvinist yoke and embraced the new, liberal doctrine. The Universalists didn't stick, however, and in 1860, an enthusiastic Methodist minister and his wife came to town. At that time the congregation didn't have a settled pastor—although they had often heard itinerant Quaker preachers from Albion and China—and so they invited the Methodist minister and his wife to stay. The Methodists held their ground until the twentieth century, when the church further morphed to become a Union church. Later, under Maggie's leadership, the church became an open and affirming church in which everyone—regardless of religious persuasion and/or sexual orientation—was welcomed.

The Sovereign Union Church is much larger than it looks from the outside, since it encompasses mostly one large room with an expansive cathedral ceiling and elongated leaded windows stretching nearly from ceiling to floor. The initial effect upon entering is one of uplifting brightness, most likely the effect intended by the town's hope-filled early settlers. A plush burgundy carpet covered the aisle separating two rows of white pews, which had been recently upholstered with soft, wine-colored seat cushions running the length of each pew. Up front, the elevated altar bore the traditional empty cross, and beneath the altar rose up the mahogany lectern where Maggie preached.

Nellie made it to church with about twenty minutes to spare, looking becomingly flushed from her hike through the woods and carrying into the building only three or four souvenirs from the forest—balsam tips and pine needles in her hair—as a clue to her route. She entered the church to find twenty-five or thirty congregants ahead of her, chatting in little groups. A single pillar candle burned cheerfully on the altar, accompanied by two fresh wildflower bouquets. Nellie attempted to slide into one of the back pews unnoted, but Shirley Palmer spotted her and broke away from the group. The spry old woman approached before Nellie had a chance to sit down.

"I was hopin' you'd be here, dearie, though I told Asa I thought probably you'd stay to home. 'Young folks don't go to church, nowadays,' I said to him. Glad to see I was wrong."

"I always go to church," Nellie replied, feeling justified in this declaration since she had attended church once with her mother the last time she was home.

"Tut, tut. I remember many a time when you stayed to home, dearie. I always wondered what yer Ma was at—lettin' a young girl like you stay to home by yerself. Anyway, yer here now and that's what counts. You ain't gonna sit back here all alone, now, are you?"

Nellie stuck out her chin by way of a reply. She further solidified her position by dropping down into the seat behind her. She slid the leather strap from her pocketbook off her shoulder and laid the modest purse several inches away on the seat next to her, thereby protecting her personal space from any other well-meaning congregant. Nellie's feint was altogether lost on the chatty matron, however.

"Wal, leastwise you won't be completely alone, dearie. Most folks don't sit up front. Thems that did has died and t'others ain't moved up yet. Probably never will, now that I think on it."

Nellie spotted a far-away-look in the matron's eyes. "Don't worry about me," she said hastily, attempting to ward off what looked like the launch into a personal reminiscence. "I'll be fine."

"Good 'nuff, dearie," Shirley said, adjusting her church hat, a fifties black felt tilt with a fuchsia plume. "There was somethin' I was agoing to say, but forgot what 'twas." She bent over and with claw-like hands grasped the tired green hymnal from the rack in front of Nellie and handed it to her. "Anyways, we're doing five hymns today—jest to take up time, you know. The numbers is up thar on the board like usual." Her voice dropped conspiratorially. "Last time we hed this minister fill in fer yer Ma we was all done by quarter to twelve. The coffee warn't even done perkin' and Maude dinn't hev the pies cut up. Oh, Lord—dinn't that throw us all into a tither! We're makin' sure this time that don't happen agin … and if it looks like Reverend Millar's runnin' long, why, we'll jest axe hymn number five. I put 'The Old Rugged Cross' at the end—it's kind o' a dispiritin' tune, ain't it? But Mabel Young likes to see it on the program once or twice a year. She don't need to have it sung, though. 'Twas her Ma's favorite."

The older woman paused to catch her breath and Nellie, whose cold shoulder was unthawing thanks to Shirley's indefatigable good humor, politely picked up the baton. "The Old Rugged Cross is a bit of a downer," she agreed, vaguely recollecting the hymn was peppered with words like 'blood,' 'sin,' and 'slain.' Until she had left for Hathorne she had been a member of the church's scanty choir, dissolved since by natural selection, and was therefore familiar with almost every tune in the bedraggled Methodist hymnal.

"Did you git a program, dearie?"

In response, Nellie waved the white piece of paper that served as the standard program. She opened the hymnal and began thumbing through the book, marking the five song selections with the limp satin ribbons clinging to the hymnal's spine.

Shirley leaned over and patted Nellie's arm kindly. "Then I'll see you at coffee hour, dearie. We're hevin' a real set-down dinner today—chili 'n cornbread, and salads 'n pie. Be sure to git yerself plenty to eat! Our little meetin' will start 'bout one o'clock. You don't need to stay, but 'course we'd love to have you."

"I'll stay," Nellie promised, smiling. She was beginning to feel affection for the earnest, good-hearted woman, who appeared so eager to attend to her comfort.

Shirley departed in search of her husband, who had mysteriously disappeared. "Good thing he ain't got my car keys," was her exiting remark. The pianist, Courtney Danforth, who was also one of the town's rural route postal carriers, began warming up on Miss Hastings' angelic-sounding Steinway. Miss Hastings had willed her beloved Steinway to the church upon her death. Hearing the music, the little clutches broke apart and made their way to their long-established seats. Nellie returned a smile or two, and waved at Rebecca, whom she noted was alone.

So, Wendell Russell didn't go to church! Nellie could almost see the old chicken farmer winking at her over this transgression.

At the last minute, Doctor Bart slid into the pew next to her, casually removing her purse and placing it on the other side of him. "Phew! Thought I was going to be late. Thanks for saving me a seat."

Nellie tried not to laugh as she glanced around the half-empty church. Saving him a seat? What a goose! Nevertheless, she felt happy to see him.

"You've got some pine needles in your hair," he said, removing the offending debris. "There, that's better."

"Shhh! It's about to start," she said in sotto voce. "We're doing five songs today." She pointed meaningfully to the hymnal in the wooden rack in front of him.

"Right. Thanks." He availed himself of the hymnal, opened the book and stared at it helplessly.

"Number twenty-seven is first," she whispered.

The organist moved into the prelude and a restful peace settled over the congregation. Nellie closed her eyes and relaxed. Listening to the vibrant opening notes of the piano, she recognized "Let Us Wander Where We Will," a Unitarian-Universalist hymn she had once performed solo in church with Miss Hastings as accompanist. She swayed back and forth, allowing her sensibilities to meld with the music. The words of the hymn, a lovely poem by Robert Louis Stevenson, came readily to mind:

Let us wander where we will,
something kindred greets us still:
something seen on vale or hill
falls familiar on the heart.

Dew and rain fall everywhere,
harvests ripen, flow'rs are fair,
and the whole round earth is bare
to the sunshine and the sun.

And the live air, fanned with wings,
bright with breeze and sunshine brings
into contact distant things,
and makes all the countries one.

As she sang to herself, Nellie felt as free as the wandering swallow of Stephenson's poem. Her heart rose up to catch the high notes, her perfectly pitched soprano tripping lightly back down the scales following the direction of the piano. When the song ended a hush fell over the little congregation. Regretfully, Nellie opened her eyes and became aware that—she had been singing out loud!

"That was beautiful," Metcalf whispered, taking her hand in his and squeezing it.

Nellie was nearly overcome with embarrassment. Fortunately, Reverend Millar filled the awful void by standing up to speak. He moved through the announcements without mentioning Nellie's gaffe, thereby removing the spotlight from her and turning it onto himself.

After the service ended, Rebecca and several others came over to thank Nellie for her singing. By that time, she had begun to feel better about her blunder. "Miss Hastings and I rehearsed that hymn so many times when I heard the familiar opening notes, I just couldn't stop myself," she explained to her mother's neighbor.

"Nor should you have," said Rebecca, giving her a quick hug. "What a wonderful treat for us! Too bad your mother couldn't have been here to hear you. Next time!"

"Sure," said Nellie. "Why not?"

But … would there be a next time for her? Wouldn't she depart Sovereign just as soon as her mother returned home? Wasn't that her plan?

Why did she suddenly feel sad at the thought of leaving her mother's friends behind?

Doctor Bart returned from speaking to a separate little group and lightly touched her shoulder. "Time for lunch," he said. "I'll stay and have some, too. That way I can give you a ride home."

"You don't need to stay," she protested. "There's a ministry committee meeting after lunch and that could take some time. Please don't waste your entire afternoon here with me."

"A little bird told me the meeting won't take long. Besides, I never miss an opportunity for a free meal."

Not being able to think of any other reasonable excuse, Nellie accepted his offer. She didn't want to walk the entire three miles home from church by way of the road, and she certainly didn't want to take the chance of running into the bearded stranger again by cutting through Henry Trow's land.

Lunch was prepared in the church's commercial kitchen, which was located in the attached banquet hall. This addition to the church had been built in 1920 when the 18th amendment to the Constitution was passed in order to provide a local, alcohol-free gathering place. After Prohibition was repealed, the church utilized the space for suppers and fundraising events, as well as for meetings.

Nellie helped herself to a bowl of chili and a steaming piece of cornbread, and seated herself at one of the eight-foot banquet tables. The chili was excellent—just the right temperature and spiciness, with melted cheese on top—and she found the cornbread especially fresh and tasty. "I've never had such good cornbread before," she said to Hannah Shorey, Metcalf's great-aunt and housekeeper, who was sitting across the table from her. "Shirley told me you made it, Aunt Hannah. What's your secret?"

"An old family recipe," Aunt Hannah replied. "The recipe has been passed down in my family for generations." She was a grandmotherly-looking, white-haired widow in her mid-seventies, a sister to Metcalf's beloved grandmother, who was now deceased. "But I grind my own cornmeal, too, and I think that makes all the difference."

Nellie was impressed. "Isn't grinding corn difficult?"

"It would be if I didn't use an electric grinder," Aunt Hannah allowed, with a wink. "Metcalf bought me one for my birthday. Coincidentally, that was when I started keeping house for him at Miss Hastings'."

Nellie laughed, and helped herself to a second piece of cornbread from the cloth-lined basket currently making the rounds of the table. "When my mother gets home she won't recognize me," she joked. "I'll be twice my usual size."

Shirley Palmer leaned forward. "Dearie, you could put on ten pounds and still be the size of a shadow!"

When the luncheon crowd dispersed, Maynard Nutter, the retired farmer with whom Gray Gilpin's mother lived, moved a wooden podium to the front of the room. Shirley, who was president of the ministry committee, banged on the podium twice with a wooden gavel. "I hereby call this meetin' to order," she announced. Nellie listened as Shirley outlined the particulars of the situation to the five other members of the committee, even though, she suspected, all five were as familiar as she was with the few facts. Maggie had disappeared and no one knew where she had gone or when she would be back. "I say we continue to pay Maggie's salary," Shirley suggested, in conclusion. "We ain't short on cash—thanks to that legacy from Miss Hastings—and we kin afford to hire speakers to fill in as we likes. Poor Maggie never hed no paid vacation, not since she come here sixteen years ago."

Maynard Nutter leaned back in his chair. "Ayuh, she deserves a good long vacation," he spoke up. "Poor gal works her heart out, more 'n she gits paid fer, too. I know thet fer a fact."

Nellie observed the proceedings quietly. Finally, however, she felt compelled to speak up. "But my mother was only a part-time itinerant when we first came to Sovereign," she pointed out. "I'm sorry—is it OK I speak?"

"Certainly, dearie."

"I'm sure Mother never thought she was earning vacation time until you brought her on full-time a couple of years ago."

"And she didn't get no vacation, neither," proclaimed Maynard Nutter. He crossed his arms over his burly chest and gave Nellie a defiant stare.

"Poor Maggie does need a sabbatical," Ruth Woods allowed. "We should have seen it sooner." Ruth was the wife of John Woods, chairman of the Board of Selectmen, and well-respected in her own right. "She's certainly had a very challenging two years, what with the loss of all our dear friends. Peter's death must have been the last straw."

"Oh, my, yes!" agreed David O'Donnell, with a theatrical flutter of his hand. "Miss Hastings, Clyde Crosby—your Merlon, Hannah. And don't let us forget dear Ma Jean! I say let the poor thing take as much time as she needs."

"I know she was mighty kind to me when Mabel Jean passed away," Maynard said, gruffly. He fumbled for his handkerchief and blew his nose loudly.

Aunt Hannah folded her hands on top of the table. "When Merlon was dying, Maggie came over every afternoon to sit with me," she added, quietly. Her bright blue eyes filled with tears. "She didn't say a word. She just held my hand. She was there the night Merlon died, too, and the next night—until Jane could get away."

"Merlon was a good man."

"Thank you, Maynard."

There was a respectful quietude as those gathered remembered those who were no longer with them: Miss Hastings, Peter Hodges, Merlon Shorey, Clyde Crosby, Mabel "Ma Jean" Brown. Nellie glanced around the little group, registering their sacred sadness. She felt a growing sense of pride in her mother. The role of minister in a small town—pastor, spiritual advisor, friend—gained in significance in her estimation. It was becoming obvious to her that Maggie was an integral part of her little community. All those afternoons and evenings Nellie had been left alone at the old schoolhouse her mother had not been out gallivanting but had been holding someone's hand, or offering a prayer or a joke, or whatever the situation warranted. Nellie had always discounted her mother's calling, thinking the ordained ministry was an outmoded, antiquated profession, kept alive only in books and by the BBC. Now, however, 'Maggie the Minister' became real in her eyes. Nellie was surprised by how moved she was at the discovery.

Maynard Nutter pushed himself up from the folding metal chair. The old dairy farmer pounded his fist against the table. The butter jumped. "I make a motion we continue to pay Maggie's salary for as long as she sees fit to be gone!"

"I'll second that," cried David O'Donnell, leaping up.

Shirley lifted the wooden gavel up midair. "All in favor of the motion—raise your hands!"

All six members of the ministry committee raised their hands.

"It's a vote!" Shirley pronounced, banging the gavel down. David O'Donnell, the secretary of the ministry committee, reclaimed his seat and faithfully recorded the results in his book.

Maynard slumped down into his chair and straightened the butter. "I move we adjourn," he added. Without waiting for a second—or a vote—he turned to Aunt Hannah. "Got any o' thet apple pie left, Hannah?"

Nellie remained ten or fifteen minutes after the meeting ended, chatting with various members of the committee, who seemed genuinely interested in her and her life. Out of the corner of her eye she spotted Doctor Bart leaning up against the kitchen wall, arms folded across his chest, patiently waiting for her. She knew he was probably hoping the kindness of the townspeople would rub off and encourage her to stick around. But she was sure—at least she thought she was sure—that Sovereign was only a pass-through place for Nellie Walker.

CHAPTER 7
Doctor Bart

Doctor Bart—Metcalf Bartholomew Lawson—was the descendant of two longtime dairy farming families from Albion, a sleepy community nestled between Winslow and China. When Metcalf and his sister were eight and ten respectively, the dairy industry in Maine had been failing for more than a decade and the Lawsons had fallen into debt. Rather than sell the family farm, Jane Lawson, who had a master's degree in library science, went back to work fulltime to augment her husband's milk check. Her job at the state law library in Augusta was meant to last until Metcalf came of age, at which time he would take over the farm from his father, like his father had done before him, and his father before that.

Metcalf developed a proclivity for medicine rather than farming, however. His father, a reasonable, realistic, hard-working man, was proud of his son's decision to become a doctor and urged the youth to pursue his dreams. Secretly, Jane, the daughter of dairy farmers herself, was disappointed in her son's choice of careers, but she knew enough of Metcalf's steadfastness—and of her husband's determination not to fetter his son with emotional chains—to attempt to try and change his mind. Doctor Bart's father lived long enough to see him graduate from medical school, but not much longer. The cows were sold, yet Jane Lawson stubbornly clung to the old place, her husband's family farm, in the event an agriculturally-minded grandchild appeared on her doorstep one day. Metcalf's sister had married a man from New York and had spawned three children in that far away state so there was not much hope there. But Jane had not given up on the possibility of netting grandchildren from her son, especially since he had taken up residence in Sovereign and … since Nellie had returned to town.

There had been many a heartfelt discussion over the years between the second cousins—Maggie and Jane—about their two offspring. Hopes had been shared; dreams described; castles in the air built upon little more of a foundation than the fact that one woman had borne a son and the other had birthed a daughter, and they appeared to enjoy each other's company. Of these matchmaking schemes Metcalf was completely in the dark. His feelings for Nellie had matured organically over the years, evolving from that of a protector of the forlorn little girl to that of a lover of the mature and graceful young woman. Nellie, on the other hand, had always been sharp-eyed and somewhat suspicious of the motives of others, especially her mother. She had easily seen through her mother's frequent attempts of late to dangle Doctor Bart and the good things of the world in front of her eyes. Maggie was about as subtle as bear bait; she thought. But Nellie also knew Metcalf wasn't to blame for her mother's machinations—he was so good he wasn't even aware of them, in fact—and therefore she allowed herself the luxury of continuing to trust him, as she had always done.

Driving home from church, Nellie remembered to ask Doctor Bart about the stranger she had met in the woods. She didn't tell him any of the particulars of their chance meeting or of the man's radical views on land ownership, though. Why take the chance of inciting trouble when no trouble was warranted?

"That must have been Walden," Metcalf replied, slowing as he maneuvered his truck from the paved road down onto the dirt Cross Road.

"Walden? As in Thoreau's Walden?"

"That's what I assume. He's been in town a couple of months. No one knows much about him, except he peddles mushrooms to fancy restaurants in southern Maine and New Hampshire."

"On what pond does Walden live?"

"Wendell lets him live in the old Nutt place in exchange for some carpentry work. You remember the Nutt place, don't you Nellie?"

"I do," Nellie replied, thoughtfully. The Nutt place was the oldest house in Sovereign still standing—barely. The house was situated on the western edge of Wendell Russell's land below the Millett Rock and had been abandoned for many years. "The last time I saw the place the roof had a big hole in it. How can anyone live there?"

"Walden has fixed the roof and the broken windows, too. Wendell is getting the better end of that deal, I'd say. He wants to sell the place when the economy picks up, as a nest egg for Rebecca and the baby. In the meantime, it's a win-win for both men. You needn't be afraid of Walden, Nellie. I've met him a couple of times and he seems pretty harmless. A bit arrogant, perhaps, but harmless."

"I'm not afraid of him; I was just surprised to see him."

Doctor Bart chuckled. "Surprised to see a woodsman type in the Maine woods?"

"Well, he's not exactly a woodsman like Leland Gorse, is he? He not only looks like Henry David; he looks as though he could quote Henry David. And that *is* surprising around here."

"Ouch," said Metcalf, wincing. "I didn't realize you had such a poor opinion of us local men. I'm not sure I could quote Thoreau, either, except perhaps that marching to a different drummer passage: 'If a man does not keep pace with his companions, perhaps it is because he hears a different drummer. Let him step to the music which he hears, however measured or far away'." He glanced over at Nellie in the passenger seat. "How'd I do?"

"That was perfect, as you very well know. Does Walden have permission to take mushrooms from Mr. Trow's land? Because that's what he was doing when I ran into him today. I noticed the property is posted, too."

"Probably not. But I'm not going to be the one to report him. I haven't met Henry Trow myself but he has the reputation of being a curmudgeon. From what I've heard, he'd probably take Walden to court for trespassing."

They reached the schoolhouse and Metcalf switched off the truck's engine. "Mind if I come in? There's something I want to speak with you about."

Nellie immediately detected a change of tone in his voice. Her pulse quickened. Was this … it? The proposal she had been worried about?

"Sure," she replied, heart fluttering. She popped open her door, trying to recall the precise words she had decided she would use to refuse him. She wanted to let him down gently, but firmly. She didn't want to hurt him, but he must know she was never going to marry him.

Nellie gave the truck door a shove shut. She froze, unable to think of a single word. He was standing there on the other side, waiting for her. He smiled when he saw her looking at him, but it was his frank, familiar smile, not the starry-eyed gleam of a besotted lover. She returned his smile weakly and moved toward the shed.

Once inside, Nellie busied herself with the coffee maker in order to stall for time. She knew Doctor Bart preferred coffee to tea and decided she could use a cup of coffee herself. She felt somewhat drained after her walk through the woods and her conversation with some of the more enthusiastic members of the ministry committee.

She started to pour water into the drip coffee maker and the outmoded machine immediately hissed and spit hot bursts of steam in her face. She quickly moved back.

"Here, let me do that," Doctor Bart said. "There's a trick to it." Nellie stepped aside and Metcalf took the pot from her hand. He opened the cover and began pouring water slowly and intermittently. The coffeemaker gurgled like a well-fed baby and soon the brown liquid dripped down through the filter, filling the kitchen with the fragrant aroma of fresh coffee. "Patience," he said. "That's all it takes."

"Never my strong suit," Nellie replied, a bit miffed that he knew the foibles of her mother's household better than she did. "Want some cake to go with your coffee?" she asked, attempting to assume the role of gracious hostess.

"No, thanks. I felt so guilty when Maynard asked Aunt Hannah if there was any apple pie left. I ate the last two pieces."

"Poor Maynard," she said, automatically.

"Aunt Hannah should get married again. Maynard would be just the man for her, too." He opened the cupboard to the right of the sink and extracted two coffee mugs.

"Why do you say that?"

"Because he's a steady guy—like me. Maynard took care of his mother until she died and now he's taking care of Sheila and Olivia. Sheila's really blossomed since she's been under Maynard's roof. She's finished her GED and is now enrolled in community college. Maynard babysits Olivia while she's at class."

"Pretty handy for Sheila."

"There was a rumor once Maynard never married because he was sweet on Ma Jean," Metcalf continued. "I never believed that, though."

"Some people only love once," Nellie opined, stupidly.

Why had she said that? She didn't ascribe to that belief and she certainly didn't mean to give him an opening!

"Is that so, Miss Marianne? Well, I'm afraid I can't agree with you there. I'm with Elinor Dashwood on the efficacy of second loves and second marriages. Everyone needs to love and be loved and if widows and widowers had the opportunity I think most would marry again, no matter how much they cared for their first spouse. In fact, it's a testament to the original spouse—and a happy marriage—if a person wants to marry again. Sugar?" He reached into yet another cupboard and pulled out a pottery sugar bowl, for which Nellie had in fact been searching.

"Sure."

Doctor Bart set the sugar bowl on the table. "Sit down, Nellie. You're beginning to make me nervous, hovering around like the cat. Now what? Do I have something on my face?"

"I'm just surprised you know your way around a kitchen so well," Nellie replied, tartly.

The good humor suddenly dissipated. "I've spent a lot of time in this kitchen lately," he said gravely, "while your mother was undergoing chemotherapy. She elected oral chemo so she wouldn't have to go into Bangor or Waterville for the IV drip. That's why Maggie's medical copays were so high. I came over when I knew she was going to be here alone—Peter gave me the heads up whenever he went to Winslow to help Bruce hay. Leland and Rebecca took turns, too. There were days when your mother spent most of her time in the bathroom, so I made myself at home."

Nellie felt as though she had been duly—and deservedly—chastised, although he had not said a word that could be interpreted as a reprimand. She felt guilty thinking she should have been the one helping Uncle Peter care for her mother so that Maggie didn't need to depend upon the kindness of her friends and neighbors. "I'm sorry, that was stupid of me. Of course I should have been here."

"I don't see that at all. And your mother certainly never implied that."

Nellie sat down. She tossed her wayward hair over her left shoulder. "What was it you wanted to ask me?" she prompted him. Any topic was better than this one, which pointed out so clearly her failure as a daughter.

"Not ask you, exactly," he replied. He poured out two mugs of coffee and set them on the table. "I want to tell you about my plans for Miss Hastings' house." He pulled up a chair.

So, he wasn't going to ask her to marry him? Not today, anyway. "Oh, is that all," she said.

Doctor Bart's face fell. Too late, Nellie realized her mistake. "I'm sorry—I didn't mean that like it sounded."

He toyed with his teaspoon, avoiding her eyes. She had wounded him with her thoughtless remark. When would she learn to think before she spoke!

He looked up. "This is important to me, Nellie, and I was hoping for your support. But … never mind. You probably wouldn't be interested, anyway."

"Please! I want to hear your plans for Miss Hastings' place. I promise, I won't laugh at you, if that's what you're thinking."

"I wasn't thinking anything of the kind. I know you won't laugh at me. I just, well … I've been thinking of opening a free medical clinic ever since I was in med school, a place where people without insurance could go and receive care. It suddenly dawned on me Miss Hastings' studio might make be the perfect place?" He glanced apprehensively at Nellie, attempting to gauge her opinion. "What do you think about that?"

Nellie's eyes widened. She inhaled a quick breath. A free medical clinic? The proposal was so like Doctor Bart she was surprised she hadn't seen it coming. But then, she had been caught up with thinking about herself since she'd returned home. And when had she ever given much thought to him and his hopes and dreams? Once again, Nellie felt a sense of personal failure.

She sat up straighter in her seat, determined to be a better person, a better friend. "I think that's an awesome idea! The set-up at Miss Hastings' house is perfect for a medical clinic," she added, encouragingly. "She'd be thrilled to know what you were going to do with her place, too."

Doctor Bart's face broke into a boyish smile. "You really think so?"

"Oh-my-God—I can see it! Patients can enter through the front door. The hall has the built-in coatrack and the tiny bathroom Miss Hastings installed for us students. She made us all wash our hands before we sat down to play her Steinway, you know. The studio is perfect for your exam room and the front parlor will make an awesome reception area. By the way, how did you end up with all of Miss Hastings' lovely parlor furniture?"

"She left it to me in her will, and the Oriental rug, too, although I can't imagine why."

"Did you ever tell her about your dream to open a free medical clinic?"

He thought a moment. "Maybe I did mention the idea once."

"I knew it! Miss Hastings never forgot anything any of us ever told her."

"Well, she certainly didn't expect me to give music lessons in the studio," he added, wryly. "I can't carry a tune in a bucket."

"She didn't expect everyone to be musically inclined. She had a knack for discovering where our individual talents lay. She could read between the lines and find a person's 'sweet spot,' as she would say. Obviously, when she read your sweet spot she liked what she saw."

"You paint a very endearing portrait of her, Nellie. I'm sorry I didn't get to know Miss Hastings until I became her doctor this past year. So tell me, Miss Organizer—for I know without Miss Hastings' prescience that organization is one of your key talents—what do we do first?"

"First, we make a list," Nellie replied, smiling. She hopped up and retrieved the yellow legal pad from her mother's desk, as well as a ballpoint pen. She reclaimed her seat, glanced down at her mother's nearly illegible scribbling on the top page and ripped the sheet off. She crumpled the yellow paper into a ball and tossed it into the trash. "Let's start with the exam room," she said, pen poised over the clean page. "What do we need there?"

Doctor Bart tilted his chair back on two legs. "An exam table, for starters. I'll look in Uncle Henry's and see if I can pick up a used one. I'll check Craig's List, too."

Nellie carefully wrote 'Exam Table' on the top line of the yellow paper. "Next?" she prompted.

"Medicine cabinets. We'll need at least two, one for supplies and a locking cabinet for medications. I can probably beg all the drug samples we need from those pesky pharmaceutical reps who're always chasing me at the clinic in Unity. Then we'll need a stainless steel instrument table, at least one biohazard container, rubber gloves and maybe a glove holder."

As they worked, Nellie's gaze alternated between her list-making and Doctor Bart's happy and excited face, which had suddenly blossomed like one of his antique roses, making him appear much younger than his years. The idea floated through Nellie's mind that maybe, just maybe, thirty wasn't so old after all.

Half an hour later Metcalf let his chair back down onto four legs and inspected her list. "Holy cow! That's pretty long. Do you think we have enough room for everything?"

Nellie laughed, recalling her most recent job in the hinterlands of Nicaragua. "If you could see the size of some of the hovels I've been working in over the past year with Clean World Water you'd think you had enough room for an entire hospital in Miss Hastings' studio."

"No kidding?"

"No kidding. I do have one concern, though, Metcalf." In the fervor of the moment she used his first name, much like she had always done growing up. But Doctor Bart appeared not to notice the slip or mind it if he did.

"What's that?"

"Won't this free clinic interfere with your job? How are you going to make a living?"

He smiled at her concern. "Don't worry, Nellie, I haven't lost my head completely. We'll start by offering office hours on Fridays and Saturdays—my days off. If someone has an emergency, not life threatening, of course, I'll see them anytime they can find me home. After that, we'll just take it one day at a time." He reached across the table and clasped her hands warmly, keeping them within his own firm grasp. "I've been thinking about this for so long and now you've given me just the encouragement I needed. I knew I was right to confide in you. You will help me get the clinic up and running, won't you, Nellie?"

"Just try and stop me!" she replied, happily. Now, this was a proposal she could accept! "When do you think we can open?"

"Let's shoot for a week from Friday. That's ridiculously soon, but suddenly I feel like being ridiculous. You know I can't pay you, Nellie …"

"Oh, don't even think of paying me," she cried. "Just letting me help you get started is payment enough."

"That's my girl! I knew you wouldn't disappoint me."

Nellie detected a subtle shift in the husky tone of his voice and she suddenly awoke to the intimacy of the situation. Dusk had fallen outside as they had been talking and the kitchen was illuminated only from the delicate light of a compact fluorescent bulb burning in the corner lamp next to Maggie's rocker. Soft beguiling shadows crept around the room, encircling them, drawing them together. Metcalf leaned closer, looking deeply into her eyes. Nellie knew he was about to commit himself. She leapt up and switched on the overhead light—and the spell was broken.

Doctor Bart blinked and leaned back in his chair. He glanced up at the regulator wall clock. "Wow, I didn't realize it was so late. You've probably been wanting to get rid of me for the past hour."

"Don't be silly. I'm as excited as you are about the clinic," she assured him, yet she deliberately remained standing. It *was* time for him to go. "Frankly, I'll be glad to have something to do with my extra time," she added. "Now that the ministry committee has decided to continue Maggie's salary, I don't need to rush out and get a paying job. I can help you get the clinic up and running while I'm waiting for Mother to return. I have enough money to tide me over until I go back to Clean World Water."

He stood up slowly, unwinding his long limbs from the chair. "You've decided to go back, then?"

There was an unmistakable note of longing in Metcalf's voice. Nellie could almost hear him thinking: "Instead of staying here with me?" He must have been hoping she would remain in Sovereign this time. She must make it clear to him that—whether she stayed in Sovereign or not—they could never be more than good friends. But she couldn't bring herself to disappoint him tonight, not when he had been so happy!

She began to wonder if she could work closely with Doctor Bart over the next few weeks, knowing he loved her, yet also knowing she didn't return his feelings. Wouldn't that be asking for trouble? Wouldn't their physical proximity put him at greater risk for being hurt in the long run? There was no risk to herself, of course, unless—unless she learned to love him!

"I think, yes, I think I will go back," she announced, abruptly.

"I see," Metcalf said. "Well, thanks for the coffee and the encouragement. I better hit the road." He reached for his tweed driving cap, which he had placed earlier on the stenciled pine chiffonier beneath the oak mirror. "It's good to have you home, Nellie, even if it is only for a short time. It's great to see you as part of the community, too. Sometimes I think you don't realize how important it is to be part of a caring group of people, whether it's in Sovereign or someplace else. I hope you find that for yourself someday."

"Me too," replied Nellie, thoughtfully. "Me too."

CHAPTER 8
The Clinic

During the following week, Nellie found organizing the clinic a welcome diversion from wondering and worrying about what she would do when her mother returned to Sovereign. Would she stay or would she go?

She was an expert at project organization, which had made her valuable in the field with Clean World Water. But she wasn't one for long-term planning, especially where her own life was concerned. She had attended Hathorne Prep because she had wanted a classical education and because she had wanted to get out of Sovereign. After graduation, she had proceeded to college because that was what students at Hathorne did. She had applied for the internship with Clean World Water because she wanted to travel and she had stayed with them because they had offered her a job when there was nothing else on the horizon. Her plans for the future were hazy, ill-defined. She feared she had fallen into the thoughtlessness trap the mysterious stranger—Walden—had alluded to. She had never thought—really thought—about what she wanted to do with her life. Instead, one thing had led to another and she had naturally followed the path of least resistance.

Now, however, Uncle Peter's untimely death—and her mother's abdication of responsibility—had interrupted this cycle of thoughtlessness, had woken her up, so to speak. She had taken a family leave of absence from Clean World Water—explaining that her step-father had died—and her boss had assured her that her job would be waiting for her. But … did she want to go back to Clean World Water? What if her mother was gone for several months? How might she feel then?

Maggie had now been gone nearly two weeks and still there was no word from her. No note, no word where she was, what she was doing, when she would return. It was too soon, Nellie convinced herself, to make anything other than short-term plans.

When she arrived at Doctor Bart's house on Wednesday, she discovered Aunt Hannah busy doing laundry. Metcalf had told her Hannah cooked his meals and cleaned up after him, but Nellie was surprised to see the elderly lady doing such physical work.

"Let me help you," Nellie offered, when she saw Aunt Hannah struggling to carry a heavy load of wet sheets from the washroom to the outdoor clothesline.

Hannah gratefully set the wicker basket atop the kitchen table. "Thank you, my dear. I must admit, the basket gets heavier every week."

"Why don't you use the dryer?"

"Miss Hastings never installed a clothes dryer, and Metcalf, well, he never thinks about things like that."

"Surely someone else could do his wash, if he hasn't got time to do it himself?"

"The truth is—I asked if I could keep house for him. Frankly, I need the money and I enjoy having something to do. When Merlon died, I ended up with $700 a month from Social Security and Merlon's ridiculously small pension from the shoe shop. I suppose I should be grateful to get even that, but it does make me mad to think he slaved at that shoe shop sixty years and all he got when he retired was sixty dollars a month."

"Oh-my-God! Sixty dollars a month? That's only a dollar a year. How horrible!"

"That's one of the reasons I'm so glad Metcalf is opening his clinic. You'd be surprised at the number of retired people like me in Sovereign who can't afford regular medical care or the cost of their prescription drugs."

"I had no idea things were so bad," Nellie said. She hoisted up the willow wicker basket and rested the bottom against her slim thigh.

"Most young people don't. But, then, it isn't all a bed of roses for you, either, is it, Nellie? Especially now your mother's gone off. Here, let me get the door for you, my dear."

Nellie walked home from Doctor Bart's late in the afternoon, enjoying the light breeze that floated up the ridge, gently tousling her silken blonde hair. Strolling along she thought about Aunt Hannah and her sad story of genteel poverty. Funny, when Metcalf had told her about opening up his clinic, she assumed his patients would consist of families with children and young people like herself. Because she wasn't close with any older people she had been completely ignorant of the current circumstances of the elderly in

Maine and across the United States. She had seen her friends struggle to find jobs in their field after college—many of them continuing to wait tables because career jobs were still scarce—and she herself was basically no more than a glorified intern at her own position. But she had never once thought of how her friend's grandparents were doing during the Great Recession and its aftermath, because she had no grandparent of her own.

How much she had missed in life! All because her mother, for some reason or other, had kept her father's identity a secret. Nellie vowed to herself she would track down her father, no matter how long the search took or how much it cost. She could only pray he was young enough so one or both of his parents might still be alive. She was going to get grandparents, one way or another!

When she reached home, Nellie automatically paused at the roadside mailbox and pulled open the rusty metal lid. She removed a sheaf of letters and advertising brochures and flipped through the stack, looking for bills. In the middle she discovered a colorful post card of the Eiffel Tower. Breathlessly, she flipped the card around, immediately recognizing her mother's careless scribble on the back. She scanned the brief note: *Miss you. Love, Mom.*

That was it?

No postscript? No mention of where Maggie was? How long she might be gone!

Nellie examined the French postmark, attempting to distinguish the name of the town where the card had been mailed. *Le Puy-en-Velay.* Le Puy? Why did that town sound familiar?

She typed 'Le Puy' into her smartphone's search engine and several links popped up. She clicked on the Wikipedia link and scrolled down through the history of the small city in south-central France, searching for a clue—and she found one: Le Puy was one of the four French starting points of the Camino de Santiago.

The Camino de Santiago, route to Santiago de Compostela—the Way of St. James!

Oh-my-God—had her mother gone on a pilgrimage?

Nellie immediately telephoned Doctor Bart and told him the news. "It would be just like Mother to do something as foolish as to think she could walk from Le Puy to Santiago de Compostela," she added, unable to keep the bitterness from her voice.

"Is that far?"

Nellie tossed the mail onto the kitchen table. "Eight hundred miles!"

He whistled. "That's pretty far."

"You're not kidding. Walking the Way from there would take Maggie two or three months, especially in her condition."

"Well, your mother's in pretty good health overall, although the radiation and chemo did take a toll on her. Of course, she could afford to lose a few pounds."

"If she's walking the Way of St. James, she'll lose more than a few."

"What's so special about this place she's walking to?"

"You've never heard of the Way of St. James?"

"Sorry, no. Who is James?"

"James was the first disciple and one of the founders of the early church. He was martyred in Jerusalem and his physical remains were taken to Santiago de Compostela in northern Spain and buried there. I'm not sure why. The pilgrimage Maggie's on retraces this route. During the Middle Ages pilgrims could earn indulgences for their sins by walking the last two hundred kilometers to the cathedral. Maybe they still can. I don't know much about Catholicism."

"You know a lot more than me. But Maggie isn't Catholic," he pointed out.

"Many non-Catholics participate in the pilgrimage to Santiago de Compostela—pilgrimages are very hip. Like I said, this is exactly the sort of thing Maggie would do."

"I guess walking off one's grief is as good a way as any."

"She could at least have left me a note!"

"You're too hard on her, Nellie."

"Probably. Just don't tell me I'll understand someday, when I become a mother, because I'm pretty sure my mother was a daughter once and she never understood me—her own daughter!"

"You're too close to the situation, Nellie. This has nothing to do with you and everything to do with Maggie. Your mother has what I call 'sick cat syndrome.' She wants to go it alone. A sick cat crawls off under a bush someplace and doesn't return until it's completely healed. In the meantime, there's no sense going to look for the cat, because you won't find it."

As if on cue, Boots rubbed up against Nellie's leg. She automatically reached down to pet the cat.

Sick cat syndrome? She could actually visualize that. The metaphor was helpful in coming to understand her mother's idiosyncrasy.

"You're pretty good," she remarked. "Did you ever consider becoming a doctor?"

He chuckled. "Ever since I was about eight. Speaking of which … are we ready for Friday?"

"I hope so," she replied, "because we've got four patients scheduled already!"

Nellie arrived at the clinic an hour before the official opening. She rearranged Miss Hastings' antique furniture in the parlor for the tenth or eleventh time, as well as the toys in the children's area. Then she sat at her desk and prepared her forms for the day, going over her plan of action. Just before nine o'clock she ran out to check the signage once again. She had made and posted several small yard signs pointing the way to the rarely-used front door, as well as a large red "CLINIC" sign for the door itself. Still, Metcalf had worried that tradition would outweigh the signage and the townspeople, used to visiting Miss Hastings through the shed, would continue to enter the same old way despite Nellie's signs.

"You can't teach old dogs new tricks," he pointed out.

"But many people in town took piano lessons from Miss Hastings," Nellie reminded him. "We all knew we had to come in through the front door."

"Tell 'em they'll have to wash up their muddy boot prints after themselves and they'll use the correct door fast enough," Aunt Hannah had advised. So Nellie had added one small sign to the other lawn signs, which humorously alerted patients what the penalty would be for entering through the wrong door.

Gray's mother Sheila and her toddler Olivia were the first patients, entering at exactly nine o'clock. Sheila glanced around, impressed by the elegance of the front hall and parlor. "Mighty fine," she said. "I ain't never been inside before. Always wondered what the place looked like."

"Come on in and take a seat," Nellie encouraged her. "I've got some paperwork for you to fill out."

"Thanks. I've got my money right here, too." Shelia sat down in a comfortable, plush armchair and settled Olivia onto her lap. The child stuck her thumb in her mouth and kicked out her fat legs.

"We'll get to that later but now, I need some information about Olivia. She's here for her first dose of measles, mumps and rubella, and her second dose of Hepatitis A and B, right?"

"Right."

Nellie handed Sheila the clipboard with the standard medical questionnaire attached. "Want me to take her? Maybe she'd like to play with some of our toys while you fill that out?"

"Sure, thanks." Sheila lifted the toddler and held her out to Nellie.

Nellie hoisted Olivia up into her arms. "Boy, she's a lot heavier than she looks!"

"She don't miss many meals," Sheila replied, laughing. "Maynard spoils her, too. He's always givin' her cookies 'n candy."

"That's what kids are for, right?"

Sheila nodded. "Maynard's awful good to both of us."

Nellie sat Olivia down in the play area she had created, which included a plastic beach pail and shovel, wooden blocks, stuffed animals, books, and much more. The child immediately overturned the plastic pail and merrily began filling it with the blocks.

By nine-thirty Doctor Bart had dispatched his first patient, with nary a whimper from the exam room. Nellie, who was sitting at her desk recording Sheila's twenty dollar donation, noted that when Oliva left the exam room she was happily sucking on a green lollipop. After the front door had closed behind them, Doctor Bart strolled out of the exam room, hands in the pockets of his white coat, the ubiquitous black stethoscope draped around his neck. He was obviously pleased with himself.

"I see you resorted to the traditional coercion with Olivia," Nellie said. "I thought candy was bad for kids' teeth?"

"That's not my provenance. I'm a doctor, not a dentist," he replied, smiling.

The ten o'clock appointment had been claimed by Helen Crump, an elderly friend of Aunt Hannah's, who had booked a regular check-up. Miss Crump, a thin, pioneer-looking spinster, was dressed in a long denim skirt, black leather lace-up boots, and a buttoned up cotton cardigan. An unfortunate curvature of the spine tilted her upper body nearly parallel to the ground. She pulled herself slowly along with a wooden cane looking much like a tortoise on the move. Nellie met Miss Crump at the front door and helped her up the granite steps. She settled the older woman into the State of Maine rocker and pulled a matching straight-back chair up beside her so she could assist Aunt Hannah's friend with the paperwork.

"Now … when did you last see a doctor, Miss Crump?" Nellie asked, her pen poised over the clipboard.

"I ain't never seen a doctor," Miss Crump replied, clutching the cane between the folds of her long skirt. The sweater pulled tight, revealing only too clearly a well-defined humpback.

Nellie quickly averted her eyes from the humpback. She glanced down at the clipboard to check Miss Crump's birth date, which she had recorded when the appointment was booked. *January 20, 1924.* Nellie did some quick math. "You're ninety-two-years-old? And you've never seen a doctor!"

Miss Crump slowly raised her neck like a majestic old snapper. "Why should I?" she challenged. "I ain't nevah ben sick."

Nellie was amazed to discover, upon further inquiry, Miss Crump not only still drove a car, but also had feasted her entire life on foods doctors discouraged most people from eating, such as fried chicken, bread and butter, ice cream, and chocolates. "I save my chocolates fer bedtime," she admitted. "Needhams is my favorite. Tell Hannah I could use some more."

Nellie obliged Miss Crump by jotting a note for the housekeeper.

Doctor Bart spent nearly an hour with his second patient, diagnosing nothing more serious than osteoarthritis and osteoporosis. He opened the locking metal medicine cabinet and removed several unit dose packs of an anti-inflammatory drug. "I want you to try these for your rheumatism, Miss Crump. Take two a day, with food: one at breakfast and one with your supper."

Miss Crump regarded the pills with suspicion. "What air they?"

"An anti-inflammatory medicine. Something to help with your arthritis," he said louder.

"I ain't deaf."

"Sorry."

"Wal, if ye think 'twill help me …?"

"Try them, Miss Crump, and then you come back and tell me."

"I ain't agoing to pay to see ye twice young man."

"This is a free clinic, Miss Crump. No payment is necessary. We do accept donations, but only from those who can afford to give."

"I kin afford my fair share," she said, stuffing the packet of pills into the right-hand pocket of her skirt. She grasped her cane and hoisted herself up. "I brung a chicken for ye. They told me down to the general store thet ye'd take a chicken. Thet a fact?"

"I am accepting chickens," Doctor Bart said gravely.

"Good 'nuff. Wal, hep me out, 'n I'll git Henrietta fer ye."

"Henrietta? I hope she's not a particular pet…?"

"She ain't. I got plenty more to home."

With Metcalf's assistance, the elderly woman hobbled back out to her vehicle. "Thar she is," said Miss Crump, pointing the end of her cane toward the back seat of her 1964 Dodge Dart.

Metcalf swung open the back door and carefully lifted the lid of a slated wooden crate. A bright-eyed white hen with a deep red comb cocked its head and stared angrily at him. She clucked loudly and flapped her wings, attempting to fly away. He slammed down the lid, but not before sawdust and white feathers scattered everywhere. "Sorry," he apologized. "Would you like me to clean up the mess?"

"Lord, no! Jest take the dang bird 'n let me git agoing," she snapped. "I'll be wantin' my crate back, young man so don't go throwin' it away, neither." Miss Crump maneuvered herself behind the steering wheel, stuck her cane over on the passenger side, and roared the car to life. The ancient, eight-cylinder engine shook and the entire car began to tremble like a wild beast.

Doctor Bart took the hint and hastily removed the crate from the back seat. He slammed the door shut with his foot and watched, horrified, as the old lady backed out into the road without checking to see whether or not any traffic was coming. Nellie wandered out and stood next to him, watching as Miss Crump sped off down the Russell Hill Road.

"Phew," he said. "She just made it."

"I can't believe she's still driving," Nellie mused. "She can barely see over the steering wheel. She must be in terrible pain, too."

"Not necessarily. Sometimes those tiny fractures in a patient's spine are painful, but more often than not they're painless. In Miss Crump's case, the fractures probably happened over such a long period she didn't notice. It's too bad, too, because she could have been treated for the osteoporosis and avoided the kyphosis altogether."

"Kyphosis?"

"Her Dowager's hump." Henrietta squawked and fluttered, and Metcalf set the crate down onto the grass. He dusted off his hands.

"I saw that Dowager's hump—poor thing! I certainly wouldn't want to walk around with a hump on my back."

"I doubt you'll ever have to worry about that, Nellie. You carry yourself like a model. Maybe you've missed your true calling?"

She frowned and shook her head. "You know I don't like to have my picture taken."

"I do, but I don't know why."

"Some trauma in early childhood, no doubt," she replied, lightly. She raised her face to the sky. "Doesn't that sun feel good!"

He regarded her upturned face thoughtfully. "Do you remember what it was?"

"Oh, please. It wasn't any one thing. I think I just got tired of all Mother's minister friends—most of them unmarried and childless—treating me like one of the Seven Wonders of the World. Somewhere along the way I started to feel like a freak."

"That's unfortunate, because you're certainly not that."

She spotted a loose feather on his white doctor's coat and reached over and brushed it off. "You're prejudiced. You knew me before my hair came in."

He laughed. "I see you're not too traumatized. Obviously, you've got a good grip on the situation. You were definitely cute, though. Do you remember my nickname for you?"

"Wasn't it 'Drool Baby'?"

"That was Mom's. Mine was 'Boo-Boo Bear'."

"Right. I prefer yours, thanks."

The chicken squawked. Doctor Bart leaned over and picked up the crate. "Well, what should we do with Henrietta?"

"Don't look at me," she replied, smiling sweetly. "You're the one who said you'd take chickens, Doc Martin!"

Rebecca pulled into the end of the driveway just as Nellie escaped back to her desk. Doctor Bart's neighbor coasted up to him and rolled down her window. "Good heavens! Is that a chicken? Don't tell me …?"

He nodded, still clutching the crate in his arms. "Miss Crump's copay." The chicken squawked again.

"Sounds as though she isn't very happy?"

Doctor Bart peered closely through the slats. "Say! This doctor business is really paying off. Henrietta just laid an egg."

Rebecca laughed and leaned out the car window so she could admire the prize. "Oh, what a perfect egg!"

"And here I was thinking an egg was an egg."

"Shame on you, Doctor Bart! And you a country boy, too. Would you like me to take her over to Trudy's? One more chicken won't mean anything to them, and I'm going there, anyway—just as soon as you accept my invitation to dinner tomorrow night. You'll bring Nellie, too, of course."

"Sounds more than a fair trade," he said, relieved. "Where would you like me to set the crate, which, by the way, Miss Crump wants back?"

"Of course she does. Put Henrietta on the back seat, please. Dinner is at six o'clock, but come any time after five. You can come earlier, but I can't guarantee Wendell will be cleaned up by then."

Doctor Bart balanced the crate on the back seat and pushed the car door shut. "Thanks for the invite, and thanks for taking Henrietta off my hands. See you tomorrow," he concluded, waving Rebecca off.

Nellie, when informed of the dinner invitation, was pleased to have been included, but not so pleased Rebecca had thought to invite her and Metcalf as a couple. Did everyone in Sovereign know her mother's hopes in regard to her and Doctor Bart? Was the entire town in league against her?

CHAPTER 9
Walden

During the course of the clinic's first day, six scheduled patients showed up and were handily dispatched by Doctor Bart. Fortunately, no fowl other than Henrietta was presented as payment. Just before four o'clock, when the clinic was due to close, Nellie heard the front door open. She glanced up to see the stranger from the woods, Walden, entering the clinic. His face was pale beneath the full beard and he was holding a bunched-up bandanna tightly against his upper arm. He was obviously in pain.

She jumped up. "Oh-my-God! What happened?"

"An accident," he replied, grimacing. He pulled the blue bandana away from his arm, revealing a torn, blood-soaked shirt. "Stupid me. I picked up some bird shot," he added.

"Did it go off?" Nellie asked, in her ignorance.

"You could say that."

Hearing voices, Metcalf exited his exam room, where he had been cleaning up for the day. He glanced at Walden's bloodied flannel shirt and his face became inscrutably bland. "In here," he directed, motioning with his right hand. "Up on the table, please, Walden."

Nellie followed them into the exam room, anxious to discover what had happened. Obnoxious or not, she hoped the stranger would be OK.

"Take off your shirt," ordered Doctor Bart, opening a cupboard and searching for gauze and bandages. He glanced at Nellie over his shoulder. "Nellie, why don't you leave us?"

Nellie was disappointed. "You might need my help," she suggested.

"I don't mind if she stays, Doc," said Walden, struggling to unbutton his shirt. He had set the blood-soaked bandana down onto his lap so he could use both hands, and the stain on his flannel shirt was spreading. "But the wound is pretty ugly—she might faint."

Metcalf snapped the cabinet door shut. "Don't worry about Nellie. She's worked in third-world countries under physical conditions you and I wouldn't be caught dead in. She's not going to faint at the sight of a little blood. Isn't that right, Nellie?"

Nellie nodded. Her heart gave a little leap at Doctor Bart's unexpected praise. Without further ado, she turned to the task at hand, expertly helping Walden shrug out of the long-sleeved flannel shirt. She hesitated before removing his tattered T-shirt, however, since she knew that would cause him considerable pain. But she quickly deduced the T-shirt would have to come off as well. Carefully, she freed both arms and pulled the tight shirt over his head, exposing a burly and quite hairy chest. Thick red blood oozed from several small holes on his well-muscled shoulder and already the skin around the area was starting to turn a nasty black-and-blue. Nellie commanded her eyes to stay focused on the wound and not wander over his bare chest.

Metcalf drew on rubber gloves and stocked the rolling prep table with sanitized tools and supplies. He liberally doused several sterile gauze pads with hydrogen peroxide and began cleaning the wounds. The strong, pungent odor of the antiseptic soon overpowered Walden's sweaty, masculine scent, much to Nellie's relief.

"How did this happen?" Doctor Bart asked, tossing several bloodied gauzes into the trash.

"I had a run-in with some birdshot. I lost."

Metcalf harrumphed, and Nellie's curiosity deepened.

"Who was on the other end of that birdshot?"

"I'd rather not say."

Doctor Bart squeezed two folds of skin together hard and Walden winced in pain. "Sorry, the pellets are in deeper than I thought," Metcalf said, pulling back. "I'll have to give you a local anesthetic. I need to get them out and clean the wound completely so it doesn't get infected." He reached into the locking cabinet and retrieved a glass vial filled with a clear liquid. "How are you with pain?"

Walden grinned, revealing a set of neat white teeth in the middle of his beard. "No better than most men, probably. Medication appreciated."

Nellie hid a smile. Men were such babies!

Doctor Bart flipped the vial upside down and measured the anesthetic into a syringe. He squirted the air out, and returned the bottle to the stainless steel stand. "Close the door, Nellie, just in case someone comes in. And get me some iodine, please."

Within fifteen minutes Doctor Bart had removed five small metal pellets of birdshot from Walden's arm, and cleaned and dressed the wound. From the supply cabinet he gathered up some sterile bandages and a tube of antiseptic cream and handed everything to Nellie. "Pack these up for him, please." He turned to Walden. "I don't suppose you have any medical supplies at home?"

"Not likely," the mushroom man replied, stepping down from the table. "Not unless they were left there eighty years ago." He retrieved his bloody T-shirt from the back of a chair. "Can I pay you in 'shrooms, Doc? I've got some nice chanterelles. That's what I was collecting when the, uh, bird shot found me."

"You can keep the mushrooms if you just tell me the truth. Listen, Walden, if someone took a shot at you—that's a serious crime. You've got to report it."

"Aw, he didn't mean to hit me. He was just trying to scare me away. I could tell he was trying to fire over my head, but he's short and, well, I'm not."

"Someone shot at you!" Nellie exclaimed, shocked. A glimmer of the truth began to reveal itself to her. Still, she couldn't imagine anyone in Sovereign who would do such a thing!

"He, who?" pressed Doctor Bart. "Henry Trow?"

"Maybe. Maybe not." Walden attempted to pull the tight cotton shirt on over his head.

Nellie stepped forward to help him. Walden was nearly a foot taller than her, so she had to stand on tiptoe to work the shirt over his head. She accidentally swayed against his burly chest.

"Steady," Walden said, sardonically. He gripped her slim hip with his left hand and held her tightly against him for several seconds.

Startled by his audacity, Nellie glanced up. She read cynical amusement in his flashing brown eyes. He thought she had fallen against him on purpose!

She jerked away from Walden's grip, blushing, but not before noticing Metcalf had averted his eyes. Oh-my-God. Did he think she had brushed up against Walden on purpose, as well?

Doctor Bart retrieved some unit dose samples of antibiotics and handed them to the bearded woodsman. "Here, take these, too. Come back and see me next week, unless you develop chills or a fever before that. There's still a risk of infection. Come see me right away if that happens."

"OK, Doc. Thanks." Walden added the pills to the bag Nellie had put up for him.

"I'm done with him now, Nellie. He's all yours."

She glanced up at Metcalf anxiously. Was there a double entendre in his remark? Surely he couldn't think she was *that* kind of woman?

Nellie abruptly exited the exam room. She sat down behind the safety of her desk, an oak monstrosity that had once belonged to Miss Hastings' father, superintendent of the corn shop. She had unearthed the solid, flat-top desk in the cottage's attic and some of Metcalf's friends had helped them swap out the desk for the parlor couch. Nellie immediately set about preparing Walden's paperwork.

The wounded woodsman ambled out of the examining room moments later. He placed the palm of his good arm against the desk and leaned down. "So … when are we going to continue our little debate, Nurse Nellie?"

"We're not," she said, in a frosty voice.

"No?"

"No. Take your arm off my desk, please."

"Oh, I get it," he said insinuatingly. "The good doctor's your boyfriend, right?"

"No—yes. I don't know." Suddenly, Nellie was confused by his musky proximity. He was even more compelling up close and personal than he had been in the intimacy of the woods. She commanded herself to remain calm and professional, no matter what provoking things he might say or do.

"Well, which is it? A guy likes to know these things."

Nellie ignored his question. She stuck the sharp edge of the plastic clipboard up against his stomach and pushed him back up. "Here. Fill this out."

"I can't. I'm right-handed." He turned and perched on the edge of the desk. "I need your help, Nurse Nellie."

"Go sit over there and I'll help you fill it out," she said, pointing to the rocker on the opposite side of the waiting room.

"Do you think that's far enough away?" Nevertheless, he obliged her by folding his tall frame into the rocker. Walden began to rock slowly back and forth, and the old chair released a steady stream of protests: *creak, creak, creak.*

"What's your real name?" she inquired, not sure which was more annoying, the man or the chair.

"Walden," he replied, without batting an eye.

"Walden," she repeated, unable to keep the sarcasm from her voice despite her vow to remain professional. "And your last name?"

The stranger stopped rocking. He stroked his bushy brown beard thoughtfully. "Pond," he replied, straight-faced.

Nellie threw up her hands. "Walden Pond? Of course! Why did I even bother to ask?"

She helped him finish the medical questionnaire as quickly as possible, certain most of the information he provided was false. She made a follow-up appointment for Walden and scribbled out an appointment reminder. She walked over and handed the card to him. "We're done. You can go now."

"Thanks for your solicitude, Nurse Nellie." He pushed himself up, towering over her.

Nellie took several quick steps back and nearly tripped over the plastic bucket Olivia had left on the floor. She caught herself, however, just as Walden grasped hold of her by the elbow with his good arm. She shook him off. "I'm fine, thanks."

He regarded her lazily, hands on hips. "I'll drop off the chanterelles tomorrow," he said. "I know where you live."

"Don't knock yourself out," Nellie retorted.

"Don't worry, honey, I never do."

She gritted her teeth and clenched her fists. Arrogant, insufferable man!

CHAPTER 10
Not an Anonymous Sperm Donor

On Saturday at the clinic, Doctor Bart saw three scheduled patients with minor medical conditions and treated two walk-ins: a black eye and a bee sting. By the time Nellie cleaned the waiting room and prepared the paperwork in the event Doctor Bart received an emergency call during the week, she discovered it was after one o'clock.

"Time to close up shop," Doctor Bart said, packing his stethoscope away in his little black bag. "I think we made a good showing for our first two days. How did we do for donations?"

Nellie examined her notes. "Sixty dollars in cash, two jars of pickles, a loaf of whole wheat bread, and Henrietta."

"I think we can scratch Henrietta," he said, drily.

She smiled. "I'll change that entry to one fresh egg, then."

He sat his doctor's bag into a nearby chair. "I couldn't have done it without you, Nellie."

"Yes, you could have," she contradicted him. Nevertheless, she was pleased by Metcalf's compliment. He obviously had put yesterday's incident with Walden behind them.

He perched comfortably on the edge of her desk. She cautioned herself against mentally comparing him to the provocative and magnetic woodsman, but failed. If only Metcalf would be a little more manly! He might have a chance with her then. A woman does like her man to be manly. But Doctor Bart was always so serious and thoughtful, as though he was about to tell her that her cat had died.

"What are you doing this afternoon?" he asked.

"Laundry, dishes, housework. The usual Suzie Homemaker stuff."

"Would you like to come with me?"

"Where to, Doc Martin?"

"I thought we'd drop in on our new neighbor, Henry Trow. I want to try and throw some oil on those troubled waters between him and Walden. You can help me further the cause of peace."

"Because I'm a pacifist?"

"Because you're a pretty woman."

"If anybody else had said that to me I'd say they were a sexist. But you …"

"Are not a sexist," he finished for her. He rose up off the desk. "I just think a comely female presence might help keep the old gent on his best behavior."

Nellie retrieved her fleece jacket from the back of her chair. "But will it keep you on your best behavior?" she teased.

"I'm always on my best behavior, aren't I?"

"Yes," she replied, feeling some of the air go out of her balloon. And that's so the problem, she thought, sadly. Walden would have taken the opportunity to pat her bottom, at least.

"Well? Will you come?"

"Sure. Why not? I've wanted to meet Mr. Trow since I got home, but for some reason or other …"

"Because you've been helping me," he said, smiling.

"… I just haven't found the time. But do you really think it's a good idea to try and make nice between him and Walden? He's so arrogant; Walden, that is. I have a feeling anything we do might backfire on us."

Doctor Bart's face became serious. "I can't let the shooting go unremarked, Nellie. I have a legal obligation to report a crime." He picked up his doctor's bag.

"Maybe it was an accident, like Walden said?"

"Mr. Walden Pond is hardly the standard bearer for Truth. Most likely he doesn't want the incident reported because he doesn't want to highlight his mushrooming activities in the area, which have been innocuous until now. But the next shot Henry Trow takes might put Walden's eye out—or worse. Before I report the incident to the authorities, however, I want to hear Mr. Trow's side of the story."

Doctor Bart elected to drive up to his neighbor's, even though the old Lovejoy place was less than a mile away. He explained to Nellie arriving on foot would weaken the impression they were trying to make and therefore weaken their ability to influence their new neighbor. Nellie climbed up into the passenger seat of his old pickup, and Metcalf, after making sure she was safely tucked inside, closed the door behind her.

Nellie had purchased two magnetic door signs for his truck, advertising the name of the clinic—*Songbird Free Medical Clinic*—with the address, telephone number, and a picture of a singing bird perched on a rose bush. She had applied the signs to the truck for the first time that morning. After closing Nellie's door, Doctor Bart stood back to admire them. He and Nellie had mutually agreed upon the name of the clinic, both of them wanting to recognize and remember Miss Hastings, who had once performed on the stages of New York as a precocious child prodigy, *The Songbird of Sovereign*.

"What do you think?" Nellie asked, through the open window.

He smiled at her appreciatively. "I think we make quite a team."

Metcalf went around and slid into the driver's seat. Before fastening his seat belt, he turned to her. "I think you should know—I've made some inquiries about your birth and, with Mom's help, learned a few interesting legal facts. I thought I'd bring you up to speed on the drive there."

She sat up straight, instantly on the alert. "Good facts or bad facts? Listen to me—I sound like Glinda, the Witch of the North: 'Are you a good witch or a bad witch?'"

He chuckled and started the engine. "Neither good nor bad, just some facts. For example, did you know in the state of Maine, if a baby is born out of wedlock the birth father's name can't be listed on the birth certificate, not unless he and the mother sign a notarized AOP—Acknowledgement of Paternity—form?"

"No, I didn't know. How long has that law been in effect?"

Doctor Bart put the truck in reverse and backed out of the driveway. "Since the year before you were born. So, unless Aunt Maggie and your father were married …"

"They weren't."

"… your mother couldn't have listed your father on your birth certificate, even if she had wanted to—not without his consent." He changed gears and motored slowly up the road. "The law did give her the option to go to court, force him to take a paternity test, make him man up to his responsibilities, so to speak. But, according to Mom, once the putative father is identified he has legal rights to the offspring."

"Putative! What kind of horrible word is that? Isn't 'puta' the Spanish word for whore? How nice!"

"Now, Nellie, don't get your back up."

"The state regards my mother as a whore and I shouldn't be offended?"

"The etiology of the word isn't Spanish. 'Putative' is an old English legal term for 'birth father'—it probably came over on the Mayflower with your ancestors." A gray squirrel darted out and Doctor Bart swerved onto the left side of the road to avoid hitting the rodent. The creature flipped around and started back the other way and Metcalf slammed on the brakes. The truck came to a standstill. "Sorry," he apologized. "Sometimes they just can't make up their minds."

Nellie relaxed her grip on the door strap. "No problem."

The squirrel finally scampered across the road and up a maple tree. He disappeared with a wag of his bushy gray tail. Metcalf released the brakes and maneuvered the truck back into the travel lane. "The fact that your mother didn't take your father to court," he continued, "suggests two possibilities. First, she didn't want him to know about you and thus kept him ignorant of his rights, or, second, he wanted to remain anonymous and she abided by his wishes. But why any woman would willingly raise a child by herself is a mystery to me. Do you know if your mother ever applied for any kind of public assistance, like TANF?"

"Welfare? Mother was way too proud for hand-outs!"

"TANF isn't a hand-out—it's a hand up," he corrected her, lightly.

"Well, I'm pretty sure Maggie never asked anybody for anything, except maybe Uncle Peter. Why do you ask?"

"Because in Maine the law requires a woman who applies for TANF to identify the father of her child. The state doesn't want to pick up the tab for an additional burden if there's a delinquent father out there financially able—but perhaps not willing—to provide for his family. Maggie would have had to name your father, and then the state would have gone after him, probably with a cotton swab to prove his paternity. If your father was abusive, however, and Maggie had been able to provide documented proof of such abuse, the state would have waived the paternity identification requirement and Maggie would have received aide without him knowing of your existence."

"No man ever abused Mother," Nellie stated flatly.

"You can't be sure of that. You weren't around, remember?"

"I know she wouldn't have stayed with an abusive man. I've heard her preach several times on domestic violence, how women need to get away from those kinds of guys."

"Sometimes that's hard to do, for many reasons."

"I know—although not from any personal experience," she amended hastily, not wanting him to get the wrong idea. "Still, I think my father was probably just an anonymous sperm donor. I never had any kind of a hint growing up he was anyone Maggie knew personally or even I might know, not after Uncle Peter was ruled out, anyway."

Doctor Bart remained silent, hands gripped on the steering wheel, eyes straight ahead on the road.

"Wait—you know something, don't you? What is it you're not saying?"

He slowed the truck so he could maneuver a right-hand turn into the paved driveway entrance to the old Lovejoy place. "I'm sorry to burst your bubble, Nellie, but your father wasn't an anonymous sperm donor."

"How do you know?" she challenged.

"Mom told me. I asked her about your father point-blank. She admitted she knows who he is—I think she even knows him herself—but she promised Maggie never to reveal his identity. When I tried to pump her for more information, she shut down like a dead battery."

"Oh-my-God! Aunt Jane knows who my father is," Nellie cried, "and she won't tell me?"

"I'm sorry, Nellie. But you have to respect her right to keep the promise she gave to your mother."

"What about *my* rights? Doesn't anybody care about me?"

They pulled up in front of the brick house. Doctor Bart put the truck in park and switched off the ignition. He reached for her hand. "I care, Nellie," he uttered, energetically. "And I'll do everything within my power to help you find your father. One way or another, we'll find him."

CHAPTER 11
Henry Trow

Nellie, still miffed at Aunt Jane's pig-headed determination to keep her mother's secret, pulled her hand away from Doctor Bart's. They were sitting together in his parked truck in front of the brick homestead. Suddenly, the venerable mahogany door of the old Lovejoy place swung open. An elderly, gray-haired man limped out onto the granite stoop and squinted at them, trying to read the sign affixed to truck's door.

The man was short—as Walden had described Henry Trow—about five-foot-five or six. His face appeared frozen in an expression of despair, the sadness of his heavily-lidded eyes highlighted by bushy gray eyebrows stretching across the bridge of his nose. He was dressed neatly, if a bit uncharacteristically for Sovereign, wearing a navy lambs wool vest over a plaid cotton shirt, wrinkled khakis, and leather scuffs.

Doctor Bart popped open his door and stepped out. "Hello, Mr. Trow?"

The man nodded. "Who are you?"

Metcalf approached the granite steps. "My name is Doctor Bart and this is my assistant Nellie Walker." He motioned for her to come and join him. Nellie, recollecting her role, hastily hopped out and moved to his side. "Mind if we come in a few minutes to speak with you?"

"What about?"

"It's a medical issue; I'd rather we spoke in private."

"I think my neighbors are a little far removed to overhear us," Mr. Trow remarked wryly, nodding in the direction of the cemetery. "What did you say your name was?" He asked, batting away a pesky deerfly.

"Doctor Bart. I just opened the medical clinic in the yellow cottage down the road."

"Well, just so you know, Doctor Bart, I have a DNR on file. Don't bring me back if you're ever called up here, whatever you do."

He swung the heavy door open and moved back inside, keeping a watchful eye on the deerfly.

Doctor Bart, regarding that as an invitation, grasped Nellie by the elbow and steered her up the granite steps. "Thanks for taking the time to see us, Mr. Trow."

"Time is about all I have left, young man."

Inside the brick house, the front hall was cool and quiet. The foyer was illuminated by soft natural daylight filtered through olive-colored sheers, which hung over the two sidelights on either side of the door and the transom window above. The filtered light was calming and grace-filled, lending an aura of yesteryear to the homestead. Nellie glanced around eagerly, curious to see whether the old Lovejoy place still retained the glory of the family, who, until this last generation, had stubbornly clung to the house, furniture, and every acre of land—except for the ten-acres donated for the schoolhouse—through the Depression of the thirties, the antique boom of the seventies and eighties, and the land speculation of the nineties. She hadn't been inside the house for nearly a decade, not since elderly Mrs. Lovejoy had passed away, intestate, thereby setting up a nasty squabble among her six grandchildren over the proceeds of the property. Either the "kids" had finally come to terms or had been ordered to sell by the court, because Shirley Palmer had informed Nellie after church on Sunday that Mr. Trow had purchased the estate mostly intact.

Doctor Bart followed the older man as he hobbled down the hall, past the elegantly-curved mahogany staircase and into the kitchen. Nellie held back a minute to take stock. Some of the antiques were missing, she noted—such as the stately Isaac Pearson grandfather clock that used to greet every guest like a distinguished doorman—as well as the two folk-art oil paintings of the original Lovejoy ancestors. Matching squares of lighter paint on the wall leading up the staircase revealed where the paintings had hung for more than a hundred and fifty years.

Had the paintings gone to one of the heirs? Or had they been sold separately to raise cash?

Nellie suddenly realized she was lagging behind. She hurried to catch up with the two men. When she reached the cherry-wainscoted country kitchen, she found a small fire burning in the woodstove. She was glad to see the familiar nickel-plated black Majestic cookstove. At least this old friend had remained with the house.

"Have a seat," invited the old man. "I'll put some water on for tea."

"That's very kind of you, Mr. Trow," Metcalf began. "But …"

"We'd love some tea," Nellie interjected, flashing the elderly man her sweetest smile. Might as well do her part.

Henry Trow's hooded eyes lit up and he returned her smile. His bushy eyebrows straightened out and his facial wrinkles relaxed. When he turned his back to draw water for the teakettle, Nellie shot Metcalf a meaningful look, and indicated with a bob of her blonde head he was to take a seat at the table. Obediently, Doctor Bart sat down and folded his hands on the tablecloth. Nellie pulled out a chair for herself, perched on the edge of it and peeked under the red-checked tablecloth, where she discovered, to her delight, the original walnut drop-leaf table. Old Mrs. Lovejoy had told Nellie she had been born on that table.

She dropped the tablecloth and rotated in her chair slightly to face Mr. Trow. "I hope we aren't interrupting you …?"

"No, no. It's good to have company, young lady." Mr. Trow set a box of herbal tea bags on the table, three silver teaspoons, a bag of store-bought cookies, and a jar of Wendell's honey. "I bought this from an odd duck down the road," he said. "I thought the man was something of a braggart at first, telling me his was the best honey around. Turns out he was right."

Nellie laughed and picked up the familiar jar. "That's Wendell," she said, admiring the honey's golden glow. She replaced the jar on the table. "Wendell Russell," she continued. "He doesn't mean to brag. That's just how he is." She smiled to herself, recalling how—not so very long ago—she too had thought Wendell an 'odd duck.' "He's really very nice, when you get to know him."

"Well, he's got himself a pretty wife; I'll give him that. So there's got to be a good bottom to him."

Nellie selected a teabag. "Are you married, Mr. Trow?"

Her question appeared to take him by surprise. He paused. One blue-veined hand gripped the back of an empty chair for support. "I was married, for nearly fifty years," he said, finally. "My wife died two years ago. Bless her! Cancer," he elucidated, gruffly.

"I'm so sorry!"

"I couldn't bear to live there without Gerry—the place didn't seem right without her—so I sold everything and came up here."

"You must miss her very much," added Doctor Bart.

Mr. Trow's right leg wobbled and he clutched again at the chair back. "Damn knee! I knew I should have gotten myself a new one before I left home, but couldn't bring myself to go through surgery by myself."

"Would you like me to take a look at that sometime?" Metcalf offered.

"Might be a good idea. Where did you say your office is?"

"The yellow house about a mile down the road. The clinic is in the front. We're open all day Friday and Saturdays until one o'clock. You don't need an appointment—although Nellie would probably prefer you to have one—you can walk right in."

"Maybe I'll just do that, Doc."

"You were telling us about your decision to move to Maine," Nellie gently prodded him.

"Oh, yes. I was going to say the only problem is—it's even harder up here without her than 'twas in New Hampshire. "

The water on the cookstove began to boil, and he turned his back to them to attend it, but not before Nellie thought she saw a tear in his eye. Mr. Trow poured out three mugs of hot water, serving Nellie first. She thanked him, taking the opportunity to study his weather-lined face. She felt sorry for him, almost positive he was very lonely. Surely he hadn't shot Walden on purpose?

"Well, Doc, what's your mission today?" inquired Mr. Trow, pulling out a chair. "Looking for money for that new clinic, I suppose?" He selected a tea bag, ripped off the foil and plunked the bag into his cup.

Doctor Bart cleared his throat. "This isn't easy for me to say, Mr. Trow," he said carefully, "but I had a patient yesterday whose shoulder was full of birdshot. My patient wouldn't say who was on the other end of the shotgun, but …"

"Good God! You don't mean I hit him?" Henry Trow's hands trembled. "I only meant to fire over his head—scare him off."

"He's got a pretty tall head, Mr. Trow—and birdshot has a way of spreading out. I'm afraid you did hit him. He's going to feel mighty sore for a few days."

"I didn't mean to hurt anyone," Henry Trow cried. Dismayed, he hid his face in his gnarled hands. "Gerry would be so disappointed in me," he sobbed.

Moved, Nellie leaped up and threw her arm around the old man's shoulders. "We're not here to convict you, Mr. Trow, we're here to help you," she assured him, with a little hug.

He looked up; his blue eyes were filled with tears. He patted her hand. "That's very kind, young lady. I do believe you are here to help me."

Nellie gave him another hug and resumed her seat. Mr. Trow searched through his pockets for his white handkerchief and blew his nose.

"But why take a shot at Walden?" Metcalf persisted. "What did you hope to accomplish? Was it because he was stealing mushrooms from your land?"

"I don't give a damn about the mushrooms," Mr. Trow swore, stuffing the damp handkerchief back into his pocket. "I just wanted to be sure he didn't come any closer, not after what he did to Jasmine's calf."

"Jasmine?"

"My wife's favorite cow who gave birth three weeks ago. The other day that cowardly reprobate doused the calf with some kind of acid to get back at me for ordering him off my property. He about burned that calf to death."

"Acid? Like hydrochloric acid?" Nellie asked, aghast.

Henry Trow nodded.

"Surely you don't mean to say Walden threw acid on one of your young stock?" Doctor Bart queried, dismayed.

"That's just what I mean. Damn reprobate!" His eyes watered again and he retrieved his handkerchief.

Nellie was shocked. Could Walden have done such a thing? An image of the mysterious stranger's face sprang to mind and she did think she could see a streak of cruelty in him.

"I'd already warned him off my property twice before," Mr. Trow continued, "but he kept telling me it wasn't my land. I told him I'd show him the title deeds but that didn't matter to him—he's got some quixotic idea about land ownership. The irony is that I would have given him permission if he'd asked—I've never been stingy with anything, especially my property. But that reprobate wouldn't lower himself to ask for permission because it goes against the grain of his philosophy."

"Tell me about the calf," probed Doctor Bart.

"Wednesday afternoon I went out to check on Jasmine's little bull calf—Gerry and I raised a few Scottish Highlands in New Hampshire and I couldn't bear to sell her favorite cow so I brought Jasmine and a bred heifer to Maine with me. Anyway, Wednesday I couldn't find the calf in any of his usual haunts. I don't know how much you know about Highlands, Doc, but when they're newborns the mothers often hide their calves in the woods or the tall grass, just like the wild deer do. Anyway, when I finally found the little fellar, he was a mess, full of maggots, the hide on his backside blacker than a burnt steak."

"Oh-my-God," Nellie breathed. "How horrible!"

"What makes you think it was acid?" Doctor Bart pressed.

"You come take a look at, Doc, and you tell me what else would cause these third degree burns. The only thing it could be is some kind of acid."

Metcalf rose up. "Let's go have a look. I'd like to see it."

Henry Trow pushed himself up from the table. "Follow me." He grasped a cane standing in the corner by the open doorway and shuffled out through the long woodshed into the attached barn. Doctor Bart followed and Nellie brought up the rear.

The old barn was stuffed with sweet-smelling square bales of hay, some of which were broken open, making the floor slippery underfoot. "Watch your step," cautioned the old man. Nellie saw a superannuated John Deere tractor, still in good condition, parked next to a built-in wooden grain silo. A wild cat darted around the corner.

Mr. Trow hobbled past the first horse stall, which was empty, but Nellie spotted a wide-horned Scottish Highland cow through the partially-opened double Dutch door on the next stall. The shaggy red cow was hitched to a post and was calmly chewing her cud. Her head swung around as they approached and she offered a faint lowing moo. In the far corner of the stall Nellie spied a blackened little bunch, which she knew was the burnt calf. The hair on the poor creature's back had been completely scorched off leaving behind a leather-looking blackened hide that did indeed look as though the calf had been doused with hydrochloric acid.

Could Walden have done such a thing? To such an innocent creature!

Mr. Trow opened the bottom café door and carefully stepped inside. "Come on in, just take it slow. Jasmine's hitched. She's usually very friendly but she's mighty protective of her young 'un."

Nellie, who had been standing next to Mr. Trow, entered first. She went immediately to the calf, scooched down and patted its head, which had somehow escaped being burned. "Poor thing," she cried. The calf bleated feebly and Jasmine's head swung around protectively.

Nellie's nose tingled from the foul odor of the calf's burnt hair, which overpowered every other odor in the stall, even the cow manure. She gazed anxiously up at Doctor Bart, who was measuring the damage with his eyes. "Isn't there something we can do?" she pleaded.

"Get my bag from the truck," he said, tersely. He knelt down beside the calf.

Nellie scrambled to her feet, knowing Metcalf had gone into what she described as 'Doctor Mode.' When he was in Doctor Mode he assumed a highly-focused tunnel vision on the problem at hand and everything else in the world disappeared off stage. If she told him she would marry him when he was in Doctor Mode he would simply nod and continue with his work, completely oblivious, remembering nothing of her promise when he awoke, as though he had been in a trance the whole time.

Metcalf moved his capable hands over the calf, checking the extent and the nature of the burns. The calf whimpered slightly, and the mother cow strained at her chain. She raised her head and mooed anxiously.

"Alright, old girl," Mr. Trow reassured Jasmine. "He's a friend; he's here to help us."

"Did you call a vet?"

"Two or three of 'em. The earliest anyone could get here was Monday. The last vet I talked to told me how to clean up the maggots—you can see where I shaved the little bugger—and suggested I get some penicillin from the farm store, which I did."

"I've got something stronger than penicillin in my bag. This animal has a very high fever. I've got some burn cream back at the office, too. It's for humans, but vets use basically the same thing."

"Thanks, Doc. I'm mighty glad you came by today." The old man patted the cow's hairy forehead and whispered a few words of endearment in her ear. The cow visibly relaxed.

Nellie returned, handing Metcalf his black medical bag. "Is he going to be OK?"

Doctor Bart placed the bag on the scuffed-up barn floor and removed the liquid antibiotic and a small syringe. "He'll make it," he assured them both. "You've done everything right, Mr. Trow." He gave the calf a shot in the neck, rubbed the injection site to disperse the antibiotic, and carefully recapped the sharp needle. "This burn isn't caused by any kind of acid, though. This calf was struck by lightning."

"Lightning!" Nellie exclaimed.

"I don't believe that for a minute," the old man stated baldly. "You're trying to protect that reprobate."

"I assure you, Mr. Trow, I'd be the first to call for Walden's prosecution if I believed he was guilty of such a heinous crime. But he's not. Lightning strikes are not as uncommon as you might think around here. I grew up on a dairy farm in Albion and we lost several cows to lighting strikes over the years. Calves sometimes survive, though. Now, if my memory serves me correct, we had a bad thunder storm last week …"

"I remember it," cried Nellie. "The thunder woke me up!"

"… and this little fellow must have been standing too close to a tree. The lightning entered his body just above his tail here," Metcalf pointed to the burnt area at the end of the calf's spine, "and then traveled up his backbone. The burns wouldn't have been so bad except for the fact Scottish Highlands have long hair. The calf's hair caught fire and burnt down around his sides."

"I never heard of such a thing," fumed Mr. Trow. "You're making that up."

"Let's see, shall we? If I'm right, there should be two matching burns on his front legs where the lightning exited his body. If I'm wrong, there won't be anything but hair there."

Nellie watched in breathless fascination as Doctor Bart gently rolled the calf onto its side and straightened out the two front legs. He pushed aside the long red hair above the calf's knees and revealed—two matching round blackened burns!

Aghast, Henry Trow released the cow's head and slumped back against the tie-up post. "My God! I not only shot him—I falsely accused him," he cried. "What have I done?" He put his head in his hands and began blubbering.

Nellie's heart went out to the old man. She made a move to comfort him, but Metcalf grabbed her by the arm and stopped her. He pulled her close to him so Mr. Trow wouldn't overhear what he had to say. "Let him cry, Nellie," he whispered in her ear, his lips lightly brushing against her temple. "Sometimes tears are the best medicine."

CHAPTER 12
Enter Julian Mills

"It's on days like these when I really miss Maggie," Doctor Bart said during the drive down to the old schoolhouse. "She'd know exactly what to do to help Henry Trow."

"What could Mother do?" Nellie replied curiously. "He's obviously got some anger issues and needs to see a good therapist."

"I think you'll find when you get to the bottom of his anger it all stems from one source."

"And that is …?"

"He's mad at God, angry his wife predeceased him. He might also be angry God did nothing while his wife was suffering and dying from cancer. We humans have been blaming God for thousands of years, unable to understand how a loving God could allow things like pain and suffering to exist."

"Why does God does allow pain and suffering to exist?"

"I certainly don't know the answer to that. Nobody does. But Maggie knows how to be present with people who are exploring that question and help them find some peace. Mr. Trow's affliction calls for a good minister, not a good therapist."

Nellie frowned at her own ignorance. More and more she was beginning to realize the value of her mother's vocation. Growing up she had only witnessed a small segment of her mother's work, never seeing the big picture. "I guess I only saw Maggie wrestling with what she was going to say in her sermon every Sunday, not the other things she did for the community," she admitted. "Mother usually tried her pastoral message out on me, to test my reaction before she took it to church. Finally I figured out what she was doing and made myself scarce whenever I spied one of those yellow legal pads coming out. I'm surprised you know so much about the ministry, though, being a doctor and all."

"Any doctor worth his or her salt has a healthy respect for the ministry. We see patients and their families during times of deepest despair—when our hands are tied; when there's no hope, nothing left for us to do—and I'm always grateful when I see a member of the clergy arriving."

Doctor Bart pulled into the schoolhouse yard and shifted into park. He turned to Nellie. "Seems to me Mr. Trow almost had you convinced Walden was guilty of throwing acid on his calf. I must say that surprised me, Nellie. I thought you liked Walden?"

There was no misunderstanding the hope in his voice. Nellie knew Metcalf, while honest to the core, was also a man. "I'm not sure whether I like him or not, but I don't dislike him," she replied, carefully. "Not yet, anyway. But I do think he's got a streak of cruelty in him and it wouldn't have surprised me if he had done something awful to that poor calf."

"Walden—cruel? You must have seen something in him I missed, but I yield to your feminine intuition. Mostly because that's what I want to hear," he added, quickly.

Nellie had her hand on the doorknob but she let it drop and burst into laughter. "You can't help it, can you?"

"Putting my foot in my mouth?"

"No, silly, being honest."

He unconsciously tapped his hand against the steering wheel. "I guess not. Somewhere along the way I discovered the thing to be gained by lying or prevaricating isn't worth as much as my opinion of myself. To tell you the truth, Nellie, I think we've all got a cruel streak in us, as well as a bunch of other unflattering human characteristics. Walden isn't such an unusual representative of the human species. Not many people actually practice what they preach."

"You do," she said. The words popped out without thought on her part but nevertheless she knew them to be true. He was steady, selfless, and disinterested. Unfortunately, he was also slow, plodding, and boring. By comparison, Walden, with his streak of cruelty (or perhaps because of it) excited and intrigued her.

"I'm far from perfect," he admitted.

"I don't mean you're perfect, but …"

"Ah, I knew there was a caveat!"

"… but you do what you say you're going to do. And you don't rush to judge anyone, either. In fact, just the opposite. I think you go out of your way to make excuses for people, like you just did for Walden."

"Well, I know things aren't always as they appear on the surface so I try not to take them at face value. I give people plenty of time to hang themselves."

Nellie smiled. "How did you get to be such a good guy?"

"You can thank my Grandma Lawson for that. She lived with us; rather, we lived with her until she died. My father took over the family farm when my grandfather passed away. Whenever I went astray, she'd take me in hand and—whack!—thump me back into shape." He demonstrated by slapping his palm loudly against the steering wheel.

Nellie's eyes narrowed. She wasn't sure whether he was teasing her or not. "She didn't physically beat you?"

"Yep. Grandma Lawson kept a leather razor strap hanging on the wall next to the kitchen sink just for that purpose. All of us grandkids were terrified of it. When I was about nine or ten I quietly moved that ugly old strap into the shed so it was out of sight. Gram never said a word about it. She simply hung a towel over the hook instead. But she was a good deal kinder to my sister and me after that. The razor strap never returned to the kitchen, either."

"I guess having a big family isn't all a bed of roses," Nellie remarked.

"You can't have roses without thorns, Nellie. But don't despair—we'll find you some thorns of your own. It just might take some time. Speaking of time …" he glanced at his watch. "We'd better get going or we'll be late for dinner with the Russell's."

Nellie opened her door and slid her legs out onto the running board of the truck. "What should I wear?"

He absently ran his hand through his unruly red curls. "I'm hardly the authority on women's clothing. Just remember you'll be sitting down to dinner with Wendell Russell and dress accordingly."

"So, no pearls but an oversized flannel shirt and grease-stained jeans?"

"Not quite that. Say … a pretty dress."

She made a little face. "I don't do 'pretty'."

"A plain dress, then. Whatever you do—do it fast. I'll be back to get you in forty-five minutes or so."

Nellie entered the shed to find a small basket containing chanterelle mushrooms, neatly wrapped in a cotton napkin. The handwoven, handled basket had been left on the bench beneath the Shaker peg rack and held perhaps a pound of the precious, funnel-shaped orange fungi. Nellie folded back the blue napkin and held the basket to her nose, inhaling the delicious apricot scent of the mushrooms.

She had been so preoccupied with the plight of Henry Trow and his poor calf she had forgotten all about Walden's promised 'copay.' In truth, she had never taken his offer seriously, believing him to be the kind of man whose promises were like monopoly money, colorful but worthless. Nellie searched in vain for a note. When she didn't find one she was disappointed. A note from Walden would have given her more insight into his character.

Although pleased the woodsman had kept his promise, Nellie felt uncomfortable knowing Walden had entered the shed in her absence. No doubt he hadn't wanted to leave the mushrooms on the stoop where the delicate fungi would be victimized by the hot western sun. But in her mind he had violated a personal boundary by entering her house without permission.

Suddenly, she felt as though someone was watching her. It was an eerie sensation. What if Walden was still in the area? What if he had been lurking in the woods, waiting for her to return?

She shuddered, and quickly turned and slid the fat bolt on the inner shed door, locking it. She certainly didn't want him entering the house while she was in the shower. How creepy!

About forty minutes later, as Nellie was attaching the first of a pair of gold-hoop earrings, she heard a sharp knock on the shed door. She realized she had forgotten to unlock the door for Doctor Bart.

"Coming," she called out to him. Earring in hand, she made her way toward the shed in her nylon stocking feet.

For her evening attire, Nellie had settled on a sleeveless black knit dress—her ubiquitous little black dress that went everywhere with her—and a tan cashmere cardigan that fell just below her hips. She had initially wanted to arrange her hair in a loose bun but decided the style was too formal for the occasion and instead pulled her long silken strands into a casual ponytail. She paused in the kitchen to slip into her black Mary Janes.

Three rapid knocks came again, this time louder. "Oh, good heavens," Nellie breathed. She threw the bolt and opened the double-crossed door. "I said I was com …." she broke off, startled to see not Doctor Bart but a distinguished-looking gentleman perched on the door stoop. Nellie was so surprised to see someone of his ilk in Sovereign she clung to the edge of the door speechless.

"I hope I'm not interrupting?" he began, in a friendly, easy manner. His voice was deep, resonating, and perfectly modulated.

There was something familiar about him, but Nellie couldn't put her finger on it. "You must be Nellie," he added.

She rolled the unhooked earring into the palm of her hand and put her hand behind her back. "I'm sorry—do I know you?"

"You tell me," he said, with a disarming smile.

Nellie regarded him carefully. He appeared to be in his mid to late sixties, with sculpted silver hair and a tanned face that bespoke tanning beds and hair salons. He was tall, not as tall as Walden but about Ryan McDonald's height, and carried himself with a dignified air. His aquiline nose and prominent cheekbones lent his face an aura of breeding and class distinction. The gentleman—for 'gentleman' he obviously was—was wearing an expensive tailored sports coat over a black turtleneck and pressed khaki pants. She was almost sure they had never met, yet his eyes seemed maddeningly familiar. "I'm sorry, if we have met, I don't remember who you are," she apologized.

He laughed, flashing a perfect, white smile. "Now, that's a blow to my ego. So much for the world-wide fame my publisher is always boasting about."

Suddenly, an image popped into her head, a black and white studio portrait from the back of a book jacket. He had been much younger then, but Nellie was sure now her mysterious gentleman was Julian Mills, the author of several best-selling books from the nineties, among them "The House by the Side of the Road" and "A New Archetype for the 21st Century."

"You're Julian Mills!" she exclaimed.

He bowed slightly. "At your service: author, teacher, preacher, and Doctor of Divinity."

Oh-my-God—Julian Mills? Her Hathorne classmates would never believe it! When they had been in high school, Julian Mills was on a par with M. Scott Peck and Eckhart Tolle. Lately, though, his popularity had waned, not having had a best-seller in many years.

He held out a manicured hand, and Nellie, quickly transferring the earring she had been clutching into her left hand, accepted his proffered handshake. "I read your books when I was at Hathorne Prep," she gushed. "They were so meaningful, so easy to understand. You made spirituality seem fascinating and compelling, especially compared to the dry theology textbooks my mother keeps around here. No wonder they were best-sellers!"

"You flatter me, Nellie," he replied, but he was obviously pleased. "We should make you part of our marketing team. I'd be lying, however, if I didn't admit my original intention was to bring the concept of spirituality down to a level ordinary people could understand."

"Well, you were entirely successful," she affirmed. "But ... how do you know my name?"

"No mystery there. Your mother and I shared some classes at Bangor Theological Seminary. I was at Bangor two semesters while working on my Doctorate. Maggie and I haven't been in touch much lately, but I heard from her after you were born and she told me she named you after her grandmother. Such a lovely name—Nellie. So, how is your mother? Is she at home?" His eyes probed the interior of the shed, searching for other signs of life.

Nellie hesitated, wondering how to respond. How much should she tell Julian Mills about Maggie? While she didn't doubt his story, she had reservations about how close he and her mother had actually been. She knew he was not one of her mother's close friends from Bangor Seminary for if that had been the case, she would have known Julian Mills had been a classmate of her mother's. True, his books had been published when Nellie was a young child, and later, when Nellie had been old enough to discuss his work intelligently, she had been away at prep school. Nevertheless, it was hard for her to believe Maggie would have passed up bragging rights to a famous author like Julian Mills. Easier to believe her mother had known him before he had become famous and Julian Mills had simply become lost among her clergy acquaintances.

Since Nellie could remember there had always been ministers and rabbis from a variety of religious denominations fluttering around their home, much like the slightly annoying moths of late summer. They would come and go, in a wide variety of surplices, robes and stoles, many of them disappearing for years as their callings led them to churches and synagogues in far-flung places. Nellie had long since given up attempting to remember most of their names or even figure out who was who in this strange phalanx of spiritual gurus. But Julian Mills? If her mother had ever mentioned him, she would have remembered!

In the end, Nellie decided to play it safe and protect her mother's privacy. "Mother's not here at the moment," she allowed.

His hazel eyes narrowed slightly and she was almost sure he knew she was giving him an evasive answer. She thought of what Metcalf had said about prevaricating and blushed slightly. Nervously, she twisted the lone earring around in her hand.

"But I'm keeping you," he said, catching sight of the earring. "I'm the one who should apologize. You're going out?"

Nellie nodded. "Some friends are having us over for dinner." She had automatically included Metcalf in her reply, since they had been invited as a couple. But she realized the moment the word 'us' escaped her Julian Mills would assume she and Maggie were going out together. She blushed again. This time she hadn't meant to mislead him.

"May I call again? Perhaps some afternoon next week?"

His question took her by surprise. "Uh, sure … that would be great. I volunteer at the free medical clinic on Friday and Saturday, though."

"Good for you. I'll be sure to avoid those days. Tell Maggie I'm looking forward to seeing her again. We'll have plenty of time to catch up. I'm staying in town for a while, trying to finish my new book. Would you believe I found the solitude I've been searching for on Craig's List? And it turned out to be a remote cabin in Sovereign, Maine, of all places."

They said their goodbyes and Nellie shut the door behind him. She leaned her back against the wooden door, relieved to have navigated difficult waters. But what would she do next week if Maggie still wasn't home? If only there was a way she could reach her mother! She had heard nothing from Maggie, excepting that one cryptic postcard from Le Puy.

Still, she was thrilled to have met the legendary Julian Mills. She was eager to learn the genesis of "The House by the Side of the Road," which was one of her favorite books from high school. Perhaps they would even have deep philosophical discussions like she and her friends used to have at Hathorne. Nellie could hardly wait until later that evening when she could text her old high school classmates. She would do a group text and tell them all the exciting news so they could talk about it altogether. Who would believe it—Julian Mills, world-famous author—right here in Sovereign, Maine? Maybe Sovereign wasn't the end of the world after all!

Nellie suddenly recollected the dinner date and hastily returned to the house. She paused briefly in front of the antique oak mirror to attach the gold-hoop earring. She dashed to the bathroom. A few minutes later she heard the familiar sound of Doctor Bart's truck. She had left the shed door unlocked this time so he could let himself in.

She put the finishing touches to her makeup and exited the bathroom to find Metcalf already in the kitchen. He was examining his freshly-shaven face in the mirror. She smiled to herself as she saw him. Silly boy!

She made a little noise and he quickly moved away from the mirror, but not before a rosy-red flush stained his fair freckled face. "Oops, caught me," he said.

Nellie thought he looked more like a besotted teenager getting ready for his first date than an experienced medical doctor. How sweet!

"You look great," he said, admiring her outfit.

"Thanks. I take this little black dress everywhere with me. With the right accessories it can be perfect for any occasion."

"Including sitting down to dinner with Wendell Russell?" he remarked, smiling.

"Including dinner with Wendell Russell."

Nellie realized with a little thrill that Metcalf was looking particularly handsome this evening. His wet curls made his hair seem darker than usual, a comely auburn color without too much of that carroty red she detested. She spied a remnant of white shaving cream under his chin and stepped forward to wipe away the offending blob with her fingertips. Their eyes met and locked. A shared, unspoken intelligence leaped between them. She heard a roaring in her ears, confounding her senses, as though everyone in the world had decided to speak to her at once. Before she could gather herself together he reached out and pulled her close to him, murmuring her name, his voice low and thick with emotion.

Her breath caught in her throat. She swayed against him, flesh meeting flesh, bone meeting bone. Her lips parted slightly to receive his kiss. Suddenly, she was released. Her eyes flew open and she stumbled slightly, catching her balance on the back of a kitchen chair. The spell was broken. She watched as he walked away, back to her.

Why had he let her go? Why hadn't he kissed her, when she was so obviously willing? Oh-my-God—had she been *too* willing?

She observed him nervously, waiting, wondering.

He moved to the chiffonier and retrieved her black clutch from where she had set it earlier. He held the purse out to her, casually, as though nothing extraordinary had occurred between them. "Ready to go?"

CHAPTER 13
The Heart and Soul of Sovereign

In addition to Nellie and Doctor Bart, Rebecca had invited the usual suspects to her dinner party: Ryan MacDonald and his wife Trudy, and Trudy's father, the loquacious woodchopper Leland Gorse. Six-month-old Alice Rose MacDonald had accompanied them, too, and was already slumbering in the old wooden cradle Wendell had brought down from the open chamber and polished up in preparation for his and Rebecca's baby. Aunt Hannah and Gray Gilpin had also been invited to the impromptu dinner party.

The others were all present and milling about the large country kitchen by the time Nellie and Metcalf arrived. She was glad to see Gray, pleased he had taken some time off from the general store. She was eager to share with Gray the fact that she didn't have a sperm donor for a father, but decided the information could wait for another day since it wasn't exactly table conversation. Nellie made her greetings to the others and presented the basket of chanterelles to Rebecca, who was making gravy at the gas range.

Rebecca set her wooden spoon into a ceramic spoon holder and grasped the basket by the handle. She folded back the blue napkin and peeked inside. "They're lovely," she exclaimed, poking among the orange-colored, fruity-scented chanterelles. "Should we have them for dinner?"

"I was hoping you'd say that," Nellie replied.

Rebecca placed the basket onto the counter, and leaned closer to Nellie. "Would you mind prepping them?" she whispered. "I think Wendell would scrub them to death. He's not exactly up to speed with mushrooms."

Nellie, grateful to have something to do, took the mushrooms to the black slate sink and went to work. She gently brushed the soft dirt from the mushrooms with the potato brush, and, using a sharp knife and wooden cutting board, sliced up the fungi for sautéing in olive oil. As she worked she became aware Doctor Bart was idly watching her, helping himself at the same time to some of the hors d'oeuvres set out on the kitchen table. The hors d'oeuvres included some of Trudy's soft cheese and a mix of fresh vegetables from Wendell's garden: broccoli, carrots and cauliflower. Scotch Broom Acres, the MacDonald family farm, had recently broadened their business of selling organic butter, milk and eggs to include soft cheeses. Nellie had already tried some at home and found them to be delicious.

At six o'clock, at Rebecca's behest, Wendell ushered everyone into the great room, a combination living-dining room that had been the mainstay of the post-and-beam house since the place was built. The oak dining room table had been expanded to seat eight comfortably and was covered with a woven beige tablecloth. The table was set with Wendell's grandmother's best china, the 'Flying Turkey' pattern from Johnson Brothers, which featured a beautifully-colored wild turkey in shades of rust, blue, green, beige and purple taking flight from a delicately sketched tree. The gleaming silverware repeated the flickering flames of four candles, which rose up from silver candlesticks of differing heights. In the center of the table—between the candles— a shy wildflower bouquet posed, diffusing a tantalizing variety of scents throughout the room. Nellie thought she had never seen a more charming table setting.

"I'll be right in with the mushrooms," Rebecca called from the kitchen.

Nellie hesitated, unsure where to sit. Wendell, who was wearing a fresh flannel shirt, clean jeans and red suspenders, moved to the head of the table. He leaned against the back of his chair, surveying his guests with satisfaction. Noting Nellie's plight, he patted the pressed-back chair to his right. "You kin sit next to me," he said. "I don't bite—much." He grinned, his gold tooth flashing.

Nellie felt herself relax. She was grateful for the old chicken farmer's good-hearted humor, which helped make her feel at home. She knew when she was nervous she had a tendency to pull back into her shell, appearing queenly and unapproachable. "Thanks, Wendell," she replied. She smiled at him—not one of her artificial beams—but a sincere smile of gratitude.

She sat down and spread the cloth napkin in her lap waiting for the others to join her. She assumed Metcalf would sit next to her and glanced over at where he was talking with Ryan. The two men were chatting and laughing over some new antics of Henrietta the chicken. Her heart skipped a beat as she observed Doctor Bart. Metcalf looked so handsome this evening, almost as handsome as Ryan!

Rebecca called out for her husband, and Wendell excused himself and returned to the kitchen. Shortly thereafter he and Aunt Hannah began ferrying dishes to the table. Taking center stage was a standing rib roast, cooked to perfection. This was followed by a steady stream of dishes including luscious red garden tomatoes, sliced and topped with a drizzle of olive oil and fresh basil; mashed potatoes with chopped parsley; the last of Wendell's sweet corn, with whole kernels scraped from the cob and smothered with Trudy's home-churned butter; an interesting-looking broccoli and nut dish; a fragrant loaf of whole wheat bread straight from the oven; and a variety of pickles, dilly beans, homemade jams and jellies. Nellie, who prided herself on her knowledge of fine cuisine, knew there wasn't a farm-to-table restaurant in New York or Boston with a better offering this night.

She glanced over at Metcalf. Surely he could see dinner was on the table? Why didn't he hurry up and sit down?

Unfortunately, Doctor Bart dawdled too long and Gray dropped down into the vacant seat next to Nellie. "Hey, didja hear the news? The white deer is back," Gray informed her. A genetic quirk in the local whitetail deer herd had spawned multiple manifestations of a rare albino-looking deer over the years. In Sovereign, the white deer were scrupulously avoided by local hunters, who venerated them for their beauty and the good luck the townspeople believed the genetic aberration signified. Unfortunately, whenever a white deer was reported to the world at large, out-of-town hunters and hunters from Away flocked to the area hoping to collect taxidermy trophies.

"I thought you shot the white deer? Of course, I know that was an accident," Nellie amended hastily, as a look of discomfort flashed across Gray's face.

"Yeah, I didn't mean to. Mike Hobart—ya remember him? Lila's husband?—he actually kilt Tinkerbelle, so as I didn't git hurt. He said not to worry 'cause there'd be another white deer someday. I can't wait to tell Mike he was right."

Nellie congratulated him. "That's good news, Gray. Where did you see the white deer? I never got to see Tinkerbelle, so I hope I get a chance to see this one."

"I seen 'im in the field ovah next to John Woods' house." The venerable First Selectman lived on the other side of town. "If ya wanna see 'im, Nellie, we ought-ta go out lightin' deer tomorrow night, 'cause that's the last day we kin go for awhile. Thet's perfect, too, 'cause Grandpa is comin' home tomorrow."

"Lighting deer? I'm not sure I know what that is."

Gray laughed at her ignorance. "Geez, Nellie, you been gone longer 'n I thought. Doncha remembah? The law allows us to shine spotlights in the fields at night lookin' fer deer—long's we ain't got no gun in the vehicle—up until September fust."

"I do vaguely remember something about that, now that you mention it."

Trudy, who was sitting down near the opposite end of the table, overheard them and leaned forward into the conversation. "That sounds like fun, Gray. I'd like to go, too. We used to light deer when I was a kid, but I haven't been in years. I know Ryan has never been, either."

"What's that?" her handsome husband replied, pulling up the chair at the end of the table opposite Wendell. Metcalf disappeared into the other room to wash his hands. "Now, what haven't I done?"

"Light deer," replied his wife, smiling.

"Yeah, ya ought-ta go with us tomorrow night, Ryan," Gray encouraged the attorney. "It's wicked fun! We count how many deer we see 'n each field 'n if we git lucky we might jest see the white deer."

"What—is it hunting season already?" Ryan asked.

"Aw, we ain't huntin' deer—we're jest spottin' 'em. Geez, yer as numb as Nellie!"

"Spotting them? I see. Well, now it's as clear as—mud. Sounds rather barbaric to me, but whatever you're doing, I'm game."

"Are you calling us barbarians, Sir?" Trudy challenged her husband.

"No, Ma'am," he replied meekly. "I believe if you check the record you'll discover I ventured to suggest the *practice* of lighting deer seems a bit barbaric."

"That *is* what he said," Nellie felt obliged to point out.

Trudy turned her playfully stern countenance upon Nellie. "Don't defend him Miss, or you, too, will have to pay the penalty."

"Penalty?" Her husband assumed a look of concern. "What penalty?"

"You'll see tomorrow night, Sir, when our excursion commences."

"That's very reassuring."

Nellie, who initially had been going to decline Gray's offer, now thought the outing sounded amusing. "But can we all fit in one car?" she asked. "Aren't there five of us, at least?" Naturally, she included Metcalf in her head count.

Gray's face fell. "We can't fit in my truck, thet's fer sure."

"No problem," Ryan demurred. "We can take my trusty steed, which seats six comfortably. I'll drive and the rest of you can tell me when I'm having fun."

His wife pinched him. Ryan grabbed her hand and held it prisoner in his lap. They gazed lovingly into each other's eyes. Nellie, watching them, felt a pang of loneliness. Would she ever find someone she could love like that?

Rebecca bustled into the room carrying the dish of savory-smelling mushrooms. "Sorry, but these were worth waiting for." She moved the potatoes aside and made room for the mushrooms on the table. Wendell stood up and gallantly held the chair out for his wife. She sat down at his left hand, across from Nellie. The old chicken farmer resumed his seat at the head of the table. By now everyone but Doctor Bart had found a seat. Leland Gorse, Trudy's father, had appropriated the open seat between his daughter and Rebecca, and Aunt Hannah had taken the seat at Ryan's left. The only chair remaining open was situated between Gray and Aunt Hannah. Nellie, out of the corner of her eye, thought she discerned a look of disappointment on Metcalf's face when he returned from washing his hands and discovered he wasn't going to sit next to her. Perhaps she should have saved him a seat, but … wouldn't that only have encouraged him?

Nellie was afraid she might have suggested more than she meant earlier in the evening when she had responded to him physically. But that slip had only been a momentary hormonal lapse. She was sure—at least she thought she was sure—Doctor Bart was not the man who would ultimately win her heart.

Outside the great room windows dusk had stolen the color from the sky, replacing the bright blue with soft shades of grays and purples. One of the south-facing windows was open allowing a light breeze to filter pleasantly through the room, causing the flames of the candles to flicker like fire flies. A reverential hush descended on the table.

Rebecca held out her hands, palm side up. "Shall we give thanks? Maggie usually does the honors, but tonight I think we should each offer our own silent prayers."

Nellie took Wendell's and Gray's hands and felt an almost electric sensation as the circle of warm hands met and closed. She bowed her head, suddenly overcome by emotion. She closed her eyes and gave thanks to God for all of her new friends, who had welcomed her back into the fold so affectionately. Her mother's face popped into her mind and she wondered where Maggie was tonight. Was she alone? Nellie added a heartfelt plea in her prayer to bring her mother home as soon as possible so she might finish her healing work in the safety and security of such a loving group of friends.

Wendell shifted in his seat, letting go of Nellie's hand at the same time. She used her free hand to brush away the tears that had gathered in her eyes. She glanced up at Rebecca's brunette head, which was still bowed, as were most of the others. It suddenly occurred to Nellie she was sitting in the center of Sovereign, the very heart of the community. Until Miss Hastings' death, that house—the little yellow cottage—had been the understood emotional center of town. Miss Hastings' legendary unconditional love, her generosity, her spiritual presence had created a lynchpin of sorts that held the community together. But now that Miss Hastings was gone, Rebecca, with her gift for making people feel at home, had, without conscious effort, returned the old Russell homestead to its former prominence. Miss Hastings had once told Nellie that Wendell's grandmother, Addie Russell, in her day had been "the heart and soul of Sovereign." Nellie had never understood what that had meant—until now.

Rebecca inhaled deeply, concluding her prayer. She lifted her head and smiled warmly at each of her guests in turn. Her bright blue eyes were filled with joy. "OK, everyone," she urged "dig in!"

CHAPTER 14

In the Company of Friends

Rebecca picked up the warm dish in front of her and proffered it to her neighbor at the table. "Mashed potato, Leland?"

"Ayuh," said the woodchopper, licking his lips. "Don't mind if I do." He accepted the heavy bowl of fluffy spuds and dug into it with enthusiasm. He was lean and lanky and sported a full head of hair—wild gray feathers that tonight had been slicked down with fragrant Wildroot hair tonic. Leland still cut wood for a living, even though he was pushing eighty.

"Try the mushrooms," Nellie encouraged Wendell, who she noted was dubiously examining the dish of sautéed chanterelles in front of him. "They're fresh from the woods."

He suspiciously sniffed the sautéed fungi's apricot bouquet. "Wal, you know, I ain't much fer slimy stuff."

"Slimy stuff?" Nellie repeated, amazed. "These chanterelles are a delicacy! In New York, people would pay twenty-five dollars a pound for them."

Wendell flashed his signature grin. "Maybe we kin send 'em to New Yock. I could use the twenty-five dollahs." He passed the bowl onto Nellie without helping himself to the mushrooms.

"He's a lost cause," Rebecca admitted to Nellie, sighing. "I've been trying to get Wendell to eat mushrooms for years. Even telling him Leland likes them doesn't help."

"'Tain't much of a recommendation at-tall."

The food was passed around the table, floating on a fluctuating tide of cheerful voices. When the plates were filled and the food settled onto the table the dining room became silent, except for the ticking of the mantle clock and the pleasing sound of silverware clinking against china. The candles flickered and spat. After a few minutes, Leland broke the quiet. "Ain't hed no bettah piece o' meat since I kilt my last deer," he declared, popping another bit of beef into his mouth. He masticated loudly.

"Father, please," Trudy reprimanded, softly. Leland abruptly closed his mouth.

"Thank you for coming, Leland," Rebecca said. "You know how Wendell and I love to feed our friends." She smiled across the table at Nellie. "We're so pleased you could join us, too, Nellie. By the way, where did you get the chanterelles? I was too busy to ask you when you came in. Did you gather them yourself?"

Nellie felt Doctor Bart's eyes upon her from two seats down. She hesitated, unsure how much she should reveal about Walden and his run-in with Henry Trow. She was mindful of the laws about patient confidentiality, having recently been schooled by Metcalf before the clinic opened.

"Bet 'twas from thet queer fellah thet's all-ways scoutin' mushrooms ovah to the town woodlot," Leland cut in, before Nellie could reply.

Ryan shot his father-in-law a dubious look. "How do you know he's been mushrooming in there? You're not harvesting in there again, are you? You know John warned you about that."

Leland's eyes widened innocently. "Not me! I jest goes in thar now 'n then ta keep my eye on thet old wolf pine, makin' shore no one else cuts 'er."

"Pass the butter, Ryan," Gray spoke out.

Ryan obligingly sent the butter moving down the table toward Gray. "Keeping an eye on the old wolf tree, hmm," he said to his father-in-law.

"Thet's the God's honest truth, son. Ain't no bigger tree this side o' the Mississippi. 'Twould be a shame to lose 'er."

"Do we need more butter?" Rebecca worried, laying her napkin on the table and starting to rise up.

Wendell stopped her. "Eat yore dinnah, Mrs. Russell. I'll go 'n git the buttah."

Rebecca obeyed, and Nellie had almost decided her problem had evaporated, when, surprisingly, Doctor Bart spoke up. "Walden left the chanterelles at Nellie's as his copay for services rendered yesterday."

"Oh, dear! I hope he didn't hurt himself in the woods," said Rebecca. "I see him in there quite often."

"Unfortunately, he took a few pellets of bird shot in his shoulder. It was an accident. Henry Trow was trying to scare Walden off his land and it worked—the hard way." Metcalf proceeded to tell the story of Mr. Trow's calf that had been struck by lightning and the misunderstanding that arisen from the freak accident.

"Poor man!" Rebecca exclaimed. "To have lost his wife *and* to have a calf struck by lightning? I wish I'd known sooner, I would have invited Mr. Trow to dinner."

Wendell set the extra butter on the table. "What 'bout Walden? He's the one thet got shot," he pointed out.

"I'd have invited Walden, too, of course—although that might have been a bit awkward."

"To say nothing of the fact that it would have removed a very interesting topic of conversation," Aunt Hannah added. She turned to Doctor Bart, who was sitting on her left. "Why does Walden trouble himself—and Mr. Trow—by taking mushrooms from posted land? Aren't there plenty of mushrooms elsewhere?"

"My guess is Walden enjoys pushing the envelope. He has some interesting notions regarding land ownership, more akin to a Native American than a native Mainer. Such philosophy is bound to bring him grief. Hopefully, he won't be shot at again, though."

"Are his ideas on land ownership so far-fetched?" Nellie asked, somewhat timidly. She had not mentioned her woods meeting with Walden to Metcalf or anyone.

Metcalf smiled wryly. "The answer to that question depends on who you ask. If Walden ventured to propound his particular philosophy in the Millinocket area, say, he'd probably be drawn and quartered for such liberal views."

"Why's that?"

"Well, I can't speak for them specifically, but generally I'd say it's because they live and work in the North Maine Woods—and have always been given access to the land—thus they have a sense of ownership. Unfortunately, the times they are a changing. The land is being sold off and the locals are losing the rights they've always taken for granted: the right to hunt and fish, to snowmobile, and to lease camps on paper company land. Some of them have built pretty grand year-round homes on land they don't own and could possibly lose."

"Oh-my-God," said Nellie.

"And yet they refuse to permanently protect that land," Ryan added, with energy. "The Millinocket area's economy has been shattered since the paper mills were shut down, yet the locals continue to derail any effort that remotely resembles an attempt to turn the North Maine Woods, which is the largest wilderness east of the Mississippi, into a national park. In the meantime, large chunks of paper company land have been sold off to so-called 'Kingdom Buyers' and private investors."

"If something like a national park isn't done soon that valuable resource will be lost to everyone," Doctor Bart agreed.

"This is the first time I've heard about a national park," Nellie said, with real urgency in her voice. "Is the proposal for real?"

"Very real," declared Ryan, who was a big supporter of the proposed park.

"I don't understand … why would anyone be opposed to a national park?"

"Well, many Mainers don't see the national park the same way we do, Nellie," Metcalf replied. "They might not realize what they have to lose."

"How could that be?

"Because the land has always been open and available to them. All of us have a tendency to assume that what's available will always be available."

"Ayuh," said Wendell, setting his fork on the rim of his plate. He leaned back. "Thet's a fact. You don't know what you've got 'til she's gone."

"I know what you mean," Nellie mused, recollecting how she had felt when she realized she was trespassing on Henry Trow's posted land, land which she and her mother had always taken for granted. "A national park sounds like the perfect solution. The land will be protected and the locals will have jobs."

"I do believe that statewide the tide is turning. The park will eventually happen," Metcalf predicted. "In the meantime, we have our own struggles here with our own land issues, such as hunters wanting to hunt on posted land."

"Or take mushrooms," said Trudy, smiling.

"Exactly."

"It's the age-old story, isn't it? The struggle over land," said Ryan quietly. "One wonders why it's preyed upon, here and all around, when in the end man only keeps a little piece of ground."

"Sad but true," concluded Metcalf.

"Did you write that?" Rebecca asked curiously. "It's a very compelling sentiment."

"To be perfectly honest, I stole it. That was part of a longer poem written by a Maine author, whose name escapes me at the moment. I picked up one of her books at some quaint shop in

Lincolnville and the book opened to that poem. Those four lines have stuck with me ever since."

"Didja buy the book?" Gray asked.

"I'm embarrassed to admit, Gray, I did not buy the book. I do feel badly about that now. The author is probably a struggling poet who can't afford the paper she writes on, which by the way is no longer manufactured in Millinocket thanks to the mill closings. The author probably lives nearby, but I wouldn't know her if I ran into her at your store."

"Well, find out who she is and I'll invite her to dinner, too," Rebecca said. The whole table laughed.

When everyone was finished eating, Rebecca rose to clear the table. Nellie instinctively got up to help. After she had removed all the dishes, at Rebecca's request, Nellie poured out coffee and tea for the others. Rebecca returned to the table a short time later carrying a warm apple-cranberry pie, the sight of which elicited 'Ooos' and 'Ahhs' from her guests.

"What kind o' pie is thet?" Leland asked.

"Father, that's not polite," Trudy admonished him.

"But perfectly acceptable," Rebecca replied, sitting down and smiling at Leland. "This is Hannah's famous apple-cranberry pie—she baked two for the occasion." She plated a big slice and handed the pie to Nellie. "Hannah told me to serve you first."

Nellie gratefully accepted the plate. Thick, rose-colored filling oozed out from under a flaky crust, emitting a spiced apple scent. "Thanks, Hannah. I've never had apple-cranberry pie before. This looks yummy."

"I just hope the pie's sweet enough," Aunt Hannah worried. "I used an early apple, which has a tendency to be a bit tart, and some frozen cranberries from a friend down in Troy."

Nellie took a bite. "Mmm, totally awesome!" She set her fork down, not wanting to eat her pie until everyone else was served.

"I'll take a piece twice thet size," Leland said, thumping the butt of his fork on the table.

"Father!"

Leland remained unruffled. "I'll wait my turn, 'course." He glanced over at Nellie. "Betcha cain't tell what these things has got in common."

"I'm sorry—what?"

"I'll list off sum stuff for ya 'n you tell me what they has in common."

Nellie was intrigued by Leland's word game. "Are they Maine things?"

"Wal, mostly."

"I'll take that bet, Leland," interjected Doctor Bart. "I don't think you can stump Nellie. She might have lived out of state for a while but she's still a true Mainer."

Nellie's heart fluttered at this unexpected praise. He was so good! How unfortunate she was more attracted to rascals.

"Now, what's your bet, Leland?" Metcalf continued. "What does Nellie get if she guesses correctly?

Leland scratched his head. "Wal, how 'bout I take 'er ovah to the town woodlot ta show 'er thet Wolf Pine?"

"Nellie?"

Nellie regarded the woodchopper with sincere interest. "What makes that tree so special?"

Leland leaned forward in his chair. "By Gawd, you ain't nevah seen a pine tree so big," he exclaimed. "She taped twelve feet breast-high twenny years ago."

"You mean—the tree trunk measured twelve feet around?"

"Twenny years ago," he cried, hands reaching for the ceiling, as though thanking God for such a majestic specimen of timber.

"How did it get so big? Shouldn't someone have cut the tree down long before this?"

Leland appeared shocked. "Cut 'er down? Gawd Almighty. She's a seed tree!"

Nellie felt adrift in a sea of ignorance. "A what?"

Doctor Bart took pity on her. "Seed trees are the mature trees woodcutters leave behind to ensure regeneration of the forest," he explained. "In this case, Leland's tree has more value as a pine cone producer than anything else since it's probably too big for the saw mill."

"Yep. Them fellas as got regular saws cain't cut more 'n twenny-five, twenny-six inches," Leland affirmed. "Thet wolf pine 'uld throw off boards way bigger'n thet!"

"In that case, I'd love to see your tree, whether I win the bet or not. Can we measure it again?"

"Ayuh—we'll tape 'er 'n see how much she's growed in twenny years," he said, happily.

Doctor Bart proffered his hand across the table to Leland. "Bet accepted, then, Leland." The two men shook hands.

"I hope your faith in me isn't misplaced, Metcalf," Nellie remarked, smiling a bit nervously.

"I'll take my chances."

Rebecca caught the rarely-used given name. "Metcalf?" she repeated, curiously.

"My first name," Doctor Bart explained, somewhat abashed.

"I wondered about that. I think I heard your mother use the name before. Where did 'Doctor Bart' come from?"

"My middle name is 'Bartholomew'—still uncommon but not as idiosyncratic as 'Metcalf,' which I always have to explain. They started calling me 'Doctor Bart' when I went to work at the clinic in Unity, but Nellie has known me since she was a baby and I'm probably lucky she calls me that rather than 'Cawkaw', which was her original handle for me. Now, Leland, give her your best shot. What's on that list you were talking about?"

The others at the table turned to Leland. He scratched his head. "Wal, let me see …" He squinted and stared up at the ceiling. In less than a minute he had gathered his thoughts together. "I got 'er now," he announced.

"Go ahead," Metcalf encouraged.

Leland eyed Nellie. "Ya ready? Heah goes: Crow Egg, Blush-in' Bride, Ma-lin-da," he drawled. He said each name slowly, as though attempting to teach her a foreign language. "Eve-nin' Pah-tee, Duch-ess, Dish-a-roon, Shi-a-was-see, Tom Putt, Ca-ba-shea, Genesee Flow'r, Bel-bo-ro-doo-skoe, 'n Titus Pippin. I think thet's nuff ta stump ya. What has them things all got in common?"

Nellie thought a moment. "Could you repeat that?"

"Not likely."

Everyone laughed. Nevertheless, Leland did manage to repeat his list.

Shiawassee? Crow Egg? Certainly they were very strange names, with a good dose of Native American to them. But Nellie was sure she had never heard any of them in her life. How frustrating! Probably everyone else at the table knew what he was talking about. She didn't want to look as though she was ignorant of her home state, however, nor did she want to disappoint Metcalf, so she resolutely put her mind to work on the problem.

Tom Putt? Titus Pippin? Titus Pippin!

When Nellie was young, Maggie had always called her a 'pip,' explaining that the sobriquet, short for 'pippin,' was an affectionate nickname her grandmother, an elementary school teacher like Miss

Hastings, had used to call her young charges. Maggie had also told her the meaning of the word: a 'pip' or 'pippin' was an apple seed.

"Apples?" Nellie guessed. "Are they all apples?"

Leland slammed his hand against the table. The silverware clanked. "By Jay-sus, she got it rite," he cried.

The others clapped and Gray hooted. Metcalf reached around Gray to pat Nellie on the back. "Good girl! I knew you wouldn't disappoint me," he said, proudly.

After the dessert dishes were cleared away and the candles extinguished, Rebecca, at the encouragement of her husband and several others, sat down at the piano and began warming up. The great room was soon filled with the sound of music. The guests began to congeal around the upright piano, but Nellie, who loved to sing, suddenly found herself being drawn off to a quiet corner by Leland.

The woodchopper's face betrayed an expression of deeply-rooted anxiety, much different from the up-beat excitement he had displayed at the table. "Ya heared anything from yer Ma, lately?"

Nellie knew her mother and the uncouth woodsman were old friends. In addition, she was mindful of what Doctor Bart had said about Leland helping her mother through her chemotherapy. As a result, she felt no compunction revealing to him what little she knew about Maggie's status. She told Leland about the postcard she had received from France, adding that she suspected her mother had gone on some sort of pilgrimage.

"I wished she'd asked me ta go with 'er," Leland said, dolefully, after hearing the news.

"She'll be fine by herself," Nellie reassured him. "Mother's very capable, you know."

Leland laid a large paw over his heart. "'Tain't her I'm worriet 'bout." But Nellie knew he was jesting and his primary concern was for Maggie.

Without forethought, Nellie reached for his age-spotted hand. The knobby, weathered member felt rough and callused to her tender touch. "When I hear anything you'll be the first to know," she promised him. She squeezed Leland's hand and released him.

Tears filled Leland's eyes. He fumbled for his handkerchief and blew his nose. "Yer a good gal," he said. "I'd know anywhars you was Maggie's daughter, even if I ain't nevah seen ya afore."

Rebecca began to play "Let Me Call You Sweetheart" and Leland took Nellie by the elbow and escorted her to the piano, where they joined the others. Nellie, eager to loosen the stays on her soprano, began to sing. Shortly she found herself harmonizing with a full-throated, deep baritone. She traced the voice back to its owner and was startled to see the baritone belonged to Wendell. He caught her expression of surprise, and winked.

Rebecca played on. They sang a variety of old-time classics such as "More Than You Know," "In the Good Old Summertime," and "Memories of You." The impromptu concert broke up about ten o'clock, when Rebecca laughingly declared herself played out.

Nellie retreated to the kitchen in search of her sweater. She hummed the last tune to herself and smiled when she realized she had never enjoyed herself as much as she had this evening in the company of her new friends.

CHAPTER 15
Expectations

Nellie rode to church with Rebecca the next day. Even though she enjoyed hiking through the woods—and the weather was still relatively mild—she had decided, especially after their conversation at dinner last night, that she wouldn't cut through Henry Trow's land without his explicit permission. She would go visit him again soon and ask his permission.

She and Rebecca separated at the church parking lot, Rebecca going to speak to some friends just arriving. Nellie entered the church alone and spotted Shirley Palmer and two or three others of the ministry committee. She gravitated up front to say a few words.

Shirley greeted her with outstretched hands and a beaming face. "Ain't I glad to see you agin, dearie," she declared. "Church is becomin' a regular habit fer you, ain't it? Yer Ma would be right proud o' you."

Nellie smiled at the matron's enthusiasm. "Don't get your hopes up," she allowed. "Mother would be the first to say I'll let you down."

"Thar ain't no disappointin' this ole grandma," Shirley cried, "cause I ain't got no expectations fer you—no, none at-tall. 'Tis a remarkable refreshin' way to live—without ex-pect-tations—'specially when one's livin' with a man like my Asa. I was like to broke my heart a thousand times afore I larnt to look fer nuthin' from 'im. When you ain't got no real ex-pect-tations, you ain't nevah a-going to be disappointed, dearie." She patted Nellie's arm with her gloved hand. "Take it from me—that's the best way to live."

"I'm sure you're right, but, honestly, I've never given it much thought," Nellie admitted. Idly, she wondered when she had been disappointed last. She realized with a little shock the letdown had occurred the prior evening, when Doctor Bart had failed to kiss her.

This revelation sent a slight electric current through her torso. If she had been disappointed—she must have expected him to kiss her!

Had she wanted to be kissed? By Metcalf!

Feeling confused and flustered, Nellie rather hastily broke away from Shirley Palmer and the others and made her way to the back pew. She claimed her seat and glanced around, looking for Doctor Bart. He had been present at the last two church services, although she had easily discerned by his awkwardness and unfamiliarity with the service that he rarely—if ever—attended church.

Up front, Courtney Danforth leaned slowly and gracefully into the grand piano and the church was soon filled with the peaceful and restful sound of Debussy's "Clair de Lune." The regular shuffle of feet ensued as worshipers hastened to their seats. Nellie heard the front door slam and turned round expecting to see Metcalf slip into the pew beside her. Instead, John Woods, the First Selectman, strode up the center aisle and folded his tall frame into the pew next to his wife, Ruth.

Once again, she felt a pang of disappointment. Where was Doctor Bart? Why wasn't he in church today?

When Metcalf had dropped her off last night, he had mentioned nothing to her about a prior engagement on Sunday—excepting the lighting deer excursion planned for that night, in which he had good-naturedly agreed to participate. Nor had he walked Nellie to the door. She tried to convince herself she wasn't disappointed about that, too—but failed.

After church, Nellie decided to walk up and visit her new neighbor. In addition to getting Mr. Trow's permission to use his land, she also wanted an update on the lightning calf's condition.

Mr. Trow appeared glad to see her, ushering Nellie into the kitchen with his awkward hobbling gait. "Sit down, young lady. Make yourself at home." He gestured to a seat at the table, hovering anxiously at her elbow, his bushy eyebrows quivering. "Can I get you a cup of tea?"

Nellie accepted the tea but declined his offer of store-bought cookies. He made a wry face as he put them back into the cupboard. "I don't blame you for passing up those little bits of pasteboard. I never ate a store-bought cookie in my life until Gerry died. And now that's all I eat. My daughter keeps telling me I need to find myself a good Maine woman, but I'm not ready for that." He settled himself into his captain's chair.

"You must miss your wife a lot," said Nellie.

"I do. I never knew what a treasure I had until I lost her."

"Funny, we were just speaking about that very same thing last night."

"I don't know how my daughter thinks I could replace her mother."

"Oh, I'm sure that's not what she means—she just doesn't want you to be alone. And … and the women in Sovereign *are* excellent cooks," Nellie added, in a hopeful fashion. "They've been bringing me cakes and casseroles since I came home." She briefly explained she was housesitting until her mother, the local minister, returned to town. Fortunately, Mr. Trow was too wrapped up in his own affairs to ask how long Maggie might be gone or why she had left town.

"I can't believe it's been two years already," he continued, returning to his wife. "When you get to be my age, the days drag so slowly but the years go rushing by like freight trains."

Nellie smiled empathetically, but said nothing. She knew he was lonely and simply needed someone to talk with, mostly to listen.

"But I wouldn't dream of offending any of the local women by refusing their baked goods," he continued, shaking himself out of his lethargy. "I certainly don't want to appear standoffish to my new neighbors."

"No, no—not that," Nellie agreed. She couldn't possibly tell him he already had the reputation in town of being a curmudgeon.

"You say the women are good cooks, eh?"

"*Very* good." Nellie set down her tea mug as an idea occurred to her. "You know, the church has an annual Harvest Supper coming up. Why don't you plan on attending? You'll be able to meet everyone and try some of their home-cooked food at the same time."

Mr. Trow's eyes opened wide with obvious interest. "Is that like a Grange Supper?"

"I'm not sure. I don't know what a 'grange' is."

"You've never heard of the Order of Patrons of Husbandry, young lady? I must say I'm surprised at that, living out here in the country as you do."

"I … I didn't grow up here," Nellie lamely excused herself.

"Well, you missed one of the best things going about country life, then. The Grange is a fraternal organization that encourages folks to get together to promote the well-being of their agricultural communities, towns just like Sovereign. I've been on the look-out for a good grange supper and I see the Benton Grange still has 'em on a regular basis, but I was wondering about Sovereign. Gerry and I used to go to the one in our town. Lots of home-cooked food and plenty of good conversation with good people. It was always a fine time."

"That does sound like our Harvest Supper. Everything is homemade or homegrown, I assure you. There are casseroles, baked beans, salads … and about a dozen different kinds of pie to choose from for dessert. I know because I wait tables at the Harvest Supper, when I'm in town."

He threw his right arm up onto the table and leaned towards her. "Young lady, you've given me a great gift," he declared.

"I have? What?"

"Something to look forward to! At my age, a good meal and a piece of homemade pie are worth their weight in gold."

She smiled. "I'll take your word for it. I'm still at the age where I'm watching my weight."

"Well, don't watch it too hard or you'll slip away to nothing." Mr. Trow patted his ample midriff. "Which is obviously not my problem."

"I'll check with Shirley Palmer—she's sort of the town's social guru—and get back to you soon with the time and date."

"Do, dear! My mouth is watering for that piece of homemade pie already."

Nellie thought about Aunt Hannah's scrumptious apple-cranberry pie from the prior evening and what Rebecca had said about inviting Henry Trow to dinner. It was too bad Rebecca hadn't thought of it sooner because he would have appreciated the invitation. She felt badly for him, lonely and apparently lost due to the death of his wife. She remembered what Metcalf had said about 'sick cat syndrome' and realized in a way the elderly gentleman was a lot like her mother. Perhaps, before the church supper rolled around she would ask Aunt Hannah to bake him a pie, to tide him over. She was sure the good-hearted widow would oblige; however, she wasn't sure whether or not it was fair to add another chore to Aunt Hannah's already full plate. Nellie wished she knew how to cook. Perhaps Aunt Hannah would teach her? No, no—that would only be more work for Aunt Hannah!

Nellie chatted with her new neighbor for nearly an hour before putting forward her special request. "Do you mind if I use your land, Mr. Trow? I'd like to walk in your woods, if I may. The old schoolhouse where we live was cut from the original Lovejoy purchase and I've always felt an affinity for the woods in back of our place."

Mr. Trow was very generous. "Go where you want, when you want, Nellie. I wouldn't have posted my land at all if it hadn't been for that young hooligan. By the bye, have you heard an update on his condition?" he added, anxiously. "I'm so ashamed I lost my temper and took a pot-shot at him. I never would have done such a thing if Gerry was still alive. She was my moral compass. Helped keep me on an even keel, you might say."

"I'm sure Walden will be OK," she reassured him. "Doctor Bart said his wounds were minor."

Mr. Trow tapped his teaspoon against the tablecloth. *Tap, tap, tap.* "I suppose, the least I could do is pay for his medical care," he said, thoughtfully.

Nellie couldn't allow that. "Walden didn't pay anything," she reminded him, feeling slightly guilty about disregarding the basket of chanterelles the woodsman had left as a copay which, she felt sure, had been harvested from Mr. Trow's land. "Songbird Medical Clinic is a free clinic."

"Nonetheless, I want to make a donation." He rose up and went to his writing desk. When he returned to the table, he handed Nellie a check.

Nellie stared at the face of the check, flabbergasted. "Five hundred dollars! That's way too much money. We can't take this." She passed him back the check.

He pushed her hand away, chuckling. "Young lady, that so-called 'free clinic' of yours is going to cost somebody a boatload of money. If you want to keep your doors open you'd better get used to having your hand out. The first rule of non-profits is 'Never turn money away.' You tell that doctor boyfriend of yours there's plenty more where that comes from, too, if he needs it."

Nellie almost blurted out Doctor Bart wasn't her boyfriend, but stopped herself just in time. She certainly didn't want to enter into a discussion with her new neighbor about why he wasn't her boyfriend.

"Besides," Mr. Trow continued, "thanks to the fund managers of my retirement account I have more money than I know what to do with. By the looks of some of the houses in this neck of the woods you'll have plenty of patients turning up on the door stoop of your free clinic."

Nellie thought of Miss Crump and knew Mr. Trow was right. Certainly, there were many residents of Sovereign who needed free medical care. "It might not be tax deductible," she cautioned him, fingering the sharp edge of the paper check with a delicious sense of accomplishment. "Ryan MacDonald—he's our local attorney—he's still working on our 501(c)3 non-profit application."

Mr. Trow waved away her concern. "Never mind that. Since Gerry's death I know what's important in life and it isn't a tax deduction, although I admit there was a time when those meant a lot to me."

Before Nellie left for home he took her out to the barn so she could visit Jasmine and her calf. Lightning had made great progress overnight, he said, thanks to the high-powered antibiotics Doctor Bart had administered Saturday afternoon.

To her surprise, Nellie discovered the calf alert and standing up. To her further surprise, she discovered why Metcalf had been delinquent at church—he had spent the morning attending the calf. According to Mr. Trow, Doctor Bart had stopped by the old Lovejoy place around nine o'clock with the promised burn cream. After checking the calf's temperature and administering a second shot of antibiotics, he had meticulously cleaned and dressed the calf's burns, cutting away as much of the blackened, leathery skin as he could.

That was so like Metcalf, to remember a promise! She herself had forgotten all about the burn cream.

Also, it was just like Metcalf to follow-up with a patient, even a four-legged one. Of all the people Nellie had ever known, Doctor Bart was the most dependable. She remembered Shirley Palmer's discourse about expectations breeding disappointment and suddenly realized that the woman with Metcalf for a husband would have very few disappointments in life. He was the polar opposite of Asa Palmer, who often made his wife the butt of jokes by taking drastic measures to hide from her.

On the walk home, Nellie's thoughts returned to the plight of the lonely widower. She felt sorry for Henry Trow, but what could she do, except visit him occasionally and include him in some of the community's activities, such as the Harvest Supper?

The germ of an idea began to take root and grow in her mind. The more she thought about it, the more she thought relieving Mr. Trow of his solitary situation was both possible and laudable. By the time Nellie reached home she began to fear she might have inherited some of her mother's proclivity for match-making. She had certainly never wanted to be anything like her mother, and yet it was a shame to let a perfectly good match-making opportunity go to waste!

CHAPTER 16
Lighting Deer

The expedition to 'light deer,' which Nellie was looking forward to, had been scheduled for dusk that Sunday evening. Sunset was at seven-thirty and shortly before seven o'clock Nellie spied the lights of Ryan's late model sedan flash into her driveway. She removed twenty dollars from her purse, stuffed the bill into her jeans pocket just in case, and collected her fleece from the shed. She exited the ell, closing the shed door tightly behind her.

Nellie headed for the back seat of the black sedan but Trudy swung open the front passenger door. "Sit in front with us," she suggested, sliding across the bench seat closer to her husband. "There's going to be six of us altogether. We invited Sarah Palmer to go with us."

Sarah Palmer was Shirley's great-niece, the young woman who had been portrayed as the same age as Nellie and eager to make her acquaintance. Nellie had since met Sarah twice at church and once at Ma Jean's and had perceived Shirley had stretched the truth a bit. Sarah was twenty-five at least, and, rather than encourage Nellie's overtures, the other girl had greeted her with a cool diffidence that offered the most barren soil for the seed of intimacy. Nellie racked her brains trying to think what she might have done to offend Sarah. In the end, she wrote off the cold shoulder as the usual female jealously of her natural good looks. In contrast to Nellie, Sarah was a plump, overly-coiffed blonde with a shrill voice and a sharp disposition.

"Where's little Alice?" asked Nellie, glancing into the empty back seat.

"She's home with my father. Believe it or not, he's a wonderful babysitter." Trudy was wearing an off-white turtleneck sweater that complemented her closely-cropped brown hair. Her hazel eyes sparkled and her face was flushed with excitement. Nellie thought she was the poster child for a happily married woman.

"Buckle your seat belt," Ryan reminded Nellie, who immediately obeyed. He threw his right arm over Trudy's shoulders, taking the opportunity to give his wife's ear a fond pinch. She smiled up at him as he backed the car out of Maggie's driveway.

They motored quietly but comfortably up the Cross Road in the gloaming. Overhead the trees touched, rendering a dusky colonnade effect to the drive. When the rows of trees ended and the car crested Lovejoy Hill, however, the sunset was resuscitated in a saffron glow to the west. Nellie saw Saturn sparkling in the gray-purple haze to the east. "How beautiful," she murmured.

"Mmm," agreed Trudy.

Ryan pulled the car out onto the Russell Hill Road. "Any word from Maggie?" he asked.

"No, I'm afraid not. She never was a very good correspondent."

"She's probably afraid of pestering you to death," Trudy said. "I know I'm going to have to work hard not to be one of those clingy mothers who smother their children."

"No worries. I won't let you be a smothering mother," said Ryan.

Trudy laughed and sought her husband's eyes in the rear view mirror. "You? You're the worst offender! You can't let Alice Rose out of your sight for a minute, and if she even burps at night you leap up out of bed as though the house is on fire."

"I'm a light sleeper," he defended himself. "Besides, there could be a fire, you know."

The couple's light-hearted banter continued until they pulled into Doctor Bart's driveway. Metcalf spied them and exited the cottage carrying a light-weight jacket hooked over his shoulder. He opened the door behind Ryan, bent his head and climbed in.

"Need me to pull the seat forward?" Ryan asked.

"I'm fine, thanks." Nevertheless there was a slight grunting sound as Doctor Bart arranged his long limbs.

Nellie felt some of the air leave her balloon. There was that disappointment again! She realized she had been unconsciously looking forward to sitting next to Metcalf. Obviously, Ryan and Trudy were not privy to Maggie's matchmaking scheme for her and Doctor Bart or they would have arranged the seating accordingly.

Nellie consoled herself with the fact that at least she could see and talk with Doctor Bart from their opposing positions. Had he chosen the seat directly behind her, her enjoyment of the outing would have been seriously diminished.

Trudy turned around and smiled at Metcalf. "Maybe you should move over behind Nellie?" she suggested. "She's half a foot shorter than Ryan and Gray doesn't need that extra leg room."

"Hey, good idea," Metcalf replied. He let himself out, walked around the back of the sedan and repositioned himself behind Nellie. He buckled his seat belt.

Oh, good grief! She might as well have stayed home.

They picked up Sarah Palmer next at her great-aunt's house. Sarah was out the door before the car even came to a stop in the driveway. She was wearing a short summer skirt with a skimpy, tight-fitting red top, which, in Nellie's eyes, seemed more appropriate for a dance than an evening driving around town shining a spotlight on wild deer. Shirley, wiping her hands on her apron, came out onto the side porch to see her niece off. "Toodle-oo!" she called cheerfully, waving in the dusk. A little brown bat darted out from some upper region in the old farmhouse and Shirley quickly stepped back into the well-lit kitchen.

When Sarah entered the automobile and closed the door behind her the car instantly filled with the cloying scent of perfume. Nellie's nose tingled and her throat constricted. She coughed. Out of the corner of her eye she saw Ryan and Trudy exchange glances. Ryan quietly opened his window several inches.

"I'm so embarrassed," announced Sarah, when the car door was safely closed behind her. She settled herself into the seat behind Ryan and pulled down her skirt. "Aunt Shirley always treats me like a teenager going off on my first date."

Nellie thought that might be because Sarah acted like a teenager going off on her first date, but kept the conclusion to herself. Instead, she uttered a greeting, which the other girl ignored.

"I think it's very nice," said Metcalf, "the way Shirley treats you. It shows how much she cares about you—that you're a very special niece."

"You always know the right thing to say to make a girl feel comfortable, Doctor Bart," Sarah gushed.

Nellie felt like gagging. Oh, good grief!

Metcalf laughed off Sarah's praise. "I'm not sure Nellie would share that opinion of me—would you Nellie? I think sometimes I'm too hard on her, saying exactly what I think."

"Nellie? Oh, I wondered who was slumped up next to Trudy. Hiya, Nellie."

Nellie gritted her teeth.

"Aren't you going to say 'Hello' to Sarah, Nellie?" Doctor Bart asked.

"Sarah Louise," the other girl corrected him, lightly. "That's what my friends call me."

"Pardon me—'Sarah Louise.' That's much prettier than just plain old Sarah."

Sarah giggled. "I should hope so. 'Plain old Sarah' isn't very flattering."

Nellie was entirely forgotten in their banter. She, who was no stranger to the wiles of a woman who would say anything and do anything to secure a man, understood now what she had done to offend Sarah—she had returned to Sovereign, thereby presenting Sarah with a rival for Doctor Bart's affections.

In five minutes they were at Gilpin's General Store. "Who's covering the store tonight for Gray?" Ryan asked his wife.

"His grandfather. Ralph and Maude came back from Winslow on Friday so Gray wouldn't miss any more classes." Trudy pointed to the double-glass front door. "Here he comes now—he must have been watching for us."

Gray sauntered over to their vehicle. He hesitated, unsure where to sit. In a flash, Sarah threw open her door and slid over next to Doctor Bart, vacating the seat behind Ryan. Gray took the hint and clambered in. Sarah coquettishly glanced up at Metcalf. "This is fun, isn't it?"

"Hey," said Gray, "I brought the light." He hefted up a black plastic hand-held spotlight to show his comrades. "Twelve million candlepowah! She's got two different settin's—high and low. Maybe ya bettah run it, though, Trude. Yer in the hot seat. Whatcha think?"

Trudy agreed to handle the spotlight and Gray took a few minutes to show her how it worked. Ryan idled the car in the parking lot of the general store while the duo consulted. He caught sight of an acquaintance and rolled down his window so he could speak with him. Nellie, wanting to give Sarah a hint about the perfume, also slid her window down. Her stratagem backfired, however.

"Brrr, I guess I should have brought a sweater," Sarah exclaimed, with an exaggerated shiver. "Do you mind if I snuggle up next to you?" Nellie didn't have to look around to know Sarah was talking to Metcalf, not Gray Gilpin.

But Doctor Bart was either clueless or disinclined to accept Sarah's advances. He passed her his jacket. "Take my coat," he offered. "I'm not cold." He draped the light-weight cotton jacket around Sarah's shoulders without waiting for a response. "Better?"

"Oh, sure," Sarah replied, sullenly.

Nellie bit her lip, trying not to laugh aloud. Poor Sarah! She was going to have hard work chasing after Doctor Bart. He was so completely unaware of feminine attentions.

Nellie rolled up her window. What did she care if Sarah Palmer set her sights on Metcalf? It wasn't as though she wanted to marry him herself. She was just concerned about the well-being of a family friend, that's all, and Sarah was obviously a poor choice of partner for Doctor Bart. Would Sarah help him build up the Songbird Free Medical Clinic, for example? Would she understand and appreciate his gravitas? Would she accept him as he was and not try to change him? Nellie doubted it.

And Metcalf was so clueless he really needed someone to look out for him. Perhaps Nellie could find a suitable partner for him, someone of the same ilk who shared his desire to help others. She ran through her head all the available—and suitable—females she knew of from school and work.

Suddenly, she was smote by a vision of her mother. Oh-my-God ... was she match-making again?

What was happening to her? Was she turning into her mother?

Ryan's acquaintance said his 'goodbyes' and walked off. The attorney closed his window and turned his attentions back to his wife. "You got that thing figured out yet?"

"I think so."

"I hope so—I don't want you to blind any of us."

"Such confidence, Sir! Which reminds me—the time has come for your penalty," she proclaimed. Trudy rested the spotlight in her lap and retrieved something from the cloth bag at her feet.

Ryan rolled his eyes. "I was rather hoping you had forgotten that, Ma'am," he said, meekly.

"I never forget. Besides, this will be fun." Trudy switched on the car overhead light revealing a handful of plastic head boppers, each with two spring-held antennae. The antennae sported grotesque protruding monster eyes in a variety of colors. "They light up," she added, clicking on one of the battery-operated switches. Immediately, two bulbous eyes shone a sickly pea-green. "Some of them flash, too."

"Awesome!" Gray exclaimed, leaning forward. "I'll take that green one." Trudy obliged him by handing it over.

Ryan groaned. "You're not serious? You want me to wear that! Where on earth did you get those things, Gertrude?"

"I found them in the attic last week when I was looking for kids' toys," she said, smugly. "My mother bought them for my eighth birthday party. They were quite a hit."

"I can only imagine."

"I remembered them this morning. I thought if we were going to light the deer the least we could do was give the deer a show in return."

"There is a madness to your method, Ma'am."

"I hope you don't expect me to wear one of them things?" Sarah spoke up. "The headband would muss up my hair for shore." She cupped her coiffed blonde hair-do.

"Don't worry, Sarah Louise. I've only got five sets."

"I'll take the red one," said Nellie. Trudy handed her the red-eyed head bopper and Nellie immediately flipped the switch to the battery-operated LED lights. She slid the monster eyes over her hair and pulled down the visor to examine her appearance in the mirror. The red antennae lights bobbled with the slightest movement of her head. "Cool!"

"Wicked cool," echoed Gray.

"You'd better hurry," Trudy urged her husband, with a twinkle in her eye. "They're going fast. Do you want to be left with Mr. Pink Eyes?"

"God forbid!" Ryan said, grasping the blue head bopper out of her hand. He joined Nellie and Gray and soon the vehicle was filled with colorful bobbling lights. He attempted to peer through the front windshield, which was now a polychromatic kaleidoscope. "I'm not sure I'll be able to drive like this."

"Try, Sir. It's not like there's a lot of traffic," Trudy said, wryly. She twisted to face Doctor Bart. "Since you have not offended the arbiter's sensibilities, you are saved from the dreaded pink eye." She handed him the jiggling yellow head bopper and placed the pink one over her own head.

Metcalf gamely slipped into his monster eyes. "Am I wearing the thing correctly?"

"Your light's not on," Trudy pointed out.

"I switched it on. Maybe it's malfunctioning?"

"What a shame," muttered Ryan. "Interested in a trade, Doctor?"

"Maybe it's a flasher?" suggested Gray.

Sure enough, within a few seconds Doctor Bart's monster eyes popped on, lighting up the back seat with a glowing phosphorescent yellow.

"Brother, you are one of us," Ryan allowed, putting the car in gear. "I'll stick with Old Blue Eyes, I guess. Where to first, Gray?"

Gray directed Ryan to the North Troy Road, which was about half a mile from the general store. When they reached the first field on that road, he instructed Ryan to pull the car over to the shoulder. Trudy, taking her cue, hoisted up the spotlight, making sure the powerful light was pointed away from everyone in the vehicle before she switched it on. She swept the field slowly with the spotlight.

Nellie held her breath. Unsure of what she was looking for, she carefully followed the swath of light, which widened out over the field. Suddenly, three sets of green eyes popped into the light. "I see them!" she cried.

Trudy stopped the spotlight and held it on the three deer. The deer bodies were barely visible—like shadows in the early daylight. The deer remained transfixed; three sets of green eyes never blinked.

Ryan regarded the glowing orbs suspiciously. "How do we know that's not aliens?" he asked, only half jesting.

Gray snorted with laughter. "Thet's what they looks like. I knew they was heah," he added, proudly, "thet's why I brung ya's heah fust. I spotted 'em two days ago. She's a doe with two little uns, right?"

Trudy confirmed Gray's guess.

"Why don't they run away?" asked Sarah, addressing Gray. She batted her mascara-laden eyelashes at him.

The youth was momentarily flustered. Until that moment, Sarah Louise had largely ignored him. He suddenly had some empathy for the deer caught in the spotlight.

"Deer freeze when confronted with bright light," Doctor Bart spoke up, relieving Gray from his embarrassment. "They never see light this bright in the wild so when the spotlight catches their eyes deer are literally mesmerized. That's one of the reasons there are so many deer and vehicle collisions."

"I got deer whistles on my truck to warn 'em I'm comin'," Gray said, recovering his composure. "Ya ought-ta git some, Sarah Louise."

She batted her eyes at the youth again. "Maybe you could get me some, huh, Gray?"

"Yeah, maybe."

Trudy released the captive deer from the spotlight and searched through the rest of the field. No more alien eyes appeared.

"That's three," she said, switching off the light. "Who's keeping track?" She reached into her cloth bag again and pulled out a pen and a small notebook.

"I will," said Nellie. Trudy handed over the pen and notebook.

"You thought of everything, didn't you?" asked Ryan, impressed.

"Preparedness is my middle name, Sir. Isn't that why you married me?"

The little group with their colorful fluorescent monster eyes bobbling motored slowly around town, stopping and starting at every new field. As they proceeded along they counted the whitetail deer population, Nellie faithfully recording the number, sex and approximate age of each animal spotted in her little notebook. When they reached the fields near John Woods' house, at Gray's urging, Trudy moved the light to the animal's bodies in order to check the color of each deer hide. Unfortunately, all of the hides were brown.

"Sorry Gray," Trudy said. "No white deer tonight."

"What's our tally now?" Doctor Bart asked, curious.

Nellie checked her notes. She maneuvered around in the seat to face him. "Forty does, fifty-two skippers and fawns, and two dozen young bucks."

"That's … one hundred and sixteen deer."

"Thet don't even count them big bucks 'at stays in the woods 'til late," said Gray.

Doctor Bart shook his head in disbelief. "Amazing."

"I never would have believed it, either," Ryan said. "This expedition is actually turning out to be quite fun."

"I told you so," said Trudy, smugly. "I hope the deer are enjoying their show, too!"

Ryan swung the sedan back into the travel lane and accelerated slowly. When he glanced in his rear view mirror he spied blue flashing lights. "Oh, oh—someone's in trouble." He pulled back over to the shoulder of the road, expecting the police car to speed on past. Instead, the officer pulled up behind the black sedan, blue lights still flashing. The siren blared briefly then swallowed itself with an alarming slurp.

Ryan yanked off his head bopper, switching it off. He caught Gray's eyes in the mirror. "Are you sure this is legal, young man? I didn't stop to check the game laws—I just took your word for it."

Gray hastily snatched off his own monster eyes. "Yep. 'Til midnight tonight—thet's September fust, ain't it?"

"It's not a game warden behind us; it's a state trooper," said Trudy, who had been carefully examining the other vehicle. She removed her head bopper and snapped off the pink light. Nellie followed suit.

Ryan rolled down his window as the uniformed officer approached, gravel crunching underfoot. "Something wrong, Officer?" Ryan asked.

"May I see your driver's license and registration, please?"

"Certainly." Ryan reached for his wallet. "The registration is in the glove box. Could you get it out, please, Nellie? It's in a black plastic sleeve."

"Sure." Nellie scrabbled through the glove box, found the plastic sleeve and passed it to him.

The state trooper examined both documents with his flashlight. He handed them back to Ryan. "Do you have any guns in the car, Sir?"

"Certainly not. Is there a problem, Officer?"

"Well, we received two separate reports of some queer flashing lights over here. Just wanted to be sure there wasn't something funny going on."

"Nothing funny going on here," Ryan assured him.

Suddenly, Doctor Bart's monster eyes, which were still atop his head, inopportunely flashed on, illuminating the interior of the car with a ghastly yellow glow.

Immediately suspicious, the officer bent down and peered past Ryan's head into the back seat. "Doctor Bart!" he exclaimed, surprised.

"Hello, Leroy," Metcalf replied, sheepishly. "Lovely night for a ride, isn't it? How's Sue?"

CHAPTER 17
No Old Folks Home for Chickadees

About the time our little group of friends was entertaining the officer of the law on the other side of town Rebecca and Wendell were settling themselves into their comfy featherbed for the night. The downy featherbed, a family heirloom, had been hand-stuffed by Wendell's Grammie Addie with duck feathers and down secured from a local farmer in exchange for a six month's supply of fresh eggs. The feather bed remained on the old four-poster year-round, regardless of season. Every now and then a sharp quill worked its way out from the blue-striped ticking and poked Rebecca in the softest part of her flesh. She had learned not to pull the offending feather out, however, since that imprudence would only widen the hole through which the precious down might escape. Instead, she worked the deserters (always feathers, never down since true down has no quill shaft) back into the mattress.

Wendell snapped off the nightstand lamp. A pastel white light from the waxing gibbous moon gave faint illumination to the bedroom. Rebecca, in her cotton nightgown, snuggled her pregnant body closer to her husband. She savored an unexpected moment of unalloyed joy, one of those unforgettable moments as rarified as the air on Mount Everest. The feeling was so exquisite she hardly dared breathe lest the moment evaporate.

Nevertheless, Rebecca found herself wanting to share her joy with her husband. "I feel so happy tonight! I don't think it's the hormones, either."

Wendell made an empathetic grunt. Not wanting to give short shrift to Rebecca's happiness, however, he tucked his wife into his arm and gave her a friendly squeeze.

"I'm so grateful for everything God has given me," she continued, toying with a button on his striped pajama top. Her soft brown curls splayed across his shoulder. "Sometimes I think of my life before Lila and I moved to Sovereign, and I can hardly understand how we stood it so long. We were used to living in fear back then, I guess—fear we would lose our jobs, fear we wouldn't be able to pay the bills, fear we wouldn't be able to put food on the table."

He fondled one of her curls. "Course you ain't got nuthin' to worry 'bout now. We gots plenty o' string beans in the cellar 'n squashes in the garden."

She giggled. "We'll have plenty of baby food then, won't we?"

"One wintah when I was a kid we et nuthin' but squash 'n venison for six months."

"Goodness! Why?"

"Cause Pappy spent all Grammie Addie's egg money on a new hoss. Warn't she agitated. Made him peel thet ornery squash every dang day 'til he figgered out he warn't much of a hoss tradah."

Rebecca smiled to herself. She loved to hear Wendell's stories of growing up at the old Russell homestead with his grandparents, cousins, and the hired hand, Bud. She placed her husband's right palm against her very pregnant belly. "What will he look like, I wonder?"

"Who?"

"Our baby, silly! Just think of all those different genes swimming around in our gene pools. When I think of the people who have gone before us—like Grammie Addie—it just boggles my mind."

"Jest's long's she don't come out lookin' like ole Pap."

"*She*, Mr. Russell?"

"Wal, you know, you kin have yore hopes, Mrs. Russell, 'n I kin have mine."

"Goodness! Did you feel that? That was a kick!"

Wendell grinned. "Ayuh, I think 'twas."

September brought a rush of cooler weather, encouraging many of the townspeople in Sovereign to dust off their woodstoves. Nellie had been using her kitchen woodstove intermittently, since the old schoolhouse was heated entirely by wood, but she had not yet needed to start the living room stove. Not knowing the last time Maggie had had the chimneys cleaned, Doctor Bart arranged for a chimney cleaner from Lewiston to come, and Nellie actually went up on the old tin roof for the first time in her life. She watched the chimneysweep clean both chimneys with a long-handled wiry black brush. The flexible handle stretched nearly down to the ground. The chimneysweep was a funny little man, about half a foot shorter than Nellie, and of French Acadian extraction. He was dressed in black from head to foot and wore special sneakers, which gave his step a quick bouncing motion like a songbird hopping across the grass.

"Dere, she set for anoder season," the chimney cleaner declared, after vacuuming up the black, acrid-smelling creosote he had knocked down to the bottom of the chimney. The iron door to the chimney clean-out was situated in the dirt cellar at the bottom of the chimney. Mr. Pelletier (pronounced 'Pell-kee,' Nellie discovered much to her astonishment) was courteous and thoughtful, accessing the cellar via the metal bulkhead to keep the granular black dirt, of which he was wearing his fair share, from tracking up the house.

Nellie paid him with a check from Maggie and Uncle Peter's joint account. Her stepfather's name had been officially removed from the account but Nellie was still awaiting new checks to arrive with her and her mother's names on them. In the meantime, with a heart-felt pang, she crossed out Peter's name from the top of the check and added her own. "How often do we need to do this, Mr. Pell-kee?" she asked, ripping off the check. They were standing outside the bulkhead, near where he had parked his big black rig that boasted a sign for *Pelletier & Daughter, Chimneysweeps.* Nellie had previously ascertained that his daughter's help was limited to inspiration, since she was only three years old.

"Some peoples say may-be too, tree time a year, but one time she be good 'nuff for you, may-be, Mam'selle." Mr. Pelletier unselfconsciously wiped his grimy hands on his black pants and brushed the dirt off his bare muscular forearms. He accepted Nellie's check, folded the paper in half and stuffed it into his pants pocket.

"I don't remember my mother ever having the chimney cleaned before …?"

He chortled, and leaped up into the bed of his truck, where he began systematically attaching the long-handled brush to a special rack.

"Did I say something funny, Mr. Pell-kee? You can probably tell—I'm new at this chimney cleaning stuff."

"Yor moder, she probbly use de old-timer way to clean chimbney, may-be."

"Oh? What's that?"

"Good hot chimbney fire—too, tree time a year. Keep de creosote down. Tank God dose old-timers die or I got no business."

"A chimney fire! I thought that's what we were trying to prevent?"

The chimneysweep made a little dissing motion with his left hand. "What we tink dangerous to-day was run o' de mill in yor granddaddy day," he declared, with a snap of his blackened fingers.

"Good ting for me time move on." He hopped down, stuck the covered pail of creosote into the back of his truck, and drove off. Nellie watched the chimneysweep disappear up the road in a cloud of dust, wondering at her ignorance of Maine life. They didn't teach chimney cleaning or any other "real life" skills at Hathorne!

On Wednesday afternoon, Nellie had a date to visit Aunt Hannah, an engagement she had very much been looking forward to. The two women had discovered while helping out at the clinic they shared a love of quilting. Aunt Hannah had been sewing quilts for more than fifty years, frequently giving them as wedding or baby gifts to friends and family members. Nellie, although a novice quilter yet to sew her first quilt, was a member of the hip New York City MOD Quilt Guild, which was founded in 2010 as a place for modern quilters to connect. Aunt Hannah had promised to show her a variety of quilts, including some family heirlooms more than two hundred years old, and she was excited by the prospect.

Rebecca had an obstetrical check-up in Bangor on Wednesday and dropped Nellie at Aunt Hannah's modest antique cape around two o'clock. "I'll pick you up about five," she called, as Nellie waved her off.

Nellie knocked on the door to the glass-enclosed front porch, and waited. When no one came, she let herself onto the porch. Evidence of Aunt Hannah's adroit handiwork was evident everywhere on the comfortable porch. Three gay rag rugs decorated the gray painted floor and two matching rockers wore saris of multicolored afghan throws. A vintage tumbling block quilt, pieced together with a kaleidoscope of diamond-shaped swatches (most likely rescued from the scrap bin) hung against the white house wall separating the two kitchen windows.

Nellie peered in through the front door and saw Aunt Hannah busy at the stove. She rapped on the glass.

Aunt Hannah turned around. "Come in, dear," she called. She glanced back at the double boiler on the stove and wiped her hands on her apron.

"Mmm, smells heavenly!" Nellie said, closing the porch door behind her. The scent of chocolate permeated the quaint country kitchen. She had never visited Metcalf's great-aunt before and was immediately charmed by the kitchen's gleaming wainscoted panels and tartan brick plaid wallpaper. A variety of antique copper cooking implements and a curious collection of cookie-cutters hung down from the wooden beams.

"Thank you, my dear. I'm making Needhams," Aunt Hannah replied. "They're Metcalf's favorite candy."

Nellie approached the stove. She peered over Aunt Hannah's shoulder into the top pot of the small double boiler. "Your friend Miss Crump mentioned Needhams, but I didn't know what they were."

"My heavens, Nellie," Aunt Hannah exclaimed. She picked up a wooden spoon and gently stirred the melting chocolate. She made a slight adjustment to the temperature of the gas and returned the spoon to the ceramic spoon holder. "Don't tell me you've never heard of Needhams? And you, from Maine!"

"I guess my mother fell down on the domestic engineering part of the job."

"Well, well. We won't blame Maggie. She had a lot more important things on her mind than making Needhams, I know that for a fact."

"Believe me, Aunt Hannah, chocolate is never far from my mother's mind. May I have a taste of the candy?"

The widow loosened a tinkling laugh. "This is just the chocolate for the coating. The candy center is in the fridge. I let it set up overnight. If you'd like to help me, you could cut the mix up into the squares for dipping…?"

Nellie needed no further encouragement. She washed her hands, and, at Aunt Hannah's direction, sliced the solid white mixture into one-inch squares. Some scrids of the candy center dropped from the knife and Nellie popped them into her mouth. "Yum! What's the center made of?"

"Potatoes."

"Oh-my-God—you're joking. This is so not potatoes."

The tinkling laugh was repeated. "That's the reaction I get from most people when they first hear the ingredients. But I assure you it's true. This is my sister's secret recipe, but all Needham filling recipes are basically the same: flaked coconut, melted butter, sugar, vanilla and mashed potato. You see, these were a treat even poor Mainers could afford during the Depression."

"Why are they called 'Needhams' if it's your sister's recipe? Was that her name?"

"No, our maiden name was 'Craig' and Laurel—that's my sister—her married name was 'Metcalf'."

"Right, I knew that. So, where does the name come from, then?"

"Our mother told us the candies were named for the Maine minister who invented them, a Reverend Needham. Apparently, he used the candy as a way to entice people into his church."

"Did it work?"

"Let's just say the candy outlived Reverend Needham's congregation."

Nellie laughed, and finished slicing the last square. "OK, what's next?"

"Next, we dip the squares one by one into the melted chocolate—like this." Aunt Hannah inserted a toothpick into one of the coconut-potato squares and dipped the candy into the melted chocolate. "Just dip it under quick … and then we let the excess chocolate drip off. I use dark chocolate but you could use milk chocolate." Aunt Hannah placed the dipped chocolate onto a cookie sheet covered with wax paper and removed the toothpick. "When they're all dipped, I'll set the chocolates on the back porch to cool. I've got a card table out there ready for them. By the time you leave this afternoon you'll be able to sample them." Metcalf's great-aunt adjusted the heat under the melted chocolate and stepped away from the stove. "Would you like to try?"

Nellie nodded eagerly. She carefully dipped a square into the melted chocolate as she had seen Aunt Hannah do.

"That's it—let the chocolate drip. Perfect!"

Nellie admired her handiwork. "Cool! I can't wait to try them—I love dark chocolates." She selected another square and repeated the process.

"Metcalf prefers dark chocolate, too. My sister used to wrap two Needhams up in wax paper—Laurel made hers the traditional size, two-inch squares—and put one in each of his coat pockets when she sent Metcalf home from visiting her. It was Laurel's special way of telling him she loved him. He was her favorite grandchild, you see."

"How sweet—at least for him, anyway. He's told me how much time he spent with his Grandmother Metcalf, about her roses and all."

"Yes, they were quite a team. I don't put the Needhams in his coat pockets, of course. That was their special thing and I wouldn't want to infringe on Metcalf's memory of his grandmother. But I do make Needhams for him from time to time."

"I'm sure he appreciates it. I know I would!"

While the chocolates were setting up, Aunt Hannah gave Nellie a tour of the house. Quilts of every conceivable style, form, and material decorated her walls, chairs and beds, including several log cabin patterns, a beautiful floral Dresden quilt, crazy quilts, a delicate handkerchief quilt made from vintage ladies handkerchiefs sewn by one of Aunt Hannah's ancestors, block quilts, star quilts and many more.

They spent nearly half an hour in the upstairs landing, where Aunt Hannah's sewing nook was cozily situated in the south-facing foyer looking out the window onto the Bog Road, the back road to Troy and Carleton Pond Bog. Aunt Hannah's calico cat Agnes was curled up in a wicker basket under a modern sewing machine. A black Singer treadle machine squatted in a corner, forlorn and forgotten. Several quilts lined the wallpapered upstairs hall and tall piles of fabric flanked the walkway, threatening to topple over and stop traffic if they weren't used soon. "Help yourself, if you see any material you like," Aunt Hannah offered generously. "I'll never use all this fabric if I live to be a hundred and fifty."

Nellie gathered up a small armful of vintage cloth from six or seven piles. "Thanks, this should motivate me. I've been looking for inspiration for my first official quilt."

"Marden's Department Store has a good selection of cloth, too. We should go there sometime. You'll need some cloth for the backing. Once or twice a year I treat myself to a stroll through their fabric department, just for kicks. I certainly don't need any more material, but … Marden's prices are awfully attractive. I've been thinking of making another Marden's run soon. Would you like to go with me after the clinic closes on Saturday?"

"It's a date," said Nellie. The cat awoke, yawned and stretched. Nellie scootched down to pet the calico creature. "I can't believe you've sewed so many quilts," she said, rising up. "There must be twenty in your house at least."

"Thirty-four, at last count," Aunt Hannah replied, placing her hand on the aged staircase bannister in preparation for their descent. "I've sewn a lot more than that," she added, "but I've given most of them away. I can tell you where every single quilt has gone, too."

"How do you keep track of them all?"

"I keep a Quilt Journal—a record of each quilt, where the material came from, who they went to, etcetera, etcetera. The latest number is on my desk there." She indicated a spiral bound notebook lying atop a small oak secretary next to the antique sewing machine.

"The latest number?" Nellie repeated, curious. "How many notebooks do you have?"

"Thirteen."

"Oh-my-God. OK, I'm definitely going to start keeping track of my quilts. But I doubt I'll ever make as many as you have."

"You're still young, my dear, and life is a lot longer than you think for. You've got plenty of time to catch up to me. I never set out to sew so many quilts, but the years kept rolling by and the quilts followed faster than my babies. You'd be surprised how many quilts you can sew in fifty years, especially after the kids leave home."

Aunt Hannah descended the stairs with a slow step, and Nellie followed, caressing the well-worn bannister as she went, enjoying the wood's exquisitely smooth feel beneath her hand. Idly she wondered how many other hands had contributed to the bannister's alchemy. The wooden steps, too, dipped in the middle, offering evidence of a legion of users. When she reached the bottom stair, she noticed what looked like the head of a silver dollar recessed into the square finial of the painted newel post. Nellie ran her forefinger over the tarnished coin, the face of which was somewhat obscured by wear. "What's this? If you don't mind my asking," she added. She stepped down onto the hooked rug and turned to examine the post.

"That was Merlon's great-great grandfather's mortgage—what's left of it, anyway. In the old days when they paid off their mortgage or their bond for a deed they burned the paper and stored the ashes in a hole bored into the top of the newel post. If the post was hollow—this one isn't, I don't believe—the paper was rolled up and hidden inside. Then the hole was plugged with a decorative bit showing they finally owned their home. Some people used special mortgage buttons made from ivory or scrimshaw, but Merlon's ancestor decided a silver dollar would do just as well. It must have been a momentous day for them, paying off their mortgage."

"I can't even imagine owning a home. I'm still paying off my student loans. Do people still use these things? I don't remember ever seeing anything like it before."

Aunt Hannah shook her head. "Mortgage buttons were pretty well abandoned by my grandparents' day."

Nellie ran her fingers over the faded coin. She wondered how many other old houses in town had so-called 'mortgage buttons' and made a mental note to check the newel posts on the staircases at Henry Trow's and Rebecca's, two of the oldest houses in Sovereign. She certainly wouldn't be visiting the Nutt place—which was in fact the oldest house in town—not as long as Walden was living there.

She turned away from the staircase and came face to face with Aunt Hannah's massive front door. It was four-foot wide at least. The window lights on either side magnified the door's abnormal girth. "Why is your front door so wide?"

"So they could get the coffins out of the house."

"Say no more," said Nellie, laughing. "I can see it, already—six fat men, three on each side, sweat pouring down their faces, desperately trying not to trip as they carried the heavy coffin over the door stoop and down the granite steps."

"You've got a quick mind, my dear. That's a very accurate description of Merlon's grandfather's funeral, which was held in the front parlor. Until forty or fifty years ago wakes and funerals were always held at home."

"Is that why funeral homes in Maine are called 'funeral parlors'?"

"I wouldn't be surprised but that was a way of making families feel more comfortable with the funeral home's services. You see, it used to be everything revolved around the family's home—nobody on the farm went out to work or to have babies or even to die. Everything happened right at home."

"Sounds heavenly! Wouldn't it be great if we could get back to that kind of life?"

Aunt Hannah sighed. "I'm afraid I won't live long enough to see that happen, my dear. Perhaps it will be different in your lifetime, though. The Internet has made quite a difference."

The two women retired to the front porch, which was toasty warm thanks to the heat of the sun through the south-facing windows. They drank a cup of tea and sampled the Needhams. "Dee-licious," Nellie pronounced, wiping melted chocolate from her fingers and mouth with the paper napkin Aunt Hannah had given her. "I can see where Needhams could become seriously addictive."

"Perhaps I should have used a little more paraffin," Aunt Hannah worried. "The chocolate wouldn't have melted in your hand so quickly."

"Don't change a thing, Aunt Hannah—they're perfect! I would have licked my fingers except I was trying to be polite. That's half the fun of eating homemade chocolates."

Aunt Hannah set her tea cup down and stood up. "I'll go put some Needhams up for you to take home. The rest I'll take to Metcalf, well, except maybe one or two I'll sneak for myself."

Nellie followed her into the kitchen and leaned against the counter as the widow wrapped up six Needhams. "May I have your recipe, Aunt Hannah? I'd like to try and make some myself."

The older woman hesitated. "I don't usually share my sister's Needhams recipe—it's never been out of the family, you see. But in this case, I think we might stretch the precedent and say your relationship at the moment is, well, close enough." Aunt Hannah essayed a conspiratorial smile.

Her remark and the way she said it gave Nellie pause. Was Aunt Hannah, too, in on Maggie's plot to marry her off to Doctor Bart? She hated to disappoint Aunt Hannah—she was such a nice lady!—but Nellie wasn't going to marry Metcalf just so everyone wouldn't be disappointed.

The two women resumed their rockers to await Rebecca's return. It was pleasant sitting on the enclosed front porch, watching the wild birds feed at the feeders. The warm porch emitted a comforting, homey scent much like Nellie had always supposed a grandmother's house would smell. She rested her head back against the chair and began to rock. Two of the front windows were open and she could hear the birds chirp and chatter. She had discovered in her short time at home nearly every household in Sovereign fed the birds and some even fed the wild deer in winter.

As Nellie rocked, a thought occurred to her. "Why do you work so hard, Aunt Hannah? I know you said you needed money and all, but that doesn't explain the quilts, the committee work at church, your volunteer work at the new clinic…?"

"I'd tell you, my dear, but it's rather a silly story."

"Please … Aunt Hannah," Nellie encouraged. "I'd really like to know."

"Well, if you insist ..."

"I do!"

Aunt Hannah folded her hands in her lap. "One day, not long after Merlon died, I rose up from my afternoon rest to go to the bathroom," she recounted. "My right hip pained me terribly; I could hardly put weight on it—I have bursitis and arthritis, you see, which acts up when the weather is bad. I thought to myself how much easier my life would be if I just gave up and got myself a wheelchair. Why did I keep pushing myself so hard when I had so little left to live for? Then, as I sat on the toilet, I happened to glance out the window and my gaze rested upon a little chickadee perched on my forsythia. I hate that bush because it keeps growing and growing and if I don't cut it back every spring it'll soon be bigger than my house. But the birds love it, especially the chickadees. Anyway, that little chickadee was trying to wrestle open a sunflower seed. I watched that precious bird struggle with the seed—much like I wrestle with my forsythia bush—and soon I forgot all about my pain. I began to wonder what happened to old chickadees too worn out and too tired to feed themselves. 'There are no Old Folks Homes for chickadees,' I reminded myself. I suddenly realized how much better I had it than that poor bird and gave myself a good talking to. I vowed then and there to keep pushing to do as much as possible lest I become nothing more than a worn-out old chickadee that at last falls to the earth dead because it's no longer able to fly or strong enough to wrestle open a sunflower seed."

CHAPTER 18

The Minister's Daughter

When Nellie returned home from Aunt Hannah's with her treasures, she found a bright white business card stuck in the crack of the shed door. The card was embossed with gold lettering that read: *Julian Mills, Doctor of Divinity and Author at Large ~ "Faber est suae quisque fortunae." (Every man is the artisan of his own fortune.)* On the back of the card Doctor Mills had scribbled a telephone number and a note saying he was sorry to have missed her. Presumably, she was to give him a call, most likely to arrange his second visit.

Nellie carried the pasteboard card into the house and set it along with her vintage cloth and Needhams onto the kitchen table. She wished Julian Mills had provided her with an email address instead of a phone number. To Nellie, the idea of actually talking on the telephone seemed old-fashioned and outmoded. She much preferred texting and messaging either on her cell or via Facebook to speaking with someone. Sending Julian Mills a friendly text message was likely a waste of time, however. If he was anything like her mother, he didn't know how to text.

Maybe she should just ignore him? Maybe he wasn't going to be around long? Nellie again wished her mother was home or at the very least there was a way she could contact Maggie. It had now been more than a month since her mother had disappeared. Nellie had tried several times to email her mother—asking Gmail to notify her when the emails had been read. To date, none of them had been opened. Obviously, Maggie wasn't checking them.

Nellie felt uncomfortable meeting with Julian Mills alone. She wasn't worried about her personal safety for he was old enough to be her grandfather. She just didn't want to be the sole focus of his attention. She had been alone with some of her mother's pastor friends many times when she was young and had disliked not only their pontificating but also the way they had quickly become enamored of her, as though they had never seen or spoken with a young person before. Nellie thought she had read once that Julian Mills led a secluded life in Santa Fe, New Mexico, but she couldn't remember whether or not he was married and had a family. Childless clergy were the worst, in her opinion. They were always trying to project their dashed hopes and dreams upon the Theological Offspring of other clergy.

Nellie picked up her phone and googled Julian Mills. She scrolled down past the Amazon book listings for him and his author's profile until she came to his website. She clicked on the link and quickly read his biography. It was just as she feared: Julian Mills—orphaned at age ten, ordained at twenty-seven, called as pastor of the largest church in California by forty, world famous by fifty—had never married and had no children. He currently resided in a spiritual compound in Santa Fe, but travelled frequently around the globe giving inspirational speeches and promoting his books.

No, she certainly didn't want to meet with Julian Mills alone. But who else was there she could invite to help take the attention off her? She cast her mind over the roster of her new friends in Sovereign and admitted to herself most of them would not even know who Julian Mills was. Worse, they might be awed and intimidated by his compelling presence. Nellie certainly didn't want to subject any of her new friends to a star-struck embarrassment. Ryan would have been the best choice, of course, except if she invited Ryan she would have to invite Trudy. And that invitation might open the door to Leland. The next thing she knew she'd end up with half the town of Sovereign at her dinner table!

If only one of her friends from Columbia or Hathorne lived closer! But Nellie's nearest friend lived in Connecticut and worked in the City and likely wouldn't relish a seven or eight hour drive to the backwoods of Maine to have dinner with her, even to meet Julian Mills. That left Nellie no choice but to invite Metcalf. Whether or not Doctor Bart had ever heard of the world-famous author—and Nellie figured it would have been impossible for him to graduate college without at least reading "The House by the Side of the Road"—he'd be able to hold his own sitting down to dinner with the famous author. In the twenty-two years Nellie had known Metcalf, she had never once had to blush for him, which was more than she could say for most of the other Maine men of her acquaintance.

Why did everything and everyone in her life always seem to point her in Doctor Bart's direction? Was the entire cosmos in league against her?

Nellie became aware the kitchen was cooling off. She closed the window over the sink and decided to light a fire in the woodstove. She went out to the woodshed to ferry in several armloads of wood, taking the opportunity to admire Uncle Peter's handiwork. Maggie had never stacked wood so neatly. Still, Nellie had never realized until now how much time and effort her mother had spent over the years keeping the place warm for them. Nellie's sole responsibility as a child had been to fill the woodbox, a task she had quite often managed to shirk. Her mother, in addition to picking up Nellie's slack, always started the fires in the two woodstoves and kept them going, cleaned the stoves out, purchased the six to eight cords of split firewood every year, and stacked the wood in the woodshed. Uncle Peter had occasionally helped Maggie but most of the burden had fallen on her mother's shoulders. The longer her mother was away from home, the higher Maggie rose in Nellie's opinion. Perhaps if she stayed away until Christmas Nellie might actually come to admire and respect her mother again!

She defrosted one of the condolence casseroles for her dinner and enjoyed her solitary meal by the flickering light of two tapers she had relocated to the kitchen from the living room. She scrolled through her email and listened to tunes on Spotify while she ate. After dinner she pushed her plate away, snapped on the overhead light, and retrieved her mother's hanging wall calendar. She had taken over the calendar for her own personal engagements. Nellie perused the calendar in search of a suitable date to invite Julian Mills and Metcalf to dinner.

The next day, Thursday, would be too soon, of course, and besides—she had previously designated Thursday as 'harvest the garden day', assigning herself the task of harvesting and canning the dozens of ripe heirloom tomatoes. Two days ago she had dragged down from the cupboard over the refrigerator her mother's vintage gold-colored Presto pressure cooker and found a note taped to the heavy lid, a note Maggie had left reminding herself to purchase a new sealing ring. Nellie had purchased the large rubber ring at Gilpin's yesterday and had since washed up jars in preparation for the tomatoes. When finished on Thursday, the tomatoes would join the canned string beans, peaches, jams and jellies, and other culinary delights her mother kept in the basement storage cupboard, awaiting parole in winter. So, tomorrow the dinner was definitely not going to happen.

Nellie paused to enjoy one of her Needhams and then resumed consultation of the calendar. On Friday, she was volunteering at the clinic. Saturday she was not only working at the clinic, but also she had a date with Aunt Hannah to go fabric shopping at Marden's in the afternoon. Sunday meant church, and after church Nellie had been invited to Sunday dinner at Scotch Broom Acres with Ryan and Trudy. On Monday afternoon the Ladies Corn Shop Museum Auxiliary, of which Nellie was now a member, was meeting at the treasurer's house. Those meetings, which always included an afternoon high tea, dragged on into the late afternoon and Nellie certainly wouldn't have time to prepare a dinner after that. Perhaps, Tuesday?

The tea kettle on the stove whistled and Nellie rose up to pour herself a cup of tea. She returned to the table and retrieved the calendar. No, Tuesday was no good, either. She had been invited to play in the regular round-robin of cribbage down to Gilpin's General Store with Maynard Nutter, Asa Palmer, John Woods, and several others from the little group of men her mother had fondly dubbed the 'Old Farts.' And that left next Wednesday—a week away—as the earliest possible date Nellie could host a dinner for Julian Mills and Metcalf. How had her life gotten so busy? This was crazy!

The times before when she had been home visiting, Nellie had always been bored. She'd never been able to find anything fun to do and as a result had spent most of her time in her room or curled up in the rocker next to the woodstove watching YouTube videos. Had anyone asked her even a year ago she would have said Sovereign was the dullest place on Earth. Now, however, she rarely had time to herself. How had this about-face happened?

Nellie wasn't sure how to explain the transformation, yet she suspected it was because she was here without her mother. She was no longer an extension of Maggie, no longer handicapped by that awful epithet she'd always hated—the 'Minister's Daughter.' No, she was simply Nellie Walker, a person in her own right, just like she was at school and at work.

After washing up the supper dishes, Nellie returned her apron to its hook by the refrigerator and glanced at the old regulator clock to check the time. She thought about telephoning Julian Mills, but decided to put it off, even though she had selected a tentative dinner date. She wanted to talk with Doctor Bart first, ensuring Metcalf was free next Wednesday evening so she wouldn't be alone with the legendary guru who would no doubt inquire about her goals in life and freely offer his advice when she failed to deliver them. Nellie still hadn't made up her mind what she was going to do when her mother returned or even where she was going to go next. At the moment, while she was enjoying her life in Sovereign, she couldn't visualize remaining here year-round. Nor was there any gainful employment for her had she wanted to stay, and Nellie very much wanted to continue her work with non-profits and NGOs.

Knowing she had about an hour of daylight left, Nellie decided to walk up to Henry Trow's. She'd gotten into the pleasant habit of dropping in on her new neighbor, sharing a cup of tea with him and going out to the barn to see Lightning's progress. She smiled to herself as she realized the irony in the fact that she never worried about spending time alone with Mr. Trow, even though he quite often focused his attentions on her and broached the very same questions she dreaded deliberating with Julian Mills. Perhaps it was the fame that made the difference?

"What did you say these are called, Nellie? They're about the best chocolates I've ever eaten," he declared, popping the rest of a Needham into his mouth. Nellie had given Henry Trow half of her cache, planning to make some of the chocolates soon herself. "Mmm, mmm, good!"

"Needhams," she replied. She explained the origin of the name to Mr. Trow, pointing out the interesting fact they were made with Maine potatoes.

"You're joking—potatoes?"

Nellie nodded, feeling a new sense of pride in her home state. "It's a Maine thing."

"Well, whatever they're made of—these chocolates are better than my wife's. You know I'd never admit that if it wasn't true. You be sure and tell your Aunt Hannah how much I enjoyed 'em and tell her she can come cook for me anytime!"

"I might just do that," said Nellie, smiling smugly to herself. The Needhams and an introduction to Aunt Hannah were part of her little match-making scheme. "Have you ever heard of Julian Mills?" she continued. She had uncovered during the course of their many conversations the fact that her new neighbor had been a high school history teacher in New Hampshire before retiring, and he was widely read. It had suddenly occurred to her he might make a good fourth at her dinner party.

Mr. Trow's bushy eyebrows puckered. "That quack! I tried to read one of his books once but I got so disgusted with all that pseudo-religious stuff I tossed it into the trash."

Nellie was dismayed. "Which book was that?"

"I think it was his second book, 'A Friend to Man.' Gerry bought it after we saw him on Oprah hustling the thing. What a fake!

He was decked out completely in white and acted as though he was more important than God. His teeth were so bright they almost put my eyes out. Don't I hate that kind of posturing! Your mother isn't like that, is she?"

Nellie shook her head. "No way! You'd never know she was a minister. She doesn't wear a robe or act like she's trying to save the world or anything. Still, I think she does a lot of good. I know she does, actually," she amended hastily, recollecting all the stories her new friends had shared with her about Maggie's good works. "She runs naked through the goldenrod every August, too," she added, as an afterthought. "It's a fundraiser for the corn shop museum."

Henry Trow chuckled. "Well, well. That gives me something else to look forward to, doesn't it?"

Their conversation moved on naturally to other topics and Nellie didn't mention Julian Mills again. Mr. Trow certainly wouldn't be a good fourth at a dinner party given in his honor!

When Nellie returned home she telephoned Metcalf. "Are you free for dinner next Wednesday evening? I want to have you over for dinner, to meet Julian Mills, you know."

"Don't feel obliged to include me, Nellie. I'm not such a fan of Julian Mills as you are, although I did like 'The House by the Side of the Road.' Why don't the two of you just enjoy yourselves? I'd only be a third wheel."

"I don't want to be alone with him," she replied, feeling slightly annoyed. Why did she always have to explain everything to him?

"I see," he said, slowly.

Nellie could tell by the way he said it he didn't see at all. How was she to explain it to him? Why was Metcalf always so clueless?

"I'm not worried he'll put a move on me or anything …" she began.

"I should hope not. He's old enough to be your father."

"More like my grandfather, actually. But that's not the point. I feel funny sitting down to eat with him all by myself. You know I don't like to be the center of attention."

"I don't think you'd have to worry about that. From what I know of him, Julian Mills likes to hog the limelight."

"Please, Metcalf. You wouldn't be in the way, really. You'd be like … like the third wheel on a tricycle—much needed," she concluded.

"You know I can't say 'No' to you, Nellie. I'll put it in my calendar. You might need to remind me, though."

She groaned to herself. Really? How could he ever hope to get himself a wife if he couldn't keep track of his own engagements?

"Good grief! How could you forget? What else do you have to do next Wednesday night?"

"Read horticultural books. See you Friday, Nellie."

Work at the Songbird Free Medical Clinic had fallen into a satisfying routine. Nellie welcomed the patients, wrote up their paperwork, and turned them over to Doctor Bart. Sometimes she assisted him, but more often not. At the end of the exam Nellie bade them farewell, usually collecting a modest donation and always the grateful appreciation of those who couldn't afford medical care anyplace else.

On Friday morning Doctor Bart had three appointments and one walk-in. At noon, he and Nellie shared a sit-down lunch prepared by Aunt Hannah. Shortly after one o'clock, Walden walked in, right on schedule for his follow-up appointment.

Nellie offered the bearded woodsman a half-hearted smile, not sure whether Walden was going to be friendly or facetious with her. "Thanks for the chanterelles," she said, after he had appropriated the black state of Maine rocker. "They were great. We sautéed them in olive oil."

"Did your boyfriend like them?" He flipped nonchalantly through the pages of an old Down East magazine.

"I told you—he's not my boyfriend."

"No, you didn't say that. You said, 'yes' and then you said 'no' and 'I don't know.' How's a guy supposed to interpret that?"

"He's not my boyfriend," Nellie elucidated hastily, stealing a glance over her shoulder at the closed door of the exam room. Doctor Bart was currently treating an elderly man with shingles. "And, yes, he did like them. There were eight of us at dinner, though. Not just him and me."

"Did I ask?" He tossed the magazine back onto the end table and stood up. He stretched, his head nearly touching the embossed tin ceiling of the parlor.

"I thought you might like to know. You inferred that, anyway. Please don't sit on my desk." Nellie said, as he moved to perch on the edge. She scooted her desk chair back until the wheel hit the wall behind her.

He rose up obediently. "Are you scared of me? You are scared of me!"

"Maybe a little. You're very big, you know."

"I have big feet, too. And you know what they say about men with big feet."

"You're disgusting. Go sit down."

He ignored her directive. Instead, he leaned an arm on the oak desk in an insinuating fashion. "What's a girl like you doing in a place like this? I know you're not from around here, Nurse Nellie. I can tell by the way you carry yourself and by the way you talk. I can't figure you out, though. Are you in Sovereign because your boyfriend's here?"

"I told you—he's not my boyfriend."

"Sure. Keep telling yourself that. I've seen you two together."

Nellie glowered at him but could think of no cutting retort.

His wounded shoulder becoming tired, Walden straightened up. He returned to the rocker and put his feet up on the table.

Nellie suspected the move was deliberate, to show her their size. "You're an ass. And that table belonged to a very dear friend of mine, Miss Hastings. She's dead now. Take your feet off it!"

"What does she care about her table if she's dead?" Nevertheless, Walden removed his feet, lowering them slowly to the Oriental rug. "You never answered my question. Why are you here?"

"Why are *you* here?" she challenged, turning the question back on him.

He leaned back and fondled his full brown beard. "I'm following in Thoreau's footsteps, natch; keeping a journal about my days in the Maine woods. Don't you want to know whether I've mentioned a certain nymph who came strolling through the woods one August morn?"

"Not really," she replied, in a bored voice.

"Someday, you'll be able to tell your grandchildren how you met me in the woods in Sovereign, Maine. Play your cards right, and you could be telling *our* grandchildren how you met me."

Nellie flared up instantly. "You're a conceited …!" she broke off, suddenly spying Doctor Bart standing in the doorway, his patient half-way out the front door. How long had he been standing there?

"I'm ready for you Walden," he announced, removing his hands from his pockets. "Bring me his chart, will you, Nellie?"

The tall woodsman meekly rose and followed Metcalf into the exam room. He took his seat on the exam table and casually unbuttoned his shirt.

"How's your shoulder? Any pain or stiffness?"

"No. She's healing nicely, thanks, Doc." Walden tossed his button-up over the nearby chair and pulled off his T-shirt, baring his chest. Nellie entered the room with the clipboard and he gazed at her suggestively.

Nellie quickly averted her eyes. She set the clipboard down on the counter and waited for Doctor Bart's next directive. When he said nothing, she remained standing quietly in the background.

Metcalf removed the make-shift bandage Walden had applied to his own shoulder. He cleaned and examined the wound, pronouncing it healing well. "Just continue to take it easy for another week or so," he advised. "Don't split any firewood."

"No worries, Doc. My wood's all in for the winter."

Nellie felt as though someone had kicked her in the stomach. Walden was planning to stay around all winter?

Doctor Bart appeared equally surprised. "You're staying here this winter?" he asked, voicing Nellie's thoughts.

Walden reached for his T-shirt. "Yeah. Why not?" He pulled the blue cotton shirt back over his head, covering up his burly chest. "I've got the old place spruced up, at least enough for me to live in."

"Well, just tread lightly around Henry Trow," Doctor Bart cautioned. "I've spoken with him—he won't be taking any more pot shots at you. But don't goad him unnecessarily."

"I won't be doing much mushrooming in winter, Doc," Walden pointed out.

"You know very well what I mean. I'm not going to report the incident this time, Walden. I can't see any good coming from that. But if something else happens I'm obliged to go to the authorities."

"I'll mind my manners around the old gent, I promise."

Nellie clenched her hands. Between the two of them they made it sound as though Mr. Trow was a complete nut-case and not a lonely old man who believed he was defending a helpless, wounded calf. "You won't have to worry about Mr. Trow," she declared hotly. "He feels a lot worse about the shooting than anybody else."

This time it was Walden's turn to appear surprised. He was reaching for his flannel shirt, but he paused to shoot Nellie an inquiring glance.

"Nellie's become quite fond of her new neighbor," Doctor Bart explained. He told Walden the saga of how the calf had been struck by lightning. "Mr. Trow was only making sure you kept your distance," he added.

Walden whistled. "Struck by lightning, was it? And the thing lived?"

"So far, anyway. That calf's burns are going to take a lot longer to heal than your pellet wounds, though." Doctor Bart ripped off his rubber gloves and tossed them into the trash.

Walden slipped off the table and shrugged into his flannel shirt. "When are you coming to visit me, Nurse Nellie? You need to return my basket so I can make my copay for today."

Nellie glanced quickly at Doctor Bart, who was washing his hands. He appeared to deliberately open the water faucet full bore so the water splashed loudly in the stainless steel sink.

"I'll bring the basket here tomorrow," she replied. "You can pick it up next time you're in the area. I forgot to bring it to work with me today."

"S-u-r-e you did."

Nellie bit her lip. She stole another look at Metcalf. She didn't want to marry Doctor Bart, but she didn't want him to get a wrong impression about her, either. She wasn't the kind of woman who slept around.

"Don't worry about the Doc, Nurse Nellie. Why should he care? You already told me he's not your boyfriend."

Metcalf wiped his hands with a paper towel. He was smiling, but Nellie could tell it was a forced smile. She was so angry with Walden she could have filled him full of birdshot herself. Detestable ass! Who did he think he was, coming into this small town and upsetting everyone? If only there was something she could do to take him down a peg! Give him a much-needed attitude adjustment.

Well, there was one surefire way to make a man like Walden reverse course and disappear out of her life forever. When she was fifteen she dubbed this technique the 'nuclear method.' She had utilized the nuclear method many times over the years to disburse unwanted suitors and it had never failed her yet.

She pulled herself up to her full five-feet, eleven-inches, adopting as rigid a pose as possible. "Did you know?" she challenged him. "My mother's the local minister. I'm the minister's daughter."

"No kidding?" Walden replied, completely unfazed. He continued to button his shirt. "What a coincidence! My father's an Episcopal priest."

CHAPTER 19

Enlightened Decisions

"Jay-sus, Nellie—wake up! Yer lettin' 'im peg ya ta death," Leland Gorse cried. "Ya ain't payin' attention at-tall." The agitated woodchopper was standing next to the rickety old card table, observing Nellie and John Woods play. Since he was to take on the winner, he preferred to play Nellie for the Tuesday cribbage championship rather than his old buddy John.

Nellie shook herself back to the present. She glanced down at the hand she had dealt herself and then at the cribbage board. Good grief! She was certainly falling behind. She would have to pay more attention going forward. She hated losing at anything, but especially at cards.

John Woods, the lanky First Selectman, shifted his long legs beneath the squat table. He leaned back in his chair, offering her a sophic smile. "Pay him no mind—he's always this way." He carelessly tossed a card onto the table in front of him. "Eleven," he said, beginning the hand.

"C'mon, John! Thet ain't fair," Leland declared, hotly. He whipped out a blue bandanna and began mopping the sweat from his brow. "Yer takin' advantage o' her."

"Settle down, Leland. You know the rules we play by."

"I'm sorry—what?" said Nellie, who wasn't exactly sure what the two were talking about.

"House rules at Gilpin's allow for an ace to be worth either one or eleven points," the selectman explained, "as long as the value remains the same throughout the playing and scoring."

Nellie glanced down at the table. She hadn't even registered he had played the ace of spades. "What does the American Cribbage Congress have to say about that?"

John Wood shrugged. "Never asked."

Nellie reviewed her cards again, frowning thoughtfully. His unexpected lead had confused her. She wondered what else the house rules encompassed, in addition to shape-shifting aces. "Sixteen," she said, playing the five of diamonds.

"Twenty-two," John Woods responded, laying down the six of clubs.

Leland moved around in back of Nellie. He peered anxiously over her shoulder at her hand.

Nellie reviewed her cards. "I'm afraid that's a Go," she said, sighing. "All I have left are face cards."

John Woods smiled mysteriously and produced the four of spades. "Twenty-six for three," he said, pegging the three-point run. He laid down the three of hearts. "And twenty-nine for four," he continued, moving his peg ahead four more slots. He then played his final card, which was the two of clubs. "And thirty-one for seven."

"Seven! How did you get seven?" challenged Nellie, unable to follow his scoring.

"The five-point run plus two more for last card and the Go." Woods jubilantly skipped his peg up the cribbage board. "And … that puts me out."

Nellie groaned. He had pegged fourteen points on her! She tossed the rest of her cards onto the table in disgust.

John Woods leaned forward, a satisfied expression smoothing out the wrinkles on his long, weathered face. "You're next, Leland."

"By Gawd, John, 'tweren't fair," Leland vowed, almost hopping up and down with agitation. "Nellie ain't up ta speed on our rules, yit. She's still green."

"Either sit down and play or shut up, Leland. Take your pick."

Nellie rose and offered her seat to Trudy's father, who grudgingly accepted the cane-seated chair. She moved over to the wooden bench by the picture window and plopped down onto the long cushion. She leaned back against the solid wood and gazed at the cozy fire in the corner woodstove, which was keeping the front of Gilpin's General Store toasty warm. The nook in which she was sitting had been the designated spot for the Old Farts to congregate since the place was first built a hundred years ago. Nellie enjoyed this rare moment alone in the usually busy nook. The clock over the register had chimed four o'clock about half an hour ago sending most of the men scurrying off to their early suppers. Only Leland and John Woods remained. The Old Farts had graciously invited her to join them this Tuesday, mostly because they could beat her at cards, she suspected now.

The fall rains had commenced and Nellie, suddenly feeling the chilly dampness, moved down the bench closer to the woodstove. Ralph Gilpin, Gray's grandfather, sidled up to her, his rubber soled shoes squeaking on the humid wooden floor. He wiped his hands on his apron. "Kin I git ya somethin', Nellie?"

"No thanks, Mr. Gilpin, I need to head home soon."

Nevertheless Nellie remained staring into the flames for another ten minutes. She turned over in her mind her latest dilemma, which was not the loss of the cribbage game but was rather an ethical dilemma. Metcalf had told her over the weekend he had been unable to unearth any other information about the identity of her birth father, beyond the fact that her male parent was a 'real' person and not an anonymous sperm donor; however, during the course of their conversation, Doctor Bart had also informed Nellie that, according to Aunt Jane anyway, her mother had always kept a personal journal. Aunt Jane, who steadfastly refused to reveal any further information, suggested Nellie look for clues to her paternity in Maggie's private diaries.

"I'm not telling you this because I think you should take Mom's advice," Metcalf had stated, carefully. "That's an ethical dilemma you'll have to wrestle with yourself. I'm telling you because I said I would pass the information on to you."

"But do you think I should read Maggie's journals? Assuming I find them, of course."

"Sorry, Nellie—only you can answer that question. I can't tell you what's right for you. That said, however, I can imagine if I was in your situation I might be tempted to read them, certainly."

"Oh, don't even try and pretend you would read Aunt Jane's journals, Metcalf, because I know you wouldn't."

"Well, maybe not," he admitted. "But it doesn't necessarily follow that a breach of privacy is never warranted."

Nellie had been wrestling with the issue ever since. Should she read her mother's personal diaries? Or should she not? She had found the journals—having so far convinced herself at least looking for the diaries was not a breach of privacy. The 8½ by 11 notebooks were stashed in chronological order in the bottom drawer of Maggie's desk. They were all neatly marked #1 through #18, and dated from August of 1987, five years before Nellie was born, with the last entry penned on day of the Corn Shop Museum opening, three days before Uncle Peter died.

As she held Journal #6 in her hand—the journal leading up to her birth—she had all she could do to stop herself from opening the red cover and immediately searching out the entries around the time of her conception. The answer to her parentage could be hers in a matter of moments. Everything she had wondered, everything she had wanted to know might be revealed in black and white.

Her hand trembled. She fingered the red cardboard cover lovingly. The journal held the secret to her father. Her father! Perhaps even grandparents!

"Ya waitin' to play cribbage, Nellie?" Gray asked, interrupting her from her reflections. He slipped out of his wet raincoat and draped it over a chair by the fire. He had just returned from class at Thomas College in Waterville.

Nellie started. "Ah, no, I'm out already. Leland is playing John Woods for the championship." She automatically adjusted her ponytail.

"No surprise theah."

"Sorry I can't stay and chat, Gray, but I'm headed for home."

"No problem. I gotta work, anyway."

"See you at the Harvest Supper this Saturday?"

"Yeah, I got the night off."

"Not me. I'm waiting tables, as usual. But it's always a lot of fun." Nellie took her raincoat from the brass hook and slipped into the yellow slicker.

"Hey, did thet old guy evah find ya? Shaap-lookin' dude? He come in heah a coupla weeks ago. I been meanin' ta ask ya. I told him thet yer Ma was gone off but thet you was ta home."

"Do you mean Julian Mills?"

Gray shrugged. "Don't know. Didn't know the dude."

"Tall? Distinguished looking? White teeth?" Nellie cringed as she mentioned the 'white teeth,' but she knew that little detail was something Gray would have latched onto.

"Yep, thet's the guy."

"He found me, thanks." As Nellie pushed her way through the exit door she congratulated herself on not inviting Gray to join them for dinner tomorrow night. Imagine, recognizing the world famous author Julian Mills only for the whiteness of his teeth!

Nellie elected to wear her little black dress again to entertain Julian Mills. This time, however, she put her hair up in an elegant bun and carefully selected some sophisticated accessories, including a gold necklace and matching gold earrings.

She had decided to bake a ham for dinner, having found a locally-smoked shoulder in her mother's freezer. Accompanying the ham would be squash from the garden, baked potato, and some of Wendell's Brussels sprouts. She had attempted her first pie for dessert, blackberry, after discovering ten quarts of blackberries in the freezer. Aunt Hannah had given Nellie a recipe for both the filling and the crust. It was a simple dinner, certainly. But to Nellie, who rarely cooked the task of pulling everything together on time seemed almost monumental. She was nervous and she knew it.

She had just returned to the kitchen after setting the pie in the shed to cool, when she heard a knock on the outer door. It was Julian Mills, of course. Metcalf would have let himself in. Nellie kicked herself for not asking Doctor Bart to arrive half an hour earlier. Why was he always late! She checked her face and teeth in the mirror and, finding no obvious flaws, went out to greet the author.

Nellie welcomed Julian Mills into the shed, where he gave her a fatherly kiss on the cheek and an autographed copy of his newest book. Pleased, Nellie invited him into the kitchen. She proudly stood the book up on end on the stenciled chiffonier so visitors to the house would be sure to see it. Rather than give Doctor Mills a tour of the place, which wasn't much, after all, she offered him a glass of wine. Alcohol was rarely imbibed in Sovereign but Nellie hadn't missed it. Tonight, however, was a special occasion. When he accepted, she poured them both a glass of White Zinfandel. "Cheers," she said, lifting her glass.

The two clinked glasses. Julian Mills took a sip. "Very nice," he pronounced, to Nellie's relief. She had already discovered how difficult it was to pair smoked ham with wine and had settled on the Zinfandel mostly because she was fond of it herself.

Julian Mills set his wine glass on the table. He pulled his car keys from his jacket pocket and placed them on the chiffonier next to the book. "Do you mind? The rental tag is rather cumbersome."

"Please, make yourself at home. I've got some hors d'oeuvres in the living room, if you'd like?"

"Sounds lovely, Nellie."

She saw him glance at his reflection in the mirror. 'Vanity, thy name is man,' she thought smugly to herself, perhaps not recalling how often she and her mother had availed themselves of the very same mirror.

Julian Mills followed her into the living room, where Nellie had placed the hors d'oeuvres and fancy cocktail napkins on the coffee table, along with a small bouquet of fall wildflowers. She had put together a simple hors d'oeuvre plate of raw veggies from Maggie's garden, combined with crackers and cheese. The author glanced around the room and, without waiting for an invitation, settled himself into Uncle Peter's antediluvian armchair.

Nellie seated herself on the edge of the couch, being careful to keep her knees together. "I'm sorry, I guess Doctor Bart is running late," she apologized. She had told him when she had invited him that an old family friend would be joining them. "He probably had an emergency at the clinic."

"I thought you said your clinic was only open on Fridays and Saturdays?"

"Doctor Bart works at the medical clinic in Unity full-time, too."

"Busy man," said Julian Mills. He placed his glass of wine on the coffee table and leaned forward to help himself to a cracker and some soft cheese.

"That cheese comes from one of our neighbors," Nellie said, feeling proud of her agricultural community. "Scotch Broom Acres. Trudy makes the best butter in Maine, too."

"How nice." Doctor Mills glanced around the living room, taking in every little detail. "And where's your mother this evening?"

Nellie had decided the tack she was going to take discussing Maggie with him. She would admit her mother was away for a prolonged period—since Julian Mills seemed to be staying in town for a while and Maggie's absence would be noted—but she would not give any explanation as to where her mother had gone or why. "She's away at a spiritual retreat—no phones, no internet. She'll be sorry to have missed you, I'm sure."

He offered up a maddeningly mysterious smile, but said nothing. Nellie made several attempts at erudite conversation, but found it was much more difficult conversing with Julian Mills than she had expected. After twenty minutes of floundering she ditched her hope of having a deep philosophical discussion with him—at least for this evening—and began to worry instead whether she would be able to make it through dinner without embarrassing herself. His penetrating discernment and pointed questions regarding herself and her mother made her feel as though everything she did and everything she said was on display. What on earth was keeping Metcalf?

Suddenly, a conversational course occurred to her. "Did you marry my mother?" she blurted out.

Julian Mills, who was taking a sip of wine, snorted the liquor back into his glass. Some of the rose-colored beverage spilled down the front of his white dinner jacket.

Appalled, Nellie leaped up. "I'm so sorry! Let me get something for that." She rushed into the kitchen, wetted a dishcloth, and returned to the living room, only to find he had sopped up the wine with his cocktail napkin. She held out the dishcloth to him, but he declined.

"Thank you, I'm fine," he said. He blew his nose, crumpled up the napkin and laid it on the coffee table with disdain. "I'm not sure I understood your question, however."

She dropped the dishcloth onto the floor and kicked it under the couch. "What I meant to say, was …" she continued, smoothing her dress beneath her as she reclaimed her seat, "… was Mother told me one of her old friends from Bangor Seminary had performed the marriage ceremony for her and Uncle Peter. I was just wondering if that was you?"

"Ah!" He sat back in the recliner looking extremely satisfied. "So? She finally put old Peter out of his misery, did she?"

There was a note of sarcasm to his voice Nellie found disturbing. Was Julian Mills denigrating Uncle Peter for his steadfast devotion to her mother? What kind of spiritual guru impugned unconditional love? Wasn't unconditional love one of the foundation stones of Christianity?

But then, hadn't she herself once made fun of Uncle Peter's puppy dog-like devotion to her mother? And weren't spiritual gurus human, after all?

Nellie decided to let his innuendo pass without comment. "They were married in the spring," she replied. "I wasn't present; I was in Nicaragua." She briefly outlined her job with Clean World Water.

While Nellie was talking, Doctor Mills leaned forward with obvious interest. "You don't make Sovereign your home, then?" he asked, taking a bite of his cracker and cheese.

She shook her head. "I'm just house-sitting now while Maggie's away. There's no central heating and ..." Nellie broke off. She had been about to say, "And the water pipes might freeze if Mother doesn't come home soon." But she certainly didn't want to go there.

Julian Mills acutely picked up on her hesitation. "And?"

"And … I haven't lived here since I was in eighth grade," she concluded the sentence lamely. "I went to Hathorne Prep for high school and graduated from Columbia in May." Nellie herself took a sip of wine, feeling she had made a laudable recovery.

"My, my!" he pronounced, with satisfaction. "Hathorne Prep and Columbia, eh? But … anyone can see you don't belong in

Sovereign, Nellie. You possess natural gifts and abilities that are going to take you far in this world. That is, if you continue to make enlightened decisions. You've played it smart so far by spending as little time as possible here. Knowing your mother as I do, I'm sure the decision to go to a private prep school was your own. I congratulate you on your perspicacity."

Now, had Julian Mills insinuated Nellie belonged in Sovereign, she would have thrown that insinuation right back in his teeth. But to be told she did not belong here somehow irritated her even more. Nellie bristled and felt her self-confidence return. "As a matter of fact, I wish now I had spent more time in Sovereign," she replied, coolly. "They're all very good to me here, inviting me to dinner, beating me at cards, letting me sing during church service even when no one else is singing, taking me out lighting deer. In fact …" she broke off, suddenly hearing the bitchy tone of her voice. Where had that woman come from? That Nellie hadn't surfaced since the first week she had been home!

"I'm sorry; I don't know what came over me," she apologized. She anxiously smoothed away an imaginary wrinkle on the skirt of her little black dress.

Julian Mills' piercing hazel eyes kindled with ready-made compassion. "Say no more. I empathize with you completely. We all have times when our tongues run away with themselves. Tell me, Nellie, what are your plans for the future?"

The dreaded question! What *was* she going to do when Maggie returned? If there was an enlightened decision lurking nearby Nellie certainly couldn't see it yet.

CHAPTER 20
"He's Not My Boyfriend"

Fortunately, a rap on the kitchen door announced Metcalf's arrival, relieving Nellie from having to answer Julian Mills' question about her future. She hopped up. He rose also out of courtesy. When he got up, the springs in Uncle Peter's armchair emitted a loud *poing*, further adding to Nellie's embarrassment.

"That's Doctor Bart at the door," she said. "I'll be right back." She disappeared quickly around the corner, and heard a reciprocating *poing* as he reclaimed his seat.

Metcalf was whistling when Nellie entered the kitchen. He smiled at her, and tossed his cap onto the oak chiffonier. "You look good enough to eat. And I'm a hungry man!"

"Where have you been?" she whispered, coming around the table next to him so Julian Mills wouldn't overhear their conversation. She could smell the clean, refreshing scent of his soap. For some reason, much to her dismay, she felt herself near tears. The evening was so not going as she had hoped! She wanted to creep into the comfort of his arms and hide until the author had departed, leaving just the two of them. Why had she invited Julian Mills to dinner in the first place?

Metcalf noticed her dismay. "I had an emergency at work," he said. "Didn't you get my text?"

Her phone was laying on the chiffonier between his hat and Julian Mills' car keys. She moved to the antique commode and checked her messages. "Not until now."

"Sorry. I should have called on the landline. I brought us some sweet cider," he continued hopefully, pointing to the gallon jug of cider he had deposited on the sideboard. "From Maine-ly Apples in Dixmont. Just pressed."

"Thanks, but we're drinking wine. Listen," she begged, "go in there and keep Doctor Mills entertained while I put dinner on the table." She pointed meaningfully toward the living room. "I'll bring you in a glass of wine."

"Cider for me, please."

"Whatever! Just help me out and I'll never ask you for anything else as long as I live, I promise," she added desperately.

Metcalf reached out for her. "What's wrong, Nellie?"

She pulled away from him and wildly turned to check the ham, which was sizzling in the oven, filling the room with a smoky scent. He caught her and gently drew her back, folding her to his chest like a distraught child. "Hey, it's OK. No matter what's happened, it's not the end of the world, is it? What was it Miss Hastings used to say? This too shall pass?"

A sob caught in Nellie's throat. "Yes," she said, tears in her eyes. She relaxed against him. Just for a moment! She would allow herself to take a crumb of comfort—but only for a moment. She snuggled closer.

His arms tightened around her. He rested his cheek against her silken bun. She sighed. Why couldn't life always be this good?

"Ah-hem," Julian Mills coughed politely from the doorway. "I hope I'm not interrupting?"

Nellie jerked back. She attempted to step away from Metcalf, but he stubbornly clung to her hand. Nervously, she made the introductions. He finally released her so he could shake hands with Julian Mills. "The living room," she hissed in Doctor Bart's ear.

Metcalf moved easily toward the other room. "I'm glad to meet you Doctor Mills," he said. "I've read some of your books."

To Nellie's relief, the famous author followed Doctor Bart back into the living room. She hovered close to the open doorway, eavesdropping momentarily on their conversation.

"Naturally."

"I really liked 'The House by the Side of the Road'."

"Am I to presume, then, Doctor Bart, you didn't enjoy my other books?"

Metcalf laughed. "Well, perhaps I didn't enjoy those so much as the first, since I'm afraid I can't remember them."

"Wonderful endorsement. Remind me to pass that along to my publicist."

Oh, good grief! She had better get the dinner on the table as soon as possible.

In fifteen minutes, Nellie called them both back into the kitchen. Julian Mills graciously waited for Nellie to be seated before sitting down. She had initially thought of asking him to offer grace, but a little voice told her to discard that idea. She quickly mumbled a few words of blessing herself. When she looked up, she found the author's eyes boring into her. Did she have something on her face? In her teeth? She wanted to hop up and check herself in the mirror, but was able to restrain herself.

She opened her napkin and folded the cloth square over her lap. She felt her anxiety rising. Why was she so nervous? So what if the dinner was a flop? What did she care?

"Is this your first visit to Sovereign, Doctor Mills?" Metcalf asked, passing the dish of buttery squash across the table to him. "Careful, the bottom's hot."

"Yes, this is my first visit to your lovely town. I never ventured out into the hinterlands when I was here before working on my Doctorate at Bangor Theological Seminary." He helped himself to a small spoonful of the soft orange squash.

"Actually, this isn't my town. I'm from Albion. I just moved to Sovereign this summer. My mother and Maggie are second cousins."

Julian Mills leaned forward, almost rudely examining Metcalf's freckled face and rust-colored curls. "Jane? Jane Metcalf?" he guessed. "Is she your mother?"

"Yes," Doctor Bart replied, surprised. "Metcalf was my mother's maiden name. She's Jane Lawson now. She took my father's name about ten years after they were married. I'm not sure what prompted that change of heart, but it made life much easier for me as a kid. Do you know my mother, Doctor Mills?"

"I met her once or twice," he allowed, picking up his fork. He smiled sardonically, baring his perfect white teeth. Nellie, watching him closely, thought Julian Mills resembled the Cheshire Cat about to swallow himself.

"Funny, she never mentioned you."

"Jane never liked me. Small town prejudice, you know." Julian Mills speared a slice of ham with his fork and lifted it onto his plate.

Doctor Bart drew back in surprise. Nellie could tell he was clearly nettled by the affront to his mother. "Bread, anyone?" she asked, attempting to defuse the awkward moment. She grasped the wicker bread basket and waved it beneath the author's nose. "I baked it myself."

"Thank you, no. I limit my carbohydrates."

"Metcalf?"

Julian Mills' black eyebrows lifted. "Metcalf?"

"It's an old family name," said Doctor Bart, defensively. "I like it."

Good grief! Things were really at a bad pass when Doctor Bart was defending the very name he had always hated!

The pathetic meal limped along. The two men continued to verbally spar and Nellie found herself playing peacekeeper. She began to regret she'd invited Doctor Bart, more for his sake than for her own. In fact, she was beginning to regret she had suggested a dinner party at all. What did she care about impressing Julian Mills, anyway? Wasn't he her mother's friend? If the truth was known, she had enjoyed herself much more at Rebecca and Wendell's little dinner party than she was enjoying herself this evening!

After the main meal Metcalf cleared the table while Nellie cut up the pie for dessert. Unfortunately, the blackberry filling hadn't set. She must not have used the correct amount of corn starch. Since the pie was watery she decided to dish it up at the counter, just in case. She didn't want to drip purple blackberry juice on Doctor Mills in addition to the White Zinfandel.

The bottom crust was soggy, making the fruit pie difficult to plate. "I'm sorry it's such a mess," she said, placing the best looking piece of blackberry pie on the table in front of her guest. "I'm just learning how to cook."

Julian Mills leaned back in his chair. He inspected Nellie's pinched, white face. "My God, what has your mother done to you? Do you realize that's the fifth time you've apologized to me? And I've only been here …what?" He glanced at his watch. "Less than two hours."

Nellie felt defeated and chagrined. "Have I? I'm so sor…" she broke off, realizing she was about to apologize for apologizing too much.

In a flash, Metcalf was standing by her side. "Nellie's just anxious to make a good impression," he said, defensively. He gave her limp right hand a reassuring squeeze. "Although why, I'm not sure."

"Metcalf, don't." She groped for her chair and sat down.

Doctor Bart remained standing. "Perhaps in your world, Doctor Mills, it's amusing to point out one another's foibles. Here in Sovereign, however, we don't enjoy making sport of our neighbors."

"Nicely done, Doctor Bart."

"Coffee or tea?" asked Nellie, feebly.

Somehow or other she made it through the next half hour. At eight o'clock, the author looked at his watch and declared it was time for him to depart. The two men rose up simultaneously. They nodded stiffly to one another. Metcalf stayed where he was while Nellie walked Julian Mills out to the shed. She offered him her hand. "I'd apologize," she said, smiling wryly, "except I'm afraid that would do more harm than good."

"You have nothing to apologize for, Nellie," he assured her, keeping her slim hand within his own slightly longer than was necessary. "I must say that was a very enjoyable—and enlightening—dinner. I only hope I haven't stepped too heavily on your boyfriend's toes."

"He's not my boyfriend," she said. The phrase had become so routine with Nellie it just popped out; however, the moment she said it she wished she could call it back. Her words made it sound as though she was trying to distance herself from Doctor Bart because of his behavior this evening. Instead, she was proud of him for being her champion.

"Frankly, I'm glad to hear you say he's not your boyfriend. I was rather worried you were fond of that chap. The world is a big place, Nellie, and you'd be making a big mistake tying yourself down to one of the local yokels at your tender age. Remember what I said about enlightened decisions."

Immediately, Nellie's back was up. "Any girl in the world would be lucky to have Doctor Bart for a husband," she declared. "He's kind, considerate, thoughtful, and …"

"And boring, am I right? I am right. You don't need to settle for a husband, Nellie. Not with your natural talents and gifts. But, we won't argue the point tonight. May I call again?"

Nellie was completely taken aback. The great Julian Mills wanted to visit again? He must want to see her mother very badly! "Well, I'm not sure when Maggie will be home …?"

"Never mind Maggie—she had her day," he said, somewhat cruelly. "I'd like to get to know *you* better."

What could she say? She wanted to get him out the door as soon as possible. She'd deal with the consequences later. "Sure. Why not?"

He offered her a brief but elegant bow. "Jusqu'à ce que nous nous reverrons, ma belle enfant—until we meet again my beautiful child." He turned on his heel and departed.

When Nellie re-entered the kitchen she found Metcalf slumped back in his chair, one arm resting on the kitchen table. She had never seen him as discomposed as he had been at dinner and suspected he was angry with himself for losing his temper. Why had she placed him in such an awkward position in the first place? Metcalf had wanted to stay home, but naturally he would never refuse her a favor. But … how could she possibly have known the two men wouldn't get along?

He rose up. "I'm sorry, Nellie. Forgive me?" he begged, taking a step toward her.

"Don't be silly, Metcalf. You don't need to apologize for anything—you were only trying to protect me. That man was a perfect ass!"

"Still, there's no excuse for poor manners. I don't know what came over me. He certainly wasn't what I expected him to be. Something about him just rubbed me the wrong way. I can't quite put my finger on it, though."

"Let me help you. How about … he was supercilious, obnoxious, vain, and worst of all, a stuffed shirt. I can't believe he's the author of 'The House by the Side of the Road,' can you?" Nellie began clearing the dirty tea cups from the table.

"Perhaps our expectations were too high?"

"Certainly, if we expected him to have a shred of common courtesy."

"You're too hard on him, Nellie."

"Listen to yourself! You're making apologies for him already. That's so like you, Metcalf. Hand me that teacup, will you? By the time I've got the dishes done up you'll be telling me the whole thing was your fault."

He smiled, and handed her the desired cup and saucer. "Probably it was my fault." He blew out the candles. The black wicks glowed, filling the air with the scent of charcoal.

Nellie added the saucer to the little stack of plates. "See, there you go! And I haven't even started washing up, yet." She carefully added the teacup to the semicircle around the plates. She pulled the dishpan out from under the sink, turned on the hot water tap and squirted some liquid soap into the plastic dishpan. She swished the soap around until the plastic pan was full of fresh-smelling suds, and stopped the water. "Could you get me my apron, please? It's hanging next to the fridge."

Doctor Bart obligingly retrieved Nellie's apron from its hook and brought it over to her at the sink. She raised her sudsy hands and he slipped the granny-style apron over her head. He took her by the elbow and faced her toward the sink so he could tie the apron's bow in back. When he was done, rather than move away, however, he remained standing close behind her, so close Nellie could feel the moist heat from his body. His right hand lingered possessively on her hip. A sensual energy radiated from his taut muscles and her female hormones screamed to life. She made the mistake of turning around to face him, thereby exposing herself to the naked desire in his eyes.

"Nellie …?"

Her arms, of their own volition, slid around his neck. How she ached for him! She pressed her firm breasts against his muscular chest, forcing him to encompass her. She was suddenly aware of a deep-seated longing for him and pressed still closer.

"Oh, my darling," he groaned. "You don't know what you do to me." He kissed her cheeks, her forehead, her temples, her neck. She reveled in his caresses. Lovingly, she ran her fingers through his short red curls, murmuring his name, half swooning. He pulled the pins from her hair, shaking free her silken tresses. He grasped her by the shoulders and tilted her chin, forcing her to look up at him. She trembled, knowing her eyes would betray the aching desire she felt for him. He uttered a triumphant cry and swept her into his arms. He masterfully pushed her back against the iron sink unit, demanding her complete surrender. His mouth sought hers and she responded eagerly to his kisses.

Suddenly, a rush of cool air entered from the shed. She heard a distant cough. "Excuse me for interrupting this Moira moment, but I forgot my car keys."

Julian Mills had returned!

Nellie was so surprised she would have fallen to the battle-scarred floor had not Metcalf held her tight. Still cradling her in his arms, he swung them around so he was the one facing the arrogant intruder. Nellie shivered, feeling as though they had been doused with ice water.

Julian Mills observed Nellie and her disheveled hair with an amused expression on his face. He jingled his keys. "I found them. Don't worry, I'll let myself out." He turned to leave, but paused momentarily in the open doorway. "By the way, Nellie—I thought you said he wasn't your boyfriend?"

CHAPTER 21
Like Ripples in a Pond

The agony of that moment! Nellie felt so ashamed she had hardly dared look Metcalf in the face. The very touch of his fingertips accused her. Every muscle in his body stiffened the moment those awful incriminating words left Julian Mills' lips: "I thought you said he's not your boyfriend?"

After the door had closed, Metcalf, with cold courteousness, set her aside as though she was a mannequin, not a flesh and blood woman. Still shivering, she fumbled to retrieve her hairpins from where he had dropped them onto the kitchen table. Surely, if she could get her hair back under control her life would follow?

"When did you tell him that, Nellie?" Metcalf demanded.

"What?" she mumbled as she gathered up her hair, the hairpins in her mouth. She knew full well what he was referring to, though.

"Was it when you walked him to the door, just now? Did you assure Doctor Mills I wasn't your boyfriend, then?"

She expertly wound her tresses into a bun and attached the bobby pins.

"And not five minutes later you wrapped your arms around my neck and begged me to kiss you?"

"Metcalf … please!"

He ignored her and moved stiffly over to the chiffonier. "What kind of woman are you? If I'm not your boyfriend, what am I? Some kind of temporary paramour? A place-holder until the right man rides into your life on a white horse?"

"Don't say that!"

"Would it have mattered to you at all who I was tonight? Or was I simply the man of the moment—someone who could serve your sexual needs? Perhaps Walden would have served you just as well. Probably better." He retrieved his cap.

His words stung her, but Nellie knew she deserved them. Her soft hazel eyes filled with tears. She held out her hands to him. If only he would take her in his arms again, all would be well!

Doctor Bart ignored her nonverbal pleas. He placed his hat over his rust-red curls—those same curls through which, only minutes before, she had been lovingly running her fingers. He clicked open the door to the shed. "I need some time to think. Goodbye, Nellie."

And then he was gone.

She stumbled to the window, watching him stride down the walk, her entire being aching for him. She closed her eyes and mentally willed him to return—to reach his truck and falter, to feel the pull of her love and come back to her. Instead, he climbed into his vehicle and started the engine. The truck tires ripped up the gravel drive. He was not coming back. She had deeply wounded him, perhaps beyond repair.

She sank down into her mother's rocker, covered her face with her hands, and wept. What must he think of her? A loose woman? A tramp!

Half an hour later she moved to her bed and sobbed herself to sleep. The cat, unconcerned, curled up on the pillow next to her, purring loudly in her ear.

The next morning Nellie arose to a cold, pounding rain. She slipped into her mother's flannel bathrobe and fuzzy slippers and plodded into the chilly kitchen. The rain, thrumming like drum rolls on the tin roof, was oddly reassuring. After she had fed the cat she started a blistering fire in the kitchen woodstove. She searched through the pantry until she located the antique coffee percolator that had once belonged to her great-grandmother. Today, she would drink real perked coffee, not weak drip coffee or herbal tea.

She filled the six-cup coffee pot and set it atop the woodstove. In less than ten minutes the water began to bubble merrily up through the grounds and into the glass perk-top. She moved the pot to the edge of the stovetop so the coffee wouldn't boil over. Soon, the kitchen was filled with the fragrant aroma of fresh-perked coffee. When the coffee was done—and the grounds had settled—Nellie poured herself a cup and curled up in her mother's soft chair by the window. She lingered over the hot coffee, gazing out through the misty sheets of rain. Not one car went by. She felt safe and protected. Somehow she would get through this.

She would talk to him, make Metcalf understand. He would not spurn her—he would listen to her. She knew his love was not of a transitory nature but rather ran deep, like the bottomless spring that fed the pond where they had fished and swum together as children.

But … what would she say to him? That she loved him—even desired him—but didn't necessarily want to marry him?

The wall phone jangled, interrupting her fragile train of thoughts. Her heart leapt, but it was only Rebecca on the other end of the line, checking in before church.

Nellie had forgotten all about church, forgotten the day was even Sunday. How could she possibly go to church today!

She quickly opted for the illness excuse, which sounded lame even to her own ears. Fortunately, her neighbor was possessed of the sensitivity to read between the lines. "Perhaps I should tell them at church you have plans for the day?" Rebecca suggested. "Otherwise, you might end up with unwanted visitors making sure you're OK."

"Good idea, thanks. You won't be lying, either because I do have other plans." Nellie hung up the phone.

Yes, she had plans. Today she would examine her heart, an undertaking that was way past due. She felt like a mortgaged homeowner who has ignored countless late payment notices. But her note had been called last night and she knew she either needed to pay the debt or let the whims of fate foreclose upon her heart.

She didn't need to ask herself if she loved him. Of course she loved him! She had always loved him. Metcalf had always been there for her—the one person in her life upon whom she could always depend. Not her mother, whose work had always claimed the first priority; not her father, who had never cared enough to even show his face; not her friends at Hathorne or her classmates at Columbia. Not her colleagues at Clean World Water, either. There was only one person who had always been there for her, waiting to catch her when she fell or to give her a hand up when she wanted to climb or to applaud her efforts when she attempted something new. And that one person was Doctor Bart.

She smiled to herself, thinking how she had once disliked his given name—Metcalf. When she was young, the name had sounded so funny. But now she couldn't imagine him as an ordinary 'Tom' or 'Dick' or even 'Kyle' or 'Brandon.' No, he was definitely 'Metcalf.'

Yes, she loved him. But that wasn't the question. In Nellie's mind, the question was—did she love him enough to spend the rest of her life with him? Because if she didn't she should put him out of his misery as soon as possible. She should stop leaning on him, as though he was the only tree in the forest. She should stop taking advantage of his kindness, his good nature, and his unconditional love for her.

Still … she was only twenty-two years old! The rest of her life seemed very long and very far way, like the first star in the night sky she had used to wish upon as a child. Her hopes and dreams and aspirations had always been to travel, to go out into the world and make a difference—a small difference, but a difference nonetheless. Would staying in Sovereign with Doctor Bart, helping him—helping others—be enough for her?

Of course, there was also the distressing possibility Metcalf might not want her anymore. Her behavior last night might have shocked him into a wake-up call. The image of her he had always cherished of 'innocent little Nellie' might have dissipated, leaving in its wake the picture of a woman who trampled upon the hearts of others while attempting to meet her own selfish needs and desires.

Nellie shuddered. She tried to shake away the image of a needy, self-centered woman—and failed.

After lunch, the rain let up and Nellie decided to go for a walk to clear her head. She threw on an old yellow slicker from the shed and trudged up the muddy road, hood up over her head. At the top of Lovejoy Hill she instinctively turned toward Henry Trow's house. Her new neighbor was always generous with his time and she had discovered he was a good companion. He was knowledgeable, an excellent listener, funny, and compassionate. It was unfortunate that he'd gotten the reputation of a curmudgeon; however, her plan for introducing him to Aunt Hannah should help mitigate that.

"Never mind about the floor," Mr. Trow said, shooing her into the kitchen. "Go in and get warm by the fire."

Mr. Trow helped her out of her slicker and draped the raincoat over the woodbox to dry. She could see he was in good spirits, despite the rain. Nellie slipped out of her muddy boots and set them on the kitchen rug. Before she knew it she found herself telling him about the dinner disaster, omitting, however, the final embarrassing act in the kitchen.

"What an insufferable ass!" Henry Trow declared, setting a cup of hot tea in front of her. "Inferring Doctor Bart's mother was small-minded just because she hails from rural Maine. Talk about prejudice! I had no idea when you asked me about him, Nellie, that Julian Mills was in the area. I wish you'd invited me to your dinner party, because I would have given him a piece of my mind."

Nellie smiled sadly. "I wish I'd invited you, too. Poor Doctor Bart had a hard time of it. He kept trying to make polite conversation with him but no matter what Metcalf said Doctor Mills twisted his words around."

"I wonder why?"

"I've been racking my brains to figure that out. Probably it's nothing more sinister than the fact that he's an arrogant prig. And then when Doctor Bart finally did stand up to him, because I was apologizing too much …"

"Because what?"

"Because I apologized too much, at least that's what Julian Mills said. Five times in less than two hours."

"He kept track?"

"Apparently so. Quite accurately, too, I believe."

Henry Trow's bushy eyebrows knit angrily together. "The nerve of that braggart! Who is he to sit in judgment on you, I'd like to know? Makes me mad enough to want to dust off my shotgun."

"Mr. Trow!"

He chuckled. "Never you worry, Nellie, I learned my lesson with Mr. Mushroom. Let's just hope I don't run into Julian Mills down at the general store, thought, or I might lob a quart of milk at his head. I hope for everyone's sake he doesn't stick around long. In the meantime, young lady, I think this warrants an epicurean remedy. How about some orange poppy seed tea bread?"

"I'm sorry—what?" Nellie said, turning around in her chair, sure she must have misunderstood him.

But Henry Trow had already hobbled off to the pantry. He soon returned with a glazed loaf of sweet bread on a porcelain cake plate. He dandled the tea bread in front of her eyes. "What do you think of this, eh? Orange poppy seed tea bread."

"You're joking! Where did you get that?"

He moved to the counter, sliced a piece of the moist bread and served it to Nellie on a dessert plate. "I never joke about food. Now, take a bite and tell me this doesn't make you feel better?"

Nellie did as she was bid. She rolled the rich citrus flavor and sweet sugary glaze around on her tongue. "Mmm, this is so not store-bought." She sat her fork down on the plate. "Where did you get this?"

Henry Trow plated up a piece of the tea bread for himself. He regained his seat, the old chair squeaking slightly. He looked smug. "A little fairy baked it for me."

"Not Aunt Hannah!"

He nodded, and helped himself to a bite, extremely pleased with himself.

"But … you don't even know her. How did that happen?"

His blue eyes twinkled. "I was so impressed with those candies you brought me—those Needhams—the next day I drove down to the good doctor's, found his Aunt Hannah, and introduced myself."

"You did not," Nellie cried, shaking her head in disbelief. "And Aunt Hannah never breathed a word about it!"

"When you get to be my age—if you find something you really want—you know better than to wait for it to come to you. You go out and get it before either of you disappears. Remember that, Nellie, because you never know who's going to disappear next from your life."

Nellie remembered only too well how she had taken Uncle Peter for granted. "That's for sure," she said, sadly.

Something about Mr. Trow's advice and the way in which it was offered reminded Nellie of her mother. Suddenly, she could see Maggie in the pulpit as plain as day, her face and hands animated as she exhorted her listeners the very same thing. "My mother did a sermon on that once, on not waiting too long," she mused. "She utilized hummingbirds as a metaphor, because everyone around here keeps track of when the hummingbirds return in the spring. But Mother pointed out it's a lot more difficult to record the day the hummingbirds disappear in the fall. One minute they're here and the next they're gone. Her message was—don't wait too long to tell someone you love them or it might be too late. I wish I'd acted on that advice now."

"Your mother sounds like a pretty smart gal."

"So everyone's been telling me," Nellie replied. She applied herself to the orange poppy seed cake.

"But you're not convinced?"

"I'm a typical Theological Offspring, I think. We see a different side to our clergy parents than they present to their parishioners."

"Don't blame that entirely on the poor minister, Nellie. Most folks don't want their clergy to be human."

Nellie thought a moment. "I suppose that's true."

"Take it from me, when Death comes knocking at your door you want someone by your side who's got backbone enough to face the Grim Reaper. Not only that, but after he's walked out the door with the Love of Your Life you want a soft shoulder to cry on. From everything I've heard, your mother is an excellent minister. I'm looking forward to meeting her."

"I guess I prefer a more grandmotherly shoulder—like Aunt Hannah's."

"You won't get any argument from me on that score. I thought your Aunt Hannah very charming. By the way, Nellie, you never told me how pretty she was! And generous, to boot. I asked her to make me some of those Needhams—told her I'd pay her whatever she wanted for 'em—but she wouldn't take my money. Finally, I got her to agree to trade a fifty-pound bag of sunflower seed for one batch of Needhams, two pies, and the tea bread. Not a bad deal, eh?"

"Keep it up you'll have me convinced getting old isn't such a bad thing!"

"Getting old is as good as one makes it, I guess. I didn't used to believe that. I felt as though all the good things in life were over for me when Gerry died. But lately, well … lately I've been thinking maybe I haven't got to the end of the road just yet. Maybe all I did was turn another corner and there's still a long way to go—and a lot of pie left to eat—before the Grim Reaper makes a return visit."

Nellie was suddenly overcome with feelings of despair. She was happy for Mr. Trow and his new-found enthusiasm for life. Yet she envied him at the same time. Her life seemed so messed up compared to his.

He pushed his empty plate to the side and reached out and clasped her right hand. His blue-veined fist was soft and warm. "Now, tell me—what's really the matter, young lady," he urged, with an encouraging squeeze. "You didn't come here today for the poppy seed tea bread, no matter how much it might help what ails you."

Nellie needed no further encouragement to relieve her troubled heart. In a halting, embarrassed voice, she told Henry Trow how she had denied Doctor Bart was her boyfriend and how Julian Mills had returned to the house, and, when finding them entwined, had thrown her denial back in her face.

"I don't care about what Julian Mills thinks," she continued, wistfully.

"I should hope not," Henry Trow huffed.

"But I am sorry for what I did to Doctor Bart. You should have seen his face. He was terribly hurt. I felt like Peter, denying Jesus three times." Ashamed, she hid her face in her hands.

The old man rose up and hobbled around to the back of her chair. "Nellie, Nellie," he said, placing his arm across her shoulders in a comforting fashion. "I'm not much on Bible study but even I know Jesus forgave Peter, didn't he? The Lord knew Peter didn't mean it."

"Metcalf might forgive me but he'll never forget," she sobbed.

Henry Trow let her cry for a minute or two, and then plucked a paper napkin from the holder in the center of the table. "All done now?" he asked. When she nodded, sniveling, he handed her the napkin. "Dry your eyes—that's a good girl."

Nellie obediently wiped her eyes and blew her nose.

"You ought to know, and if you don't know by now you should, that life doesn't hang in the balance of one stupid thing we do or say, no matter what soap operas and trashy novels would have you believe. Mark my words; you'll get another chance to tell that young man how you feel about him."

She anxiously twisted the paper napkin. "How can you be so sure?"

"Because I've been around the block once or twice myself. Here—give me that thing, will you?" Henry Trow relieved her of the soiled napkin and tossed it into the trash. "But … I don't suppose you can take my word for it just because I've kicked around longer than you have, can you? I remember when my daughter was your age. She thought I was the dumbest thing on two legs. But I got a lot smarter when she started having kids of her own." He took Nellie's hand. "Come with me, I want to show you something."

Nellie meekly allowed her neighbor to lead her out of the kitchen, plodding along in her stocking feet a half-pace behind his shuffling steps. "You know I've been working on the old place," he continued, as they passed through the foyer. "I want to show you what I uncovered in the front parlor." He threw open the white painted door that led to the old-fashioned drawing room. "Watch where you walk," he cautioned, ushering her inside.

Laid down on the parlor floor was a thick plastic floor covering, overspread with white dust and shreds of recently-removed wallpaper. A stepladder stood in one corner and several wallpaper removal tools rested on its shelf. The original horse-hair plaster walls—exposed for the first time in perhaps a hundred years—jumped out, thanks to a base coat of bright yellow paint upon which some talented hand had drawn a lively, colorful mural. The folk art mural sprawled over the parlor walls, leaping across the four windows—two on the south wall and two on the west—as though each leaded-glass span was as transient as time.

Amazed, Nellie disregarded the mess and dirt and walked into the middle of the room so she could examine the mural in its entirety. "Oh-my-God! I've never seen anything like this," she said, turning to net a 360° view. "It's beyond beautiful! How did you discover it?"

"The old wallpaper was stained pretty bad so I thought I'd replace it. The other day I started peeling back the paper, and once I got going I couldn't stop. Six layers of wallpaper later—there was the mural."

Nellie's gaze alighted upon a little white church centered between the two western windows. "There's our church," she cried. "I'd recognize it anywhere." She stepped closer. "I love the way the artist painted the building; it's so fluid-looking, leaning into the wind with the trees, as though the church was part of the natural world."

"In their day, religion was part of the natural world," replied the former history teacher.

Nellie's gaze rose to where, six inches below the white ceiling, a pattern of hearts repeated itself, encircling the room like a necklace. "Such gorgeous stencils, too."

"Those were probably done by Moses Eaton. The hearts signify a new bride and groom. Perhaps the painted parlor was a gift from William Lovejoy to his bride. William was the second son of the second generation, the man who built this place."

"Very romantic! Did Moses Eaton paint the mural, too?"

"We don't think so. Hannah has been helping me with my research," he clarified, seeing the puzzled expression on Nellie's face. "She's a member of the historical society so I went to her first."

"Naturally," said Nellie, smiling.

"Hannah and I did some research and we think the mural was probably done by an interesting fellow by the name of Rufus Porter. Porter painted several murals similar to this in Sebec. He was quite a character, an inventor and publisher—he started Scientific American magazine—as well as being an artist. Rufus Porter was known to throw in with Eaton occasionally, so it's not unusual to see their artwork together. He often included local landmarks in his murals—like your church there—to keep his customers happy. Remember, William Lovejoy's father was the first minister of the church. But Porter also added some of the unusual things he'd seen in his wanderings, like those palm trees. Apparently, he was quite taken with Hawaii."

"He went to Hawaii?"

"Among other places. I told you he was an interesting fellow. Still, he must have stopped at home occasionally because he and his poor wife had ten children. But … I didn't bring you in here just to see the mural, Nellie."

"No?"

"I want you to absorb it, to 'soak it up,' as I used to tell my history students. Start back over there and tell me what you see." He directed her attention to the east wall, where they had entered the room.

Nellie moved closer to the designated starting point. "A brick house? Why, it's this place! I didn't recognize the old place at first without the attached shed and barn. And there's the Lovejoy family, all dressed up in their Sunday best. Look, here comes a little boy running out of the house, trying to catch up with the wagon."

He moved her gaze over to the north wall. "And over here?"

"That's Wendell's house—I'd know it anywhere. Do you suppose those are his ancestors walking down the road?"

"It's a good bet. Can you guess where everyone's going?"

"Church? I see a lot of little black books."

"Yep, those are most likely their New Testaments; everyone had one in the nineteenth century." He pivoted Nellie a quarter-turn so she was back looking at the west wall, facing the white church again. "And now … observe closely this time. Really step into the scene. Spot anything interesting?"

Nellie's eyes narrowed. "Why, some figures are going into the church through the side door and then they're coming out the front door. They're getting into their buggy—it looks like the same buggy. Yes, here's the little boy." She eagerly moved to the south wall following the progress of the folk art figures in the buggy. "They're going home!"

Henry Trow beamed at her. "That's right. The mural is a continuous circle. Rufus Porter knew—and you'll find out as you get older—life doesn't flow forward from us in a straight line from birth to death, but rather expands like the ripples you see in a pond when you toss in a stone. When I was a young man, I thought if I missed a chance at something, that chance was gone for good. But as I matured I came to see that life circles back onto itself. What I let slip away from me once—or even twice, like Gerry, my wife—kept circling around again until I finally smartened up enough to grasp hold of what I loved with both hands. Your young man might be feeling hurt. He might even be a little angry with you. But if he truly loves you, he'll keep coming around again. And if you truly love *him*, someday you'll wake up, just like I did with Gerry, and pull him out of the pond."

"But what if I don't pull him out of the pond?" Nellie persisted. "What happens then?"

"He'll just keep passing by and no harm done."

"That doesn't seem very fair to him! What if he wants a wife?"

"Nellie, if a man wants a wife, he'll find himself a wife. But if a man wants a particular woman for his wife … well, then, that's a different story altogether. In that case, he'll wait for her—no matter how long it takes or how many turns around the pond he has to take. Mark my words—he'll wait."

CHAPTER 22
"And Now We Roam in Sovereign Woods"

Mr. Trow's homespun wisdom helped calm Nellie's nerves and ease her concerns about her relationship with Metcalf. She thought his words to the wise were probably as efficacious as Grandmother Metcalf's Rose and Valerian Root Restorative, and certainly better than the sweet woodruff tonic her mother forced her to drink every May as a spring tonic. As a result, she returned home feeling calmer, more balanced, and even mildly happy. The cat was eager to see her, and several messages from her new friends were on the answering machine, letting her know she'd been missed at church. During the first week that Nellie had been home she had changed the machine's outgoing message, now informing callers Maggie was unavailable for an extended period of time, in order to forestall repeated calls from her mother's friends wondering why Maggie wasn't getting back to them. Since her second or third week home, all the messages left on the old-fashioned electronic device had been for her. It was good to be missed, good to be a member of a community, as Metcalf had once pointed out.

Nellie's equilibrium continued into the following week, despite the fact that the fall rains held the sunshine and blue sky at bay. Oddly enough, she found the gray days soothing and refreshing. She luxuriated in the sound of rain on the old tin roof and delighted in the sight of the misty wraiths of fog billowing across the hayfield like playful ghosts. She set up a card table next to the toasty woodstove in the living room and applied herself to her first official quilt, a baby quilt she was sewing for Rebecca's shower the first weekend in November. For the pint-sized quilt Nellie had selected a soft mix of yellows, blues, pinks, and greens, all tied in together by a white satin background. The quilt was the Seven Sisters pattern, a lovely hexagon and star design popular during the late nineteenth century. Aunt

Hannah had given her much of the material for the quilt and also the cardboard templates for the quilt's oddly-shaped triangular pieces. Although Nellie had nearly a month before the baby shower, she knew she needed to work faithfully on the project since the pattern required a lot of fussy cutting, a skill she needed to master.

Every afternoon, to clear her head and stretch her legs, Nellie took a walk. On Monday she donned her yellow slicker and strolled over the myriad of paths her mother had mowed through the abandoned hayfield during the summer. She paused atop the hill behind the schoolhouse to admire the view to the west, and momentarily felt an urge to doff her clothes and run down the hill as free as the wind, like Maggie did every August. But this rare spark of rebelliousness was extinguished immediately when she considered what Ryan MacDonald might think of her if he was to drive by and see her streaking naked through the field. Last year, Ryan had good-naturedly offered to help her mother turn her annual naked goldenrod run into a fundraiser, but that event had been cancelled this year because of Uncle Peter's death.

Nellie abandoned the mown paths and waded through the tall, sodden puckerbrush to the spring-fed pond on the edge of the field where the Lovejoy's cows had lounged in summer and where Metcalf had taught her to swim. She startled a gaggle of Canada geese on the pond, which set to with harsh honking and flapping of wings, trying to scare her away. But Nellie held her ground and eventually the geese gave up, surrendering the waterway to her and to a pair of quiet, peaceful mallards who sailed off into the tall reeds and peered at her through the dying yellowed foliage. By her third trip to the pond the mallards seemed to accept her right to be there, no longer bothering to hide themselves in the reeds.

During her daily perambulations Nellie's heart would swell with love and gratitude for the natural world around her, for her missing mother, for Metcalf, for her newly-acquired friends in Sovereign, and even for herself. She was happy to be alive, happy to take delight in little things, such as a walk in the woods, the friendship of a pair of mallards, a bountiful garden, a pretty table and a wildflower bouquet for the table. She felt as though she had been stripped of her prior delusions about life, leaving her core exposed and open to Truth. Rather than feel vulnerable, however, she felt relieved of a great burden. She was lighter, more buoyant of spirit, grateful to shed the unnecessary baggage the material world had stealthily imposed upon her over the years without her consent.

On Tuesday, Nellie received her mother's credit card bill, which revealed what she had expected: her mother had purchased a plane ticket for France; had made large cash withdrawals in Paris; and travelled by a variety of trains to Le Puy, where her credit card charges ended. Nellie was more certain than ever after reviewing the bill, which included the purchase of hiking gear, that Maggie was en route to Santiago de Compostela. As promised, she immediately contacted Leland Gorse and gave him the news.

"She ain't comin' back anytime soon, then?"

"I honestly don't know," Nellie admitted. "But I don't think so, no."

Nellie, after having walked in her mother's shoes for the past two months, had gained a much greater appreciation for Maggie. Any lingering resentment she felt toward her mother had dissipated, leaving in its place a feeling of pride that her fifty-eight-year-old mother had dared to undertake such a grueling pilgrimage on her own, especially after just having overcome breast cancer and losing her husband.

On Wednesday, Nellie decided to treat herself to lunch at Ma Jean's Restaurant. It was about a thirty minute hike through the woods out to the Bangor Road. She arrived at the restaurant around one o'clock, knowing the noon lunch rush would have cleared out by then. She was greeted by an unusually friendly Sarah Louise, who instructed her to sit where she liked.

Nellie slipped into a vacant booth and checked out the specials on the blackboard. She decided to order the mushroom quiche. Ma Jean's, under the direction of Rebecca and Maude Gilpin, was noted for using local ingredients and Nellie was curious to see whether or not Jessica Gould, the current chef, was continuing this tradition.

"You goin' to the Harvest Supper Saturday night?" Sarah Louise asked, as she settled the quiche in front of Nellie. "Careful, that top plate's hot."

"Yes, I'm waiting tables," Nellie replied, putting a fork into the fragrant, cheesy quiche and releasing a burst of woodsy-scented steam.

"Me too. I told Aunt Shirley I'd help out."

Nellie smiled at the other girl. "Looks like we'll be working together, then." She took a small bite of quiche. "This is yummy. Where do you get your mushrooms?"

"From the mushroom guy." Sarah Louise set the edge of her tray upon the table and rested her plump bare forearms against it. "You know him?"

"Do you mean Walden?"

The waitress giggled. "Yeah, funny name, huh? He brings us in mushrooms every couple of days. Sometimes he brings me flowers, too. He's cute, ain't he?"

"Do you think so?" Nellie took another bite, attempting to appear disinterested. She didn't want to get into a discussion about Walden's physical attractions.

"I think he's wicked hot. Oh, I suppose he's not good enough for you, Nellie, with your fancy schooling 'n all. But I don't care 'bout that kind of thing. They can be dumb as a board for all I care."

Nellie thought Walden was hardly the board in that duo, but said nothing. She applied herself to the quiche.

"I like macho men," Sarah Louise continued. She giggled self-consciously. "They seem to like me, too."

Nellie shuddered, recalling how not so long ago she, too, had thought macho-manliness an important quality for a mate. Thank God she had woken up!

"Besides," Sarah Louise continued, lifting up her tray, "he wouldn't waste time on you. Everyone knows you're Doctor Bart's girlfriend."

Out of sheer habit, Nellie was about to deny she and Metcalf were a couple. Instead, she took a sip of water and changed the subject.

On Thursday, Nellie hazarded a long-promised visit to the Millett Rock, which was only a few hundred yards from the Nutt place where Walden lived. She'd been avoiding the Millett Rock because she'd been avoiding Walden. But in thinking it over she realized she was giving someone she cared little about power to affect her life, and so she set out after lunch down the misty woods road.

A warm rain was lightly falling. The sound of the rain was amplified as it dripped slowly through the leaves of the trees. Nellie hiked carefully through the slippery forest, watching her step along the woods road. When she reached the ancient, weathered boulder, she paused and glanced around. Sure enough, she spied Walden coming toward her.

Nellie flipped around and began to retrace her steps. Behind her, she could hear him calling out for her to stop. She hesitated, and decided to face him. She turned around and waited for him to get close enough so they could talk without yelling over the steady rain. "What do you want?" she said, forgoing a greeting.

"I was hoping you were on your way to visit me…?"

"Hardly. I just wanted to climb the Millett Rock."

He turned his broad shoulders toward the boulder. "Let's go—I'll give you a hand up."

"Thanks, but I'll come back another time." She certainly didn't want to get in a situation of physical contact with Walden.

"Aw, don't be that way, Nurse Nellie. Look, I'm sorry if I've offended you."

His head was bare and she could see he was beginning to get wet. "This is hardly the time to talk, is it?"

"Can't we start over?" he persisted, dashing the rainwater from his forehead with his hand. "Because I have a feeling when someone gets to know you—you can be fairly decent company."

She made a dismissive noise. "I can only imagine what your idea of good company is." She pictured in her mind three or four women like Sarah Louise fawning over Walden's burly chest.

Immediately he shot back. "My idea of good company is the company of clever, well-informed people, who have a great deal of conversation. That's what I call good company. Oh, wait. That's not good company—that's the best."

Nellie was surprised by his very accurate quote from Jane Austen's "Persuasion," which was one of her favorite novels. "Oh-my-God. Where did you learn that?"

"Waterford Academy. One of my English teachers doted on Jane Austen. She had a thing for Emily Dickinson, too."

"I knew it!"

"Knew Mrs. Brown was a Janeite?" He moved so he was under the thicker cover of a nearby spruce tree.

"I knew you had a prep school education."

"Yeah, and look where that's gotten me." His face became glum and he unconsciously shifted his weight from foot to foot. "An outcast who wanders the Maine woods looking for 'shrooms."

"Don't let me hold you up."

"See, there you go again. I wonder if you realize how snotty you sound? What's the use of an expensive private education if you can't treat a guy with respect?"

The truth of Walden's words hit home and Nellie immediately felt ashamed of herself. "I'm sorry; we did get off on the wrong foot." She held out her right hand. "Truce?"

Gratified, he stepped forward and took her hand. "Truce." As if on cue, the rain stopped, the clouds parted, and a ray of sun shone down through the trees. He looked up and chuckled. "Looks like someone's trying to send us a message!"

Nellie quickly withdrew her hand. "I'm not so sure about that."

"What? You don't believe in signs?"

"No, I'm afraid not."

"What kind of Theological Offspring are you?"

"The pretty normal kind, I'd say."

"Speaking of messages," he continued, in a casual tone of voice that belied deeper emotion. "I got yours about the old gent and went to see him yesterday. Just so you don't think I'm completely without merit."

"Mr. Trow! Why?"

"I had a dark night of the soul; realized my attitude was as much responsible for the pellets in my shoulder as he was. The old gent was a brick. Invited me in and apologized profusely. He even offered to help me, not just with money, either. You were right—I think he felt worse about the shooting than I did." He reached up and lightly fingered his wound.

"How's your shoulder now?"

Immediately, his insouciance vanished. His eyes flashed. "Do you care?" he challenged.

"I …"

"Listen, Nellie, don't BS me, OK? If you want to be kind to a guy, you tell him the truth, even if he doesn't want to hear it."

Nellie remained silent, unsure what she should say.

"You know, the first time I saw you I thought we might be kindred souls." His blue eyes bored into hers. "You were walking up the Cross Road and I spotted you from the woods behind the old gent's house. I followed you—you didn't know, did you? I followed you up the hill watching you take in every little detail, not just blindly pass stuff by like most people do. And then, when I came onto you that Sunday morning in the woods and caught you sniffing the painted bolete—I thought you were the most beautiful thing I'd ever seen, with your long blonde hair falling over your shoulder and your innocent schoolgirl looks. Everything about you was perfect. Well, maybe not that sweater."

Nellie, who had been about to cut short what appeared to be a romantic declaration from Walden burst out laughing. "Oh, that awful sweater! It's not mine—it's my mother's."

"Sure it is."

"Walden, I …"

"My name is Nick—Nick Faulkner."

"Nick, then, I …"

"Did you ever read Emily Dickinson's poem about the loaded gun?" he hurried on, not giving Nellie a chance to speak. "This is really ironic. You'll love this. One of the reasons I came to Sovereign in the first place was because of this poem, but instead of finding love, I found the wrong end of a shotgun."

"I remember that poem. Isn't the gun a metaphor for Emily?"

"That's the one." He tossed back his wet hair, struck a pose, and began to quote:

'My Life had stood – a loaded Gun –
In Corners – till a Day
The Owner passed – identified –
And carried Me away –

And now We roam in Sovereign Woods –
And now We hunt the Doe –
And every time I speak for Him –
The Mountains straight reply –'

There's more," he added. "But that's the gist of it, at least for me. I always fancied that line—'And now we roam in Sovereign Woods.' So when I was visiting my sister at Colby this spring and discovered there was a town named 'Sovereign' nearby—with thousands of acres of unspoiled woods—I hitchhiked over. I wasn't in Sovereign six months before I stumbled into Henry Trow and his shotgun. Pretty ironic, huh?"

"Not as ironic as a man who can quote Emily Dickinson," Nellie replied. The moment the words were out of her mouth she regretted them.

Walden pulled up short. He looked hurt and shocked. "Wow! You just can't help that condescension, can you? I'm spilling my guts here and you can't resist the opportunity to cut me down." He plucked a bleached yellow leaf from a nearby birch tree and rolled the limp leaf up between his thumb and forefinger.

"I'm so sorry, Wal … Nick," she apologized. "I don't know what came over me. The truth is—I don't feel superior. I feel different. I grew up so differently from everyone else I always felt left out, as though I didn't belong anywhere. I think I use condescension as a shield, so I don't get hurt."

"Believe me I know just how you feel. That's pretty typical for us TOs."

"So your father really is an Episcopal priest?"

"Yeah, if you'd let me finish my True Confession, you'd know it all. Just hear me out, Nellie, and then you can turn tail and run, OK?"

Nellie nodded meekly.

"This is not bragging now—I'm just going to try and explain how it was. My parents are very liberal progressives and growing up they taught me to march to a different drummer long before I ever knew being Green was cool or Henry David Thoreau existed. There was a voice inside me calling me into the woods and I didn't feel comfortable until I was off by myself or up a pine tree somewhere. I think we all have that inner voice but most people ignore it and the voice gradually fades away. But I didn't ignore mine. Kids can be pretty cruel, though, and in junior high they started calling me Yeti. I can't blame them—I was different. I was big and I liked to be alone. I was pretty hairy by then, too." He broke off to fondle his damp beard. "My parents sent me to prep school but that didn't make anything better, just worse. I graduated wanting to be Henry David while all the other guys at Waterford were set on becoming stockbrokers or CEOs of Google. Being different has its great moments, as you know, but it's also damn lonely. I tried a lot of stuff to wash away the pain of the loneliness: acid, beamers, pot, hallucinogenic 'shrooms—that's how I got into mushrooms in the first place. I even thought about becoming a priest, like my father, hoping religion might net me some relief. Fortunately for the Episcopal Church, I decided against that. So, you can understand why, when I saw you—daughter of the local minister, taking in Mother Nature's bounty—I thought you might be the answer to a guy's prayers."

"You knew my mother was the local minister? But … why were you so rude to me!"

"Oh, did I leave that part out? That's my other fatal flaw—I deliberately shoot myself in the foot whenever I'm with a pretty women. But wait," he continued, staving her off once again. "I'm not quite done. After I saw you, I vowed I wouldn't leave town until I'd asked you out, gotten to know you. Maybe even love you. But … when I saw you and the good Doc together—saw how natural you were with one another—I was jealous. A guy doesn't need an advanced degree to know when a girl prefers another man. It about broke my heart, seeing you two together. I realized then I'd probably be alone for the rest of my life."

"But I've known Doctor Bart since I was a baby!"

"What? Are you going to try and tell me *again* he's not your boyfriend?"

Nellie hesitated. Her gaze dropped to the wet pine needles at her feet. The rust color of the needles reminded her of Metcalf's red hair and her heart fluttered at the recollection of how she had run her hands through his curls with erotic abandon. Her cheeks flushed and her respiration increased.

"Look at me," he demanded, grasping her roughly by the arm.

She averted her gaze but didn't shake him off.

"You can't look me in the eye, can you? You're in love with him. Why won't you just admit it?"

"I . . ."

"If you knew the world was going to end at midnight tonight and you had to choose one guy to be with in the final hours—one guy!—can you tell me you wouldn't pick Doctor Bart?"

Walden's words hit their mark. Nellie felt a piercing pain in her chest. She loved Metcalf! She ached for him—yearned for him! "No," she muttered, hoarsely. "No, I can't say that."

His shoulders slumped. He dropped her arm. The rolled leaf fell from his hand and floated down. Angrily, he crushed the bleached leaflet into the ground. "This is one of those times when it really sucks to say 'I told you so.' Go home, Nellie. Better yet, go tell the good Doc the truth—he deserves it."

Nellie, hearing the anguish in his voice, glanced anxiously up at him. "Are you going to be OK?"

"Don't worry about me. Haven't I just told you? I'm used to being alone."

CHAPTER 23
The Harvest Supper

"Kin I git anothah cuppa coffee ovah he-ah, Nellie?" Leland called, waving his vintage white mug in the air, trying to catch her eye. The third and final seating of the Harvest Supper had thinned out but Nellie still found herself scrambling to catch up. For some reason or other Sarah Louise had failed to show up to wait tables, leaving Nellie and Trudy alone to handle the banquet room. Although the meal was a buffet, there was still plenty to do providing drinks, clearing away dirty dishes, and cleaning between diners.

"I'll bring a pot right over," Nellie assured Leland, ferrying her heavy tray of dirty dishes out to the kitchen. Gray, who had been pressed into service by his grandmother, began emptying the tray for her. "Thanks," she said, taking the opportunity to catch her breath. She pushed back a damp strand of hair that had escaped from her ponytail. "Any sign of Sarah Louise?"

"Nope. She must'a hed a bettah offer. 'Tis Saturday night."

Nellie offered up a disdainful sniff. "I have a feeling she'd consider any offer better than actual work," she replied, unable to keep the frustration from her voice. Being one waitress short had taken most of the fun out of the Harvest Supper for her. She glanced out through the wooden screen door that separated the kitchen from the entryway where Shirley Palmer was congenially greeting the last stragglers, accepting their cash donations. "Shirley hasn't heard anything?"

"Not a peep. Sarah Louise ain't called or nuthin'."

"Well, it doesn't matter now; we're almost done."

Gray swiped the tray with a hot soapy dishcloth. "I'm all caught up, Nellie. Whyn't ya let me clear tables for ya? Grandma won't mind, not if I put an apron on." His grandmother, Maude Gilpin, President of the Ladies Auxiliary, was in charge of the fundraiser.

Nellie immediately accepted his offer. "You're a lifesaver, Gray," she assured him. She reached for the fresh pot of decaf coffee and headed back in Leland's direction.

The Harvest Supper was a major annual fundraiser for the church, usually adding three or four thousand dollars to the coffers. This year the money would be split between the church and the new corn shop museum, the food having been prepared and donated by members of the Ladies Corn Shop Museum Auxiliary, most of whom were church members. This evening's menu included baked beans and brown bread, beef and venison stew, winter bean soup, stuffed green peppers, chicken pot pie, an asparagus-pasta stir fry, and a variety of fresh biscuits, breads and rolls. In addition, there was a complement of vegetable dishes ranging from winter squash to Brussels sprouts to the traditional cabbage salad. For dessert, diners could choose from a wide variety of homemade pies for which the Harvest Supper was known and which enticed diners from as far away as Augusta. Nellie had waited tables at these annual fundraisers since she was ten and had never seen as many people as tonight. She knew the take from this evening's three seatings would exceed the haul from last year, which had been the biggest year to date.

She hurried back to the banquet table where Leland was sitting with Ryan, Rebecca and Wendell, Ralph Gilpin, Harald Young, and one or two other stray husbands whose wives were busy in the kitchen. "Sorry I took so long," she said, splashing some coffee into Leland's mug. She held up the pot. "Anyone else?"

Before any of the others could answer her, Ryan rose up and relieved her of the coffee pot. "Sit down, Nellie. I'll take over. You must be exhausted."

Nellie hesitated, considering his offer. She wanted to get off her feet, but it didn't seem appropriate. "What about Trudy?" she asked. "She's worked just as hard as me. Shouldn't you give your wife a break?"

He pointed across the room to where Trudy was already sitting over supper with Maynard Fowler, Sheila and the two children, Sheila's daughter Olivia, and Ryan and Trudy's daughter, Alice Rose. "Sheila's been watching the baby for us tonight," he explained. "As you can see, I'm not as big a draw as the kids."

Nellie smiled and allowed herself to be persuaded. "I am tired," she admitted, sinking down into Ryan's seat. The attorney gamely assumed Nellie's duties, parrying the chafing of some the other men as he did so.

"Whar's yer apron, son?" Leland asked, shoveling three spoonfuls of sugar into his mug of coffee. Leland's friend Harald Young, who was sitting to the right of him, sniggled.

"I left it at home, hanging right next to yours," replied his son-in-law. Ryan deftly refilled John Wood's coffee mug and hoisted the pot without spilling a drop. Nellie was impressed by the attorney's adroitness.

"Thank you, son," said the lanky First Selectman, leaning back in the folding metal chair and regarding Ryan with a thoughtful expression. "I'd say you've done this sort of thing before."

"I put myself through law school waiting tables," the lawyer replied. "Tuition doesn't grow on trees; at least it didn't in my neighborhood." A table of diners near the back of the room waved to get Ryan's attention, and he expertly wove through a gauntlet of empty chairs to bring them coffee.

Nellie was about to excuse herself to visit the buffet when Wendell pushed back from the banquet table. "I'll go git ya a plateful, Nellie," he offered. He rose up and hitched up his jeans.

"You don't need to do that, Wendell. I can go myself."

"Course, I was goin' thet-a-way anyway."

"Oh, let him get you a plate, Nellie," Rebecca interjected. "Wendell wants an excuse to snag a third piece of Mother Clark's Pumpkin Bread."

"Whose mother is she?"

"Mother Clark is everyone's mother, I think. She's about a hundred years old and only bakes her special pumpkin-raisin bread once a year for the Harvest Supper. Good thing Maude doesn't keep track of how much Wendell eats or she'd charge us double!"

Nellie sat back down. "That'd be great, Wendell, thanks."

"Aren't you going to ask Nellie what she wants?"

"If she don't like what I git, she ain't got to eat it," Wendell replied, flashing his gold-toothed grin. He sauntered off in the direction of the buffet tables.

Rebecca smiled at her husband's retreating figure. She glanced around the table. Seeing that the other men were deep in conversation, she leaned closer to Nellie. "Where's Sarah Louise?" she whispered. "I thought she was supposed to waitress tonight?"

"Me too," Nellie mumbled through the elastic hairband in her teeth. She gathered up her blonde hair and snapped the elastic back into place. "She's a No Show."

"You don't suppose she and Metcalf are … ?" Rebecca broke off.

Metcalf and Sarah Louise together? Nellie shuddered at the thought. It was too horrible to contemplate. "Not possible," she said flatly.

"I didn't think so," Rebecca said. "Still, one never knows."

Nellie, too, had noticed Metcalf's absence from the Harvest Supper and it had flashed through her mind—just for a fleeting second—perhaps his absence was somehow related to Sarah Louise's failure to appear. But she dismissed that notion almost instantly, clinging stubbornly to her belief that despite their current misunderstanding Metcalf still loved her.

There had been few words spoken between her and Metcalf since Julian Mills had interrupted their passionate embrace. Nellie had wanted to clear the air between them, but he had given her little opportunity to do so.

On Friday morning she had dressed for work with care and presented herself at the clinic half an hour early, thus providing an easy opportunity for a private chat before their first patient arrived. Doctor Bart, however, had remained holed up somewhere in the house. Nellie busied herself with paperwork, anxiously waiting for him to appear. But Doctor Bart appeared just in time to greet his first patient. His smile was hollow and he treated Nellie with a casual indifference that nearly broke her heart. She pretended not to notice his change of attitude and reminded herself he had a right to feel hurt and angry. She mentally revisited Henry Trow's words of wisdom and felt better. Assuredly, Metcalf would 'come around again,' although his volte-face might take some time.

Aunt Hannah arrived to collect the clinic's laundry and immediately sensed the strained relationship between the two young people. "My dear, what's wrong?" she asked, when the door had closed behind Doctor Bart and his patient. "Why is Metcalf behaving like a muttonhead?"

Nellie, reviewing her chart notes, paused to answer. "It's a misunderstanding, Aunt Hannah. Nothing to worry about."

Aunt Hannah gave her an empathetic hug. "Hang in there, my dear. He's worth it."

You're right about that! Nellie had silently agreed.

But now Metcalf hadn't shown up at the Harvest Supper and neither had Sarah Louise. Could there be a connection? Were they—God forbid!—on a date?

While she waited for Wendell to return with her food, Nellie absently played with the fresh-cut floral arrangement in the center of the table. She plucked off a few daisy petals and let them drop to the red-and-white checked tablecloth. 'He loves me—he loves me not.'

Suddenly, Sarah Louise's ingratiating words to Metcalf during the deer lighting expedition popped into her head: *"You always know the right thing to say to make a girl feel comfortable, Doctor Bart."*

She shuddered again, and deliberately tore off more petals, defrocking the poor daisy entirely.

Wendell returned and plunked a fragrant plateful of food on the table in front of her. "They was all out of thet asparagus slop so I brung ya extra beans."

Rebecca, who had been chatting across the table with Leland, overheard her husband's remark. "That's not very nice," she reprimanded him. "Jessica's Asparagus Dream is one of the most popular specials at Ma Jean's."

"Thet don't mean I got to like it," Wendell pointed out.

Nellie picked up her fork. "This is perfect Wendell, thanks." He grinned and headed off in the direction of the dessert buffet.

Leland moved his coffee mug out of the way and thumped his elbows on the table. He directed his attention to his neighbor on the right. "I heared what ya was sayin' ta John, Harald, 'n yer problem ain't with the tree yer tryin' ta cut. Yer problem is—ya ain't got yerself a real chainsaw. Ain't nuthin' under 50cc is a real saw."

"Now Leland, yore jest sayin' thet 'cause all yore saws is biggah," Harald replied. He was a crusty, white-haired crony of Leland's who prided himself on looking like a sea captain rather than a retired bakery truck driver, which is what he was.

"Thet jest goes to show how much ya don't know, Harald. Them politicians changed the law so they could pass them *toy* chainsaws off as real—'n you fell fer it."

"Don't get yourself wound up, Leland," John Woods advised. "I know a lot of boys who use smaller saws and while they're not cutting fifteen or twenty cord a year like you, those 32cc saws have their place."

Leland snorted derisively. "Ya cain't even cut a staddle with 'em, John!"

"What's a staddle?" Nellie whispered to Rebecca.

"I haven't the faintest idea."

"Thet's a small oak," Wendell answered, reclaiming his seat. He glanced across the table at his friend. "Leland ain't goin' on 'bout thet chainsaw law change is he?"

"Apparently so. It's very interesting, actually."

"You wouldn't think so if you'd heared it twenty times afore."

Leland, suddenly realizing that he had the attention of the entire table, threw out his chest and increased his volume. "If yer haulin' a full chebobbin to the mill, ya ain't usin' no dem toy ta cut yer timbah," he cried passionately.

"We'll give you that, Leland," said the First Selectman, mildly. "Now, calm down and drink your coffee. You're making a spectacle of yourself."

The woodsman ignored Woods' adjuration. "Them fellars as werk down to the big box store 'n Waterville talked my son-in-law inta buyin' one o' them things," he continued, waxing hot, "and he couldn't do a dem thing with it!"

"He the one waitin' tables?" queried one of the stray husbands innocently. Harald Young sniggled at the implied swipe at Ryan's masculinity.

"He couldn't even use the thing ta cut maple saplins growin' 'round the bahn," Leland exhorted, ignoring the interruption. "I tell you, thet law should nevah bin changed. Them kids as is jest stahtin' out don't know their head from a hole 'n the ground 'n they ain't got nuff money ta learn the hahd way, neither." He leaped to his feet and raised his arm like a politician on canvass. "I says—we needs ta do sumthin' 'bout the sit-u-ation. Who's with me?"

Nellie glanced around the table and noticed several hoary heads bobbing in tacit agreement.

Wendell, who had been listening stoically, heaved a heart-felt sigh. He lifted his dessert plate and held it out. "Leland," he interrupted, "this here's the last piece o' Maude's lemon meringue pie. Want it?"

Leland forgot all about his canvassing and dropped down into his chair. "Don't mind if I do," he replied. He took the pie plate and set to noisily devouring the poufy lemon meringue pie.

"Now what?" Rebecca asked her husband, in amusement.

"Now I go git me some mincemeat tarts."

"If you're talking about Hannah's frosted mincemeat tarts, bring me one," she directed. "No, make that two." She turned slightly in her chair and her pregnant belly caught and held against the table edge. "Oops."

Wendell raised an eyebrow. "You shore 'bout thet?"

"Just do as I say. Don't forget—I'm eating for two."

"'Tain't likely I'd forgit."

Nellie enjoyed her dinner, listening to the pleasant chatter of her table companions. Her eyes wandered fondly around the table from one familiar face to another and she was struck by the difference between how she felt about these people this evening and how she had felt the day she returned to Sovereign. She blushed for her immaturity and self-centeredness back then, and was grateful to her new friends for giving her a chance to get to know them. They had accepted her into the fold despite her initial obvious disdain for them.

When she finished eating, Nellie ventured to the dessert table, taking the opportunity to check in with Maude in the kitchen to be sure she wasn't needed. After receiving the matron's blessing, she popped out of the antiquated kitchen and spotted Aunt Hannah and Henry Trow tucked away at a small table in the back corner of the banquet room. The table was a two-seater, near the door leading to the attached outhouse, which was no longer in use. Nellie approached the couple with a smile. "I see you two hiding up here," she said, resting her hand affectionately on the back of Aunt Hannah's chair.

"We're not hiding, my dear," said Aunt Hannah, smiling up at Nellie.

"Let her think that, Hannah, if it amuses her," encouraged Mr. Trow. "Makes me feel young again to hear her talk like that—almost as though I was about to do something foolish."

To Nellie's surprise, Aunt Hannah actually giggled. "I know what you mean," she said.

"Good grief! I was just joking," Nellie blurted out. "But now I'm beginning to think I've interrupted a bona fide tryst."

"Shall we tell her, Hannah?"

"Not yet, Henry. Let me speak with my children first."

Nellie put her hands over her ears and backed away from the table. "I am so not hearing this!"

She hastily resumed her seat and ate her piece of cranberry custard pie. Most of the others at the table had drifted away. When Harald departed for the dessert table, leaving Nellie and Leland alone at the banquet table, Nellie pushed her plate away. She regarded the loquacious woodchopper curiously. How could it be that Leland, who was obviously lonely and in need of a wife, had allowed the best cook and the nicest woman in Sovereign to be stolen right out from under his nose by Henry Trow, who was after all a newcomer to town.

"Do you mind if I ask you a question?" she said.

Leland set down his coffee mug and gave Nellie a worried look. "Tain't 'bout thet tree I cut while we was in the town woodlot last week, is it? Like I told ya—'twas a widder-maker and needed ta come down."

"No, it's not about the tree. It's personal."

Relieved, Leland retrieved his coffee. "Wal, if thet's all—fire away."

"Why did you never marry again? I mean, Trudy's mother passed away when she was young, and, well …" Nellie realized with some embarrassment that she was floundering. "I was just wondering—why not?"

Leland scratched his head. "I been takin' my time, lookin' fer the right woman, I guess."

"For thirty years?"

"Wal, if she's the right woman, she's wuth waitin' fer. If she ain't, then I ain't got so long ta live with 'er, now do I?"

CHAPTER 24

He Made No Such Promise

When Nellie finished her cranberry custard pie she gathered up her plate and as many dirty dishes as she could carry and headed toward the kitchen. Gray met her with an empty tray and relieved her of her burden. "Thanks, Gray. Did you get something to eat?"

The youth bobbed his head. "Ya ain't got to worry 'bout me none, Nellie. I don't miss many meals. Gram cain't figger out how I stay so skinny."

Maude Gilpin, with whom Gray lived, was the best cook in town and Nellie herself had always wondered the same thing. "How *do* you stay so thin?"

"Wouldn't ya like to know," he replied, with a suggestive wink.

"Gray Gilpin—are you flirting with me?"

"Ha, ha. You wish!"

Nellie gave him a playful tap. He grinned and hoisted his tray. She watched for a few moments as Gray paused to collect some dirty dishes from a group of diners, making jokes and chatting with them. She shook her head, almost unable to believe how confident and mature the youth had become, just in the last year. She was used to thinking of him as a 'hobbledehoy,' a very apt word frequently employed by one of her favorite authors, the popular nineteenth century English novelist Anthony Trollope, to describe awkward young men who hadn't yet hit their stride. But Gray Gilpin today was certainly no hobbledehoy!

On the way back to her table she spotted Aunt Jane entering the banquet hall. The older woman frantically waved her over to the entry way. Nellie felt her heart leap into her throat as she immediately assumed the worst. She hurried to join her mother's best friend. "What's wrong, Aunt Jane? Where is he?"

"He who?"

"Metcalf! Is he alright?"

"Good heavens—don't alarm me, Nellie. Metcalf was fine half an hour ago when I spoke to him on the phone. He's just running late, as usual. Another emergency."

Nellie felt a rush of relief. "Thank God," she breathed, hand at her throat. She couldn't believe now how fast her heart was beating.

"Come, Nellie, you'll never make a doctor's wife if you worry every time he's running a few minutes late."

Nellie smiled, but said nothing. Even Aunt Jane assumed she would eventually marry Metcalf!

"I just wanted to speak with you about … about your father. Metcalf told me you were waiting tables, and …" Jane stepped closer to Nellie and lowered her voice conspiratorially, "… and I wondered if you'd found Maggie's journals?" She glanced around the empty entryway, ensuring no one else was present to overhear their conversation.

Maggie's journals! So … that's what this was about.

Instantly, Nellie's back was up. She stiffened her spine. "I found Mother's diaries," she replied, coolly, "but I decided not to read them. You know as well as I do, Aunt Jane, that would be a violation of Mother's trust. Besides, it's unethical."

"Pooh, don't be such a Puritan, Nellie! I swear sometimes you're worse than your mother. You need to know who your father is and the sooner you know the truth the better." She plopped her leather purse on top of the white painted windowsill and shrugged out of her rust-colored corduroy jacket. Her freckled face was redder than her short hair. "Why is it so hot in here?" she complained, pacing restlessly. "Don't you think it's hot in here?"

Nellie pointed at the adjoining kitchen door. "We just served dinner to three hundred people," she replied. "Listen, Aunt Jane, if you want me to know the truth about my father, why don't you just tell me?"

Jane wrung her chapped hands together. "I can't. I promised your mother."

"So it's OK for me to be unethical, but not you?"

"Don't think I haven't been tempted! Especially since…"

"Since what?"

"Let's just say there are extenuating circumstances in play at the moment. I'm worried you're going to get hurt. Oh, Lord! It's so hard for a person to know the right thing to do." She took several steps toward the entry door, her lithe frame moving easily over the wooden floor. She pushed open the door and peered out into the night.

"Are you expecting someone, Aunt Jane?"

"No, I'm checking on my car. I left it running. I'm not staying for supper."

Nellie began to wonder if her mother's best friend had been drinking. Aunt Jane had driven all the way up from Albion and she wasn't even staying for the Harvest Supper?

"Have you heard anything from Maggie?" Aunt Jane asked, abruptly dropping the door and turning back. The door closed behind her with a bouncing thunk.

"Just that her credit card bill came this week and validated everything I suspected—she's on pilgrimage to Santiago de Compostela."

"And there's no way to reach her, of course."

"Not unless she calls or emails us."

"That's so like Maggie—running away and leaving this horrible burden on the rest of us!"

Nellie felt her anger rising. She had accepted the fact that twenty-two years ago her mother's best friend had promised never to reveal the identity of her father. But what was so pressing now Aunt Jane felt the need to hunt her down at the Harvest Supper? "C'mon Aunt Jane, what's up? It's obvious something has happened. You say you want me to know the truth, yet you refuse to tell it to me."

"I do want you to know the truth," she cried, clutching the gold necklace dangling from her thin neck. "But …I just-can't-say-any-more."

"Then I'll never know who my father is," Nellie expostulated.

Jane opened her purse and pulled out a tissue. She daubed the perspiration from her forehead and upper lip. "It *is* hot in here," she pronounced. She stuffed the tissue into her purse and snapped it shut. As Nellie watched, the expression on the older woman's face metamorphosed from doubt to resolution. "That's not necessarily true," she said slowly.

"Well, don't expect Maggie to tell me when she gets home, because she won't. She's had plenty of opportunities to share my father's identity over the past twenty-two years and she hasn't done it yet."

"I'm not alluding to your mother. There's someone else who knows who your father is."

"Yes, but unfortunately, Uncle Peter is dead."

"I wasn't referring to Peter, either."

Nellie felt completely baffled. There was someone else who knew the identity of her birth father? Who could that possibly be? According to Metcalf, only the three childhood friends—Peter, Jane, and her mother—had been in on the secret of Maggie's pregnancy. "Who?" she challenged.

"Your father. As far as I know, *he* made no such promise to secrecy."

Nellie felt her heart skip a beat. Her father? Could it be possible her father not only knew about her but also knew who she was?

"I've got to go," Jane declared. "I've said too much."

"But—wait!"

The older woman hastily collected up her purse and jacket. "Forgive me, Nellie. Just know I'm doing the best I can for you under the circumstances." She gave Nellie a quick hug and darted out into the black night.

Before Nellie could wrap her mind around Aunt Jane's disclosure, the screen door between the kitchen and the hall creaked open. Gray stuck his head out. "Hey, Nellie. She gone?"

Nellie nodded instinctively. What had Aunt Jane meant by telling her so much, and yet so little? Why had she apologized? What harm could possibly come to Nellie from learning the truth about her birth father?

Who was he? Why hadn't he come forward and introduced himself!

"Kin ya come in heah?"

Somewhat dazed, Nellie stepped into the brightly lit, noisy kitchen. Much to her astonishment, she found a distressed Shirley Palmer sitting at the prep table surrounded by a bevy of sympathetic, clucking women. The former postmistress was weeping in heart-wrenching fashion. An eerie feeling crept over Nellie. She turned to Gray. "What happened?"

"Sarah Louise runned off with some guy. Asa went back to the house lookin' fer her 'n found a note on her pillow."

"Who did she run away with?"

Gray shrugged. "Thet's jest it—ain't no one knows who he is. 'Twas thet mushroom guy."

"You can't mean Walden!"

"Yep, thet's him."

Nellie was shocked. She would sooner have believed Sarah Louise had run away with Leland Gorse than with Walden.

Walden? Who only a few days ago had revealed he was in love with her!

That Walden had been sincere about those feelings Nellie hadn't doubted. Not even a professional actor could have offered up such an authentic performance of frustrated love. No, his feelings for her were real, regardless of what crazy and unaccountable action he had taken since.

She thought of Walden's confession of loneliness and her heart went out to him. If only she had been kinder to him! But how could she have befriended him when she knew what he wanted from her was so much more than friendship?

But why had he abandoned hope so quickly? Surely someone special would have come along sooner or later! Eventually Walden would have found a woman more of his own nature and sensitivity, a woman who would have understood and appreciated his affinity for the natural world. Someone with whom he could read Emily Dickinson. Nellie didn't condemn Walden for his impatience, but she did decry the weakness of character that compelled him to seek out someone as lonely—but much more vulnerable—than himself: Sarah Louise.

"Course Walden ain't his real name," Gray continued. "Ain't no one knows thet, nor where he come from, neithah. Not even Wendell."

"He took advantage o' my poor girl," Shirley whimpered. "Sarah Louise ain't a bad girl; she jest don't know no bettah." There was a murmuring of assent from the empathetic group surrounding her.

Nellie quickly reached a resolution. She stepped forward. "His name is Nick—Nick Faulkner," she stated in a loud, matter-of-fact voice to the kitchen at large. "He graduated from Waterford Academy in Massachusetts about ten years ago. I don't know where his home is, but his sister goes to Colby College and his father's an Episcopal priest. That should give you—give the police—enough information to track them down."

Shirley rose up and tottered over. She clutched Nellie's arm. "Oh, thankee, dearie!" She turned to her husband. "Didja git thet, Asa?"

"Yep," grumbled the Road Commissioner. "Dang fool gal," he muttered under his breath. "Ain't like Sarah Louise was born yestiddy. Now I gots ta go git 'er."

Nellie, feeling as though she had done her duty, moved back out of the limelight. When she stepped back she bumped into someone who had come in through the screen door behind her. She felt a firm hand on the middle of her back and her heart leapt. Metcalf! She swung around, so relieved to see him she nearly burst into tears.

"Hey, no need to cry, Nellie. Asa will have Sarah Louise back before we know it," he reassured her. "That is, if she wants to return, which I rather doubt." Metcalf dug into his pocket, pulled out a white handkerchief and pressed the men's hanky into her hand. "Dry your eyes—there's a good girl."

"You're late," Nellie said, smiling through her tears. "Maude's lemon meringue pie is all gone. So is the Asparagus Dream."

"Fortunately, I didn't come here for either of those things."

As he spoke, Metcalf gazed deeply into Nellie's eyes. It was impossible for her to mistake his meaning. He still loved her!

"Listen, Nellie, I'm sorry I was such an idiot the other night," he said apologetically.

"Please, don't …" she broke off, too embarrassed to talk about it.

"I've been thinking," he continued, evenly. "Maybe we should take a day off by ourselves. Go somewhere—just the two of us. Talk. Laugh. Have lunch. How about it? Would you like that?"

Nellie felt as though her heart had just given birth to a butterfly. "You mean like—a date?"

Metcalf smiled at her naiveté. "Not 'like' a date—a real date. What do you say?" He gathered up her hands within his capable ones. "Will you give me the chance to make it up to you?"

'Yes," she said, without hesitation. "I will."

"Good girl. How about I pick you up at nine?"

"Oh, wait. I just remembered—tomorrow's Sunday."

"Don't you think they can get by without you at church, just this once?"

Nellie laughed at her implied self-importance. "They always have!"

"Good. It's a date."

She felt an exquisite happiness standing in the church kitchen with him. She and Metcalf seemed to be in their own little world, while everyone else swirled around them on a never-ending merry-go-round. Shirley was directing Asa; Maude was pontificating about the proper way to put away the salts and peppers; Gray was scraping plates. Only Metcalf's face remained steadfast, firm, unwavering.

Reluctantly, she pulled her hands away from his. There were social conventions to consider and practical matters to attend to before tomorrow. "What should I wear?"

He groaned and ruffled his auburn curls with his hand. "Not the clothes question again! Where's Aunt Hannah when you need her?"

Nellie bobbed her head toward the dining hall. "She's in there, being swept off her feet by Henry Trow."

Metcalf whistled. "No kidding?"

"I kid you not."

"Wow! Some guys have all the luck."

CHAPTER 25
"You Know Where My Heart Is"

Nellie allowed Metcalf to give her a ride home from the Harvest Supper. Rather than drop her off, however, he walked her to the shed door. They stood together on the granite stoop. "See you tomorrow, Nellie," he said.

The outside light was on and a few bedazzled bugs swirled around the compact fluorescent bulb overhead. Metcalf's face was fully illuminated by the light, enabling Nellie to count every precious freckle. She idly wondered why she had ever thought redheaded men were homely. She smiled and gave him her hand. "I'm looking forward to it."

"Me too." He reached around her to swing open the shed door so she could enter. "Bye."

"Bye."

From the kitchen window Nellie watched the progress of his truck's lights up the hill until they disappeared from sight. She felt a physical sense of loss watching him drive away, an indescribable yearning emanating from unplumbed regions of her solar plexus. She knew she would see him tomorrow, but suddenly that was not soon enough for her. She wanted to be with him every moment of the day and was even beginning to suspect a lifetime wouldn't be enough time for the two of them to spend together.

Nellie realized the truth now beyond the shadow of a doubt—she wanted to spend the rest of her life with him!

The house was still warm from the fire she had left burning in the woodstove and before she filled the kitchen stove for the night she wandered into the living room to check the messages on the answering machine. Checking phone messages had become a pleasurable experience for her. She would check them several times a day, harkening back to a simpler time before the advent of texting and instant messaging. To her astonishment, there was a fragmentary message from her mother: *"Just found out … Cathy Burbury said … church … must know … sorry I …down … Kairos time … call again … love you darling."*

Her mother's tone, what Nellie could make out from the garbled message, sounded anxious. *Must know.* Obviously, there was something her mother felt was important enough to break her self-imposed silence for. But what was it? Was the phone call connected to Aunt Jane's odd visit to her at the Harvest Supper? Did it have anything to do with her father?

Cathy Burbury, the person mentioned in the message, was one of Maggie's close minister friends from Bangor Theological Seminary. When Nellie was young, Reverend Cathy had pastored a church in Portland and had visited them often. About ten years ago, however, Reverend Cathy had been called by a church in Alaska. Nellie remembered this because the mission had sounded incredibly exciting to her at the time. She hadn't seen Reverend Cathy since she'd moved away from Maine. How could a pastor living in a Fairbanks possibly know something affecting Nellie's life in Sovereign? Aunt Jane had implied that only three living persons knew her father's identity—Aunt Jane herself and Nellie's mother and father. Could Aunt Jane be wrong?

And what did Maggie mean about 'Kairos time.' Nellie knew that in New Testament theology, 'Kairos time' related to the coming of Jesus. Because she had studied Greek at Hathorne she also knew the ancient Greeks utilized two forms of time: *kairos*, the moment in which something BIG would happen, and *chronos*, which was straightforward, linear time. Her mother's reference to 'Kairos time' probably didn't mean Jesus was returning anytime soon but something BIG was about to happen.

Was Nellie finally going to learn the identity of her father? If so, what could be wrong with that?

Unfortunately, the old-fashioned answering machine didn't have caller ID nor had her mother left a call-back number. Most likely Maggie was staying in a hostel along the Way of St. James and had simply borrowed the hostel's phone. Who knew where Maggie would be tomorrow? When she would call again?

Suddenly, Nellie gave the erasure knob on the answering machine a savage twist. She listened with satisfaction to the slithering and *click-click-clicking* sounds signifying her mother's message had been erased. She was sick and tired of wondering and worrying about the identity of her father. She was wasting too much of her precious life on that apparently useless quest. If her father knew about her—and it appeared now he did—but had deliberately chosen not to reveal his identity, did she really want to know such a man? What kind of person must he be? He was probably married and had another family. No doubt he thought she would be an embarrassment to him.

Well, Nellie Walker would be an embarrassment to no man!

She vowed not to take another step in the search for her father. From this moment forward she would look to the future, not focus on the past. What did it matter what happened twenty-two years ago? How could *then* affect her life *now*?

As a result of this new resolution, Nellie slept sounder than she had for many a night. She awoke to a beautiful late October morning. When she exited her bedroom she spied a ray of sun shining through the east living room window, highlighting the colorful quilt she was sewing for Rebecca's baby shower. The shower was less than a week away. Nellie felt slightly guilty taking a day to spend with Metcalf knowing she still had the backing to apply; however, she promised herself on Monday she would pick up her work where she had left off.

She hummed to herself as she raked the coals and reloaded the stove. She set a pot of coffee on the woodstove to perk and glanced at the Regulator clock. She still had an hour before Metcalf would arrive to pick her up. She was both happy and relieved he had suggested they take this day for themselves. The private outing would give her the opportunity to make things right with him, to apologize for her share in that awful misunderstanding. Also, it gave her a good excuse to skip church. She had learned from Shirley earlier in the week that Julian Mills would be leading the church service today and while normally she would have been pleased to hear Doctor Mills speak, after his rude behavior to Metcalf she was much less enthralled with the author. Plus she felt no small embarrassment when she imagined how she must have looked when he had returned to the house for his car keys. It would be just fine with her if Julian Mills left Sovereign and she never saw him again. She must remember to tell her mother about his visit, though.

Nellie was finishing up her breakfast when the landline rang. She eagerly answered the heavy black wall receiver, hoping to hear her mother's voice. Instead, Metcalf was on the other end of the line.

"There's a special place I'd like to take you today," he said, after his initial greeting. "Near Sugarloaf. We'll have to hike in a short ways to get there, though. If that's OK with you?"

"Excellent. Now I know what to wear."

"But I didn't tell you what to wear."

"Yes, you did: jeans, walking shoes, a sweater, and a lightweight jacket, just in case."

Nellie hung up the phone, her heart singing. Soon! Soon she would see him again.

She retreated to her bedroom and found her sneakers and jeans. Finding a sweater, however, was more of a challenge. The only sweater she owned was her tan-colored, open cashmere cardigan, an elegant piece inappropriate for a hike in the Maine woods. And she certainly didn't want to wear her mother's floret fashion sweater, the one Walden had mocked. She had no other choice but to search through her mother's rather dowdy wardrobe again to see if she could locate an alternative.

Nellie found nothing but sweatshirts in the top of her mother's closet. When she peeked under the bed, however, she spied a plastic tub filled with sweaters. She blew off the dust balls and opened the cover, tossing a couple of possibilities onto the bed. Suddenly, her hand stuck something hard. She lifted up several sweaters and found an antique picture frame packed between them. She lifted the picture out and, holding it carefully by the wooden edges, turned the frame around to reveal a vintage 1920s print under glass. The print featured a picturesque rural cottage in the background and a poem penned in black cursive lettering in the foreground. Nellie had never seen the print before and suspected it had belonged to her great-grandmother, with whom Maggie had lived for many years. She tilted the frame to catch the best natural light and read the poem aloud:

Let me live in a house
by the side of the road,
Where the race of men go by-
The men who are good and the men who are bad,
As good and as bad as I.
I would not sit in the scorner's seat,
Or hurl the cynic's ban;-
Let me live in a house by the side of the road
And be a friend to man.
Sam Walter Foss (1858-1911)

Nellie recognized the charming poem from Julian Mills' first and most important book, "The House by the Side of the Road." But why would her mother keep such a delightful print packed away under her bed? Had she merely forgotten about the picture? Or was it possible Maggie—a long-time writer herself—had become envious of Julian Mills when his book was published? Had her mother tucked the vintage print away because she didn't want to be reminded of the gulf between their literary successes? Or lack thereof, in her mother's case.

Nellie set the print on the bed and returned to the task at hand. She selected a marled cotton pullover from her mother's sweaters and packed the rest back into the plastic tub. She left the print out, however, in order that she might ask her mother about it when Maggie returned. She took the framed poem downstairs to the living room and found a nail to hang it on. She thought the vintage print looked as though it belonged in the house and it was a shame not to enjoy it.

She finished dressing with only minutes to spare. Before she knew it, Metcalf was there in the flesh, standing in the kitchen. She hesitated in the doorway from the living room, her heart fluttering. He looked so boyishly handsome, so confident and self-assured! And she loved him!

He presented her with a small bouquet of late-blooming wild flowers, which included purple asters and several different sprigs of herbs. The stems were tied together by a delicate yellow satin ribbon. "How smart am I? The asters match your sweater."

Nellie sniffed the sweet-smelling bouquet. "They're beautiful, thanks. I'll just put them in water before we go."

"They don't need water. They're all set. This is a portable bouquet—a tussie-mussie. In the language of flowers, each individual sprig means something different. If you could read these flowers, you'd be able to read my heart."

"The language of flowers? Now I'm sorry I never took that botany class at Columbia. So, what's your bouquet trying to tell me?"

"Not to be impatient," he replied, with a teasing smile. "Ready to go?"

Nellie, still clutching the tussie-mussie, gathered up her other things and happily allowed Metcalf to pack her into the truck. He went around to the other side and climbed in. He started the engine and they drove in restful silence, examining their neighbor's houses as they drove past, which was usual and customary practice in Sovereign. "I see Wendell finally has his weathervane back up," Nellie remarked, pointing to the restored copper weathercock shifting slightly in the breeze atop the barn cupola. "I love the chicken! Most of the weathervanes around here are roosters."

Metcalf squinted to examine the copper chicken. "Wendell told me the chicken was his grandmother's idea," he said. He coasted the truck up to the stop sign at the intersection with Route 9 and checked the traffic before pulling out onto the main road. "Apparently, Grammie Addie didn't mind setting her own course, if you'll excuse the pun. Your mother told me once rooster weathervanes were some kind of Christian symbol, to remind the devout of Jesus prophesying Peter's denial of him—three times before the cock crows. But you'd know more about that than me."

"I would if I'd ever paid attention to any of mother's sermons. Now, I'm sorry I didn't listen," Nellie said, sincerely. "According to everyone in town, she actually had some interesting pastoral messages."

"I'm glad to hear you say that, Nellie. I always thought you underrated your mother."

"Mea culpa, I'll admit. How did Wendell's weathervane get broken in the first place?"

"A freak storm blew a tree branch onto on it twenty years ago. The weathercock—rather weatherhen—languished in the open chamber until Rebecca stumbled onto it two years ago. Wendell promised her back then he'd fix the weathervane, but he never felt motivated to make good on that promise until he found out she was pregnant. Seeing into the future gave him a new perspective on life, he told me. He's even been talking about having the entire property surveyed."

"Is a survey so unusual?"

"Well, not nowadays. But back in Pappy's time—Pappy was Grammie Addie's husband—abutting landowners would get together every year or two to perambulate their adjoining properties and agree upon the boundaries. It was a good chance to spend the afternoon in the woods with a friend and neighbor, a couple of pieces of strawberry-rhubarb pie, and a thermos of coffee."

"Sounds good to me!"

"But that was back when a man's character was as good as his word, and a handshake was more valuable than a piece of paper recorded at the registry."

"Hmm," Nellie replied, thoughtfully. She could almost see Pappy Russell and his neighbor meeting at the stone wall, shaking hands, and tramping together through the woods, thickets, and fields. She wondered about their conversation. Would Pappy and his neighbor talk about how much the blackberries were encroaching in the cuttings? At lunchtime, would they spread their handkerchiefs on the ground and sit down? Or would they enjoy their pie leaning against one of the towering pine trees often utilized as boundary markers?

Nellie knew that Pappy had been a local legend, earning a special place in the annuals of Sovereign much like his grandson, Wendell. She had come to know Wendell well during these past few months and recognized the true value of his character. Now she understood perfectly the attraction such a man would have for Rebecca. *She* would never have to wonder about her safety or security, for Wendell would provide for her and their baby, in every sense of the word.

Nellie stole a quick glance at Metcalf's countenance and her heart gave a little leap. He was so good! So kind, generous, and thoughtful. How wonderful to have someone to lean upon! Someone who could be trusted with all of her little hopes and dreams, cares and concerns.

How could she have been so blind to Metcalf's worth all those years? Thank goodness she had finally woken up!

Nellie put her nose to the tussie-mussie and inhaled again the sweet, subtle fragrance of the herbs and flowers. Ah, life was *so* good!

Metcalf turned and smiled at her. "You're very quiet all of a sudden. A penny for your thoughts …?"

She returned his smile with a coquettish look. "I was just wondering what your flowers were trying to tell me."

"Still trying to wheedle it out of me, eh?"

"Naturally. Who wouldn't want to know the secret message in these beautiful asters? Ignorant me; I didn't even know flowers could talk."

"I only know because my grandmother taught me. Apparently, in ancient times flowers and herbs were assigned a certain meaning. If one wanted to send a message to a friend or lover—but was too shy to speak out—he or she could say it with flowers and the recipient would know what was intended."

"So that's where 'Say it with flowers' comes from?"

"Exactly. But flowers speak to us in other esoteric ways, too. Have you ever heard flowers calling out to you on your walks?"

"Only to pick them."

"So, you have heard them?"

Nellie thought seriously for a moment. "Not in actual words, but I think I know what you mean."

"Are you familiar with the works of Elizabeth von Arnim?"

"Of course. She wrote 'Elizabeth and Her German Garden.' It's one of my favorite books."

"She also said, and I quote: 'Every flower is a friend and every tree a lover'. Now, there was a woman who understood the language of flowers!" They arrived at a junction in the main road and Doctor Bart slowed the truck. "Let's go via the back roads, shall we?" He switched on the pickup's directional signal.

"Since I don't know where we're going, that's fine by me. I can't believe I never knew you talk to your plants. I thought only little old ladies did that."

"Little old ladies and boring country doctors."

"Do they talk back?"

"Not in English, but in plant kinds of ways."

"Such as …?"

"Sometimes they lean forward to greet me, as though I'm a good friend or neighbor passing by."

"Perambulating the boundaries of the rose garden?"

He laughed. "You're a quick study."

"Go on, I'm all ears," she encouraged. "How else do you and your plants communicate?"

"Well, sometimes I shake hands with them," he admitted. "I can't exactly explain why. Not the roses, of course …"

"Naturally."

"… but most of the others. When a plant leans toward me—what else can I do? I feel rude walking away without at least an affectionate touch. Sometimes it seems as though one of them has something special or important to say and so I linger longer when paying my respects. Mostly, though, my plants alert me to up-coming changes to the weather. And before you think I'm completely crazy I should inform you that Linnaeus—you know who he is, the father of modern taxonomy—he once listed forty-six flowers whose sensibilities were affected by the weather."

"Flower sensibility? I don't think you're crazy. I think you've been reading too much Jane Austen! If I thought black-eyed Susans were trying to strike up a conversation with me every time I passed them by I'd never get anywhere."

"Now you know why I'm often late," he said, chuckling. "It's not always an emergency—although that's what Mom tells everyone. Sometimes it's nothing more than I have to stop and talk to my plants." Metcalf hummed a little tune. "Did you know? Lilacs were once used to divine love. If you were a fortune teller, you could make a good business out of that practice today."

"How does it work?"

"The woman in question—the one who wants to know whether she's loved—swallows a five-petal lilac floret. Most lilacs have four-petals so the five-petal is supposedly endowed with special powers. If the woman is able to cry out 'He loves me!' while swallowing the five-petal floret, then he does love her."

"What if he doesn't love her?"

"She chokes."

"Remind me not to order lilacs for lunch."

Their conversation continued in much the same light-hearted vein as they motored along through the fall countryside. The brilliant colors of October—yellows, oranges, reds—had already given way to the more muted grays, ambers, and mauves of November. When they reached the sleepy town of Kingfield, not far from Sugarloaf Ski Resort, Metcalf pulled into Longfellow's, a small restaurant near the bridge. "Are you hungry?" he asked.

"Starved! I can't believe it's lunchtime already."

"Time flies when you're talking plants. I've eaten here before and I think I can safely say you won't find any flowers on the menu. Not since nasturtiums have gone out of season, anyway."

The restaurant was quiet, bereft of tourists. Maine's foliage season had unofficially ended two weeks earlier on Columbus Day and the winter ski season had yet to gear up. The waitress seated them at a table for two situated on a heated back porch overlooking the dam and the bubbling Carrabassett River. The clear water sparkled with sun diamonds as it leaped down over the gray rocks. Nellie gazed out the window, savoring the moment. She had a presentiment that someday she would look back on this as one of the happiest days of her life.

After they had placed their order, however, Nellie noticed a change in Doctor Bart. He began shifting in his chair, as though he had something to serious to say but didn't know how to begin. Finally, he clasped his hands on the table and assumed a grave demeanor. "I owe you an explanation, Nellie, about my behavior the other night."

Nellie felt her face grow warm. "Please, don't …"

"I took advantage of you while you were in a vulnerable state. No, let me finish, please."

Nellie, who was about to protest further obediently fell silent. She knew she needed to hear what he had to say, no matter how difficult and awkward his confession would be for both of them. She folded her hands in her lap and prepared for further chagrin.

"Worse than my selfishness," he said forthrightly, his hazel eyes meeting hers, "I embarrassed you in front of an old family friend. There's no excuse for it, except … except …" He broke off and stared out the window at the dam.

"Except?" she prodded gently.

"Except … I love you, Nellie. I've always loved you—ever since we were kids." He paused momentarily but when she didn't stop him, he continued, gaining encouragement. "You were adorable, as kids go, with that chaotic yellow hair and those crazy dresses Aunt Maggie made you wear."

It was on the tip of Nellie's tongue to tell him she had selected those dresses herself. This time, however, she wisely bit her tongue, offering instead an encouraging smile. She knew nothing he could say or do would make her love him any more than she did in this moment. But she would let him have his say without interrupting him—and then she would put him out of his misery.

"I wouldn't have paid much attention to you—cuteness notwithstanding—if I hadn't seen how lonely and miserable you were. I don't want to find fault with Aunt Maggie but I think we can both agree she wasn't the most attentive mother. So I set myself up to be your big brother of sorts. I think I was fairly successful, too." He glanced anxiously at Nellie, as if seeking affirmation.

"I always knew I could count on you," she said quietly.

"I'm relieved to hear you say that," he said, leaning back. "I was afraid you'd begun to think I was persecuting you, chasing after you like a besotted teenager every time you came home."

"I never thought that."

"Despite how it might have appeared, I haven't been chasing after you for my benefit alone. At least that's my excuse. I'm almost embarrassed to admit—because it sounds so self-serving when I say it aloud—but I began to think that marrying me would be good for you. I thought, given the insecurity of your childhood, you'd benefit from my steadiness. I could give you a settled home, which you always seemed to be looking for, just never in your own backyard. But when you never gave me any encouragement—just the opposite, in fact—I thought my case was hopeless. And then poor Peter died, your mother left for parts unknown, and you came back among us. Frankly, Nellie, I've fallen in love with you all over again. I've seen a side of you I never saw before, a new maturity, a deeper compassion for others. I've also seen a new vulnerability, which is understandable given the fact that you've just lost the only father you ever had. I swore when you came home in August that I wouldn't take advantage of you in your vulnerable state; I would be there for you, as a brother or father or uncle or trusted friend or whatever you wanted, but I wouldn't pursue you as a lover until I was convinced you were able to stand on your feet again. The other night when you looked up at me I saw something in your eyes I'd never seen for me before, and … I lost my head. All my good intentions went right out the window. I would have ravaged you on the kitchen table if Julian Mills hadn't broken in on us. Probably I should be grateful to him for interrupting, but I'm not."

Unfortunately, before Nellie could hint she might have welcomed his ravishment—that in fact, she was in love with him—the waitress arrived with their food. She felt irrationally irritated that the girl had interrupted them just at the pivotal moment, postponing what appeared to be a marriage proposal. When she had first returned to Sovereign she would have been grateful for such an interruption. But her feelings for Metcalf, much like her feelings for her new friends—and even for her mother—had undergone such a dramatic transformation over the past three months she now welcomed his proposal with open arms.

How had it all happened? How had she evolved from feeling unloved, unwanted, a sideshow of sorts as 'The Minister's Daughter,' to become a cherished, protected member of a community, something greater than herself?

When she had returned to town she had been self-absorbed, selfish and a bit of a snob. Now, she would willingly set aside her own selfish desires to do whatever lay in her power to make Metcalf happy. She only wanted to have the chance to prove to him she was worthy of his goodness, his selflessness, his unwavering love for her.

"Need anything else?" the waitress asked, stepping back from the table.

"Nellie?"

"Nothing else for me," she replied, smiling at him. "I have everything I need right here."

His freckled face flushed happily.

After lunch, they motored a few miles outside the village of Kingfield until they reached a trailhead leading to the Narrow Gauge Pathway, a rail-to-trail path along the banks of the Carrabassett River. "Ready to go for that short hike?" he asked. "I have something special I want to show you."

Nellie smiled her acquiescence and he tucked her hand in his arm. They strolled companionably through the woods toward the river. Two or three chickadees followed them, flitting from tree to tree along the narrow pathway. She inhaled the fresh scent of the forest and with it a hint of frost. As they walked along they met and greeted two other couples returning to their vehicles. A lone bicyclist zipped past them on the gravel path, sending a few small stones scattering to the side.

When they reached the river, they came upon a wooden trestle spanning the wide gulf of water. Metcalf led Nellie out into the center of the bridge and stopped so she could look around and enjoy the panoramic view. Columns of trees lined the shore on either side of the river. The trees, naked of their leaves, appeared to hug themselves with spindly limbs as though trying to stay warm. Nellie, glancing to the north, thought she spied November lurking offstage and empathized with the shivering trees. It wouldn't be long now before winter swooped down upon them all with her frozen wand, turning everything myriad shades of white.

"I wanted you to see these," Metcalf said, bringing to her attention several stone cairns and ad-hoc sculptures that adorned the river bed.

The water was low and sparkling clear, and Nellie could see that fun-loving hands had created whimsical designs underwater with colorful stones. One of the fluid-looking designs spiraled on along the river bottom for nearly a hundred yards. Another was a circle of stones rising up out of the water like a mythical sea creature, holding itself upright by the volume of its own weight and cleverness of shape. "It's beautiful," she cried, attempting to take it all in at once. "How did you ever find this place?"

"I stumbled onto it quite by accident a few years ago. I've been here several times since then and every time there's something new and wonderful to discover. Come, I particularly want you to see this one. I'm not sure who contrived this creation, but I'm sure it's meant for you."

"For me?"

He said no more but led her to the opposite end of the bridge and gestured down. Nellie gazed into the crystal water and was astonished to see a large heart, ten or twelve feet across, shaped by a collection of flat, copper-colored rocks lying perfectly still upon the sandy river bottom. The rocks appeared as natural as though the spring freshet had carried the stones downriver and settled them carefully into their final resting spot.

"I know you think I'm boring, Nellie. No, don't deny it—I'm not a complete idiot. Even I realize I'm not as exciting and intriguing as someone like, say, Walden. But I do have a romantic side, too. Here's my heart; it's yours for the taking. If sometime in the not-too-distant future you think you might be ready to settle down—and if you think you can love a stuffy, boring, country doctor who talks to his plants—well, you know where my heart is. But I want you to know that if you decide your path lies with another man, I'll still be there for you. I'll lead you down the aisle or stand up with you at the altar, or whatever you want. I'll love you every step of the way from this moment until my last breath, even if I'm not the one who's walking by your side. The choice is yours, my darling."

Tears filled her eyes. "Oh, Metcalf! I …"

He stopped her. "I'm not looking for an answer today. Give a guy a little time to hope, OK?"

The look Metcalf bestowed upon Nellie as he added this entreaty was one of boyish eagerness and she had all she could do to keep from throwing herself into his arms. But some little voice emanating from her better nature made her pause. With her newfound maturity she was able to see deeper into his character and she suddenly realized that, despite his boyishness, he wasn't jesting. He was sincere. He wanted her to take some time to think about his proposal. He wanted to know for a surety that her reply was not simply prompted by the romance of the moment but rather came from a place of deep and abiding love for him.

"I'll take it under advisement," she promised, clasping his arm affectionately. "*If* you tell me one thing."

"What's that?"

"What the purple asters in my tussie-mussie are trying to say to me."

He chuckled. "You are incorrigible!"

"I know. And that's why you love me."

"That might be one of the reasons why I love you—but it isn't the only one. For your information, the aster symbolizes love and patience. Need I say more?"

CHAPTER 26

The House by the Side of the Road

On Monday, Nellie determined to finish the quilt for Rebecca's baby shower. She still had the backing to apply, so after breakfast she set herself up in the living room and began the laborious job of hand-sewing. She could have used her mother's portable sewing machine; however, she had decided from the outset she would make the quilt entirely by hand, having adopted a purist attitude toward quilting not uncommon to modern quilters. During the morning she made great progress, but in the afternoon she was interrupted by a knock at the shed door. Metcalf had told her he had a busy week coming up and warned her she was unlikely to see him, so although Nellie's heart fluttered at the sound of the knock she knew he was not the originator of the sound. She carefully secured her needle, set the quilt aside, and stepped into the kitchen. Out of habit, she glanced at her image in the mirror hanging next to the door. She spied a pink thread dangling from her hair and hastily removed it.

The knock came again, this time sounding more impatient. When she opened the door Nellie was surprised to discover Julian Mills standing on the granite stoop. "Doctor Mills!"

"Good afternoon, Nellie. I hope I'm not disturbing you. May I come in for a moment?"

Nellie hesitated. Did she really want to chat with Julian Mills? Wouldn't it be better if she told him she was too busy to see him?

He sensed she was about to fob him off. "I'm on my way to the airport and I wanted to have a few words with you before I left Maine for good. If you don't mind…?"

He was leaving? Perhaps giving him five or ten minutes was a small price to pay for knowing when the door closed behind him she'd never see him again. "Sure. Why not?"

She led him into the kitchen and offered him a chair. She was about to apologize for not seating him in the living room because of the mess, but remembered just in time his lecture to her about apologizing too much. He accepted the seat at the table and gazed at her in an expectant fashion. Nellie wavered, knowing she should offer him a cup of tea at the very least. She had been bought up under a strict small-town protocol, which was that one always offered guests appropriate refreshment no matter how ill-timed the visit or how unwanted the visitor. She attempted to shake off the protocol—even pulling out a chair for herself across the table from him—but discovered to her annoyance that she could not shirk her duty. "Would you like some tea?"

"That would be nice. Herbal, if you have it."

Nellie set the copper kettle onto cookstove and switched on the gas burner. "That's pretty much all we do have. Mother makes her own. She's always concocting some herbal tea or other."

"So … Maggie is still into herbs, is she? Witches brew, I used to say."

Nellie allowed the slur to pass. She wasn't going to be drawn into an argument with Julian Mills because that would only prolong his visit. She would hear what he had to say—most likely some message for her mother—and then send the author on his way.

She opened the tea cupboard, selected a jar of a dried herb mixture, and set it on the counter. "This is Mother's autumn mix, which I think is very nice. She makes if from dried rose hips, lemon balm, raspberry leaves, and bee balm. Is that OK?"

"That will be fine." Julian Mills settled back into his chair and unzipped his leather aviator jacket.

Nellie was relieved to note he didn't remove his jacket. She hoped that meant he didn't plan to stay long. She set two ceramic mugs on the table and busied herself preparing the tea. Although her back was turned to him, she had the eerie sense he was watching her every movement. She felt as though she was being inspected for some obscure purpose and idly wondered whether she would pass the great Julian Mills' litmus test. Probably not.

"Are you always so self-conscious?"

Startled, Nellie felt herself stiffen. "I've never liked being the center of attention," she said coolly. Fortunately, the teakettle on the stove whistled, giving her something to do. She switched off the propane and poured boiling water into the ceramic teapot, floating the colorful dried berries and green herbs to the top.

"A beautiful young woman like you! Not enjoy being the center of attention? How did that happen?"

Nellie set the steaming teapot onto the table next to the two mugs. The rosehip tea filled the kitchen with a moist, fruity fragrance. "Who knows?" she replied, attempting to shrug off his question. She rummaged through the center drawer to locate the stainless steel tea strainer. "I've never liked to have my picture taken, either. I've been that way since I was a little girl." She placed the tea strainer on the table and slid into the chair across from him. She stared boldly at him, expecting him now to censure her mother, as he was wont to do. She was prepared to pounce on him if he did.

Julian Mills accorded her a sardonic smile, but said nothing. Once again she had the feeling she had met him before. His handsome face, with its pronounced cheek bones and aquiline nose seemed maddeningly familiar. Perhaps she had met him when she was a young child, too young to remember who he was but old enough to recognize him now? If that was the case, he must have forgotten they had met or he would have mentioned it, unless of course he was one of those men who didn't consider children 'people' until they reached the age where one could converse intelligently with them.

"I was disappointed not to see you in church yesterday, Nellie. I rather expected—given your remarks about my books during my first visit—you would want to hear me speak. Perhaps I was mistaken …?"

Nellie set the tea strainer on top of one of the mugs and poured out a small quantity of tea in order to see if the tea was sufficiently infused. "I had other plans," she said. Satisfied with the tea, she filled the mug and set the hot tea in front of him. "I'd love a copy of your pastoral message—that is, if you wouldn't mind emailing it to me."

Pleased, he bobbed his carefully coiffed silver head. "It would be my pleasure."

"Honey?" She held up the jar of Wendell's wildflower honey.

"Thank you, no. Too messy."

Nellie poured out her own tea and liberally helped herself to some of Wendell's honey. She felt almost savagely happy when some of the sticky honey dribbled down the side of the jar and spilled onto the table. After a moment's reflection, however, she berated herself for such small-mindedness.

"Were you out with your young man yesterday? What's his name? Doctor Bart?"

"We went for a drive," Nellie replied, defensively.

"Very nice."

To Nellie's relief, he appeared to let the matter drop. She had been expecting a sharp reproof since she knew for some inexplicable reason the best-selling author had taken a disliking to Metcalf.

"Have you heard from your mother? I think you said she was at some sort of spiritual retreat?"

"She called Saturday night." Nellie shook off her dripping teaspoon and set it down onto the patterned tablecloth. "I wasn't here. I was working at the church—our annual Harvest Supper. She left a message, though."

Julian Mills straightened up and leaned forward. His white teeth flashed. "Did she have anything particular to say?"

His unnatural eagerness about her mother reminded Nellie of the Big Bad Wolf. She began to feel uneasy. "No, unfortunately her message was garbled."

"That's a shame," he said, with a smile that belied his words.

Nellie felt as though the two of them were playing a cat-and-mouse game—and there was no question which of them was the mouse. "Why do you hate her? Mother? You always seem so satisfied when I tell you bad news about her."

His eyes darkened. "You mistake me, Nellie. I don't dislike your mother. Indeed, I have the utmost respect for her. She's the hardest working woman I know. She's one of the indefatigable soldiers for Christ who never lift their heads up out of the trenches long enough to be shot at."

"See—right there! What do you mean by that? You start out with something that appears to be a compliment but then at the end you turn it around so it's really a dig."

"Nellie, Nellie! You're misunderstanding me, I think. You're overly sensitive about your mother, for some reason. What a merry dance she must have led you in childhood! Tell me, how often did she leave you alone while she sallied forth to save the world? You can't deny she left you home alone?"

"Why do you care?" she challenged him. "What's it to you?"

He fondled the handle of his tea mug with his perfectly manicured hands. "Ah, what's it to me? Why should I care that the lovely, gifted daughter of a friend of mine is hermetically hidden away in this anachronistic excuse for a town? Think of all the places you could go, Nellie! I could take you places you never dreamed existed and introduce you to the world's movers and shakers. With your looks and your intelligence—and some judicious instruction—in no time you'd have them all at your feet."

"I don't want anyone at my feet." Metcalf's beloved countenance popped into her head. "Well, maybe just one person. But I certainly don't care about the movers and shakers of the world. The less seen of them the better, I think." Nellie glanced at the clock. Three o'clock already! "I'm sorry; I need to get back to work. I'm sewing a quilt for a friend's baby shower this weekend."

"Very quaint."

His remark irked Nellie, giving her courage to stand up to him. "We are a bit provincial here," she retorted, "but people in Sovereign truly care about one another. I'm sorry if our lifestyle doesn't appeal to you, but that won't bother you much since you're leaving." She rose from the table, unconcerned that she had apologized yet again. She had given Julian Mills all the time he was going to get.

"I've offended you, I see. Well, perhaps another time." He followed her lead and stood up.

Nellie stepped over to the kitchen door in order to usher him out. Before he departed the author briefly paused to examine his reflection in the oak mirror, much as she herself had done a thousand times before. Her gaze instinctively followed his. Their eyes met in the mirror—and locked. Unspoken intelligence leaped from his mocking hazel orbs to her matching eyes. She heard a ringing in her ears and the ground seemed to buckle beneath her feet. Suddenly, she knew without a shadow of a doubt where she had seen his face before—it was in her own reflection!

"You!" she exclaimed, whirling around, horrified by the mirror's revelation. "Oh-my-God—you're my father!"

Everything fell into place: his mysterious comments, his sudden appearance after her mother's prolonged departure, and his intimate knowledge of Maggie's ways and her mother's childhood friends. Everything made sense now, especially his interest in Nellie and her future.

"And you're my darling daughter." He bent to kiss her on the cheek but Nellie jerked away from him.

"How could you? How could you have left us alone all these years?"

He shrugged. "Your mother and I made a bargain. I was merely upholding my end of the deal."

"I don't believe you!"

"Nellie, Nellie! Calling me a liar won't change the truth."

"You owe me an explanation. Sit down." Nellie realized she was shaking with anger. She unclenched her fists. "Please," she added, almost as an afterthought.

"Are you sure you want to hear the truth?" he asked. He slowly reclaiming his chair.

She resolutely thrust her chin forward. "Don't waste your implied threats on me. Nothing you can say will change my love for my mother. Now, tell me what happened," she demanded.

He clasped his hands atop the table and smiled at her half apologetically. "You were an accident, naturally. Nellie Walker was never meant to be! Although it pains me to admit that to your face. It was the same old story—your mother assured me she was using protection and obviously she wasn't. No doubt she was hoping to trap me into marriage. Let me finish, my dear! Our affair wasn't a lasting passion, at least not on my side, but more of a pleasurable way to spend a Sunday afternoon. When Maggie informed me she was pregnant I immediately arranged for an abortion, which was perfectly legal in Maine and would have been the logical solution given our individual circumstances. I had just been called by the largest evangelical congregation in California, while your mother was finishing up the coursework necessary to become an ordained minister. How many churches do you think want to be led by an unwed mother, hmm? Not many, as your mother found out the hard way. Did you never wonder why your mother bounced around from church to church? Why Maggie was dismissed from that cushy pastorate in Portland? Why, despite her many gifts, which I'll freely own she possesses—she's a very fine parish minister and pastoral counsellor—she ended up as an itinerant minister, driving all over the state of Maine merely to serve insignificant rural congregations like Sovereign?"

"You mean …?"

"You know what I mean, Nellie. She's not in this backwater by choice. She's here from necessity. These people don't know any better than to set an unwed mother up in the pulpit above them, nor do they …"

"She's not above them," Nellie interrupted. "My mother is not above anybody here. These people are our friends and neighbors. Mother stands shoulder-to-shoulder with them, through sickness and in health. She sits with them when they're sick and holds their hands while they're dying. She comforts those who are left behind."

"Then she's perfectly well-placed, isn't she? Your mother has found her home, such as it is." He glanced around the rustic country kitchen with an expression of disdainful contempt. "But there's no necessity for you to follow suit. The sins of the fathers—and mothers—are not necessarily visited upon the children, not now. Don't you understand? You're free, Nellie! Free to leave this domicile of darkness and come into the light, into a fruitful world where the good things of God's green earth are plentiful and easy for you to harvest. Come with me and I can put you in possession of a life most people only dream about."

He spoke with such eloquence Nellie could see how a rudderless soul might easily fall under his influence. However, she was not a rudderless soul. She was wide awake and perfectly able to recognize malarkey when she heard it. "That's bullshit," she declared. "You don't care about me. All you care about is yourself. If you truly cared about me you would have been here when I needed you; when *we* needed you," she amended.

"If you'd let me finish …"

"Tell me about this so-called deal," she cut him off, boldly. She felt ruthless, as though his failure as a parent had given her a strange power over him. Her ire had nearly reached the boiling point yet she felt in complete control of the situation. "What bargain did you make with my mother?"

He shrugged again. "Have it your way, my dear."

"And stop calling me that. I'm not your 'dear'. Now, what was the deal?"

"Simply this—your mother and I both agreed to give up something we very much desired. I agreed to cancel the appointment for the abortion, to which by the way your mother was not ethically opposed having been pro-choice for many years. She merely felt her clock was running out and she might not have another opportunity to bear a child."

"And what did she give up?"

"Maggie? Surely you must have guessed by now? She gave up all rights to the book."

"What book? What are you talking about? She's still working on her book about Maine's small churches."

He laughed in a vulgar fashion. "Don't tell me she's still wasting time on that white dinosaur! She always said she was going to turn that drivel from her Master's thesis into a book. You couldn't pay me enough to take *that* tome off her hands. No, no, I'm speaking of 'The House by the Side of the Road,' naturally. You never guessed?"

He bobbed his silver head in the general direction of Maggie's comfortable rocking chair, which was situated next to the window where her mother often sat and watched the world go by. "Open your eyes, Nellie! Can't you see the truth? It's not my life detailed in that book—it's your mother's. This just proves what I've always believed about how little we know about those with whom we live! 'Let me live in a house by the side of the road, where the race of men go by'," he quoted. "'The men who are good and the men who are bad, as good and bad as I. I will not sit in the scorner's seat nor hurl the cynic's ban. Let me live in a house by the side of the road and be a friend to man.' Sound familiar?"

"Oh-my God—Mother? Mother wrote 'The House by the Side of the Road'?" Nellie rose up in astonishment. "How could I not have seen it?"

"Before she found out she was pregnant Maggie asked me to read a manuscript she'd written the year she entered seminary," he continued. "Her Grandmother Walker—your great-grandmother—had just died and she was moved by the experience to scribble some things down. She asked for my opinion of the piece, knowing I was a published writer. I read the manuscript and immediately recognized in Maggie's charming prose a simplistic, universal theme that might appeal to the masses. So I sent the manuscript to a friend of mine who worked for a major publishing house in New York—without telling him the truth about its authorship, naturally. The publishing house came back to me with a contract and a sizeable advance."

"You're a thief and an imposter!"

"I'm not a thief. Your mother freely signed away her rights to that work. I have the paper to prove it, although I wouldn't need such proof now. If Maggie were to make a claim against me, who would believe her? The washed up pastor of backwoods church?"

"So instead of doing the right thing you decided to sit in the scorner's seat and hurl the cynic's ban?"

"Audentes fortuna juvat—'Fortune favors the bold,' Nellie. According to Virgil, and I must say I agree with him."

Amazed by everything she had heard, Nellie paced a few quick steps back and forth. "I still can't believe my mother traded away her rights to that book for … for me?"

"Would you rather she had not made the trade? That's a very depressing thought, isn't it? We wouldn't be having this lovely father-daughter chat now, would we?"

She glared at him. "You might be my birth father, but you're not my real father." She shook her fist. "Uncle Peter was my *real* father. You're nothing to me—nothing! And it's way past time for you to leave. Get out!"

Julian Mills casually eyed his Rolex. "It is getting late. I certainly wouldn't want to miss my plane."

"You don't belong in Sovereign—you belong in … in, I don't know where you belong, but not here! This town is too good for you."

"Like mother, like daughter?" he queried, snidely.

"Thanks. I'll take that as a compliment," she shot back.

Julian Mills chuckled. "Suit yourself." He pulled himself up to his full height and squared his shoulders. "Never say I didn't offer you a better choice, Nellie. A better life."

"Nothing you can offer me is better than the life I have right here, right now, today."

He zipped up his jacket and bobbed his coifed head. "Then I'll say adieu, my dear. Enjoy your life, such as it is." And then her father exited without a backward glance.

CHAPTER 27
"Something Greater Than My Own Small Self"

"Horrible, horrible man!" Rebecca cried. "You're a better person than me, Nellie. I would have tossed my cup of tea right into his smug little face." She hotly clutched the handle of her porcelain teacup as though preparing to demonstrate.

"Believe me, I thought about it. But the tea had cooled off so much I knew it wouldn't hurt him," Nellie replied, honestly. Both women laughed, which helped defuse some of the anger Nellie felt at discovering her birth father was a cad.

With Maggie still absent and unavailable, Nellie had sought comfort from the most motherly person she knew—Rebecca Russell. Her first thought had been to telephone Metcalf at work and cry on his shoulder. But she didn't want to interrupt him with a patient and also preferred to tell him the news in person. So she laid her troubles at Rebecca's door, feeling as though her female neighbor embodied the perfect combination of friend and surrogate mother.

The two women were sitting at Rebecca's kitchen table, the tea kettle bubbling merrily on the woodstove puffing steam into the room. As soon as Nellie had arrived at the old Russell homestead—in obvious distress—Wendell had risen up, tossed two sticks of wood into the fire, set the tea kettle on, and exited for parts unknown. "I'm so sorry, Nellie," Rebecca continued. "I wish there was something I could say or do to make it better. I suppose another cookie wouldn't help?"

"Couldn't make it any worse," Nellie replied, with a wry smile. Rebecca lifted up the plate and Nellie absent-mindedly helped herself to a third lemon butter cookie. "What's worse is how I treated my mother all those years," she continued. "It kills me to think of him lounging by the pool in New Mexico enjoying the income from Maggie's book while she worked two or three churches to support us.

I spent most of my life denigrating and belittling my mother—more of a handicap to her than a help—all the while creating fantasies about a man who never bothered to wonder if I had a pair of winter boots or if there was enough food on the table for us to eat. And then when I remember Maggie getting up in the night to keep the fires going, well, I … I," she broke off.

"There, there, dear. Go ahead and cry. You'll feel better afterwards." Rebecca pushed her pregnant body away from the table and stretched for her purse, which was on the windowsill. "Here's my handkerchief—it was Grammie Addie's. Wendell's grandmother used to say: 'Never underestimate the power of a handkerchief'."

Nellie accepted the purple embroidered white handkerchief and continued to cry for several minutes. When she was cried out, she wiped away her tears. She glanced down at the delicate handkerchief and was suddenly struck by its simple beauty. "Did you find this in one of the old dressers here?"

"No, your mother gave me that, although I did find a precious lace christening outfit and some handmade linen tablecloths upstairs in one of the dressers. Remind me to show them to you later. Miss Hastings gave this handkerchief to your mother, who gave it to me. There were two. Maggie kept one for herself. Open it up and you'll see Addie's initials."

Nellie unfurled the damp white handkerchief and examined the purple embroidered initials—ALR. "What does the 'L' stand for?"

"Libby. Addie's maiden name, I believe."

Nellie placed the handkerchief on the kitchen table, smoothed out the wrinkles, and neatly folded the cloth three times. "Thanks, I do feel better," she said, returning the handkerchief to Rebecca. "Maybe the handkerchief does have a special power."

"The power of love—and history."

"I get the love part, but why the history?"

"Because history teaches us that while blood might be thicker than water, it's no guarantee of respect. Family isn't someone with whom we happen to share DNA, by a chance of birth, like your father, Nellie. Family is someone who truly loves us, who cares and respects us, no matter what! That old adage about blood and water went down the drain with the Civil War, I think. We know how that turned out."

"You are so right about that!"

"History also teaches us we're not alone, no matter how lonely we might feel sometimes. The people who came before us—

even if we didn't know them personally—helped through their own lives to make our lives better."

"I'm not sure I follow you. Are you talking about my mother's parents and grandparents?"

"Yes, to some degree. But I'm also talking about Grammie Addie and Pappy, and those others who are no longer with us but whose physical spaces we now inhabit."

"Like at the old schoolhouse?"

"Yes, certainly! Do you never sense the children who used to study and play there? Or the young teachers who tried so hard to teach the children everything they knew?"

Nellie's eyebrows knit thoughtfully together. "I used to feel them, now that you mention it. But I'd forgotten all about it. The first time Mother left me alone—I was seven or eight—I was terrified. But then I heard (or thought I heard) kids laughing and shouting and playing, and that got me wondering how many kids used to go to school there and exactly where their desks had been. I went to look and found the holes in the kitchen floor where the desks had been nailed down. The next thing I knew Mom was home and I was fine. I never felt alone or afraid in the old schoolhouse after that." Suddenly, Nellie recollected the mural at the old Crockett homestead with Wendell's ancestors walking off to church with their Bibles. "And you must feel Wendell's ancestors here?"

"I do. Sometimes, when I'm in the garden weeding or picking peas, I see shadows—just the faintest outlines—of them. I try not to move too quickly or they'll disappear. Once I thought I saw Grammie Addie thinning sweet corn—she always used to plant two kernels and then weed out the weakest sprout. But when I put my hand out to touch her, she's gone. Knowing I'm standing on her shoulders—and she was standing on someone else's shoulders—makes it easier for me to see the big picture. Understanding I'm connected to something greater than my own small self helps me keep my problems in perspective."

"I like the sound of that—being part of something greater than my own small self."

Rebecca gathered up three hand-carved wooden clothespins and held them out to Nellie. "Look at these—aren't they beautiful? I found a pail full of them in the shed this morning. Feel how smooth they are. Aren't they wonderful?"

Nellie accepted the slotted clothespins and ran her thumb over one of the curved heads. "Wow, that *is* smooth! So simple and utilitarian, and yet beautiful, too."

"Wendell says each clothespin is hand-carved from a solid piece of wood, probably birch."

"Who made them?"

"Bud. He was the hired hand during Grammie Addie's day. He lived in that little cabin out back. Bud loved to whittle and was known throughout the county for his bird carvings. One of his carvings sold for three hundred dollars at an auction recently. I'm sure Bud would have been surprised to hear that!"

"Too bad he wasn't the one who ended up with the money."

"Sometimes I feel as though I have a leg in several different time periods of history. Don't you feel that way?"

"I'm feeling that now."

"Living in history gives us a richer, more rewarding life, I think."

"It's funny you should mention that because I've thought the exact same thing before, only maybe not in English."

Rebecca chuckled. "English isn't my first language, either. Poor Wendell! My first language is the language of feelings, which then morphs into an image, and then finally I latch onto words. It's an arduous translation process, sometimes. For many years, especially after my son Scott was killed, I didn't know what I felt because I didn't have time to reflect upon my feelings, nor did I want to, I suppose. One of the things Lila and I appreciated most about moving to Sovereign—in addition to the wonderful people here—was having quiet time to think. We had gotten so caught up in our hectic modern lives, and in all the terrible things that were happening around the world, we hardly had a moment to ourselves much less time for thoughtful contemplation. How much better we all would be if we took some time for contemplation at the beginning and end of every day! Those old Calvinists who insisted on morning and evening prayers attended by the whole family knew what they were doing. Oh, dear. I'm babbling, aren't I?"

Nellie shook her head, slightly discomposed by Rebecca's artless revelation. "I didn't know you lost a son," she blurted out. She had never thought much about the life the older woman had before she came to Sovereign, but if asked she certainly she would have said Rebecca had led a charmed life. Obviously, that wasn't the case. "How did he die? I'm sorry—do you mind if I ask?"

"Scott was killed in a motorcycle accident, many years ago," Rebecca replied. "I don't mind talking about it now, especially to you, Nellie. He was out with some young friends and they were partying. I suppose I should have known, but of course I never suspected a thing. Billy, the driver of the motorcycle, went around a corner too fast and lost control. They crashed into a telephone pole and were killed instantly. Scott was only fourteen-years-old."

"Oh-my-God! I'm so sorry. How awful for you! How sad for Amber, too, to lose a brother."

"It was very difficult for her. Amber was six when Scott died. She adored her older brother. When I told her Scott wasn't ever coming home again, well, she was didn't believe me at first. And then she was very angry, as you can imagine. Fortunately, I found an excellent grief counselor for us. Her father refused to get help. Two years later he died—a bitter, angry, unrepentant drunk. I never, ever thought I'd be able to recover from the horror of those days—and look at me now!" She cupped her pregnant belly with her hands, tears in her eyes. "To be given a loving husband, a comfortable home, a supportive community, and a miracle baby at this age, after all I've suffered? Well, it's too wonderful! All I can say is God is truly good."

"I'm sure you deserve to be happy! And so does Amber."

"Thank you, Nellie. She is happy. Amber was born to be a dairy farmer, I think, although she never even petted a cow growing up. God certainly does work in mysterious ways."

"It's no wonder that my mother loves it here," Nellie continued, thoughtfully. "Everyone here has had a difficult life and yet instead of being bitter about it, you're all so loving and caring. I'm beginning to fall in love with Sovereign myself."

"I'm so glad to hear you say that! I was hoping when you came back to us this time you'd have a change of heart. I know you've always thought we were a bit old-fashioned and out of touch. Confess—you did think we were a step or two out of time," Rebecca said, smiling sweetly. "Didn't you?"

Nellie's mind quickly reverted back to those first few days of her return to Sovereign. "I did feel that way," she admitted. "But … something happened to me. I'm not sure exactly what, but the change began the morning you came to see me. After you left, Shirley Palmer dropped in—just like you'd said would happen—and she brought me the yummiest chocolate cake I've ever eaten in my life. Somehow, after that cake, my defenses seemed to crumble."

Rebecca laughed, and lifted her teacup. "A toast—to Shirley Palmer's chocolate cake!" The two women clinked teacups.

Nellie took a sip of tea. "I'm looking forward to seeing Lila again," she said, returning the china cup to its delicate matching saucer. "I never really got to know her before she moved away. When are they arriving for the baby shower?"

"Friday afternoon. They're all three coming: Lila, her husband, Mike, and little Claire. They're staying here with us. This used to be her house until she gave it to me as a wedding present."

"Wow! Some wedding present."

"That's Lila, so loving and generous. I can hardly believe it's only been three years since Miss Hastings invited Lila and me to visit Sovereign—so much has happened to both of us. Last time I saw Claire, which was at Miss Hastings' funeral, she was just starting to walk. She's the spitting image of Lila, except she has blonde hair, which she gets from her father."

"He's a nice guy, isn't he?"

"Mike? He's the best. There's no more perfect man for Lila than Mike Hobart. But it wasn't all love and roses for her either, Nellie. Before Lila could bring herself to accept Mike's love she had a lot of emotional healing work to do. This house—and Mike's love—gave her the courage to tackle some demons from her past, demons that had been keeping her from the love and happiness she'd been searching for. Oh, Nellie—what is it? Did I say something wrong?"

"No, no," Nellie replied, brushing away a few tears. "I just realized I'll never have something I've been longing for my whole life."

"What's that, dear?"

"Grandparents! I was so hoping when I found my father I'd find an extended family, too. When I was a kid all my childhood friends bragged about how they were spoiled by their grandparents. And Metcalf is always telling me stories about his Grandmother Metcalf. I'm so envious! Now, I'll never have that. Julian Mills, my father—such as he is—was an orphan."

"How can you say that, Nellie? Why, you've got both a grandmother *and* a grandfather!"

"I do?"

"I've never seen a more attentive and loving grandfather than Henry Trow! And I've certainly never known Hannah Shorey to share one of her recipes. Believe me, that speaks volumes! They both love you very much. You've found your grandparents, Nellie, just not where you were expected to find them."

Nellie's face brightened. "I have, haven't I?"

"Did you ever read your mother's book, 'Hens and Chickens'?"

"No, I thought that was one of her sermons, which I generally avoid like the plague."

"The book did start as a pastoral message, but it was so well-received at church she expanded upon her sermon. The gist of her message was that when loving old hens and lovelorn baby chicks go looking for love, they'll find one another. Your mother found her special person in your great-grandmother, and Lila discovered hers in Mike's father."

"Mike's father? But I thought Lila fell in love with Mike?"

"She did. But she didn't agree to marry Mike until after she'd met his father. She'd been very close to her own father, you see, who died when she was a child. And likewise Mr. Hobart had lost his wife and had been longing for a daughter-in-law who would hopefully bring his son back home to Maple Grove. Maggie arranged for the two of them to get together and the rest, as they say, is history, or perhaps I should say 'her-story'. When Lila met Mike's father she realized she had finally found her rightful place in the world as part of the extended Hobart family. She found her nest, her home, a safe place where she could raise chicks of her own."

"That's what I've been looking for—only I didn't know it."

"But you've found it here, haven't you, Nellie? You've found a grandmother in Aunt Hannah and a grandfather in Henry Trow. And maybe, hopefully, a lover and a husband in Doctor Bart. But … I won't push you in that direction. Much as I love *love*, I'm not a matchmaker. I'll leave that to Maggie." Rebecca shifted in her chair, attempting to find a more comfortable position. "Speaking of Maggie, there's one other thing I'd like to add before you leave. It's not about Maggie specifically; it's a little aphorism about mothers in general."

"Oh? What's that?"

"Most women go through two distinct stages in their lives relative to their mothers. In the first stage, we pray to God we don't end up like her."

Nellie smiled, instantly identifying with the truism. "That's for sure! What's the second stage?"

"In the second stage—we thank God because we do!"

On the walk home Nellie contemplated with deep appreciation Rebecca's motherly words of wisdom. She was moved by her neighbor's candor in speaking of her son's death. Such openness of heart made Rebecca approachable and completely trustworthy. Once again Nellie recognized that she had been in the presence of the heart and soul of the little community. How fortunate for everyone that Rebecca had been downsized from corporate America and found a new nest in Sovereign, Maine!

Rebecca had invited her to stay for supper, but Nellie gratefully and politely declined. Wendell, worried as a mother hen, offered to drive her home, but Nellie assured him she wanted to walk, knowing she had a private promise to keep. She accepted the loan of a large flashlight—with which she was able to convince both Wendell and Rebecca she would be able to safely navigate the fall twilight without being run over either by an automobile or a moose—and departed the old Russell homestead at dusk.

The crisp late October evening was perfect for ambulation and Nellie set off up the hill in good spirits. From inside the well-lit kitchen the outdoors had appeared black, but when she stepped outside she discovered the rising first-quarter moon threw off enough white light to render Wendell's flashlight unnecessary except to alert the one lone car that motored by of her presence. Metcalf's house, formerly Miss Hastings' little cottage, was still dark. He was not yet home from work. She would call him later to bring him up to speed, but in the meantime, she was on a mission. The hayfield to her right sloped off precipitously, revealing at its western edge a bright orange glow where the night had gobbled up the sun. Nellie, examining the remains of the sunset, could see from whence the colors of Halloween—orange and black—had organically arisen.

When she reached the gate leading into the Russell Hills Cemetery, she paused to catch her breath. She leaned her arms atop the wrought iron gate, surprised and gratified to see a multitude of solar lamps glowing amongst the graves like stars in the night sky. The miniature lights gave the cemetery a fantastic look, as though the spirits of the departed were merely biding their time, waiting for God's regular evening stroll through the Garden so they too could rise up from the dead and join the procession.

Nellie pushed through the unlocked gate and entered the cemetery. The town clerk had told her the approximate location of the Yaroslavsky family's burial plot—Miss Hastings' family surname had been changed from 'Yaroslavsky' to 'Hastings' at Ellis Island—and after a few false starts she was able to locate the correct grassy sward that led to her former music teacher's grave. She trained the spotlight on the marble tombstone and read the epitaph: *Here lies the Songbird of Sovereign ~ free at last.*

She sank down onto her knees in the damp spongy grass and offered up a silent prayer. After brushing away a few tears she settled herself cross-legged in front of the tombstone and began to speak as though sitting over a cup of tea with her former music teacher. "I'm sorry I missed your funeral," she began. "But I'm glad I'm here now." She glanced around the cemetery, admiring the evocative white lights from a different angle. Her gaze returned to Miss Hastings' tombstone. "I found your note," she continued, in a softer voice. "Thanks for all those wonderful things! I can't believe you figured out so much about me during our piano lessons. I never thought about what you were learning from us while we kids were learning piano from you. And you're so right about Doctor Bart—he's just the man for me! I do love him. I just hope I'm good enough for him," she added, worriedly.

Was that a response she heard? A murmur of assurance, wafting about on the evening breeze?

Nellie shut her eyes and allowed her mind to go blank. Immediately Miss Hastings' enthusiastic, cherub-like face framed by wild black-gray curls appeared in her thoughts. She could almost hear the music teacher's cackling laughter and her high heels clicking down the corridors of Heaven. "Dahrrrling, don't you worry your head one little bit about that! You just go out there and love him … and never look back!"

CHAPTER 28
Four Heroines

When Nellie conveyed the news to Doctor Bart on Tuesday afternoon that Julian Mills was her father and that he had tried to tempt her away from Sovereign by dangling the "good" things of the world in front of her eyes, Metcalf, despite her pleadings, immediately buckled on his armor and stormed over to Mike Hobart's cabin where the author had been staying, intending to take the great man down a notch or two. Unfortunately, his adversary had already flown the coop and Metcalf shortly returned to the old schoolhouse morose and downcast. "He's gone," he reported, reentering the kitchen. "There's nothing there but dirty dishes and a lot of trash." He tossed his green-and-black checked jacket, which had served as his armor, onto the back of Maggie's rocker. "I'm afraid Mike and Lila will have quite a clean-up job this weekend. Maybe we can help them?"

"Saturday afternoon is the baby shower," Nellie reminded him. She removed a casserole from the oven and set it on a waiting plate. She had baked shepherd's pie for lunch, one of Aunt Hannah's recipes, and had been keeping it warm until his return. "You need to eat before you go back to work," she urged, setting the casserole on the table.

He pulled up a chair and she served him a large helping of the shepherd's pie. "I'll see if I can help Mike after the clinic closes on Saturday, then," he said. "It's the least I can do, since I'm partly to blame for the mess." He began picking at his food, still preoccupied with Julian Mills.

"How can you say that?" she cried.

He set down his fork. "Because I should have figured out who the fellow was and sent him packing weeks ago. Now that I look back, the truth seems so obvious. Your mother leaves town; Julian Mills arrives. He pesters you to form a relationship with him; yet offers no basis for it. He takes an immediate dislike to me; and tries to drive a wedge between us. On top of that, there was something about him that just bugged me right from the beginning …"

"Such as his insufferable attitude and poor manners?"

"… and yet it never occurred to me he was your father, Nellie. I assumed that any man who had helped create such a lovely, intelligent creature as you would have wanted to shout his paternity to the world, not keep it secret."

At these simple, yet gratifying words, Nellie, who had been in the process of pouring Doctor Bart a glass of milk, rewarded him with a shy peck on the cheek as she set down the cold glass. "My hero," she said. Her hand lingered momentarily on his shoulder.

"But I didn't do anything," he protested. Nonetheless he was obviously pleased.

"Maybe not, but if he had still been at the cabin I have a feeling his face wouldn't be quite as pretty as his author's photo now."

Metcalf chuckled. "Good thing for me Julian Mills was gone, then, or it might have been my face with the damage. He was a muscular-looking fellow for his age."

Nellie, mindful of the other important news she had to impart, applied herself to her own meal. After they finished lunch, she moved Doctor Bart's wool jacket to another chair and relocated him into her mother's rocker. He had become unusually pliant following her kiss on the cheek. "Look out the window," she directed him. "What do you see?"

"I don't know—trees, birds, blue sky. There goes a car. I think it was Shirley. Yes—she waved." He automatically lifted his hand in reply. When the car had motored up the hill he twisted around in the chair. "Was this some sort of test? Did I pass?"

"No, it's not a test. But … does it remind you of anything—sitting there? Take a moment again, only this time pretend you're Maggie. Don't look at me. You're supposed to be looking out the window!"

"Sorry. It would be easier for me to take this seriously if you weren't standing so close to me."

"Silly man." Nevertheless, Nellie stepped away from the rocking chair.

He obediently faced out the window and settled down into himself. Nellie could tell by the set of his chin that he had gone into Doctor Mode. Another car jounced past on the dirt road but this time he didn't respond to the friendly wave. Moments later he rose up and stepped past Nellie almost as though she wasn't there. She quietly followed him into the living room, where he paused in front of the framed poem by Sam Walter Foss. She could see his eyes narrow and realized he was reading the poem. When he finished the last line, he pivoted around, a puzzled expression on his face. "It's the strangest thing," he mused, "but I wonder if Maggie wasn't the author of 'The House by the Side of the Road'—not Julian Mills? The idea occurred to me the other day, when I first saw this poem, but I shrugged it off at the time as too fantastic. Now, however, sitting in her chair, seeing the world from Maggie's perspective—from a house by the side of the road—well … tell me, am I crazy?"

"You're not crazy. You are a genius!" Nellie pronounced, impressed. "What do you think? My mother is a best-selling author!"

Doctor Bart shook his head in disbelief. "But how can that be? You've always lived hand-to-mouth, the two of you. 'The House by the Side of the Road' has sold millions of copies around the world!"

"Have some dessert and I'll tell you everything," Nellie said. She led Metcalf back into the kitchen where she plied him with rosemary shortbread, another of Aunt Hannah's recipes. He ate two pieces while Nellie told him about the bargain Maggie had made with the Devil, as she unflatteringly dubbed her natural father.

"Poor Maggie," he exclaimed, when Nellie had brought her sad tale to a close. "To have been in such a position with such a man! Feeling as though she was held hostage to choose either one or the other—the baby or the book—when both rightfully belonged to her. I would have told him to go jump off a cliff, but then, I'm not a vulnerable, pregnant woman. This shortbread is very good, by the way. Do you have more milk?"

Nellie refilled his glass with the white foaming beverage that came straight from Scotch Broom Acres. She had a standing order with Ryan and Trudy for a gallon a week, plus a pound of butter and a dozen eggs.

"Still, much as I feel sorry for Aunt Maggie," he continued, without missing a beat, "I'm grateful for whatever happened that enabled you to come into this world."

"He couldn't have forced her to have an abortion," Nellie pointed out.

"Not legally, no. But men have been coercing women into doing what they don't want to do for thousands of years."

"He wasn't the least bit apologetic for what he put Mother through, either," Nellie added, hotly. She returned the milk jug to the fridge. "I don't think he ever cared for her and he certainly doesn't care about me, except as an appendage to him."

"Still, one can't help feeling sorry for Julian Mills," Metcalf allowed.

Nellie stopped in her tracks. "I knew it!" she exclaimed, hands on her hips. "I knew it would only be a matter of time before you found an excuse for him."

"Don't get me wrong—I'm not excusing his conduct," he said. He patted the chair next to him. "Come, sit by me," he suggested.

Nellie warily accepted the proffered chair. "OK, I'll bite. Why do you feel sorry for my erstwhile father?"

"Because I'm here with you—and he's not."

How could Nellie find fault with that?

Over the course of the week Metcalf continued to surprise and delight her. Every day he presented Nellie with a thoughtful and beautiful gift, as if attempting to make up for the disappointment about her father. Later that very afternoon, when Nellie was finally putting the finishing touches to Rebecca's baby quilt, the doorbell rang. She set the quilt aside, rose up and peeped out the kitchen window—wanting to ensure that it wasn't Julian Mills hovering on the stoop like the Big Bad Wolf. She spotted a floral delivery van and hurried to the shed door, where she was presented with a large bouquet of yellow roses. She wondered how Metcalf had known yellow roses were her favorite, and then remembered mentioning the fact to him when they were together in Miss Hastings' rose garden during her first week home. She was touched, but not surprised, he had remembered her preference from such a casual conversation.

On Wednesday, he dropped by shortly before noon, bringing with him lunch for two that had been put up by the local deli in Unity. "You're taking a proper lunch two days in a row?" she asked, accepting the white deli bag from him. "What about your patients?"

"I don't see patients during lunch. I see paperwork. And I'd much rather see you than paperwork."

She peeked in the bag. "Ooo, chocolate truffles!"

"Raspberry chocolate," he elucidated, smiling. "I wasn't sure what you liked, but I figured I couldn't go wrong with chocolate."

"You're so right about that!"

Thursday evening Doctor Bart came by after work and presented Nellie with a beautiful knit hat, scarf and mitten set. "It's lovely," she declared, immediately trying on the violet-colored hat and preening before the kitchen mirror. "So soft! Just the right color for me, too."

"I'm glad you like it. The set comes from Fibers of Unity. They have an alpaca farm and a shop, too. I've noticed when you walk you never wear a hat."

"That's because I don't have a hat. I can't bring myself to wear one of Maggie's odd Beanies. I can't think what possessed her to buy so many of those knitted caps."

"I think she probably got those when her hair began to fall out. I've seen some like them at the cancer clinic in Bangor."

Immediately, Nellie felt contrite. "Of course," she cried. "How could I have forgotten?"

"It's easy to forget what you haven't seen," he pointed out. "I think Maggie enjoys those strange hats."

"That sounds like Mother. I'm glad for that. Still, I wouldn't want to wear them."

"Well, now you don't have to."

On Friday morning, when Nellie arrived at the clinic, she discovered a new desk chair in place of her old one, which had been threatening to topple her to the floor for several weeks. In addition, the waiting room was full of flowers, all with her name on them. "Aunt Hannah, what am I going to do?" she wailed, when Doctor Bart disappeared behind closed doors with his first patient. There was no one else but the two of them in the waiting room.

"Why must you do anything?" asked the older woman, setting an armful of bleached white towels onto the desk. She availed herself of the nearest chair and sat down, resting her blue-veined legs.

"To stop this nonsense," Nellie said, indicating the flowers with a little wave of her hand.

The grandmotherly Aunt Hannah, who had perhaps been down this route before, was quick to respond. "My dear, this will end all too soon. In the meantime, try and enjoy it!"

"Well, it is kind of nice," Nellie admitted, twisting the new chair first one way and then the other, trying out its various features. "By the way, I love your pin." She stopped the chair at Aunt Hannah's side of the desk. "Are those Maine tourmalines?"

"Yes. Beautiful, aren't they?"

"Gorgeous." Nellie leaned closer to examine the brooch's pink and green cut gemstones with their mysterious sparkling lights. "I've never seen you wear this one before. Is it new?"

"Brand new. It's a gift from a certain gentleman caller, a mutual friend, I might add."

"Oh-my-God—Mr. Trow?"

The older woman bobbed her white head. A smile adorned her pretty face. "He's done me the honor of asking me to cook his meals and clean up after him for the rest of his life. Frankly, I don't think I can get a better offer at my age. Do you?"

Nellie was floored. "Aunt Hannah! You mean …?"

"I mean I'm no longer going to have to wrestle with that old forsythia bush every spring, my dear. Soon, we'll be neighbors!"

"Oh, that's just what I've always wanted!" Nellie leaped up and gave the older woman a warm hug. "A grandmother living next door to me."

"That's not quite what I was expecting, but I'll take that as a 'Congratulations'."

Saturday afternoon was Rebecca's baby shower and more than two dozen women of various ages—mothers, grandmothers, daughter, friends—crammed into the great room at the old Russell homestead to shower her with gifts and good wishes. Rebecca happily unwrapped a variety of delicate baby clothes, cloth diapers, linens, and other items including a 'How-to' book on child-raising, which brought hoots of laughter from her twenty-four-year-old daughter Amber. "Do you think she's forgotten?" Amber asked Trudy, the giver of the book, wiping tears of laughter from her pretty blue eyes.

"Maybe she thinks I haven't done a very good job with you, darling?" Rebecca responded, before Trudy could reply. She affectionately smoothed Amber's waist-length brown hair. Her daughter, who was a lankier version of herself, was sitting cross-legged on the floor next to the couch, keeping track of the gifts given in a small notebook.

Trudy smiled at the mother-daughter pair. "Neither of those assumptions is correct, as you both very well know. It's simply a book I found useful when Alice Rose was born. I thought you probably didn't pack many baby books when you and Lila moved to Sovereign."

Lila tittered. "Not likely!" As hostess of the shower she was leaning against the door frame, keeping an eye on the proceedings. A vivacious twenty-nine-year-old, Lila's short black hair framed her face like a chickadee's cap. At Miss Hastings' urging, she and Rebecca had relocated to Sovereign after Rebecca had been fired from the insurance company in Boston where both women worked. For a time they had raised chickens and sold organic eggs at the old Russell homestead. "We were thinking of a totally different kind of chick back then, weren't we, Becca?"

"We certainly were. Oh, Nellie—how perfectly lovely," Rebecca cried, unwrapping Nellie's quilt. Rebecca pushed herself up from the couch and held the baby quilt out for the others to see. "What beautiful colors, too! And it's just the right size."

Nellie flushed with pleasure. "Aunt Hannah gave me most of the material but I sewed it myself, all by hand. It's my first quilt—you're in my new quilt journal as Number One."

"That's quite an honor, Nellie. Thank you."

"Can I be number two, Nellie?" Amber quipped.

Everyone laughed, except Rebecca. Amber's mother resumed her seat and rather breathlessly regarded her daughter. "What makes you say that? Do you have anything to tell us, darling?"

Amber patted her mother's hand. "Not yet, Mom. We thought we'd let you be a mom first again before you became 'Grandma'."

"Well, don't wait too long," Rebecca advised. "Soon I'll be too old to be a grandmother." At this artless confession, everyone laughed.

After all the gifts were unwrapped, the guests began to depart. Nellie offered to help clean up.

"Thanks, I'll take you up on that," Lila said gratefully.

The two women gravitated to the kitchen, collecting dirty dishes along the way. Nellie carefully unloaded her armful onto the kitchen counter next to the black soapstone sink.

"I'll wash, if you dry," Lila suggested, retrieving a plastic bucket from under the sink. "That way we can chat. Seems like I never get to see you, Nellie," she mused. She ran some hot water into the bucket and began washing and rinsing a stack of dirty plates. "You're never home when I come down for a visit."

"I've been away a lot," Nellie admitted, liberating a linen dish towel from a hook next to the sink. As she began to dry the dishes she explained to Lila her job with Clean World Water.

"Are you going back to them when Maggie comes home?" Lila asked.

"No, I think it's time for me to move on to my next adventure."

Lila set a dripping crystal pitcher into the dish rack. "Is that why you've been so quiet this afternoon? Thinking about leaving your colleagues behind?"

Nellie hadn't thought about Clean World Water in weeks and had in fact been thinking of Walden, of his surprising disappearance with Sarah Louise. "No, I've been wondering why people do what they do," she admitted, honestly. "Wondering if they know why they do it—or if they're simply actuated by emotion."

"Does this 'they' have a name?"

Nellie hesitated before answering. "Walden," she said. "The mushroom man."

"The guy who ran off with Shirley's niece?"

Nellie nodded. She added another dried dessert plate to the growing stack on the counter. "You wouldn't believe how intelligent and educated Walden is! He once quoted Emily Dickinson to me in the woods one day when we happened to run into each other. Emily Dickinson!"

Lila chuckled. "At least he had good taste in poets, if not in flesh and blood women."

"I know! Can you believe it?"

Lila carefully balanced a glass upside down in the dish drainer. "And now you're wondering whether Walden consciously decided Sarah Louise was the woman for him or whether he just said, 'The heck with it,' and took off with the first warm, willing body in sight?"

"Exactly! But how *could* he have thought it through, given the results that are sure to follow? In two weeks—or less—he'll be completely bored with Sarah Louise and find some excuse to dump her! Then what will he do? What will *she* do?"

"Hmmm. Self-awareness is a great gift, Nellie, but just because we know the motivation behind our actions doesn't automatically make us better people. A selfish person uses the information about himself to further gratify himself. A selfless person gratifies others. Do you see the difference?"

Lila's words, so succinct and yet so insightful, opened up Nellie's understanding. She was immediately struck by the difference between men like Walden and her father—and men like Metcalf. "I do," she cried. "Why, I can't believe how clear everything seems to me now! Of course Walden knew what he was doing, but he didn't care—at least not about Sarah Louise. He cared about himself, meeting his own personal needs. He just didn't want to be alone anymore."

"Well, now he isn't alone, is he? At least, as you say, in the short run."

"How awful, to use someone like that!"

Lila shrugged and rinsed off the silverware. "Happens all the time, I'm afraid. Selfishness isn't limited to men, either. Although there do seem to be a lot of rascals around like your mushroom man.

Women are often attracted to rascals, too, even educated and intelligent women, who appreciate Emily Dickinson."

Nellie blushed. "If you mean me, I'm safe," she assured Lila. She assiduously wiped some spots from a drinking glass. "Although I admit there was a time when I felt a physical attraction to Walden, but I always rebuffed his advances."

"Thank goodness for that," said Lila. She dumped out the dirty dishwater and rinsed the pan. "Unfortunately, not every young woman has your discernment, Nellie. I see so many who focus on a man's looks or on his net worth, rather than his character. Never mind the rest of the dishes; they'll dry on their own. Let's go join the others, shall we?"

Nellie allowed the older girl to propel her back into the living room where Rebecca and Amber had their heads together chatting and laughing. But they broke apart and greeted the duo from the kitchen cheerfully. Lila swiped the wrapping paper and ribbons off the couch and motioned for Nellie to sit down. She meekly dropped down next to Rebecca.

"Now, Nellie … you can't leave us without giving us the scoop," Lila declared, perching pertly on the opposite arm of the couch. She threw her arm around Rebecca and gave Nellie an encouraging smile.

"What scoop?"

"What's the story with you and Doctor Bart, hmm?"

Nellie felt her face grow hot. "Doctor Bart? I …"

"Oh, don't embarrass her, Lila dear," Rebecca cried. "That's not very nice. When Nellie has something to tell us about their relationship, I'm sure she'll let us know."

Lila tittered and hopped back up. "So, it's true, then? I was just guessing about you two, but honestly, Rebecca, you are so easy!"

"You've got that right," Amber agreed. "Mom is way easy."

Nellie was grateful the attention was momentarily shifted to Rebecca, for she wasn't sure how she should respond. True, Metcalf had proposed to her—and she fully intended to accept his proposal—but she hadn't yet figured out when or how she would accept. But she should certainly tell him before making the engagement generally known!

"So, when are you going to put the poor guy out of his misery? I'm sorry, don't answer that," Lila added repentantly. "It's none of my business. I just remember those early days with Mike and, well, I guess I'm a little envious of you."

"Wow! Has the bloom gone off the rose already?" Amber asked, looking up from her spot on the floor. "You've only been married a year longer than me, Lila."

"Are you kidding? Mike dotes on me. He's always underfoot, worse than Claire, even. He hasn't changed any, but I … I have. I still remember how thrilled I felt those first few months living here—how scared and excited I got when I heard his truck coming up the hill. Where has all that romance has gone?" Lila cast a hopeful glance at the other three women. "Thoughts, ladies …?"

Amber burst into peals of laughter. "Don't look at me! Bruce used to be crazy about me but now I can't even get him to take off his barn boots before he tracks into the kitchen. He's completely incorrigible. He says he hasn't got time to stop and take his boots off when he wants something quick to eat or drink but he never considers how much time it takes me to clean up after him!"

"Oh, dear! I'm not sure I can top that, but I do have a corollary," Rebecca added, smiling. "Wendell is forever hiding my cleaning bucket, even though the doctor has told him it's perfectly acceptable for me to clean if I feel like it. You don't know, Nellie, but Amber and Lila do—cleaning helps calm my nerves. Wendell, bless his heart, won't let me do anything and I'd have been a nervous wreck today if I hadn't found the bucket on Tuesday and sneak-cleaned the kitchen floor while he was down at Gilpin's playing cribbage."

"Too funny!" Lila proclaimed, laughing. "Classic Wendell, too, hiding your cleaning bucket. I thought the old place looked pretty good, but as you know, Becca, I'm not always the 'shaapest tool in the shed.' OK, your turn, Nellie."

"Me?" Nellie gulped. What could she say? She appreciated being included in the Girl's Club, but the others were married women and she—she was still single.

"Don't tease her, Lila."

Nellie unconsciously twisted her hair into a loose bun. "Well, there is one thing about Doctor Bart," she admitted.

"Omigod, you mean he's not perfect?"

"I can't seem to get him to stop sending me flowers or buying me gifts."

Lila groaned and Amber hooted. Even Rebecca giggled. She patted Nellie's hand. "Don't worry, dear. That won't last. It never does."

The conversation continued on in the same vein for another hour, the coffee klatch ranging from men to baby names to pre-school education. Finally, Amber rose to go and Nellie followed suit.

"See you soon, Mom," Amber said, kissing her mother goodbye. "Call me when you feel the first contractions, OK? Don't wait for your water to break. I can get here in twenty minutes."

"Goodness, Amber! Twenty minutes? It's twenty-five miles from here to the farm."

"Twenty-two," Amber corrected.

"Please don't speed, darling! I'll only worry about you."

"That might take your mind off your labor pains," Amber pointed out.

"I'm not so sure about that!"

Lila began carefully gathering up the wrapping paper and ribbons from the floor so that she could recycle as much as possible. Suddenly, a thought occurred to her. She paused in her task and shot her best friend a fond smile. "Just think how different our lives would have been, Becca, if Joe Kelly hadn't fired you," she remarked.

"Oh, my! We'd probably still be working in Boston, slaving over some awful desk job. Thank goodness Miss Hastings invited us to visit her!"

"I can still remember her tweet to me: 'Old house next door falling down; take a chance – move to Maine. What have you got to lose, darling? We'll show you how to raise chickens.' I love that part! 'We'll show you how to raise chickens.' Where would we be now—all four of us—if it wasn't for Miss Hastings, hmm?" Lila glanced at the other three women.

"Thank God for Miss Hastings!" Amber agreed, with vehemence. "She was the only one who supported my relationship with Bruce when everyone else was against us. Oh, I know you only wanted what was best for me," she added quickly, as her mother started to protest. "But we sure didn't see eye to eye on what that was, did we?"

"I'm happy to admit I was wrong, darling, and you and Miss Hastings were right."

"Do you suppose Miss Hastings can see us now?" Lila whispered, with an awed upward glance.

"I hope so. I want her to know she was right about Bruce and me!"

"I hope so, too," Rebecca added. "I'd like to think Miss Hastings can see how happy we all turned out, thanks to her efforts. I just wish your mother was here with us, Nellie. I'm worried about

Maggie. I know she's grieving the loss of Peter—we all are—but she should be here with us, not out in the cold cruel world all by herself. I do hope she comes home soon!"

"Me too," Nellie murmured, wrapping the soft alpaca scarf around her neck. "Me too."

Lila gave Nellie a quick hug. "Bye, Nellie," she said. She stood back and eyed the other girl appreciatively. "It's been great to see you. I hope you're planning on sticking around a while before your next adventure?"

"I think I will," Nellie replied, offering up a mysterious smile.

"Good for you! Now, if we can just get Maggie back in the fold we'll be all set. Sovereign just doesn't seem the same without her." Lila resumed gathering up the wrapping paper and ribbons.

"When are you going back to Maple Grove?" Nellie asked her.

"Just as soon as Mike and Claire get back from the cabin. We were going to stay over another night—how I wish we could! But Mike says there's a big snowstorm on the way. If we don't drive back today we might not get home for a week."

"That's just fine by us," Rebecca said, hoisting herself up off the couch. "Wendell and I would love to have you stay—Oh, oh!" she cried, clutching her abdomen.

"Omigod! Rebecca … you're not …?"

Amber rushed to her mother's side. "Mom, are you OK?"

"I think … I think—OOOoo—yes! I'm having the baby."

"Forget the snowstorm," Lila declared, dropping her armful of wrapping paper. "I'm not going anywhere until my godchild is born."

CHAPTER 29

George's Debut and Nellie's Needhams

By the time Mike Hobart and little Claire returned to the old Russell homestead pandemonium had broken loose. Rebecca was walking up and down the length of the great room with Amber on one side of her and Nellie on the other—her contractions having increased to less than five minutes apart—and Lila was directing traffic. "That's it—breathe in! Hold it. Hold it! Now … breathe out." Seeing her husband's vehicle drive into the yard, Lila broke off the mantra. "OK, just keep breathing and I'll be back in a minute." She darted into the kitchen meeting her husband at the inner shed door. "Where's Doctor Bart?" she demanded, hand on the doorknob. "I texted you to come back right away!"

Hobart set Claire down onto the braided rug and unzipped the child's coat. "Mama," Claire said, wriggling free of her winter jacket. She stood up and tugged on the hem of her mother's short skirt. "Mama!"

Lila automatically swung the child up into her arms. Placated, Claire happily toyed with one of her mother's earrings. "Where is he?" Lila repeated, anxiously.

"I dropped Doctor Bart at his place," her husband replied, unzipping his own jacket. "Why?"

"How could you let him get away!"

"You didn't tell me to hold him hostage, honey." He shrugged out of his coat and tossed it over a chair by the table.

"Funny man. Rebecca has gone into labor!"

"Wow! No kidding?"

"Would I joke about something like that? Now, put your boots back on and go up there and get Doctor Bart!"

Rebecca, who had overheard some of their conversation from the other room suddenly cried out: "Wendell! Get Wendell, too. Oh, ooooh!"

Hobart plopped down into the nearest straight-back chair and quickly pulled on his boots. "Do we know where Wendell is?" he asked. He jerked his boot laces tight.

"Where do all the men in town go when they want to escape their wives?"

"Gilpin's," he replied with a grin. The handsome farmer stood up, grabbed his jacket, and opened the shed door. "I'm on it," he said. Before he departed, however, he leaned over and gave his wife a kiss. Claire, who was wriggling in her mother's arms, caught a handful of his thick blonde hair and pulled hard. "Ow!" he said. The child giggled with delight.

Lila gently released her husband from the clutches of Claire's chubby hands. "Hurry up! This is no time for shillyshallying," she said. Nevertheless, she smiled at him.

"Who says I'm shillyshallying?" He managed to steal one more kiss from his wife. "Don't worry, honey. I'll be back before you know it."

Hobart retrieved Doctor Bart first—Metcalf living only just up the road—and dropped him off at the old Russell homestead before going in search of Wendell. But at the general store his mission quickly became bogged down. He was first waylaid by the Organic Kidd—Tom Kidd, the certification director at MOGG (the Maine Organic Growers Group)—who exited the double-glass doors just as Hobart was entering. Hobart almost didn't recognize his old college schoolmate. Kidd's signature black hair, which in former days had been shoulder-length and greasy, was now close-cropped and clean. In addition, the man's lean and lanky frame was clothed in freshly-washed jeans and a new fleece-lined LL Bean hurricane shirt.

"Hey, hey, Hobart—whaddaya say?" Kidd asked, reaching out and catching the former carpenter by the arm.

Mike tried to shake off his old acquaintance, who in truth was no friend. "Not now, Tom. I'm in a hurry," he said, pulling his arm away.

"You're always in a hurry with me, Hobart," he said, feigning hurt. "I just thought you might wanna see a pic of my wife and kid. But, hey, I can take a hint."

Hobart hesitated; his hand flat against the cold glass door. "You got married?"

"Yeah, to Michelle Currier. She graduated Unity two years after we did. We got hooked six months ago. Surprised ya, huh?" Kidd peeled into his wallet and produced the promised photograph, which he proudly held out. "My wife's got some better pics on our Facebook farm page. Check it out sometime—Tin Pan Alley Truck Farm. We do organic veggies."

Mike Hobart accepted the photograph and squinted at the wrinkled, glossy image. "Congratulations, Tom. Is that a boy?"

"Yeah, he'll be a year old in December. Michelle keeps both of us pretty much whipped into shape." He fingered his fainéant black goatee, contemplating with momentary regret the liberties of his bachelor life.

Hobart returned the photograph. "Congratulations," he repeated, privately thinking that keeping the Organic Kidd whipped into shape would be a full-time job. "Thanks for showing it to me, Tom, but I'm on a mission so I've really got to run."

"Wait! Hobart …"

"What now?"

"Tell your wife I'm sorry, OK?"

"For what?"

"You know for what, Hobart. Do I really need to spell it out for ya?"

Mike well remembered when the Organic Kidd had lied to Lila in a malicious attempt to drive a spike into their budding romantic relationship. Fortunately, Lila had seen through Kidd's villainous plot and on the very same day she had agreed to become his wife. "OK, apologies accepted on Lila's behalf. Thanks." Hobart pushed in through the double glass doors and was relieved to see Wendell in the usual spot with the other Old Farts.

No sooner had he walked into the store, however, than Mike was accosted by Ralph Gilpin, the store's proprietor, who slipped around from behind the counter and greeted him gleefully. "Mike! Good to see ya, son. Been hopin' you'd stop by."

"Not now, Ralph. I need to fetch Wendell."

"Maude wants me ta invite ya … "

"Not now, Ralph!" To the old shopkeeper's dismay Hobart rudely pushed past him and strode over to where the Old Farts were gathered in the front facing benches.

Before he could get Wendell's name out of his mouth Leland Gorse hopped up and grabbed his hand. "Mike! Been wantin' ta ask ya 'bout thet wood on yer land. Some o' them trees need thinnin' and …"

"Catch me another time, Leland," Hobart interrupted, pulling his hand free from the woodsman's clutches.

"But me 'n the team is lookin' fer somethin' ta cut this wintah!"

John Woods stood up and proffered his hand. "Good to see you, Mike. How's Lila and Claire?"

"We're fine—I'm fine. Everybody's fine but …" Seeing there was no other hope to get his message through, he cupped his hands to his mouth: "WENDELL, YOUR WIFE HAS GONE INTO LABOR."

The crowd of old men parted like the Red Sea. All eyes turned to the retired chicken farmer. Wendell stood up and hitched up his jeans. "Wal, you know, it's about time." He grinned.

As Hobart exited the store with Wendell hard on his heels he heard John Woods' distinct voice call out: "Any bets, boys?"

Just before seven o'clock in the evening, Rebecca was safely delivered of an eight-pound baby boy. Nellie, who had never seen a baby's birth before, was both humbled and thrilled by the experience. She had momentarily held the baby when he was less than a minute old, Metcalf having unexpectedly placed the squalling child into her arms while he cut the cord. Lila and Amber relieved her of her duties almost immediately. Nellie stood to one side and watched with an indescribable longing as the newborn was bathed and inspected by Rebecca's daughter and her best friend.

Amber wrapped the clean baby in a soft, yellow receiving blanket and set him into her mother's arms. Rebecca peeked beneath the soft blanket. "Is George perfect? He is, isn't he?" she asked, anxiously. She and Wendell had decided in advance a baby boy would be named 'George Scott' after Wendell's grandfather, George 'Pappy' Russell, and Rebecca's son, Scott, who had died prematurely.

"Course he is," Wendell replied, proudly. He was puffed up like a bantam rooster. "He takes aftah his old man."

By the time Metcalf dropped Nellie at the old schoolhouse it was after nine o'clock at night and the snow was already beginning to pile up. "Are you sure you don't want me to stay with you?" he asked, worriedly. "We're supposed to get over a foot of snow."

"I'm fine, thanks," said Nellie, smiling at his fussy concern. "I've survived a few snowstorms before." She opened the passenger door. "Besides, you know the weathermen always play up the first storm. We'll probably only get four or five inches."

"We might lose power, though. Do you have candles?" Metcalf exited the truck and walked with her to the shed door. The overhead light illuminated the fast, fat snowflakes, whipping hither and thither as though each one was on its own special mission.

"Candles, oil lamps, you-name-it," Nellie replied. "I think they came with the place." She stomped the snow off her boots. "And if I have to, I can get water from the pond. Remember, this is Maggie's house we're talking about. Besides, after today I feel like I can handle just about anything."

He squeezed her mittened hands. "You were a big help with the birth, thanks."

"That was the most incredible experience I've ever had!"

"Nellie, I …" he broke off. He gazed at her with a moonstruck expression on his face, much like the deer in the spotlight from their deer lighting adventure.

Nellie noted Metcalf's blatant look of longing and—she selfishly ignored it! She didn't want to share her special day with the birth of Rebecca's baby. When the time came for her to tell Metcalf she loved him—and that she would be his wife—she wanted the day to be specially theirs, to belong to just the two of them. He had been waiting for her for years, she reasoned, he could wait a little longer.

She pulled her hands away from his and slipped out of her right mitten. She reached up to brush the accumulating snow off his short red curls. "You're getting wet," she said. "Don't worry, I'll check in with you tomorrow."

By the time the snowstorm ended Sunday night the little town of Sovereign had received sixteen inches of fluffy white snow. The early snowstorm had been widely trumpeted and therefore not many Mainers were caught off guard; however, downed trees on power lines caused the loss of electricity to 65,000 homes, including at the old schoolhouse. Nellie simply tossed more wood into the stoves and curled up on the couch with a favorite book of poetry. From the warmth of the cozy living room she watched the snow pile up outside the window and feasted on chocolates and Emily Dickinson:

I went to heaven, -
'Twas a small town,
Lit with a ruby,
Lathed with down.
Stiller than the fields
At the full dew,
Beautiful as pictures

No man drew.
People like the moth,
Of mechlin, frames,
Duties of gossamer,
And eider names.
Almost contented
I could be
'Mong such unique
Society.

On Monday, when everyone was finally plowed out, Amber returned to Oaknole, to Bruce and her farm duties. On Tuesday, Lila, Mike and Claire finally departed for Maple Grove. As a result of their departures, Nellie spent much of Wednesday and Thursday helping Rebecca with Baby George. Before she knew it was Friday again, and she and Metcalf were working side by side at the clinic.

"How are you feeling Miss Crump? Any better?" Doctor Bart asked, as he took hold of the spinster's angular elbow and helped her up out of the rocking chair. He watched as Miss Crump wobbled ahead of him into the exam room. "You seem to be moving better?"

"Yer wantin' me to tell ye them pills worked, ain't ye, young man?"

"I want you to tell me the truth, Miss Crump." Metcalf shook his head at Nellie, indicating he didn't need her assistance with his patient. Despite the slushy roads, the indomitable Miss Crump had driven over for her follow-up appointment. Nellie gave him a fond smile and returned to her work at the desk.

"Well, them pills air convenient, I'll give ye thet," she continued. "But if I had my druthers, I'd take my gingerroot tea ovah them pills any day o' the week."

Doctor Bart discreetly hoisted the elderly woman up onto the exam table. "Ginger does have anti-inflammatory properties," he allowed, moving over to the sink where he began to wash his hands. "It's also beneficial as a digestive aide."

"Ain't nuthin' wrong with my digestion." The alert nonagenarian thumped her hand-carved wood cane against the step for emphasis.

He pulled off a paper towel and wiped his hands. "Glad to hear that. Nellie says you eat a lot of chocolate. Chocolate has anti-inflammatory properties, too, especially dark chocolate."

"So yer gal ratted on me, did she? Wal, she ain't all thet bad—she did git Hannah to make me up some more Needhams."

"Nellie's job is to gather information to help me do my job, which is to help you feel better. I'm not opposed to herbal or natural remedies. In fact, I've concocted my share of them over the years."

Nellie, overhearing their doctor-patient chatter from her desk, smiled to herself. She pictured in her mind the young Metcalf and his Grandmother Metcalf laboring over their distilling contraption with which they attempted to make attar of roses. She still remembered how many roses—sixty thousand blooms!—it took to make one ounce of rose oil.

"And I've certainly eaten my share of Needhams over the years. I prefer dark chocolate; how about you, Miss Crump?"

"I like 'em black 's black kin be."

Listening to the two of them, Nellie suddenly had an idea about how she would give Metcalf her answer to his marriage proposal. She had been searching for the perfect mode, wanting to meet his unusual, straight-forward proposal with similar honesty and uniqueness. A simple but romantic response had seemed easy in theory, but had turned out to be much more difficult in practice. For the past week Nellie had been racking her brains trying to figure out what to do. Miss Crump had unwittingly given her an idea, a memorable way for her to say everything she wanted to say to him—without saying a word!

Friday evening Nellie mixed up a batch of the Needham candy centers. She spooned the mix into a buttered baking pan and set the pan into the refrigerator to harden. Early Saturday morning, before going to the clinic, she cut the mix into two-inch squares, the traditional size of Needhams, which his Grandmother Metcalf had made for him. She dipped each piece into melted dark chocolate and set them in the shed to stay cool. Her Needhams weren't perfect, but for a first attempt the candies were more than satisfactory.

Nellie would have enjoyed walking home Saturday afternoon after the clinic closed at one o'clock—the new blanket of snow giving everything a fresh, healthy look—but in order for her to execute her plan she asked Metcalf to give her a lift. Pleased, he hastened with his exam room clean-up and accompanied her out to the truck. Nellie had deliberately let the living room stove go out knowing he would offer to get the fire started for her. Immediately upon entering, he doffed his green-and-black checked jacket and disappeared into the other room with paper and kindling.

While Metcalf was thus occupied, Nellie removed two individually wrapped Needhams from the refrigerator and slipped one into each of his coat pockets, just like his Grandmother Metcalf had done when he was a boy. She zipped up the pockets and moved his jacket to the shed so the candies wouldn't melt. He dawdled for nearly forty-five minutes, but finally admitted he had work to do at home. Nellie made no attempt to detain him. Instead, she retrieved his jacket from the shed and wordlessly handed it to him. He slipped into the wool coat, gave her a quick kiss on the cheek, and departed.

With the shed door safely closed behind Doctor Bart, Nellie dashed to the kitchen window. She peeked around the flounced curtain and watched as he made his way down the snowy path to the truck. Her heartbeat quickened. Would he put his hands in his pockets?

She watched with bated breath as he climbed into his truck and proceeded to back out of the driveway. Disappointed, Nellie glanced at the old Regulator clock. Two o'clock. How long would it take him to discover the Needhams? Two hours? Four hours? A day? Two days? She hoped it wouldn't be longer than two days because the candies wouldn't be very good after that!

Feeling let down, Nellie wandered into the living room. She had left some of Hannah's colorful quilting magazines sprawled across the couch, hoping to get an idea for her next quilting project, a surprise gift for Metcalf's thirtieth birthday. She settled herself down on the couch near the crackling woodstove and began flipping through the pages of one of the glossy magazines. Soon, she was lost in a delightful reverie of quilts. Should she sew Metcalf a traditional log cabin quilt? A cathedral window? Or perhaps he'd like the court house steps design best?

Suddenly, she was startled by the tell-tale squeak of the kitchen door. She glanced up.

"Nellie!"

Metcalf was standing in the doorway of the living room, his handsome face alive with an expression of exultation. He was still wearing his green-and-black wool jacket. He reached into his right-hand coat pocket and pulled out one of the individually-wrapped Needhams. He held the chocolate candy out as though wanting an explanation, but before Nellie had time to verbally affirm her acceptance to his marriage proposal, he was across the room and pulling her to her feet.

"Say you love me," he demanded, holding her so close she could scarcely breathe. He rained ardent kisses upon her face and neck. "Say it!"

Nellie's passion for him, so long restrained, burst forth like a spring bulb forced for winter blooming. "I do love you," she cried, twining her fingers around his short red curls and pulling his head close. "I do!"

"And you'll be my wife?"

"Mmmhmm," she murmured, in his ear.

"Say it!"

"Yes, I will be your wife, Metcalf Bartholomew Lawson."

He swept her up into his arms and strode into the kitchen. He kicked open the shed door.

"Wait—where are you taking me?"

"Darling, I'm taking you home."

CHAPTER 30
"I'll Never Meddle Again"

Metcalf drove Nellie back over to his cottage, where, to her astonishment, he disappeared into the shed and returned with two sets of antique snowshoes. As he helped her into the ash and leather Tubbs he somewhat sheepishly explained he wanted to show her a medley of connecting trails he had been cutting through the woods since acquiring Miss Hastings' property.

"What? You're not going to ravish me?" she teased, as he expertly tightened the rawhide laces on her bear paws.

"Not yet, darling. I want you to see this first. I've been dying to show you what I'm doing here."

Together they tramped through the deep powder, following a trail that began off the rose garden and wound through a thicket of astringent-smelling pines. After fifteen or twenty minutes they broke out of the woods into the abandoned hayfield. They paused on the hillside, holding hands, admiring together Miss Hastings' sweet home—soon to be Nellie's home—from afar. The yellow cottage was awash in the rosy glow of the early November sunset. The windows winked, as though Miss Hastings herself was winking at them. Nellie could almost hear her former music teacher cackling with glee: "I knew how it would be, my dahrrrlings!"

"I'm making the trails for our kids," Metcalf said, his freckled face flushed with happy excitement. "Your mother has all those crazy paths down at the old schoolhouse where she runs naked through the goldenrod and all. I thought if I didn't do something similar up here the kids would want to spend all their time down there."

Nellie burst out laughing. "Tell me you're not serious! How can you be jealous of something so far off in the future?"

"I'm a very patient man," he replied, drawing her hand into the crook of his arm. "Don't you know that by now?"

"Actually, I did figure that out." She snuggled up to him. "I hate to tell you, though, no matter what we do, our kids will still rather be with their grandmother than with us. You do know Maggie will spoil them rotten?"

"Mmm, I like the way you say that—'our kids'," he said, nuzzling her hair. "Maybe we should skip the rest of the trails and go straight to the ravishment part. After all, George is going to need a girlfriend …?"

"George already has little Claire and Alice Rose. Don't you think we should concentrate on the wedding first?"

He straightened up, smiling. "I do, darling. You know I was only kidding. Still, I can't help wondering what this neighborhood will look like in fifteen or twenty years …?"

"Whatever we think will happen—probably won't. But there's one thing we can count on."

"What's that?"

"In fifteen or twenty years we'll find out!"

Suddenly, Metcalf's cell phone buzzed. He frowned and dropped her hand. "Sorry, I have to take this. I'm on call."

"No problem, Doc Martin."

The call was an emergency and Metcalf immediately went into Doctor Mode. Before she knew it, Nellie found herself bundled unceremoniously into the truck, their snowshoes tossed into the bed. He hopped in and they roared off. When they reached the old schoolhouse he slowed down in front. He leaned over and gave her a perfunctory kiss. "I'll call you later," he promised.

"I'll be here," she replied, jumping down onto the snow-covered road. She slammed the passenger door shut and waved him off. Metcalf put the truck in gear and sped off toward Unity. She watched as the pickup's taillights melted away into the gloaming. Her heart swelled with connubial pride and love. But she also experienced a new, underlying anxiety and with a little shock realized that, as the wife of a country doctor, she would always worry about him until he was once again back home, safe and sound.

A reverential feeling of humility fell over her. She closed her eyes and bowed her head. "Thank you God for all of my blessings! Please keep a watchful eye on Metcalf tonight," she prayed. "And also on my mother," she added, as an afterthought. "Where ever she is."

Dampness propelled her toward the house where friendly lights twinkled from the narrow old windows. She didn't remember leaving so many lights on. She looked up and was surprised to see smoke billowing from the center chimney. The white plumes stood out against the indigo sky. She didn't remember Metcalf filling the kitchen woodstove, either; however, she wasn't surprised by his thoughtfulness. He had probably left the lights on for her, too.

She inhaled deeply, drawing the smoky scent and the cold night air deep into her lungs. In the shed, she removed her hat and scarf, hung up her jacket on the Shaker peg rack, and stepped out of her wet boots, pushing them to one side. She opened the door into the warm country kitchen where, much to her surprise, she discovered—her mother, trying to work a fat stick of maple firewood into the woodstove! Maggie was dressed in jeans, a rag wool sweater, and one of her knit beanie caps.

"Mother!" Nellie exclaimed.

Startled, Maggie whirled around, dropping the wood, which landed with a muffled thunk on the soft pine floor, adding another battle scar. "Nellie, darling," she cried. Maggie opened her arms wide and Nellie flung herself across the room. The two women tearfully and joyfully embraced.

After several minutes of hugging, laughing and crying, Maggie pulled away to examine her daughter. She reached up and moved the hair back from Nellie's forehead. "You look happy, my darling. What a wonderful sight for a mother's sore eyes!"

"So much has happened since you left, Mother! I have so much to tell you," Nellie replied, shyly. She stole a glance at Maggie's beaming face. Funny, she didn't remember her mother being so short. But then, she couldn't remember the last time she and her mother had actually hugged.

Maggie's face fell. "Oh, no! Is this about your father?" she said, worriedly.

"Oh, please! That man is *so* not my father."

Maggie threw her arms toward the heavens. "Thank the Good Lord! If only you knew how worried I've been since Cathy Burbury told me Julian was preaching at the church. I had no idea he was even on the east coast, much less in Sovereign. I came home just as soon as I heard."

Nellie bent over and retrieved the piece of firewood her mother had dropped. "I don't understand—how did Reverend Cathy know he was here?" She expertly maneuvered the fat wood into the stove, shut the cover, and brushed the wood remnants from her hands.

Her mother's eyes narrowed. "I had about give upon on that piece. I didn't think it would fit."

"I've had plenty of practice with the woodstove lately," Nellie allowed. "Tell me about Reverend Cathy."

"Oh, yes. Would you believe? Cathy subscribes to the online Waterville Morning Sentinel and saw the information posted in our church news." As she spoke, Maggie gravitated toward her rocker by the window. "The whole thing was serendipitous, really. I got up one morning, realized it was Cathy's fiftieth birthday and decided to give her a call. When she told me the news about Julian—he was in one of her classes at Bangor Seminary, too—I almost fainted. I called you immediately, but you weren't home. Of course I couldn't call you on your cell because I'd forgotten your number and I didn't have mine with me." She dropped down into the padded rocker. "So, I take it Jane told you Julian was your father? She never liked him."

"Aunt Jane didn't tell me, although she badly wanted to. When push came to shove, however, she couldn't break her promise to you." Nellie settled into the straight-back chair closest to her mother's rocker.

Maggie's eyes widened. "Then how … ?"

"In the end, *he* told me—rather, I figured it out. Vanity of vanities—all is not vanity!" she misquoted impishly, nodding at the oak mirror over the chiffonier. "There's the guilty party."

Maggie regarded the mirror. "My grandmother's old looking glass?"

"Yep. I made the mistake of glancing into the mirror the same time he did. Do you know how vain men are? Well, maybe not all men," Nellie amended hastily, thinking of Metcalf.

"I certainly know how vain Julian is."

"After I guessed the truth, I made him tell me everything, *everything*," she emphasized. "Oh, Mother! How could you trade away all the rights to your book?"

Maggie slumped tiredly. She began to rock back and forth. "Because I was young and stupid," she admitted. "And I felt like a fool because my birth control failed. Oh, my God, do you know how difficult it is to talk about birth control with your daughter?" she cried, stopping the chair. "No, of course you don't, but let's hope you do someday. Anyway, all I really wanted was for Julian to disappear out of my life. I'd already discovered what a miserable cad he was …"

"My sentiments exactly," Nellie said, through gritted teeth.

"… but he threatened to stay and make my life miserable—our lives miserable—unless I cut a deal with him."

Nellie rose up and switched on the gas under the copper teakettle so they could have a cup of tea. "Keep going. I'm listening."

Maggie, realizing what Nellie was doing, pushed herself to her feet. "Sit down, darling. I'll make us some tea, just like old times."

"No, Mother. It's time you let me take on my share of the responsibilities." Nellie gently pushed her mother back into the comfy rocker. "Anyway, keep talking. I want to hear your side of the story." She leaned back against the kitchen table.

Maggie acquiesced and settled into her chair. "Well, when Julian suggested I trade the piece of writing I'd scribbled after my grandmother died for his parental rights, I thought that was a cheap and easy way to get rid of him. After I signed away my rights to the manuscript, he vanished. Vamoosed! As though he'd never been there at all."

"Did he make you promise not to tell me who my father was?" Nellie asked, curious.

Maggie nodded. "I had to promise not to tell anyone—especially you. But Peter and Jane already knew, so Julian forced me to ask them for the same promise. Jane understood and easily gave her word, but Peter—poor Peter! He wanted me to tell Julian to go to the devil and promised he'd take care of us both. Unfortunately, I was stiff-necked and stubborn back then. I thought I could do everything by myself. I finally extracted the necessary promise of secrecy from him, which Peter deeply regretted. So many times over the years he wanted to tell you!"

"I wish he had," Nellie said, sadly.

"But you know Uncle Peter and his integrity. He'd never break his word once he'd given it. But even worse than that—Julian made me promise never to say anything bad to you about your 'Father.' He didn't want me to poison the well in the event someday—like now—he decided to return and claim his child."

"I'm not sure he was going to claim me. I think he was just inspecting me to see whether I made the grade."

"No doubt he was weighing the cost of revealing an illegitimate child against your potential value to him."

"I'm sure I failed that test!"

"Do you know, this second promise turned out to be much more difficult to keep than the original?" Maggie mused. "I couldn't say anything bad about Julian—and I certainly couldn't say anything good—so I ended up saying nothing to you about your father at all. As a result, you were free to make up all sorts of romantic stories about him and I was powerless to stop you. How could I say anything unless I told you the truth? What a twisted state of affairs our lives became!" She gave her head a rueful shake and the knit navy cap she was wearing slipped to one side. Maggie reached up and pulled the hat off, revealing angelic tendrils of white hair.

"Your hair!" Nellie cried, shocked. She had been so happy to see her mother she'd forgotten all about the cancer diagnosis and chemotherapy. "Sorry, I didn't mean that like it sounded. Your hair looks great. How are you feeling?"

"Never better. Well, not since I was fifty, anyway." Maggie ran her fingers through the short white fuzz. "It's just beginning to grow back. Of course it was too much to hope my hair would come in brown." She tossed the knit cap onto the seat of a nearby chair. "Now, where was I?"

"Maybe you should have Doctor Bart take a look at you tomorrow," Nellie suggested worriedly. "Just to make sure you're OK."

Maggie waved away her daughter's concern. "There'll be plenty of time for doctoring later. Oh, I know what I wanted to say—I wanted you to know why I didn't fight him for the book. When we made our bargain, Julian didn't tell me he'd already received a publication offer and an advance for my manuscript."

"That doesn't surprise me."

"Later, when 'The House by the Side of the Road' came out and I realized what he'd done, I did think about taking him to court. But I couldn't afford a lawyer at the time much less could we afford the personal scrutiny of a public legal fight. I decided to leave well enough alone. You and I had just moved to Sovereign, and I felt as though we'd finally found a home."

"We did find a home," Nellie avowed. "Both of us." She set a mug of steaming tea onto the windowsill by the rocker and paused to examine her middle-aged mother. Overall Maggie did appear much healthier than when Nellie had last seen her. Her mother's face was tanned and she appeared to have lost fifteen or twenty pounds. "You've lost weight," she pointed out. "Was that a result of the chemo, too?"

"I wish," Maggie replied, chuckling. "No, that came off the hard way. Walking the Way of St. James does that to you." She took a sip of tea. "Oh, that's perfect, thank you. Just the right amount of Wendell's honey, too."

"I knew it!" Nellie declared, with no small amount of pride. "I knew you were on a pilgrimage."

"Of course I was, dear. Didn't you get my note?"

Nellie set her own mug of hot tea on the table. "What note?"

"The note I left in my desk, with my phone and house keys."

In a flash Nellie recollected the yellow legal pad that had been lying under Maggie's cell. She vaguely remembered there had been some ink scribbling on the pad; however, thinking that was the beginning of one of her mother's sermons, she had set the pad aside without reading it. Later, when she had Metcalf were making plans for the clinic, she had torn the top sheet of yellow-lined paper off and tossed it into the trash.

"Mea culpa," Nellie said, sighing. She pulled out her chair and sank down. "Sometimes I'm my own worst enemy!"

Suddenly, Maggie's attention was arrested by Boots the cat, who had meandered into the kitchen while the two women were talking. "Look who's come to greet me!" she exclaimed, clasping the cat to her ample breast and giving the feline a fond squeeze. "Suzette!"

Nellie's eyes widened. "Suzette? Metcalf told me that thing was a boy. We didn't know his—her—name, so I named her Boots."

Maggie laughed heartily. "Good thing Doctor Bart went into general practice and not veterinary medicine! He never could find the balls on a cat. It's not easy to do, you know."

Nellie shook her head in amusement. "You haven't changed a bit, have you, Mother?"

"Should I have?"

But no sooner had the words left Maggie's lips when a change fell over her. Her precociousness was abruptly replaced by the gloom of an overly-chastised mind. She unceremoniously dumped the cat out of her lap and stood up.

"Did I say something wrong?"

"I should have changed!" Maggie proclaimed. "I did a lot of soul searching on my pilgrimage and frankly I didn't like what I saw. I saw a woman who thought she knew all the answers for people who weren't asking her any questions." She began pacing back and forth across the well-worn kitchen floor, where hundreds of fidgeting schoolchildren down through the decades had once scuffed their leather boots against the wide pine boards. "I've made up my mind," she continued, with some vehemence. "No more telling others how to live their lives or handing out advice like homemade cough drops. I'm all done with that. I'll never meddle again!"

Nellie tried not to smile. She knew full well her mother would break that promise. She was no different than an errant schoolboy who, after having been caught red-handed dipping a girl's pigtail into an inkwell, repeats the prank the next day—on the very same girl! "Right," she said, drily.

"I mean it," Maggie declared. "No more dishing up unwanted and unwarranted advice."

Nellie took a sip of her tea. "Isn't part of being a minister giving advice?"

"Spiritual insight, darling. Not advice. They're two different things."

"Kind of splitting hairs, isn't it?"

"And another thing," Maggie cried, as though Nellie hadn't spoken. "I'm through meddling in the romantic affairs of others. No more match-making for me. After all, just look at the mess I made of my own love life. Wasting all those years when I could have been with Peter! We were so happy when we finally got together, too." She teared up.

Nellie, overcome with a new urge to comfort and protect her mother, quickly rose up and wrapped her arms around Maggie's shoulders. "I miss him too," she said. "Uncle Peter was my *real* father."

"Oh, Nellie! Peter would be so proud to hear you say that." The mother and daughter embraced. Tears flowed freely for several minutes. Maggie broke away first. She composed herself, daubing her eyes with a cloth napkin from the kitchen table. The napkin was one Nellie had used for several meals, but she held her tongue.

"From now on," Maggie continued, "humility—not vanity—is going to be my guide. Maybe, over time, I'll even make up for my past meddling."

Nellie groaned inwardly when she heard her mother's well-known buzzword, 'vanity.' Did that mean all the mirrors in the house were going to be grounded again? She shot a quick glance at the antique oak mirror hanging next to the door, which she still patronized despite the fact the mirror was the guilty party that had revealed the identity of her father. "Hmm," she replied, unconvinced.

There was a slight pause, as both mother and daughter became lost in their own thoughts, Maggie wondering at the greatness of her new resolution and Nellie wondering how long it would be before her mother broke that resolution. Nellie didn't have long to wait.

"By the way," Maggie said, perking up. "Don't you think Courtney Danforth would make Gray an excellent wife? I just saw the two of them together over at the general store. She's a bit older than he is, of course, but Gray is so mature for his age." Her eyes sparkled with the old familiar interest and excitement Nellie knew so well. "And besides …"

"Mom!" Nellie protested, laughing.

Maggie stopped and stared intently at her daughter. An expression of surprised pleasure spread across her face. "Do you know—that's the first time you've called me 'Mom' in seven years, two months and …" she broke off and glanced at the hanging wall calendar "… fourteen days!"

"I didn't know you were keeping track."

"Me either!" Both women laughed. "Gray and Courtney? What do you think? Not bad, eh?"

"What about your new resolution not to match-make?"

"That's not really match-making," Maggie prevaricated. "We'll just give a small dinner party and invite both of them. What happens—happens. I won't meddle, I promise. We'll have Wendell and Rebecca, as soon as she's feeling well enough to go out, that is. Gray told me the wonderful baby news! And we'll also invite Leland, and Ryan and Trudy. With you and me, that will make nine of us." Her spirits fully resuscitated, Maggie reclaimed her rocker and happily began ticking items off on her fingers as she rocked. "We can have baked stuffed lobster—I can get some from my friend Jason on Isle au Haut—Bakewell Cream biscuits and a fresh cabbage salad. Unless you've eaten them, I've got four cabbages down in the root cellar. And we'll have a blueberry pie and homemade vanilla ice cream. What do you think?"

Nellie felt love and gratitude for her mother welling up in her heart. Why would she want Maggie to be anything other than the wonderful woman she was? "I think it's a great idea, Mom," she affirmed. "But …" she broke off, unsure how to proceed. She had noted one glaring omission from the guest list and wondered why.

"But what?"

"You left out Metcalf," Nellie pointed out. "Don't you want to invite him to our little dinner party, too?"

Maggie pulled a long face. "You heard what I said. I'm all done matchmaking. Poor Doctor Bart! But, it's no use. I'm done throwing him at you." She sighed deeply. "I give you my word."

"Oh, is that all? That's great, Mom," Nellie said, smugly.

"You don't have to sound so cheerful about it," her mother replied, tartly. "You know how I've always wanted him for your boyfriend."

"Well, he's certainly not my boyfriend."

"I know that. Don't rub it in."

"Because … he's my fiancé!"

Surprised, Maggie's hands flew to her face. "Stop it! You're pulling my leg."

"I am so not pulling your leg, Mom. I love him," Nellie proclaimed, proudly. "He's the best man in the whole world, and—I'm going to marry him!"

"Oh, my darling!"

Epilogue

We needn't tarry any longer at the old schoolhouse—wondering how soon after that conversation with my darling daughter she and my godson Metcalf tied the knot (soon), or whether or not during our proposed little dinner party Gray Gilpin and our church pianist and rural letter carrier became romantically entangled (yes)—because Time has marched forward six months to reveal her secrets. Now, after a record-breaking cold and snowy Maine winter, Mother Nature has once again turned back on the fragrance of the pines. So much has happened since my return from my pilgrimage I can hardly comprehend it!

First, in a move that surprised everyone in Sovereign, Walden and Sarah Louise returned to town. Whether he or she (or perhaps both) got cold feet, no one knows for sure. What we do know is that one day Sarah Louise was back at her job waiting tables at Ma Jean's and living with her aunt, and Walden was back living in the old Nutt place and harvesting balsam tips and making wreathes (in lieu of mushrooms) to sell to his out-of-state patrons. When Walden heard of Nellie's engagement, he stopped in and offered her his sincere congratulations. And although I've vowed not to match-make, I do feel as though we're under some sort of obligation to reward Walden for having repented of running away with Sarah Louise. I've been keeping my eye out for a more suitable companion for the bearded woodsman and do believe I've found someone; however, as that story has yet to unfold perhaps we will revisit Walden again someday in the not-too-distant future.

On Christmas Eve I performed the marriage ceremony for my beloved Nellie and our kind, considerate country doctor, Doctor Bart. Today they make their home—and a joyful place it is—in Miss Hastings' former cottage, where they treat the sick and sick at heart in their Songbird Free Medical Clinic. During her wedding Nellie wore the same elaborate hand-wrought lace veil Miss Hastings' mother wore when she was married in the old country. When helping to set up the clinic Nellie had found the veil and some exquisite hand-embroidered linens in the bottom drawer of the walnut dresser in what had been Miss Hastings' bedroom. Underneath the veil was a white envelope with Nellie's name scribbled on it. Seeing her name Nellie felt no compunction in opening the envelope. Inside she discovered a scented notecard from her former music teacher gifting Nellie the precious veil and the other items in the drawer. Miss Hastings, whose perspicuity for seeing into the future was legendary, had long thought Nellie and Doctor Bart belonged together and had placed her bets accordingly.

Not long after their wedding, I joined the hands of Henry Trow and Hannah Shorey. That wedding took place in the newly-renovated front parlor of the old Lovejoy place, the room with the beautiful antique mural. I love that mural because it portrays Time as an endless, ever-expanding loop, and all one needs to do to change the direction of her life is to get in her horse and buggy and drive to Sovereign, Maine. Needless to say, Nellie is thrilled to have her 'grandparents' so close at hand and spends as much time with them as she does with me!

I have never seen Wendell as happy as he has been these past six months, squiring his new family around town. The old chicken farmer is still as 'shaap' as ever and has recently promised Rebecca he will try to live to be one-hundred-and-ten, in order that he might meet George's grandchildren. Not to be outdone, Leland immediately declared he would live to be one-hundred-and-twenty, by which he intends to signify he'll live at least as long as his buddy Wendell. Thankfully, my good friend Leland shows no sign of expiring anytime soon. Over the past winter he yarded out as much firewood as ever with Cain and Abel from woodlots he owns and from those, well, he does not own. For my part, I hope both Leland and Wendell will live to be one-hundred-and-thirty because I've had my fill of funerals for a while.

Little George Russell is growing faster than the horsemint in his mother's rhubarb patch. Rebecca, who is the epitome of happy motherhood, is not only a new mother but also will soon become a first-time grandmother. Amber didn't know it at the time, but she was pregnant at her mother's baby shower. Nellie is now hard at work on her fourth quilt (Metcalf's birthday quilt was number two and my 'Welcome home, Mom' quilt was number three) for Bruce and Amber's baby. Peter would be thrilled to know another generation of Hodges-Gilpins will soon be running free and wild along the banks of the Sebasticook River in Winslow, where we used to play and where

Peter lies buried. I go to the cemetery sometimes to visit him, but not as often as I thought I would. Time does heal; time and the love of family and friends.

Trudy and Ryan have expanded their Jersey herd to keep up with the growing demand for their organic milk, butter and cheese. In addition, Trudy just revealed to me that before this year ends Alice Rose will have a baby brother or sister to play with at Scotch Broom Acres. Not to be outdone, Lila and Mike will be adding another cousin to the pack of Hobarts in Maple Grove in Aroostook County. Those young pips have a way of multiplying! Who knows? Perhaps the children of our little group of friends will grow up, fall in love, and marry one another.

There's a spot in the Russell Hill Cemetery, near Miss Hastings' grave, where I sit these heady May afternoons and ponder the next phase of my life. From this high vantage point one can see for miles. The town sprawls across the tableau below like a well-loved picture book, offering glimpses of what is quintessential Sovereign: fields, frog ponds and woodlots; the general store; the Millett Rock; the church; the cornshop museum; and the mysterious mist rising up from Black Brook. What cannot be seen by the naked eye, however, are the kind and loving hearts of the people in our little hamlet, this frost pocket of goodness. A hand-carved wooden sign hanging in the kitchen of the old Lovejoy place sums up their character best: 'He who enters is a Stranger—but once.'

A flycatcher flits from a purple lilac bush to the iron flag holder at the gravestone nearest me, her brown tail bobbing up and down as though trying to catch my attention. The refreshing breeze flaps the folds of the little American flag under her feet. I can smell the sweet scent of the lilac blossoms intermingled with the soft pine fragrance wafting from the nearby woods. In the distance, amorous wood frogs chatter about their love lives. The sun feels warm against my face.

For some reason, Miss Hastings' tweet to Lila—the catalyst that initiated the entire Sovereign saga—springs to mind. The message, a spark plug of sorts, was one the former music teacher regularly deployed to unsuspecting down-at-heart individuals long before the advent of Twitter. I still remember the thrill I felt seventeen years ago when I opened Miss Hastings' lavender scented notecard and apprehended her looping scrawl: *"Our church needs you, darling! Take a chance—move to Sovereign. What have you got to lose? We'll show you how to raise chickens."*

Sadly, Miss Hastings is no longer with us to change someone's life with a wave of her benevolent wand and the promise of poultry. Instead, I sit at night hunched over my desk, scribbling away on my new yellow legal pad, trying to figure out how to issue that same warm-hearted invitation in 100,000 words or less. Perhaps, after all, shorter is better.

Take a chance, my friends. What have you got to lose? Our hearts and our doors are always open.

We'll show you how to raise chickens! But the rest of the story is up to you.

The End

www.TheSovereignSeries.com

The Sovereign Series of novels (and complementary cookbook) by Maine farmer and author Jennifer Wixson offer a nostalgic glimpse into a kinder, gentler world and suggest a new paradigm for life in the twenty-first century. Set in the mythical farming community of Sovereign, Maine (pop. 1,048) the stories feature a lovable cast of characters who weave in and out of the books like good friends dropping in for a cup of tea.

Book 1, Hens & Chickens (White Wave, Aug. 2012)

Two women downsized by corporate America (Lila Woodsum, 27, and Rebecca Johnson, 48) move to Maine to raise chickens and sell organic eggs, and discover more than they bargained for—including love! Hens & Chickens opens the book on Sovereign and introduces us to the local characters including the old chicken farmer Wendell Russell, the retired music teacher Miss Hastings, the handsome carpenter Mike Hobart, and the Gilpin clan. A little tale of pips and peepers, hens and chickens, love and friendship, Book 1 inculcates readers with delight and contentment, a sensation not unlike that feeling described by Ralph Waldo Emerson as "a certain cordial exhilaration…"

Book 2, Peas, Beans & Corn (White Wave, June 2013)

The romance of a bygone era infuses Book 2 in the Sovereign Series when Maine Army Guardsman Bruce Gilpin, 35, returns to Sovereign with the secret dream of restarting the town's old sweet corn canning factory. He's aided in his new mission by the passionate organic foodie Amber Johnson (21, Rebecca's daughter), who reawakens his tired heart. The course of their true love is muddied by their well-meaning mothers, however, and by the arrival of Bruce's ex-wife and the handsome corporate attorney Ryan MacDonald, who hits town to rusticate. History pervades this little tale of hummingbird moths and morning mists, horse-drawn sleighs and corn desilkers, and the words of the poet Emily Dickinson, who could have been describing Sovereign when she once wrote: "I went to Heaven – 'Twas a small Town."

Book 3, The Songbird of Sovereign (White Wave, July 2014)

She's the most popular resident of Sovereign, Maine yet no one in this rural farming community of 1,048 souls has ever known the story behind Miss Hastings' seven decades of dedication to children. In Book 3 of the Sovereign Series, Maggie the minister sets out on a quest to plumb the mystery of Miss Hastings' past before the retired music teacher – nearing her 89th birthday and in failing health – departs this world forever. But Maggie has a mystery of her own, a conundrum that might upset the apple cart before she can uncover the rest of Miss Hastings' story! The Songbird of Sovereign moves effortlessly back and forth through time, from a poignant first love at a central Maine sanatorium in the 1940s to a merry winter picnic in the present day Maine woods. Two intertwining story lines come together in a stunning and inspiring conclusion.

Book 4, The Minister's Daughter (Aug. 2015)

Although tall, blonde and beautiful, Nellie Walker, 22, (daughter of Maggie the minister) is also self-centered and a bit of a snob. When a tragic event leaves Nellie alone in the world she returns to Sovereign—a place she's always hated—to pick up the pieces of her mother's life. Helping Nellie through this dark time is the compassionate country doctor, Doctor Bart, 29, whose affection for her has long been suspected (and promoted) by her mother. But stiff-necked Nellie wants to choose her own partner and the mysterious stranger Walden, known locally as the "Mushroom Man," has piqued her interest. Who is this mysterious stranger? And why has his unorthodox view of land ownership created such a stir in Sovereign? The Minister's Daughter is filled with the stuff that makes Maine wonderful: hand-made quilts, forgotten history like mortgage buttons, Needhams (chocolates), old-fashioned roses and herbs, wildlife watching, and so much fabulous food you'll begin to wonder whether or not you can reach Sovereign in time for suppah!

The Sovereign Series Cookbook (late 2015 or 2016)

A companion to the novels, The Sovereign Series Cookbook contains recipes for all the mouth-watering foods described in the books. Recipes include: Euna's Hot Water Gingerbread, Maude's Rose Petal and Caraway Shortbread Cookies, Miss Hastings' Raisin-Filled Cookies, and much more. The cookbook is compiled by author Jennifer Wixson with the assistance of her niece, Maine foodie Laurel Wixson McFarland.

COMING IN THE FUTURE:

Thanks to the urging of loyal fans, Jennifer Wixson recently announced there will be at least two more Sovereign Series novels:

Book 5, Maggie's Dilemma
Book 6, To the Waters & the Wild

Visit our website for more information on

www.TheSovereignSeries.com

Jennifer Wixson

Maine farmer and author Jennifer Wixson writes from her home in Troy where she and her husband (fondly known as the Cranberry Man) raise Scottish Highland cattle. A graduate of the School of Hard Knocks, Jennifer also admits to a Master's degree in divinity from Bangor Theological Seminary. You can follow her on Twitter @ChickenJen and find the latest on her writing at: www.facebook.com/Jennifer.Wixson.author.

Visit our website for more information on

www.theSovereignSeries.com